SUDDEN THREAT

A.J. TATA

VARIANCE
ARKANSAS

Library of Congress Catalog Number –
2009930797

ISBN: 1-935142-08-9
ISBN-13: 978-1-935142-08-9

Cover illustration: Larry Rostant
Cover layout: Jeremy Robinson and Stanley Tremblay
Interior layout: Stanley Tremblay
Map: Jackie McDermott
Edited: Shane Thomson

Published by Variance LLC (USA).

www.variancepublishing.com

Visit A.J. Tata on the web at: www.ajtata.com.
Author's website designed by www.alifelski.com

In Memory of:

Command Sergeant Major Jerry Lee Wilson
Captain Bill Jacobsen
Major Doug Sloan

This book is dedicated to the memory of three soldiers killed in combat, two in Iraq and one in Afghanistan. These men are role models for all of us.

CSM Jerry Wilson was command sergeant major during my last six months of command of the Second Brigade, 101st Airborne Division. Jerry, a tall, strong man from Thomson, Georgia, was killed in Mosul, Iraq, in 2003, during Operation Iraqi Freedom. Jerry's heart was as large as he was tall, and as I said at his funeral in Thomson, we must all endeavor to earn his sacrifice.

Bill, who also served with me in the 101st Airborne Division, was killed the next year during the devastating attack on the dining facility near Mosul, Iraq, while serving as a Stryker Brigade company commander. Bill was a six-and-a-half-foot-tall Mormon who loved his soldiers. In the streets of Mosul, he was an icon among both his troops and the Iraqi people. He was the best officer with whom I have served. Speaking with Bill's wife and their four boys at his funeral near Charlotte, North Carolina, I again vowed to live up to the sacrifice of the many good men and women who were fighting both in combat and on the home front.

Doug served with me in the Eighty-second Airborne Division and Tenth Mountain Division and was killed by an improvised explosive device in Afghanistan in 2006, three months after he was scheduled to leave company command, but his soldiers had asked their commander to keep him in place. Kneeling in front of Doug's rifle, helmet, smiling photo, and identification tags at his memorial service in Konar Province, Afghanistan, on a crystal-clear day amidst the towering Hindu Kush, I wept, proud of Doug's courage and the fact that he had achieved the highest praise a man can seek: subordinates who demanded his leadership.

Jerry, Bill, and Doug were the kinds of leaders soldiers loved to follow. They were selfless men who courageously and valiantly answered the call to duty. Men and women like them are not uncommon in our military. Indeed, they are a reflection of our society and the values of our nation.

The sacrifices of these men should galvanize all of us to recognize the reality that, indeed, freedom is not free, and we have enemies who seek to destroy our way of life.

And if you've read this far and don't turn another page, that's okay by me. Google Jerry, Bill, and Doug, and you will understand the sentiment that these men stirred in those around them.

If you choose to read on, this work of fiction attempts to capture the grittiness of combat against a realistic geopolitical backdrop. Any thriller must have a stage on which to play out, and that stage must be based on current events. In addition to the disclaimer that this book is, in its entirety, fiction, including all of its characters, I want to add that *Sudden Threat's* only purpose is to entertain. It is not a political statement and in no way, shape or form represents any official opinion of the government. *Sudden Threat* is the first in a series of books that follows the paths of two brothers, Matt and Zachary Garrett, CIA paramilitary operative and U.S. Army officer, respectively.

As for me, I am a soldier. I believe in and endeavor daily to accomplish the country's strategic aims, I despise and have fought the enemies of our nation, and I know the threat we face.

Late at night, as thoughts of combat and training spin through my mind, I'm always left with the images of Jerry, Bill, and Doug. So, if I've been able to capture a little bit of the qualities of men such as these in the characters of the main protagonists, then I will have succeeded.

ACKNOWLEDGEMENTS

The publication of this book would not have been possible without the friendship and guidance of Rob Hobart and Brad Thor. Rob's professionalism and years of dedicated, selfless service are the foundation for a character readers will discover in *Rogue Threat,* the sequel to *Sudden Threat,* and books beyond. Rob introduced me to Brad, who has simply been an unbelievable mentor through the publication process, not to mention a first-class friend and best-selling author.

I am deeply grateful to the Variance publishing team, Tim Schulte and Jeremy Robinson, who decided to take a chance on an Army officer who has enjoyed writing for the past fifteen years in his "spare" time. They absolutely live up to their goal of being an "author friendly" publishing house.

An author could not ask for two better editors than Bob and Sara Schwager, who have diligently compensated for my inattention in grammar class and plebe, freshman year, English at the United States Military Academy. For sure, any errors in the book are mine alone.

I also need to thank Rick "The Gun-Guy" Kutka for his weapons technical expertise and for his years of service to our nation.

To my entire family, who have been so incredibly supportive of me over the years during military deployments and the usual roller coaster of life, I say thank you. My parents, Bob and Jerri Tata, in particular have been steady supporters of my writing even when life seemed to get in the way.

And to Jodi Amanda, as you say, *all ways and always.*

SUDDEN THREAT

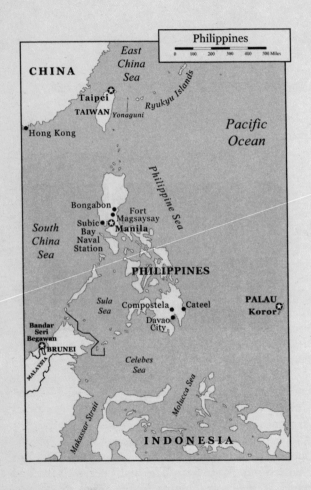

PROLOGUE

NANGAHAR PROVINCE, AFGHANISTAN, DECEMBER 12, 2001

Matt Garrett pulled his white Gore-Tex hood over his forehead, warding off the biting winds that sliced downward from the 14,000-foot peaks of the Tora Bora Mountains and rifled through his layered Afghan garb like invisible sheets of ice. As he turned his head slowly to check on his three other men, the snow was more like pellets fired sideways at his face by enemy weapons.

Holding in position a mile inside the Pakistan border, overlooking a small, nameless village, he studied the hand-held monitor and watched the grainy, barely discernable Predator feed as it followed the ambulance that had passed through Torkum gate, the fabled Khyber Pass. The ambulance turned north on a small road out of Peshawar and then the video feed was lost due to the raging storm.

It was December 12, 2001 and Matt had led his team from Jalalabad through the rugged, snow-jammed trail north of the pass that separates Afghanistan from Pakistan while the Eastern Alliance, fortified by a consortium of special operators and some of his cohorts from the CIA, attacked into Tora Bora. The night before, Matt had stared at the map hanging in the small shack near Jalalabad airfield as he listened to the fight raging in the windswept mountains.

Then he heard the announcement of a cease fire.

"Bullshit," he had said. "Head fake."

Matt figured that with all of the assets watching and listening to Al Qaeda in the mountains, he would form a supporting effort. His study of Bin Laden always led him to a small village in Pakistan. The one he presently viewed through the scope of his M24 sniper rifle.

Matt had pointed at the map with his team and said, "If he doesn't go the back way out of Tora Bora into Parachnir, he's going there." His finger had smacked the map north and west of Peshawar. "We've got enough dudes up in the mountains; this is where we're going."

Then as they were about to move, an Eastern Alliance checkpoint reported the pearl of intelligence to General Ali. An ambulance had appeared from nowhere in the snowstorm and was passing through Torkum Gate, heading east.

"That's him. Get Pred feed over it now," Matt had instructed. The Predator was unarmed and could only monitor. Matt's hunch, headquarters determined, was not the main effort.

Tora Bora was the focus and therefore received the balance of the armed assets.

Four men and two mules had walked all night from a drop-off point near the border. They shivered and struggled to keep their bottled water and Camelbak hydration systems from freezing. After a quick recon, Matt had selected this rocky crevice with superb fields of fire into the village.

Matt plugged a cable from his sniper scope into a USB port in his small handheld satellite communications device. He was transmitting his sight picture back to Langley, but he also knew that the national command authority in the White House situation room and the national military command center in the Pentagon routinely tapped into the CIA video; all in the name of post-9-11 intelligence sharing.

Matt could not give a rat's ass about who was watching the video feed.

They want proof? They can watch the bullet pass through his brain.

They were perched high above the village nearly 500 meters away. The driving snow provided ample cover, especially with their white gilley suits that lay atop them. Two of his men were faced outward, securing their position from any passerby. Tony Macrini, known as X-Ray, lay next to him peering through a larger scope, confirming what Matt was seeing as well as providing redundant digital confirmation of the kill.

"Pred lost them, but they're heading this way," Matt said, confidently.

"Roger," Macrini said, then spit some tobacco into the bone-white snow. The brown juice disappeared instantly beneath a fresh layer.

Bones and McKinney tapped Matt every fifteen minutes. One tap meant all ok; two taps meant there was a problem. Better with minimal talking.

Matt's heart quickened just a bit. Though he was experienced, to know that he potentially had the shot on Al Qaeda senior leadership elevated his nervous system slightly. That was good, he thought. He wasn't nervous or anxious, but there was something nagging at him.

He had been told to call in approval for any sniper shot on AQ senior leadership. *It's okay to drop a bomb on a cave and kill the dude*, Matt thought, *but I can't pull this trigger without approval?*

"Movement," Macrini said.

Matt shifted his scope marginally and picked up two men with AK-47s slung across their backs standing outside in the snowstorm.

"That's it," Matt said. Pulling into the view of his scope was a makeshift ambulance with a large, red cross on either side. It slowly wound through a defile and pulled to a stop in front of the larger adobe structure in the nine-building village.

Men clambered out of the ambulance and opened the back door, extracting a stretcher. After the AK-47-clad stretcher bearers pulled the litter from the back, a short man wearing wire-rim spectacles stepped carefully from the compartment into the snow.

Matt watched as the wire-rimmed, spectacled man rapidly ushered the precious cargo into the large building. Momentarily losing sight of everyone, Matt was pleased when they placed the stretcher on a table juxtaposed to an open window.

"I've got the shot."

"You've got the shot," Macrini affirmed.

Matt deliberated in his mind. *Make the call, not make the call?*

"You've got the shot," Macrini said again, emphatically, as if to say, *screw the call.*

Before Matt could ruminate any further, his earpiece crackled with the sound of a distant incoming radio call.

"Garrett, standby."

"Don't answer it," Macrini cautioned. "I don't like it."

"They can see my feed, they know we can talk."

"Garrett, standby, acknowledge immediately." Matt didn't recognize the voice through the wind and static, though he assumed it was some bureaucrat seventeen times removed from his low level status as an operator. He registered that the voice could be coming from any of the outstations: Langley, the White House, the Pentagon, and God knows whoever else might be watching. The 8,000-mile screwdriver was going cordless.

"I'm telling you, man," Macrini warned. "You know anything good to ever come from head-quarters?"

Matt looked at his friend, a former Marine Force Recon scout. Macrini's beard, like his own, was thick. He wore a pakol and tan and green blankets beneath the white sheets they used to conceal their position.

He turned back to his sight picture and lined up the black dot of the cross hairs on the middle of the patient's torso. The medical team had stripped the man, a very tall man, down to his long johns. The white shirt was stained red on the left side. Shrapnel, maybe a bullet, Matt figured. The scope traced the body and then the black dot landed on the bearded face, actually just to the side of the elongated nose and just beneath the dark, brooding eyebrows. The eyes, though, seemed compassionate, or perhaps he had the faraway look of a wounded deer.

Matt nodded to his battle buddy, exhaled steadily and placed an exposed trigger finger on the trigger mechanism. He found that spot where he would have no pull on the weapon, just straight back, not moving the weapon, sending the bullet directly where the cross hairs were resting. He closed his eyes briefly, retreating into that inner sanctuary that allowed him complete focus. Opening his eyes, all he saw was the black dot and the man's face looming large in his sight picture, the way that a slow-spinning curve ball might look to Tony Gwynn, the greatest batsman of all time.

"Homerun," Matt whispered.

"Homerun," Macrini confirmed.

"Do not fire! Do not fire! Kill chain denied!"

"What the hell?" Macrini said, rolling away from the scope and yanking out his earpiece.

Matt didn't move. He was in his zone. Everything was in slow motion; his breathing, his trigger finger beginning the squeeze, the movement of the patient's head turning toward him, exposing the worn prayer callous on his forehead.

"Take the shot!" Macrini growled.

"Do not fire! Kill chain denied!"

"Take the shot!"

With the good angel on one shoulder, Macrini, and the bad angel on the other, the anonymous voice, Matt closed his eyes.

I've got the shot.

"This is a direct order. Entry into Pakistan was not authorized. Kill chain denied. Violation will be prosecuted."

I've got the shot. I'm close.

"Take the shot!" Macrini demanded.

Matt exhaled again, keeping his sight picture, and squeezed the trigger at the same time a JDAM missile exploded perilously close to his position.

"Holy shit!" Macrini shouted, covering his face. Bones and McKinney turned toward Matt, who was still in his zone.

The bomb's detonation created a bright orange fireball that mushroomed into the sky nearly 100 meters from his position.

"Closer to us than the shack," Matt said to his three teammates.

He looked at Macrini, who stared back at Matt and shook his head.

"We were punked."

"Roger that," Matt said.

"Kill chain denied, Garrett. Return to Jalalabad for new orders."

Phase I: Chasing Ghosts

CHAPTER 1

The one time my country asks for a head on a platter, Matt Garrett said to himself as he recalled the nightmarish scene in Pakistan. He let out a heavy sigh, watching the sun dip behind Mount Apo, just to the west of Davao City, Republic of the Philippines, on the island of Mindanao. From the freezing snow to the humid backwaters. From the epicenter to the periphery.

I had the damn shot!

Disappointed in himself, he shook the memory from his head and crushed a smoldering butt under the sole of his dingy work boot.

Keeping his gaze fixed on the gray evening, he noticed a few destitute, but nonetheless workman-like, Filipinos scurry around the concrete fishing piers that abutted Davao Gulf, a horseshoe expanse of water adjacent to the Celebes Sea.

Pulling the ratty Dodgers baseball cap down over his forehead, Matt shook off a bit of his clinging anger and discreetly strode next to a shack, watching the activities—nothing out of the ordinary. He had been cycling between Zhoushan Naval Base, China, and Davao City for over two months. Tonight, he had been given instructions in the form of a text message from his handler to meet a dockworker who would provide him information.

A few short months after being mysteriously

yanked from Pakistan while in hot pursuit of Al Qaeda senior leadership, Matt was now trying to locate a large number of unmanned aerial vehicles (UAV) called Predators. They were just being put to good use in the War on Terror, and it appeared that someone had traded this technology to the Chinese for financial motivations. Either that, or the Los Alamos debacle had contributed to the satellite imagery that indicated the Predators were being built and tested near Zhoushan. He had developed a lead in China when he suddenly received a message from his handler that there was a significant find in Davao City; and so here he was. *Every time I'm close, I'm moved*, Matt thought to himself.

Matt was large, a college shortstop, and looked comfortable in his cargo pants and khaki shirt. He tugged at the Dodgers baseball hat again and hid his eyes behind Oakley sunglasses.

"Muggy," the dockworker said to him in Tagalog.

"Always in the evening," Matt said in Mandarin.

A hazy mist rolled off the bay, distorting the presence of hundreds of fishing vessels. A gull stood guard atop a pylon and flapped its wings once, as if to shiver, though the temperature was in the nineties.

"Got any cigarettes?" the man asked, this time in Mandarin also. That was the key, he had been told.

He turned and looked at the slight Filipino. Matt, standing over six feet, towered above the diminutive man, who was shorter than five and a half feet. The contact had black hair and brown eyes, the norm in that part of the country.

"Sure. Here." This time in English. Matt grabbed his rumpled pack of Camels and held it out to the source, who took two, glancing at him for approval. Matt nodded.

"Running out of time," Matt said. He watched the man put a cigarette between yellow teeth and strike a match. Once he had lit the cigarette, the man shook the match and tossed it on the pier. He looked in both directions, then nodded at a ship across the harbor.

"See that tanker?"

Matt looked past the rows of red and gray fishing ships in the direction the man had nodded. He saw several tuna rigs, then could make out a large black-and-red merchant vessel. It looked more like a container ship or an automobile carrier. He guessed the contact had mistaken it for an oil tanker.

"What about it?"

"Japanese. Leaves tonight. Didn't off-load anything, but Abu Sayyaf put something on it."

Matt continued staring at the ship and read the name on the side: *Shimpu*. That name registered with him, but at the moment he couldn't remember why.

"What was it?" Matt asked, still staring at the ship.

With his peripheral vision, Matt saw the guard remove the cigarette from his mouth and begin to speak. What followed happened quickly: The orange tip of the cigarette fell from the man's hand and dropped at Matt's shoes as his contact's body shuddered. Instinctively, Matt pulled his Glock 26 from beneath his untucked shirt and jumped onto a floating dock running perpendicular to the pier on which they had been standing.

As he leapt, he saw that the contact was prone on the pier and bleeding from a head wound. He also felt the hot wash of a bullet pass uncomfortably close as he ducked behind a junked generator, which he presumed was used as an auxiliary power unit for some of the ships. The generator pinged twice from gunshots. And Matt eyed a large Bangka boat with a roof, a ferry of some type, going somewhere.

The helmsman was removing a weathered bowline from a rusty cleat about thirty meters away. There were a few passengers that he could see; mostly fishermen, probably making their way home to

Babak on the eastern side of the gulf. He waited until the captain gave the boat a slight shove. As he watched the boat separate from the pier, he sprinted as if he were stealing third base against a catcher with a rifle arm, then did his best long-jump imitation, feet cycling through the air.

He landed with a thud on the roof of the boat, which promptly gave way and dumped him on the floor, which held.

The helmsman had put the engine into forward, and the ferry was moving slowly away from the pier.

No more shots followed him, but he thought that the ship captain might decide to take over where his other attackers had left off. The wizened man was screaming and baring his teeth, throwing his arms up in the air. Matt understood most of what he was saying and stood, brushed himself off, and pulled five hundred dollars from his wallet.

"Sorry about the roof. Buy a new boat," he said in Tagalog.

"My boat. Had for twenty-five years. New roof."

Clearly the man was bargaining with him, so Matt pulled two hundred dollars more from his pocket and handed it to the man but didn't release it. The helmsman tugged on the money with a weathered hand.

"Drop me off at the next pier up near the airport, and we're even," Matt said.

The man yanked the remaining two hundred dollars from his hand and nodded.

Much later, true to his word and the seven-hundred-dollar payment, the captain of the ship pulled into the pier normally used for fruit transshipment. Night had fallen, and Matt effortlessly leapt from the bow of the Bangka ferryboat onto the concrete pier.

He reassured himself by patting his Glock, which had stayed firmly in his hand through the fall, and which he had quickly placed in its holster while still on the floor of the boat. He walked a kilometer to the apartment he had rented, grabbed his gear, then discreetly moved another kilometer and a half toward the airport and checked in at the nondescript Uncle Doug's Motel.

Matt presumed that "Uncle Doug" was Douglas MacArthur, patron saint of all things Philippine.

He tossed his duffel on the floor, locked the door, and pulled out his satellite Blackberry.

Check out *Shimpu*. Contact KIA. New location. Standing by.

Matt sent the dispassionate note as if having contacts killed and being shot at were akin to signing an office memo or sitting in a meeting to discuss the next meeting. He removed the Baby Glock from its holster, ran his finger along the extractor, and felt the reassuring bump indicating he still had a round chambered.

Almost immediately he received a text message from his handler.

Airport. Midnight. More to follow. Feet and knees together.

Matt looked at his watch. It was 0200. *Like I'm on a wild-goose chase*, he thought, and shook his head.

Matt forwarded the text to his personal secure e-mail account; his way of keeping a journal.

"Feet and knees together" was paratrooper code for the way to survive a parachute landing. Matt understood that if you kept your feet and knees pressed firmly together, you stood a chance of not breaking an ankle or leg. If you reached for the ground with one foot, then all of your weight would come barreling onto one spot of one bone at the speed of gravity, usually resulting in a fracture.

He simply typed back: Roger.

Sitting on his twin bed with no box springs, he stared at his pistol, cycling the events of the last few hours through his mind. He snapped his head upward and whispered, "Shimpu." Remembering the meaning of the obscure Japanese word sent a chill up his spine.

"Divine wind," he said to himself.

It's what the kamikaze pilots called themselves.

CHAPTER 2

MINDANAO ISLAND, PHILIPPINES

Garrett had spent the day resting, doing a few push-ups, and chowing on combat rations. One thing about a parachute jump that Matt knew for certain was that you rarely landed in your intended location. Therefore, he needed to be rested and well fed in preparation for the abundance of energy required once on the ground.

He cinched the parachute straps, tightening them against his legs and across his back. He patted the Duane Dieter Spec Ops knife he had taped beneath his cargo utility pants, then tapped his Baby Glock and visually inspected his SIG 552 Commando rifle. He felt the reassuring weight of his 9mm and 5.56mm ammunition in his outer tactical vest. All seemed to be in good order.

What was not in good order, in Matt's mind, was the text he had just received. A group of Filipino Rangers had just been shot down somewhere over the island of Mindanao. Matt's handler had sent a text indicating that one C-130 was a catastrophic loss, meaning everyone was killed, while the lead airplane had some jumpers get away.

The question he was to answer was, Were there any survivors?

I come here looking for Predator connections, and now I'm looking for dead Filipino Rangers, Matt thought, shaking his head. It was not that the task was a nuisance; just the opposite. He knew damn

well that the soldiers who had just died were fighting
in the name of freedom.

More sacrifice.

The Casa 212 airplane bounced along the runway
and lifted easily into the sky. Matt was jumping a
square parachute so that he could steer it to a
precision landing. He had asked the pilots to put him
over the wreckage site, and he would work from
there. The reported crash site was thirty kilometers
east of Compostela.

Through a map recon, Matt had selected a drop
zone about a kilometer away. It was the best he could
do, and even at a kilometer, he believed that the
blank level-looking spot on the map was probably a
banana plantation or, worse, a recently harvested
sugarcane field. Either way, he stood a good chance
of being impaled on a freshly cut banana tree or
sugarcane stalk. Neither was a particularly good
option in Matt's view.

Once he had silk over his head, he would flip
down his night-vision goggles and steer to the best
possible landing point.

The flight from the Davao City airfield to his
drop zone took about ninety minutes, even though
the release point was only eighty kilometers north of
Davao. Matt had asked the pilot to fly south over the
water, then to circle around the island and approach
the drop zone from the north, which doubled the
flight route. He would be jumping from 3600 meters
above ground level, which would put the airplane at
about 5400 meters above sea level. The plains of
Mindanao were surrounded by jagged volcanic
mountains that ran parallel along the west and east
coasts. The heat and rainfall had, over the course of
time, spawned lush tropical rain forests on both the
windward and leeward sides of the island. Matt
would be jumping in the bowling alley between the
two ranges, which topped out at about 4300 meters,

but he would be cheating toward the eastern range, where the airplanes had last been sighted.

As they flew, Matt used his goggles to survey the landscape. Once the pilot made the turn to fly from north to south, Matt saw the city lights out of the front right of the airplane. He was standing between the pilot and copilot seats, observing through the windscreen, and assumed the city was Compostela.

"There," Matt said, pointing to his left front. He saw the faintest evidence of fire. Stepping away from the cockpit, he walked over to the port personnel door, which was open, and held on to the rails of either side, leaning out of the aircraft but staying out of the slipstream.

With his goggles, the fire was more evident. He could see the smoldering remnants of something burning. As they approached, he saw he was looking at two spots of burning wreckage.

Seems right, he thought.

He walked back to the cockpit, lifted his goggles, and said, "Just get me over those two hot spots. I'll open at about a thousand AGL and find a good location. That's where I need to be."

Paramount in his mind was the fact that there might be some survivors. He was jumping in with a small rucksack, which included a first-aid kit. He would be able to treat a few patients, but that was all. Unfortunately, Matt knew, a few might be all that were left from a plane crash.

"Okay, sir, we're over top. Anytime now," the copilot said, leaning back and looking at Matt.

"Roger. Thanks, guys."

Matt checked his gear once more, then walked off the back of the open ramp, fell forward into a swan dive as if he were going to do a belly flop, and flared his arms to stabilize his free fall.

Initially he was unable to detect the two fires he had seen from the airplane, and as he checked his altimeter, he saw he was approaching 1100 meters above ground level. He spun once, then again. On his second spin, he saw them and adjusted his airflow to direct his fall toward the wreckage.

At just above 350 meters, he pulled the rip cord on his parachute. It opened cleanly and he had good silk above him. The cool air offset the typically warm Philippine nights and felt good on his face.

He retracted his goggles from their pouch, steered them to his face, and placed the harness on his head, securing it with a chin strap. The "dummy cord" flapped against his windbreaker but would prevent him from losing the goggles should they come loose.

Through the green-shaded world of the goggles, he studied the wreckage. He saw an unpleasant sight at the southernmost airplane.

There were hundreds of people milling around the burnt remnants, but he could determine the oblong shape of the airplane and concluded that aircraft must have been the second in the order of movement. Making a snap decision at about 200 meters before landing, Matt pulled hard and steered about a kilometer away from the southern airplane and toward the northern wreckage.

The only obvious problem was that he couldn't see anywhere to land.

"Oh shit," he whispered. He realized that talking to himself while under canopy never did much good, but thankfully he caught an updraft and rode it over a small ridge. His quick-firing mind realized that the reason there seemed to be no people near the northern fire was because the terrain was too severe. They might arrive soon enough.

At 40 meters above ground level, he could see the fire burning, and its ambient light gave him enough visability to conclude that the only place he could land, if at all, would be in the middle of the plow field of the wreckage.

So, his two options were to land in burning, twisted metal or a stand of twenty-meter oaks, chestnuts, and mahogany trees.

His goggles refracted the glint of something elongated running perpendicular to his axis of descent and he realized, perhaps a bit too late, that it was the moon reflecting off water, which in those mountains could even be a waterfall.

Just as his feet were skimming the tops of the trees, he miraculously found a clearing of sorts and toggled hard into a spiral that took him into the hole. Beneath the jungle canopy, his goggles were less useful but still better than the naked eye.

His parachute caught on something, and he swung forward. He was suspended in air, oscillating back and forth as if on a playground swing set. He had his rucksack on a seven-meter lowering line, so he pulled the quick release and heard it thud into the ground shortly after.

Matt flipped his goggles back onto his head, removed a flashlight from his vest pocket, and shined it beneath his feet. He was a mere two meters off the ground.

He removed his Duane Dieter Spec Ops knife from its ankle sheath, cut one riser, then grabbed above his intended cut on the remaining riser, cut it and held on with one arm. He flipped his knife into the ground, heard it stick, then let go.

He kept his feet and knees together as he landed.

Collecting his rucksack and knife, Matt pulled a compass from his vest, set an azimuth north, and began walking quickly to the wreckage.

CHAPTER 3

Just to move maybe a kilometer had taken him nearly an hour. Where the terrain was moderately level, it was choked with dense undergrowth. Where there was less vegetation, there seemed to be impossibly jagged and steep volcanic rocks and cliffs.

Matt took a knee on the rock ledge that he had just ascended. His beacon had been the bright spot in the offing, like town lights reflecting off the clouds, though his goggles, when he could wear them, had differentiated the subtle nuances of the burning crash up on the face of the mountain through the triple-canopy forest.

Finally, he put his goggles up to his eyes and saw the smoldering ruins of half a fuselage. Looking to his left, he could see the direction from which the aircraft had flown, or tumbled, and cut a wide swath of destruction. To his right it looked like the debris field continued on another fifty meters or so until a flat wall of rock had blocked any forward progress.

Matt stood and walked carefully, scanning with his goggles in both directions as he stepped lightly over hot chunks of metal scattered about. He had seen airplane crashes before, and they were never remotely comprehensible. Could anyone ever imagine the terror or horror of plummeting in a plane into the ground? In a way, he hoped that someone could tonight; it would mean they were still alive. On the thought, he touched his rucksack, which he knew contained his first-aid kit.

He stepped over a full propeller, knelt next to it,

and touched the blade. It was warm, but not hot. The friction of the crash and the jet-fuel spillage had created fire and heat, but not everything burned.

All I'm asking for is one person to be alive, Matt thought to himself. *Just one.*

He moved toward the blackened hull of the aircraft, which was surprisingly intact, but split wide open, like a lobster tail. He entered the fuselage from the rear and immediately saw a body. The heat and smell pushed him back outside. For the first time he noticed the crackle of the fire still burning rubberized pieces of material.

Matt saw the man's hands first. It was an odd visual display as the body was actually outside the aircraft, tethered by a deployed parachute.

The flashlight that Matt shined on the scene revealed a charred static line tracing from the door of the aircraft onto the rock ledge. From there Matt saw the metal ring at the apex of the parachute and some charred silk. His eyes followed the suspension lines to the risers, which were surprisingly intact.

The hand was splayed upward toward the riser as if reaching to pull a slip. Matt moved the flashlight beam farther down the body and could see a U.S. Army combat uniform.

Shit. He sighed.

He moved quickly next to the man and saw the name tag: Peterson. Matt checked for pulse and airway, but got negative reports on both accounts. He visually inspected Peterson and saw that he had been rigged to jump and that the airplane must have crashed as he was trying to exit.

Matt saw the arrowhead patch of the U.S. Army Special Forces on the man's shoulder sleeve with airborne and Special Forces tabs above. *No one told me Americans were in this thing,* he said to himself. *What the hell is going on?*

Returning to the moment, Matt shook his head.

The seconds between life and death were so arbitrary. Why did Peterson not make it, while apparently everyone else did? His search of the surrounding area had yielded two pilots and a loadmaster. As tragic as their deaths were, Matt knew they were Filipino, which mattered, but somehow did not have the same impact on him that kneeling there looking at Peterson did.

"Who are you, Peterson?" he whispered. *And why wasn't I told about you?*

Again, he checked for pulse and any sign of life, shining the flashlight into Peterson's wide eyes. The pupils were nonresponsive, so Matt used his thumb and forefinger to slide the eyelids shut. He saw that Peterson had not been burned badly; really, just the heat from the fire had burned his parachute. The man must have died from blunt-force trauma during the crash or as he was flung from the rear cargo door.

Matt looked up and saw that the starboard wing had been sheared off and was probably a kilometer or so back in the debris field. He stood and made another lap around the airplane and into the split fuselage. He moved the bodies of the two pilots and the crew chief onto the rock ledge near Peterson's body. He pulled a GPS locator beacon and put it in the mouth of one of the men, then shut his jaw tightly. Human scavengers would be picking the place clean in less than twenty-four hours, and the last place they would look was in the throat of a dead man. Filipinos were not known for their gold fillings.

Regardless, he would send a report back to the station chief in Manila and get word to the Armed Forces of the Philippines that they had three men located in the jungle.

He could only carry one.

He carefully removed the parachute harness from Peterson and checked him one last time for signs of life.

Again, he was denied. Climbing his way out would require two hands, and so he took three twelve-foot ropes from his rucksack and slid them under Peterson's upper back, lower back, and buttocks, leaving enough rope on either side for his purposes. Next he laid himself face up on Peterson, wrapped Peterson's arms around his chest, then tied the ropes around their bodies. He rolled to all fours with Peterson on his back and then pulled his hands down and tied them with the trail ends of the lower rope. When he stood, he felt the full weight of his rucksack, which he had secured to his chest, and Peterson on his back. But his arms were free to move and pull his way out of the wreckage. To the casual observer it would appear that Matt was conducting a tandem jump or giving Peterson a piggyback ride.

Looking up at the cliff he needed to scale, Matt silently wished it were a tandem jump.

Matt heard a noise below the crash site, perhaps one and a half kilometers away. He had been at the site for an hour and knew it was time to move. He would go to high ground, as he would surely run into opposition if he initially went lower.

With Peterson on his back, he stepped into the first of many foot ledges in the rock wall that angled away from the crash site. While Peterson's weight was almost unbearable, Matt determined that it was the least he could do.

"Never leave a fallen comrade," he whispered to himself. And while he wasn't an Army officer, such as his brother Zachary, whom Matt had last seen while undergoing Langley's immersion training and a near face-lift in preparation for his current assignment, he thought that was a pretty good credo to live by. And he knew damned well that if it was Matt Garrett at the end of that parachute harness and Peterson had found him, Matt would expect the same thing.

Never leave a fallen comrade.

On that thought, he pulled and scraped his way out of the crash site until two hours later he had to stop.

The sun was beginning to crest the ridge in the east, and he had reached some sort of plateau by climbing almost straight up. He had a hole in the forest canopy through which a helicopter would be able to lower a jungle penetrator. He determined he would stop there, make contact, then figure out his next move.

He sat down awkwardly with Peterson on his back and untied the ropes. Peterson had gone to full rigor and looked strange sitting there, dead, as if he were driving an invisible car, his arms and legs outstretched.

Matt pulled his satellite Blackberry from his backpack and sent the following message:

One U.S. KIA. Peterson, Ronald W.; current grid location; airplane crashed at grid location of beacon 12, 3 AFP personnel dead at location; status on other U.S. personnel? Why not told?

He wolfed down a combat ration and a power bar, downed two bottles of water, and changed out of his sweaty T-shirt.

Sitting on the grassy mountaintop, his anger began to surface again. *First, we are pulled from Pakistan. Next, I'm moved from China. Then, I find a lead in Davao City, but have to leave. Every time I'm close, I'm moved. Now, I've got a dead Special Forces soldier.*

What is going on? He inhaled heavily and blew out the air. "No use in whining," he whispered.

He looked east, then stared down at his GPS, which displayed a map. Once he had satellite triangulation, the visual display showed that Matt was on a volcanic ridge just southwest of Cateel, a fishing village on the windward side of Mindanao.

He repacked his rucksack, checked his rifle and pistol, and stood. He could see the ocean and was momentarily struck by the beauty of the sun nosing its way out of the blue sea.

Which is why he felt the turbulent wash of the bullet before he was aware of its echo. A few more shots zipped in his direction.

Peterson's body took two shots to the chest while Matt's backpack took one. Matt spun and sighted his rifle. The shooter had been careless to miss, because now Matt could see two men trying to scale the cliff he had just climbed. In full daylight, Matt was awestruck at what he had done with Peterson on his back as he leveled his SIG SAUER on the lower man and pulled the trigger. The man tumbled backward … a long way.

Matt then shot the lead man, who had been on all fours trying to scale the cliff. After confirming the second shot, Matt studied the lead man through his sight. He was black-haired and young, and very dead. He wore a red bandanna and had ammunition strapped across his chest like Rambo. A few sparse hairs were growing along the chin, and his skin seemed smooth, almost oily. Had to be Abu Sayyaf or New People's Army.

Matt made a decision that he could probably defend his current position better than anywhere he could go, so he made only a minor adjustment in his location by moving two hundred meters to the south, where he found a series of boulders in which he could set up camp. The canopy was still open in the area and he had good visibility. It took him two trips, but he finally got his equipment and Peterson's body into the rock formation.

He opened his rucksack, pulled out his Blackberry, and stared at the blank screen.

There was a bullet hole between the T and Y buttons, as if someone had been aiming at the device.

He pressed a few buttons to no avail. He pulled his cell phone out of his cargo pocket and saw that there was no reception. No surprises in the middle of this uncharted rain forest.

Matt thought quickly. Had his handler received his last text? Assuming Peterson was not alone, there had to be some American GIs that survived … unless they were on the other plane. But that didn't make sense. Peterson would *not* have been alone, and they would have at least split six and six, so that means at least five were still alive.

I'll bury Peterson with a GPS, Matt thought, *then try to find the remainder of the team.*

"Besides, they'll probably need my help," he said aloud.

After snatching Peterson's ID tags from the beaded chain lying against the dead man's chest, he placed some rocks on top of Peterson. They would be too heavy for an animal to move. Then he placed a GPS in the dirt about ten meters from the rock formation. He pulled out his compass, shot an azimuth to the south, and determined he would follow the ridgeline of the mountain he had scaled.

As the sun rose, Matt picked his way carefully along the rocky ledge.

CHAPTER 4

SAME NIGHT, EAST CHINA SEA

With the knowledge that Matt Garrett was on the island of Mindanao, former Japanese Naicho agent Taiku Takishi, had shut off his satellite phone and begun his portion of the plan. He held on tightly to a metal rail as the Taiwanese-built and Japanese-operated Kuang Hua VI attack ship cut through the dark sea with purpose. Its gray hull burst from the swirling fog and tracked against the racing thunderheads above—a ghost ship emerging from another time and suddenly finding its way.

A storm was approaching from the north. The worst kind. The wind kicked the ocean into white-peaked swells, testing some of the small crew. Takishi's worried face reflected weakly off the cabin window as the GPS navigation device flashed that they had passed their mark. He had just completed a twenty-four-hour flight schedule and was weak from travel. Now this.

He cast a skittish glance at Admiral Saigo Kinoga, thinking, *We've come too far.*

"Admiral?" Takishi muttered, watching the radar device.

Kinoga ignored him. Takishi knew that the admiral had commissioned the craft just two years ago. It was the newest of the Japanese attack boats. Her two Mitsubishi diesel engines and gas turbines turned the two screws, getting her about thirty-five knots in the rough seas. She churned through a massive swell, pitched to the top, and rode the crest downward, only to bore through another wall of water.

Takishi doubted that Kinoga appreciated a politician such as him riding shotgun on his mission. In a way, Takishi admired the admiral, who had been a young officer in the Imperial Navy before Takishi was born. Takishi saw his own face reflecting off the windscreen in the dim cabin light; he tried to hide his fear, forcing a passive countenance.

Kinoga shut the engine. The boat yawed, listing hard. Takishi stumbled in the cockpit and saw Kinoga smile.

"What do we have for defensive measures, Admiral?"

Kinoga took measure of Takishi briefly and said, "Four Hsiung-Feng II missiles for ship-to-ship combat. If successful, they will not be necessary."

The Chinese Maritime coastal defenses were aware that a ship was about to enter its twelve-mile offshore territorial boundary. Seaman Ling, the young radar analyst, had waited, believing the intruder to be a wayward fishing vessel. He had seen, on other nights, fishing ships enter, then leave the twelve-mile limit in the East China Sea.

Ling was bored and not exceptionally interested in his day job. When not performing compulsory service as a radar analyst in the People's Liberation Army, he wrote code, hacked computers, and sold online Viagra. Now that was exciting. Watching the sonar blip appear every ten seconds was worse than watching the paint dry on the rocks he and his peers were forced to beautify on the weekends near the front gate of the base. He yawned as he watched the radar image inch its way across the red line superimposed on his screen. Still he hesitated, watching the light flash on and off, creeping forward. He fully expected the fishermen to turn away after realizing their mistake. Taiwan wasn't his concern, even if the political and military leaders of his country had declared the confederate island nation Chinese public enemy number one. They were capitalist, and so was he. *So who gives a shit,* Ling thought. *They would never attack the mainland.*

"Another boat," Ling said to his section chief, who was peering over his shoulder.

"Stealing our fish again." The section chief sighed, hardly taking notice.

Many Japanese fishermen had probed the waters as fisheries around the world declined. Chinese diplomats had sent a stern rebuke, and the Japanese government, after much debate, had put measures in place to correct the problem. Still, the boats were returning with record hauls from what seemed previously untapped waters.

Takishi's dual purposes came to fruition as Kinoga's modified vessel sat silent in the wind-whipped sea. They rocked aimlessly in the churning water. His anxiety mounted as Kinoga ordered the helmsman to turn the bow to the east.

"What makes you think we can get this close, Admiral?" Takishi asked. It sounded like an accusation.

"Mind your own business, politician," Kinoga spit. "They think we're fishing."

"Fishing? I see," Takishi said. His deal with China had increased their fishing rights along the twelve-mile border. The fishing vessels had made the People's Liberation Navy defenses less sensitive to boundary incursions.

"Are you worried about your Chinese friends?"

"Do not accuse me of conflicting loyalties," Takishi countered, perhaps the first inkling of his getting his sea legs.

Takishi examined Kinoga, a very different man from himself. Kinoga was a career seaman, waiting for the day his country could erase past embarrassments. Takishi was a stockbroker turned politician, hoping to rule Japan sometime in the not-too-distant future. They were two men with different aspirations which led to the same end state that night.

"Initiate jamming," Kinoga said harshly into a gray microphone, his voice transmitting to his reliable crew of six. Takishi stepped back as the jammers commenced the attack by deliberately sending bursts of radiation to momentarily short-circuit the Chinese radar and interrupt communications systems. It was a silent attack, and he wondered if anything had worked.

"Fire the pods," Kinoga said. Takishi held firmly to the dashboard of the attack ship as fire bellowed from the foredeck of the ship. The rockets burst away, burning brightly, momentarily silhouetting the ship against a bright fireball, then dove quickly into the water five hundred meters off stern. Nine others followed.

Ling, who had his feet up on the metal table beneath the radar monitor, slammed his chair into the floor and stood, staring at the sudden appearance of ten flashing radar indicators. *Taiwan, hell,* he thought. Ling had a horrible image of American nuclear submarines poised off the coast, ready to launch their weapons. It would be his fault. Speechless, he grabbed his section chief and pointed at the screen.

"Where did they come from?" the chief shouted.

"They just appeared out of nowhere, sir," Ling stammered, knowing his response sounded lame.

"You moron, radio the strip alert. Now!"

"**Admiral, they have** launched two bombers and a reconnaissance plane with the rest of the squadron to follow," Kinoga's Chinese linguist remarked, lifting one earphone away from his head.

Takishi snapped his head toward the admiral.

Kinoga had only two 20mm guns and four useless ship-to-ship missiles to protect his vessel. Even though the guns could fire three hundred rounds a minute, they would be ineffective against the high-tech Chinese aircraft.

"Full ahead," Kinoga said. Takishi felt the boat move slowly almost immediately after the admiral's order.

Takishi saw Kinoga watching the radar. The Chinese aircraft pursued his vessel as it strained for the safety of international waters and ultimately, the southwestern shores of Japan. Takishi knew that success depended entirely upon the avoidance of conflict or capture in Chinese seas.

Takishi settled into a calming routine, part of his jujitsu training. He watched Kinoga and his crew. In his dark blue utility uniform, Kinoga looked like any other sailor. His eyes seemed closed as he watched the radar screen. He periodically looked over the bridge of the vessel and into the black night.

"Scared, Takishi?" Kinoga prodded.

"The only thing that scares me, Admiral, is taking unnecessary risks. What happens if they capture our ship?" Takishi muttered.

"Then we die. Remember, or did the prime minister forget to tell you, that we are rigged with explosives." Kinoga grinned.

Takishi looked away, shaking his head. He began to wonder if he was in too deep, but he had made commitments to his prime minister and to others. He had no option but to continue, and there were more dangerous tasks ahead. The prime minister had guaranteed him that the emperor would crown him upon successful accomplishment of the entire plan. Thinking of this seemed to motivate him.

There were no beacons or lighthouses to guide their retreat through the dangerous seas. Black water crashed against the angled hull, spraying a thick, salty mist high into the air that opaqued the cabin glass. Takishi thought that it was like trying to look through a thin veil of milk. The ship accelerated, riding the swell, then slowed, boring through the mass of water at the bottom of the pitch, only to repeat the process.

He pushed it too far.

Kinoga smiled at Takishi.

Takishi smiled back, denying the admiral satisfaction. Yes, indeed, he would be getting satisfaction soon.

But right then he was infinitely more concerned with Kinoga's ability to outrace the rapidly approaching aircraft.

Two Chinese Shenyang J8D fighter/interceptor aircraft cut through the night sky. Last year, a J8D fighter had bumped an intruding American P3 reconnaissance aircraft, setting off a firestorm of geopolitical machinations. The MiG-21 knockoffs sucked the cloudy night through their turbines and spit it out the backside in a twirling vapor. The pilots carved through the thunderheads, feeling their way in the night as they searched for that magical bit of airspace where they could range the enemy ships with their weapons, while remaining out of harm's way from any retaliatory means the ships might possess.

Their instructions were to prevent the seaborne intruders from escaping.

They were beginning to circle the ships to the east into what was international airspace, the ungoverned common area where contests could take place fairly;

much like a dueling field. And so, after repeated warnings via their communications systems, the two fighters separated to begin the destruction of the invading fleet.

Each pilot acquired radar lock on a ship and fired a missile.

By Takishi's calculations, they had to be close to international waters and their relative safe harbor from Chinese attack. The plan was for them to turn southeast and aim toward the island of Yonaguni, whose port would indeed provide shelter and whose proximity to Taiwan would offer the intended ruse.

Then it happened. Takishi heard the steady, high-pitched sound of radar lock screeching through a speaker in the cockpit.

"What's that?" Takishi asked nervously.

Ignoring Takishi, Kinoga studied the night sky, watching the two bright flashes punch through the cloud cover and streak through the blackness, searching for an illusory target—his ship. He reached down and pressed a gray button, employing additional countermeasures. He released three SIREN electronic chafflike rockets, hoping to confuse the missiles by sending a strong electronic signal from a battery-powered amplifier floating beneath a parachute. The SIREN rockets screamed into the air, quickly deploying their parachutes and high-technology merchandise below.

"What the hell is going on, Kinoga? You went too far! Now we are in combat!" Takishi screamed.

Kinoga lurched at Takishi and grabbed the lapels of his heavy jacket. He moved his face within centimeters of Takishi's, who could smell the captain's stale breath.

"Don't question my authority on my ship!" Kinoga hissed. "I am the captain. I am in charge.

Now shut up before I throw you overboard and grieve your accidental loss before the prime minister!"

Takishi's body was limp in Kinoga's powerful grasp. His back against the wall, Takishi ran one hand lightly over the pistol inside its holster beneath his jacket.

Kinoga stepped away and returned to his duties, smiling as he watched the rockets seduce the enemy missiles, breaking the radar lock on his vessel.

Takishi silently urged the ship forward, not wanting to know how close they had come to being hit. *Let's move*, Takishi thought, as the missiles veered away and screamed ineffectively into the water, which quickly drowned their potency.

Ling watched the pursuit on the radar screen. He saw the three aircraft quickly circle to the east of the ships as one escaped into international waters. He applauded as the missiles struck two radar images. Perhaps he would not be shot if the pilots could kill them all. Plus, this was *way* less boring.

"We've hit two," the pilot called back to the central command.

"Good work. Kill the one moving east, then the rest," the section chief responded.

The pilots pulled out of their attack formation and swung east again, bearing down on the fleeing radar image. Acquiring radar lock, each pilot removed the safety from his weapons control with the flick of a gloved thumb. They had the intruding ship in their sights. Suddenly, twelve F-16 aircraft pushing squawk codes of the 401st Tactical Fighter Wing of the Hualien Air Force Base, Taiwan, intercepted the Chinese aircraft, appearing as a mass on the two pilots' radar screens and warning them that they were prepared for combat.

Outnumbered, the Chinese pilots quickly turned and re-formed to cover one another. Speeding back into Chinese airspace, the fighters were joined by the People's Liberation Air Forces and destroyed the remaining "ships" within their offshore zone, erasing any evidence of what had really transpired. They remained vigilant throughout the night, as a carrier battle group received word to deploy from Zhoushan and churn full steam ahead into the East China Sea.

Takishi managed a smile as he knew that the F-16s were actually Japanese air defense forces. He had secured the squawk codes from a Taiwanese air force general in exchange for a generous "gift."

The F-16s conducted an aerial display worthy of an air show, providing cover for the retreating vessel.

CHAPTER 5

Takishi watched Kinoga pilot his ship as they continued to tunnel through the black, salty night. They finally split the lighthouses of Kubura and Irizaki, which guided them into a port tucked safely behind the rocky bluffs of Yonaguni, the southernmost of the Japanese Ryukyu Islands and a short 130 kilometers from Taiwan. As they arrived at the small pier, Takishi pondered the night's activities. Their actions had given the impression that Taiwan was probing, if not provoking, China.

Takishi was a master strategist, and he was certain that Prime Minister Mizuzawa had chosen the proper course for his native land. With North Korea and China possessing both the capability and the intent to dominate the Pacific Rim militarily, Japan could not let a few radical Muslims divert the world's attention away from what really mattered: the geopolitical balance of power in the Pacific. His alliance with the Americans was simply a means to an end.

Having performed his duties as a teenager in the Japanese Self Defense Forces, Takishi had migrated to becoming a clandestine operative with Naicho, the Japanese equivalent of the CIA, then ventured into the banking business, where he amassed a fortune. He was an expert marksman, mountain climber, and viewed himself as the ultimate Renaissance Man. He believed that there was nothing of which he was not capable. How many times had he climbed Fuji, he wondered? Why not Everest? Perhaps his ascent up his personal Mount Everest had begun two years ago over a few beers with an old Harvard Business School classmate.

Nobody planned wars in a vacuum, Takishi knew, and he was no exception. His instructions from the prime minister had been as clear as they were vague.

"Exploit this window of opportunity to our advantage. We have China and North Korea salivating now that the U.S. is focused on their upcoming Iraq war. And we have pressing resource and economic issues that we must confront. You are a Harvard man. Help me solve them."

Takishi knew that most people recognized a window of opportunity by the sound of its slamming shut; always in hindsight. But not Mizuzawa and especially not him. Takishi was proud of the phased operation he had begun planning right after 9-11. Whether the Americans had engineered that attack or not, he didn't care. There were so many conspiracy theories about how the U.S. had invited Japan to attack Pearl Harbor, but he doubted them all. It was Japanese brilliance that had led to the most stunning victory in the history of the world, not American conspiratorial cunning.

Takishi felt relieved as he spied his Shin Meiwa US-1A float plane, a Japanese air-and-sea craft with four Rolls-Royce AE 2100 engines that drove the amphibious craft's four propellers, tethered just one pier away. The sun was already spreading its morning glow on the rugged terrain of the atoll, where Japanese explorers claim to have found a city that sank when the island broke away from the continent in the twelfth century.

A sinking Japan, Takishi thought, was exactly what they were trying to avoid.

"Satisfied, my friend?" Kinoga asked as he walked to the starboard ramp with Takishi, the morning brightness hurting his eyes.

"Yes, I am getting satisfaction," said Takishi. "I was much too bothersome to you last night, Admiral." He snapped from his reverie as he held a stanchion at the top of the ramp.

"It is good that you are not in my line of work—don't ever pretend you could handle it."

Seagulls circled nearby, hoping for the ceremonial dumping of the ship's slop bucket. Their loud squawks hurt Takishi's ears, causing him to flinch and narrow his eyes. The fresh morning air returned some coherency to his thoughts.

"If you could gather your crew, the prime minister has given me the authority to award you and your men the Imperial Cross."

Kinoga hesitated, ever suspicious. But the Imperial Cross was the highest military decoration, and his men had earned it.

"Why are you so generous, Takishi?"

"It's not my idea, Kinoga. Our prime minister instructed me that if you successfully completed the mission, your men were to receive the Cross," Takishi said, avoiding eye contact.

"Do you not believe we deserve the medal?" Kinoga scoffed.

"What I believe is irrelevant. Your men accomplished the mission, and they deserve the prime minister's compliments."

"Very well, I will be in the cockpit debriefing the men."

Kinoga assembled his six men while Takishi debarked and walked to a black limousine waiting near the pier. Inside the small room, Kinoga told his men to sit. They did so at a rectangular wooden table.

"You performed a difficult and sensitive mission for your motherland last night. You should be proud," Kinoga said, his mouth dry and sticky. "Whether you know it or not, you all have taken part in the first of a series of activities that will lead our great nation back to its rightful place. Because of your actions last night, the Japanese Empire will rise again."

The sailors, all hand-chosen by Kinoga, were weathered seamen who wanted only the best for their country. They all nodded with approval at Kinoga's words.

Kinoga then individually congratulated them, reminding them of the secrecy of the mission.

"Your prime minister will reward you highly for your accomplishments," said Kinoga, facing the table with his back to the door. He heard the door open with a metallic squeak.

Before he could turn around, a whisper shot through the room. Kinoga fell forward at his men's feet, bleeding from the skull.

Standing in the doorway was Takishi, holding a silenced machine gun at his side.

He smiled and finished his business.

"And it is good you are not in my line of work, Admiral," he said, stepping over the bodies.

Leaning over the admiral's corpse, he whispered to the man's lifeless face, "Politics? This is about national survival, my dear friend."

Takishi, who used the moniker "Charlie Watts," pulled out his satellite-enabled phone and sent a text message to his contact, "Mick Jagger."

Satisfaction.

A moment later Mick Jagger sent a return note:

Let it bleed.

Indeed, Takishi thought. *If you only knew.*

Takishi boarded his Shin Meiwa as the men in the black limousine moved to dispose of the attack boat.

CHAPTER 6

Takishi was a busy man. That morning he had flown nearly nineteen hundred kilometers from Yonaguni to Davao City, Mindanao, to meet quickly with the Abu Sayyaf leader there.

He stooped and stepped down the ladder of the Shin Meiwa. The new version of an endangered species of an airplane, with its upgraded Japanese computer avionics and GPS technology, made the vessel perfect for Takishi's purposes.

As he stood on the steaming runway, the bright sunlight and intense Mindanao heat rapped him in the face. He was tired from the previous night's seafaring activities, and the humidity further sucked his strength. Yet, he was more at home there than bouncing around the cockpit of Kinoga's attack boat. Dismissing the thoughts of killing the admiral and his men, Takishi was focused on his next task. *So much to do.*

Meeting Takishi on the tarmac was Commander Douglas Talbosa, a snake-eyed man who led the entire Abu Sayyaf movement in the Philippines, having engineered several attacks and kidnappings over the past decade. The more spectacular, the better, because the money would pour into the Abu Sayyaf coffers once they were able to post onto the Internet the images of death and destruction. Talbosa was unusually tall for a Filipino, nearly six feet, and wore an Australian bush hat with one side flipped up. Takishi looked at him and thought the man at least had some style.

That an emerging Muslim extremist terror network existed in that remote southern isle of the Philippine archipelago was no surprise to Takishi. He knew that Al Qaeda was seeking areas that lacked governance, and the hundreds of islands that constituted the Republic of the Philippines were impossible to govern effectively. The remote islands presented the perfect sanctuary ingredients: desperate, uneducated peasants, isolated terrain, and clandestine routes of ingress and egress.

Those ingredients were perfect for Takishi's plan as well.

His sunglasses shielded his eyes from the bright sun and the Filipino commander. The prop wash from the four propellers of the Shin Meiwa blew hot air against his back as he bowed. Fortunately, Takishi had worn his lightweight khakis for his final meeting with the Al Qaeda knockoff group.

Talbosa returned the bow and said in broken English, "Good news. But first, Takishi, I should show you our plans for the entire operation again."

"I only have a few minutes, Talbosa, but I wanted to make sure we had no remaining problems."

"Yes, yes, no problem," Talbosa said quickly with a heavy accent. "All operations are no problem. All good. Good news, too."

"What news?"

"We have destroyed two ranger C-130 airplanes. My deputy, Pascual, is securing them now."

Takishi reflected a moment, glad his eyes were hidden by sunglasses. *The Rolling Stones work quickly*, he mused.

"Yes, that is good news. Do you have all of the information and ammunition you require?"

"We have most of what we need. Luzon will attack the Subic ammo point. No problem. They get the ammo from Subic for us and to keep the Americans from having it. No problem."

"Okay, you run your operation however you see fit. I'm here to make sure you have what you need. And congratulations on the victory."

"No problem. And Takishi, I have been inspecting your operation as well. It appears you have no problems also?"

Takishi lowered his sunglasses and stared at Talbosa, whose face was rigid with sincerity.

"No problems." Takishi smiled.

He offered his hand to the Filipino as they approached his aircraft.

"Yes, it is all good. And remember, Talbosa ..."

"Yes?"

"When you are done, you will be justly rewarded. Perhaps president?"

"We want Muslim nation; that is all." Talbosa was nonplussed. A warrior and devout Muslim, he was akin to the Taliban, who intersected with the poppy growers to fuel their insurgency. *By whatever means possible.*

"One final thing," Takishi said.

"Yes? But hurry, I must meet with Pascual."

"There is an American somewhere on this island. It would be good to catch him and ... do as you please with him." Takishi looked down the long runway, away from Talbosa, wondering if they caught the significance of what he was saying. "Matt Garrett. He's CIA."

"I understand, Takishi," Talbosa said. "We will capture this man and make an example out of him."

"But no other Americans, clear?"

"No problems," Talbosa smiled.

CHAPTER 7

Takishi bid Talbosa farewell and boarded his plane. He fit a set of headphones over his ears as he sat in a strapped jump seat between the pilot and copilot, and told them to head to Cateel Bay.

The Shin Meiwa pulled away from the runway with a short roll, its four powerful Rolls-Royce engines easily lifting the aircraft off the concrete instead of having to fight the suction created during a waterborne take-off.

Ascending above Davao City, Takishi looked down upon the impoverished metropolis. There were a few modern buildings in the downtown area, like a pearl in a rotten oyster, but they quickly gave way to adobe structures, then to the thatch huts that dominated the outskirts of the city. Banana plantations and rice paddies formed odd geometric shapes beneath them, in stark contrast to the thick triple-canopy jungle of the highlands.

His pilot cut the trim of the tail rudder, and the plane leveled into a smooth glide. Cateel Bay was only forty-five minutes away, just northeast of Davao City on the eastern coast of Mindanao.

They flew above the tropical rain forest that dominated the mountains, which cut a jagged north-to-south path over the eastern portion of the island. A series of small agricultural and fishing villages dotted the east coast. Takishi could see groupings of thatch huts every twelve kilometers or so. Parked on the sandy shore were small wooden boats that the fishermen used for short ventures beyond the coral reef to harvest the rich waters of the Philippine Sea.

He tapped the pilot on the shoulder when he saw the horseshoe of Cateel Bay. The pilot knew the route and nodded at Takishi. They began their descent, circling down from above. The tropical blue hue of the water became more evident as they floated downward. The pilot banked the Shin Meiwa, then leveled its wings parallel to the water. With its protective coral reef nearly a kilometer offshore, Cateel Bay was the perfect area in which to land an air/seaplane. There were no waves, and the beach was sandy, allowing the craft easy ingress and egress.

The plane skidded as it always did, spraying fine mist in either direction. Another skid, and the water's friction against the pontoons grabbed the craft, causing its passengers to lurch slightly forward for a typical landing. The pilot steered the plane to the beach, where it found purchase with a gentle nudge into the sand.

Takishi turned and spoke in his harsh Japanese tongue to his eighteen passengers, telling them to stand and exit the airplane.

They came crawling from the back of the plane toward the side door in single file. Movement was difficult, as each man had his hands and feet chained together. Like a clumsy centipede, they clanked together down the ladder of the airplane, stepping into the shallow water.

To a man, they shut their narrow eyes, balking at the brightness of the noonday sun. They were relieved, however, to be out of the airplane, as the temperature had reached an unbearable 120 degrees inside the steel frame of the craft while they were waiting for Takishi in Davao City. Outside, it was only 105 degrees. Much better.

Takishi stood on the beach, envisioning himself as a futuristic MacArthur, with his gold-rimmed sunglasses and wicked smile. He pulled a revolver from his trousers and checked its payload with a quick flip of his wrist. The prisoners looked up, squinting in the bright sun, at the familiar sound of unlatching metal. With his thumb, Takishi popped the cylinder back into the New Nambu revolver. Takishi liked it because it made him feel like a cowboy. It was uniquely different from the military automatic pistols, and the curved, custom-made pearl-handled grip fit his hand rather well.

He smiled at the gang of prisoners, all Chinese, Koreans, or Indonesians who had infiltrated his homeland, byproducts of the fractional criminal element in Japan. While the black market was a nuisance to the country, these illegal immigrants were perfect fodder for his purposes.

He marched them off the beach, past the thatch huts of the fishing village, and onto a trail that led almost two kilometers into the jungle. *Yes, we shall return*, he thought to himself, smiling. Takishi relished this post-9-11 window of opportunity. The Americans' fledgling effort in Afghanistan and their obvious intentions toward Iraq opened the door for geopolitical chess moves that would overwhelm and stymie the Americans. He was part strategic military planner and part pragmatic economist: a modern-day Machiavelli.

As they walked, Filipino peasants waved at Takishi. He always brought them packages of food from his country. This time was no different as he had the pilot drop three boxes next to an elderly woman. The peasants were unaware that the food was nothing more than military combat rations. It was nutritional and filled their children's stomachs.

The Filipinos stood from cleaning fish along a straw mat and watched the entourage. Takishi looked at the children in bare feet, their legs dirty and riddled with fly bites. He smiled and waved, though it was an insincere gesture. He had no sympathy for them.

They soon entered the dense jungle and followed a worn path up the spine of a ridge to the south of a river that would lead them to a brown and green structure. There was a road that came from the north, but the shorter distance to the factory was directly through the jungle.

Once there, Takishi would introduce his friends to Mr. Abe, the manager of plant number three, who could surely use the labor. The other three Rolling Stones knew about plant number one, which manufactured small arms for the Abu Sayyaf insurgency.

But they had no clue about the other three plants, which built weaponry of a different type.

CHAPTER 8

Philippine Abu Sayyaf Commander Douglas Talbosa departed the airfield and rode in an old U.S. Army jeep toward the burning hulk of an airplane that had crashed about thirty kilometers north of Davao City in the east-central highland region of Mindanao.

He had three battalions of infantry soldiers, each consisting of roughly three hundred men. There were three companies per battalion. The unit had no organic support structure. Talbosa had done his best to create a new, loosely structured unit to supply ammunition, food, and other critical supplies to his troops deployed in the field. As a result of the Japanese monetary assistance, the Muslim army had been able to buy new supplies, equipment, and, most importantly, food. Talbosa had a two-man staff that coordinated all logistical efforts. Now with the apparent shooting down of two Philippine C-130s, he hoped they would be able to take some pictures and get more funding by posting them on the Internet. Al Qaeda was always looking to reinforce successful commanders by rewarding them with money that would propel further attacks against westernized countries.

Eyewitness accounts said one aircraft blew up in the sky, and the other discharged about thirty paratroopers before exploding into the side of a mountain. When he got a daylight report, then he might dispatch one of his few precious helicopters to survey the wreckage. But for the moment, he wanted his men to quickly inspect the smoldering aircraft hulks, if they could, and bring back alive any soldiers who made it to ground safely. Just days before their final offensive into Manila, it was critical that he get as much intelligence as possible.

The sun had risen, peeking above the jungle highlands to the east. An orange-gray shade tumbled over the eastern mountain range, the sun not yet high enough to illuminate the leeward slopes. The mountain's elongated shadow still obscured the aircraft wreckage.

Talbosa did not know exactly what he was looking for, but his men rode forward in old farm trucks and jeepneys, fancy Filipino jeeps ornately decorated with several hood ornaments and colorful velvet material around the window edges. They had painted the vehicles an olive color, but some of the troops kept the red, orange, and maroon velvet curtains hanging inside.

Two of Talbosa's battalions moved quickly to link up with the battalion that had downed the aircraft an hour earlier. Speeding along the only road in the Central Valley, they moved past what was the initial drop zone for the Ranger unit and stopped their vehicles in a rather unprofessional fashion all around the one aircraft. Black smoke billowed from the midsection, which was split in two. The wreckage gained definition as the sun burned away the dawn mist and darkness. The men who had shot down the aircraft were jubilant, and wasted no time in greeting their commander.

"Rangers?" Talbosa asked Pascual, his second-in-command, who had been in charge of the air-defense efforts.

"That's right," Pascual said, relishing his kills. "We got both planes. Only about twenty or so enemy jumped from the first airplane."

"Congratulations, men," he said to the growing

throng gawking at the smoking airplane and the charred bodies strewn about the wreckage. In no time, the men were pilfering the equipment and picking through the uniforms of the dead soldiers.

"Have one battalion stay here, another to move back to their air-defense positions, and the last one to move into the jungle to the east with me. I want them here in half an hour," Talbosa ordered. Pascual saluted and moved out, eager to please his commander once again.

Talbosa was not surprised when his men, digging around the wreckage, found the bodies of seventy Filipino Rangers. A Mindanao native, Talbosa was in his middle forties, and the drop zone was less than eight kilometers from his boyhood home. He grew up with the Abu Sayyaf and its governing ideology, not as right wing as the Taliban in Afghanistan, but not as liberal as the European Muslims of Bosnia and Kosovo. Their ideology was a more pragmatic one, based loosely around Islamic faith. Talbosa knew that not even Al Qaeda was altogether Koran-based. In the final analysis, he was convinced that the only way for his country to achieve any semblance of international respect was by aligning with the only growing insurgent movement in the world, Islamic extremism. Perhaps that would bring social and economic equality to his countrymen. Nothing else had.

He had been only ten years old in 1969, when a group of ragged Filipino soldiers appeared at his family's hut. His father worked the sugarcane plantation of one of the wealthy Filipino families, the Aquinos. Their rudimentary living quarters consisted of nothing more than a thatch hut, which sat astride the massive sugarcane field. The soldiers had told his father about the new movement that some "university students" were organizing. They needed people to fight for the cause.

"We want a better future for your son, Mister Talbosa," a wild-eyed student armed with an AK-47 had said.

The elder Talbosa had looked at his son, standing by his leg, then beyond the soldiers at the cane fields and knew that if his children were to have a better life than working eighteen hours a day in those rat-infested fields, he had to let him go. Douglas was eager to venture out, as most young boys are wont to do.

He was not the youngest "soldier," but he had showed great bravery padding along the hardened trails of the jungle, running messages, and providing warning of attacking Filipino or communist soldiers. He had soon graduated to a sparrow unit and participated in the executions of hundreds of his countrymen who did not support the cause. He had risen through the ranks the hard way, having several brushes with the grim reaper. He knew about death, and he knew about poverty. He preferred to die fighting for a better life for his countrymen than to live in a shack where the children ran scared from rats the size of soccer balls.

After his sparrow-unit experience, he had been given command of the Mindanao cell, which consisted of about two thousand loosely aligned soldiers. Now, with Takishi as wind behind his sails, he had declared himself the leader of the Abu Sayyaf movement throughout the country. One day, he believed, his army could anchor the eastern boundary of the Islamic Caliphate.

Considering his past for a brief moment, Talbosa spit into the ground, pulled the brown Australian bush hat tight onto his head, and scanned the eastern mountains for the wreckage of the second plane. Clearly, it was not visible on the western range, as the sun provided great visibility, but the eastern range was still dark. They would find it in time. It was his notion, too, that whatever Rangers had made it safely out of the aircraft would probably move to the nearest cover, and that appeared to be the eastern range. Even though the Rangers normally moved south toward Davao City to conduct raids, he figured the unit had taken too many casualties for them to pursue that option.

He radioed the battalion commander and told him to hurry. They were going Ranger hunting.

And they needed to hurry because, Talbosa knew, Matt Garrett was near the wreckage.

CHAPTER 9

JAPANESE WEAPONS PRODUCTION PLANT #3
CATEEL, MINDANAO, PHILIPPINES

"Unit number seven needs more hydraulic fluid in its lower lathe," Kanishi Abe said to the production supervisor.

"Mr. Abe," he said, pronouncing it "Ahbey," "we are operating well beyond the capacity of these machines. Less than two years old, and we have exceeded the quality-control time lines on all replaceable parts," Mr. Kuriwu said in his native language.

"I understand. We have almost met our production goals, and a new team will come in a few days to replace us. Then it will be their problem," Abe said. His comments were out of character. He considered it unprofessional to pass along unresolved problems, but this was different.

"Please patch the tubing and replace the fluid before we lose hydraulic power in number seven and exceed the parameters for safe assembly."

"Yes, sir."

Abe walked along the assembly line, watching his robots perform assembly of minor parts of a tank chassis. Wearing a white smock, he looked like the automobile engineer that he used to be. Graduating with honors from the University of Tokyo, Abe had immediately gone to work for Mitsubishi, designing most of their current line of automobiles. Recently, he had participated in developing, hell, he developed, the Mitsubishi AH-X helicopter with the new twenty-nine-hundred-horsepower turbo shaft engine.

He spoke briefly with a technician and moved along the production facility, which was brightly lit. Robots moved in short, hydraulic spurts, placing a widget here or a gadget there, and at the end of the line came a tank or a helicopter. The sound of men speaking Japanese was evident above the constant clanking of the assembly line.

How the Japanese engineers had ever constructed this plant was a mystery to Abe. Carved into the side of a mountain, it seemed more like a huge white cave to him. He was amazed and at the same time not surprised by the abilities of his countrymen. It was his understanding that there were three other similar facilities spread over the remote island. His particular plant was built into an old mining quarry. In essence, the Japanese had simply laid down a floor on the bottom and a big roof on the top. But the guts were state-of-the art robotics, pushing tanks and attack helicopters along two separate assembly lines.

He was curious how the Philippine government could afford such a massive increase in their armed forces. He surmised that the Americans were paying for all of it, and construction of the facilities was another "peaceful" way for Japan to contribute to security in the region and contribute to the Global War on Terror. It made sense, and Mr. Taiku Takishi had told him that the United Nations was exploiting the strengths of member countries to create a stronger world that could fight terrorism at its roots.

"Manufacturing is our strength," Takishi had said. Abe did not personally know Takishi other than the fact that he appeared roughly every couple of weeks with 18 new workers for him, mostly foreigners, Chinese, Korean, and a few Japanese mafia. He knew that Takishi landed his float plane in

Cateel Bay, walking the prisoners up the spine of the ridge to his plant location.

But still Abe wondered, why the secrecy? What happened to the other teams that had already rotated back?

The facility was located in the eastern mountain province of Mindanao just northwest of the small coastal town of Cateel and astride a river that provided waste runoff from the plant into Cateel Bay. He and his production team had rotated to Mindanao from Japan six months ago, replacing a team that had already been working six months. In three days, another team was to replace them, and he could go back to his family.

He paused at a water cooler and drained two cupfuls. He pulled a picture of his wife and two girls from the breast pocket of his smock and stared at it. He missed them. He wondered if his two children, ages five and three, would remember him. He had not been allowed any phone or email contact with his family and was only permitted outside of the biosphere environment to exercise for thirty minutes daily.

Abe exercised during that time, the only real stress relief he could find. He wore a bright orange Nike jogging suit when he ran. That way, no Filipino hunters would mistake him for a wild pig running through the jungle. The Japanese construction team, two years earlier, had built an exercise path through the jungle above the old quarry. It was perversely anachronistic—a modern arms-production facility with an executive jogging path in the Mindanao hinterlands, through which indigenous tribesmen occasionally wandered. The dense tropical rain forest made it seem like the facility and path both were out of place, not that the area had failed to modernize.

The top of the plant was covered with dirt, and tropical growth renewed over the past two years. The running route was a dark tunnel of trees through the thick jungle, consisting of a circular kilometer and exercise stations every couple of hundred meters where the five or six high-level technicians could do push-ups, pull-ups, sit-ups, stretching, and balancing exercises. At each station was a sawdust pit off to the side of the gravel track, with signs that described how to use the appropriate equipment. For Abe, the exercise had become the only thing he looked forward to since his plant had gone to round-the-clock production. He couldn't remember being so tired since Mitsubishi increased production in the mid 1990s in order to flood the American market.

It was nearly five in the morning and time for Abe to get four hours of sleep before checking the nine o'clock shift. During his next shift, he would sneak out and relax his mind and body, he told himself. He summoned his vice president for operations and told him to take charge while he rested. The man dutifully obeyed. Abe walked past the constantly moving assembly line, looking at the many tank chassis, marveling at the technology they were employing on these modern weapons.

He knew very little about the military. He was a pacifist, having been raised in Japan's post–World War II era. He advocated Article Nine of the Japanese Peace Constitution. He saw no need for Japan to be strong militarily when they could effectively compete in the world through economics. But he understood the need for other nations to have strong militaries, particularly countries such as the Philippines, where insurgency impeded all government headway.

He opened the door to his cubicle of a room. As the plant manager, his accommodations were less spartan than the others', but not luxurious by any stretch. Still, he had no television or radio. He was completely isolated from the outside world. The walls of the facility were as white as Abe's smock. It was a sterile environment. Music from Japanese tapes poured through speakers in the work area.

Before he entered his room, he paused and looked down the pristine white hall toward the glass door and guard station that separated the living quarters from the production area. Beyond his door in the other direction was the heavily guarded entrance. Abe felt secure with the guards there. Mr. Takishi had warned him about the rising tide of Islamic insurgency and how they would try to steal everything they had. It was good, he thought, that there were Japanese soldiers protecting his plant. He agreed that trucking the tanks at night to the port city of Davao was best, also, because it was then that they would be most secure from the wandering Abu Sayyaf bands.

He closed and locked his door behind him. His room was about seven meters wide and five and a half meters deep. He had a bed, sink, shower, and toilet area; desk area with nearly thirty books; and a closet and chest-of-drawers area. It was not unlike his dorm room at the University of Tokyo. Littered about his desk were pictures of his wife and girls. His wife, Nagimi, was a beautiful woman in her late thirties. She had black hair and a huge grin that produced dimples in her cheeks. In one picture, she was kneeling, looking up at the camera and wearing an oriental robe. Sitting at his desk, he got out his notebook to make another entry in his journal.

"April 2002. I have only three days remaining until the next team arrives to plant number three. Soon, I will joyously return home to my lovely wife and children. I can't wait. But must. I can feel the spirit of my family in my soul. Oddly, we have continued to increase production of tanks at a rapid pace. We are

making nearly twenty a day now. I hope and pray that these weapons bring peace and security to the Filipino people and help the fight against the terrorists. If in some small way, I have made the world a safer place through the production of these weapons, then I will have fulfilled a duty that I always wanted to pursue. If these weapons, however, only add to the fighting and suffering in the world, then I am ashamed of my time here and will, of course, be responsible for my actions. At the very least, I have fulfilled an obligation to my prime minister, and I am happy about that. A new poem:

The path is my way/a way to peace you say/the path is my guide/my temple to pray/it moves past me/as only I can see/my motives are/to make these people free/gravel beneath and green above/it is the dove/I hope/and not the fisted glove/that comes flying toward/these people so moored/to their misery.

Three days and counting.

Abe closed the book and placed it in his desk drawer. He had religiously written similar thoughts in the journal every night since his arrival. He thought he might try to publish his collection of poems. It was an escape for him, like writing the fabled poison-pen letter that never gets sent to whom it is directed—at least it makes you feel better, he thought. He walked to the sink area and washed his face. Looking in the mirror, he noticed new wrinkles in his face. He was aging quickly. Perhaps all of the stress and worry had gotten the best of him. After brushing his teeth, he urinated and climbed in bed. He set his alarm clock for 8:30 A.M.. That would give him enough time to wake up, shave, shower, dress, and report for the 9:00 A.M. shift. After all, the commute was short.

Lying in bed, as he thought of his two girls, he

wept silently. He had to be strong. Even though he was only a few days away from rejoining his beloved family, the battery in the clock seemed to be weak, dragging the second hand slower and slower each day. Sometimes, it almost seemed to stop.

Soon, he would run on the jungle path. That would make him stronger.

CHAPTER 10

Special Forces Major Chuck Ramsey watched Sergeant First Class Jones set up the tactical satellite radio so that he could inform Okinawa and the U.S. embassy in the Philippines that he had control of eleven of his twelve team members and one Filipino Ranger that had survived the jump.

The news was not good, but it always got worse with age. The two men quietly huddled in a thick crop of elephant grass, toying with the satellite antenna. Overhead, monkeys spoke their primordial language, screeching at one another through the green of the mahogany leaves. The blazing sun hung in its afternoon position over the western mountain ranges, its unfiltered rays blasting them with heat.

"Viper base, this is Bushmaster six, over."

"Bushmaster six, this is Viper base. Send it, over." The response was immediate and reassuring. He never doubted that it would not be, but his sense of isolation had grown as the realization of Peterson's death settled over him.

"This is Bushmaster six, we are in Las Vegas. Number two went to Montana, over." Las Vegas was the code for the rally point his team currently occupied and Montana was the unit's code for someone missing in action. Peterson was number two on the unit manning roster. After a brief pause, Ramsey heard the voice on the other end mutter, "Christ almighty." He quickly pressed the button on his handset to squelch the words. While the satellite communications were secured through encryption, the embassy was monitoring on the same frequency and he was unsure of the allegiance of some of the Filipinos who worked in the building.

"Wait one, Bushmaster." Ramsey waited, assuming the battalion commander was being paged.

"Bushmaster six, Viper six," the commander said, using his call sign. "Say again sitrep." Commanders never trusted initial reports from radio and telephone operators so always had to hear a second iteration.

"This is Bushmaster six. I say again that we are in Las Vegas and that number two went to Montana."

"Roger. Any other information?"

"Negative."

"Roger. Go Yankees, out."

"Out," Ramsey said. "Go Yankees" was the code signaling Ramsey to continue the mission. "Go Dodgers" would have meant to abort the mission. He was sure the battalion commander was just as pained over Peterson's loss as he was, but Ramsey knew the man to be a professional who realized that there were eleven other lives at stake. Plus, long radio conversations were routinely intercepted and got people killed. Ramsey passed the word that they had made contact with battalion and passed on the message of "Go Yankees." His Special Forces soldiers expected nothing less.

From his perch, he could see movement some 550 meters below. Looking at the map, he determined his location to be about twenty-five kilometers east of a small village named Compostela. They had jumped parallel to a major highway, which provided the most direct route from the northern port city of Surigao, through Davao, and to the southern tip of the island near a town called General Santos. With the searing sun illuminating the entire valley and the Abu Sayyaf seeming, for the moment, not to be on his tail, Ramsey could see that Mindanao was a beautiful island. To his north were a high

ea. I know they mine a lot of copper
here."

writing and mine shafts. Mmmm.
ernment doesn't allow much foreign
e the local dialect is Chinese. Who
y shrugged.
, else, maybe we can do some PT,"
ferring to the track.
ked at Benson, and they both shared a
amsey said, "Yeah, right." It felt good

into the ground, plucking scattered
cco away from his lip.
now. You think it would be safe to
re and check it out this early?" Ramsey
g of the thick scrub that he and Lonnie
ught through and how much easier it
e daylight.
lded.
their rucks on, and Ramsey placed
ge of the team, while he and Benson
connaissance mission. He had decided
young Filipino Ranger with them.
objected, but Ramsey insisted that he
to provide some insight into the nature
le had proven useful in finding his way
d indeed walked point on two of the
ls the team had performed.
settled the three men began hacking
ugh the jungle in search of the gravel

leted preparing his transition briefing
roduction team and now anticipated a
n the path in the wild jungle. To Abe,
rom the state of the art factory to the
stepping into a time machine. One

plains area and another range of mountains. To his west was a rain forest that rose to 2500 meters in another mountain range. He could see where several rivers converged into the southern portion of Mindanao at the site of a town called Datu Piang. Just beyond Datu Piang was another mountain range, which seemed to be the steepest of them all. From afar most of the forests were dotted green and brown. Ramsey correctly assumed the brown spots to be clear-cut areas where relentless loggers had shredded enclaves of history and time.

He did a quick map resection to verify his location. While the GPS was usually accurate, he occasionally backed up its data with his own calculations. He liked the technology, but trusted his mental processes more.

He figured azimuths to three known points that he could identify on the map, a mountain peak, a road intersection, and a radio tower. He was surprised to see the radio tower, but was glad it was there. He then converted the azimuths to back azimuths by subtracting or adding 180 degrees. Then he drew a line from each point on the map along the back azimuths. The point at which the three lines intersected was his team's location. He had them positioned on an eleven-hundred-meter mountain that separated the towns of Compostela and Cateel. That was good news. A beach near Cateel Bay was where the Filipinos were to pick up his team in three days.

"We should've gone back sooner," Ramsey said to SFC Jones.

"Shit, Major, we've been on the go since last night. That's an L-shaped ambush waiting to happen. You done right, keeping the rest of the team safe," Jones responded.

"He saved my life. He hooked me up and threw me over the ramp."

"Go easy on yourself, sir," Jones said. "You'd have

done the same for him. Plus, I ain't convinced he's dead." Jones's last statement trailed off in an unconvincing manner. They all knew.

"Lonnie had to pull me away from the wreckage last night. I didn't want to leave, but there were so many of those bastards crawling all over both planes. Our move time had come and gone, and Lonnie kept telling me we had to leave, that maybe we'd link up with Peterson later. I kept expecting to find him beneath a parachute lean-to chowing on an MRE or something."

"Stop it, sir. It's not your fault. You've done a hell of a job keeping us alive."

It was true. Six times they had come within less than one hundred meters of detection, remaining motionless, practically breathless, as the Abu Sayyaf forces quickly padded by in their ragged brown and green uniforms.

In the darkness, Ramsey and Lonnie White, the medic, had finally circled back toward the drop zone. They found the area teeming with Abu Sayyaf, making undetected access to either airplane impossible. He and White had fought their way back through the steep, rocky jungle, their return trip more painful as they carried the extra weight of Peterson's loss squarely on their shoulders. Sometimes clutching to shallow roots was the only thing that prevented them from dropping to certain death 550 meters below.

Though glad to have Ramsey and White back in the fold, the team was solemn when they saw two, not three, men re-enter the patrol base.

Ramsey stuffed his map back in his rucksack, hearing Benson approach from the north as he led his patrol back into the base camp.

Sergeant First Class Benson knelt next to Ramsey, squatting in the high, misty jungle, listening to the eerie animal sounds of monkeys and macaws high in

the trees. They had about five kilometers all they had walked back on their own Sayyaf would not c far, they had been co

"Sir, we've got so said, sweat streami painted face.

"Surprise me. I Ramsey said, pulling and stuffing a good stark and unshaven. scratched his oily br

"We found a fen It's well-groomed, v fours. There are sig on them. We didn' eyebrows. As it was about a hundred me from the recon site jogging path."

"Was the enem asked.

"They did have most others we've Asian. Like I said, checking a green n

"Tell me more

"There's not n had little pictur running. Beneath about three mete kind we used fo school."

"Yeah. How f

"That's the s to the northeast,

shafts in
and ore

"Chi
Philippir
mining.
knows."

"If no
Benson sa

Ramse
silent laug
to smile.

Chuck
chunks of

"It's 1
head dowr
asked, thin
White had
might be ir

Benson

They p
White in c
went on th
to take tl
Benson qui
might be ak
of the signs.
around and
extended pa

The issu
their way th
path

Abe had col
for the new
peaceful run
transitioning
path was lik

minute he was the classic Japanese manufacturer, the next he was an orange-clad aborigine dashing through the rain forest.

In less than 72 hours, he would board Takishi's Shin Meiwa and fly north to see his family for the first time in over six months. His happy mind pinged with positive thoughts of reunion. He continued to carry a picture of his wife and two little girls in the breast pocket of his white smock. He wanted to go for one last jog before he ventured home.

The contrast of his seeming captivity in the plant and the freedom of the running path made him feel like a wild mustang running across the great American plains. He had visited America often and appreciated the culture, having developed a special affinity for Western movies. His latest poem alluded to the American West.

The horses rear wildly/dashing up the rocky steepness/canyons, buttes, and piñon trees/scattered to the west/they scamper and buck/chased by the hatted hunter/whose greedy ropes/have no luck/the mustang gives chase/searching and seeking/the ropeman disappears/having been beaten.

Donning his bright orange jumpsuit, he informed the vice president for operations that he was going for a quick jog. He walked out of the electronic doors, passing the guard, who had fallen asleep leaning against the building. They pulled hard shifts, and he decided not to wake the young member of the Japanese Defense Force.

He stretched briefly, then hopped onto the railroad-tie stairway that led out of the old quarry and onto the jogging path. Over his shoulder, he could make out the beautiful blue waters of Cateel Bay. The beach had a pinkish hue as the sun lowered behind the mountains. With a joyous smile, he broke into a gallop.

Today, I am the Mustang.

The walk had been brutal, taking them nearly half a day to move and then reconnoiter the running path. Ramsey, Benson, and the Filipino, simply known as Eddie, had sliced their way through the jungle using dead reckoning where Benson laid an azimuth on the compass, and they all followed. Benson had not found any trails leading to the curious path this time around. The jungle was mysterious that way. What was there only minutes before was gone the next time someone looked for it. They felt confident, though, that their machetes had blazed a suitable trail for the return trip.

They found the chain-link fence and the gravel path and backed off about twenty meters to set up an observation post. Ramsey determined that they should spend some time conducting reconnaissance of the surrounding area, so they took pictures with digital cameras, radioed back to the patrol base what they were doing, pulled back into an objective rally point, and planned to breach the fence near dusk.

As the sun began to dip behind the mountain range over which they had traveled, Ramsey low-crawled to the fence, snipped a hole with wire cutters, then continued to the sawdust pit with the sign and saw that it was exactly as Benson had described it. Only this sign had a stick body horizontal to the ground, a disconnected circular head, and a perpendicular arm, like it was doing a push-up. He crawled back to the observation point, holding his hush-puppy pistol in his hand and using his elbows to propel him through the thorny vines.

Benson provided cover with the MP5. As the daylight faded into darkened hues of green and brown, they knew it would soon be time to don the night-vision goggles.

"You go now. See if you can read the writing,"

Ramsey said to Eddie. He had smooth brown skin. His face was soft and round, despite the long scar coursing across the right cheek. His brown eyes were wide with anticipation, glowing white around the edges in hopes of providing useful information to his benefactors. They had taken him into their protective custody and he felt with grim certainty that he was the only Filipino Ranger left alive on the island.

Eddie moved with precision and skill to the sign and knelt. After a brief moment, he looked at the Americans hiding in the brush, smiling and giving them a thumbs-up. He had studied the Japanese language for two years in school, before dropping out to become a soldier.

As he was about to move, Eddie heard a steady crunching in the gravel. He froze on one knee with his head turned over his shoulder like a spotlighted deer. From their support position, Benson immediately sighted the moving figure. The bright orange outfit made the person an easy target. He was nearly fifty meters away, about to make the turn onto the push-up pit. Eddie slowly lowered his body, slid under the sign, and eased himself into the first layer of scrub. He lay motionless as what looked like a well-groomed Japanese man in an orange jumpsuit came panting into the pit. He was running so fast that Eddie thought the man was going to land on him when he stopped, the man's hands spraying sawdust into the Filipino's eyes.

Benson looked quickly to Ramsey for direction, who held up his hand, motioning him to maintain status quo. The orange-clad jogger began doing push-ups, and his good form perversely, though momentarily, struck Ramsey. Head raised, not looking between his legs like so many troops have a tendency to do. He was pumping like a hydraulic machine, his head fixed on the scrub to his front. His push-ups began to slow dramatically, and it struck

Ramsey as odd that he would taper off so soon. Then he stopped and froze.

Ramsey immediately knew that the man had spotted Eddie, who, no more than two meters away from the jogger, remained motionless in the bush.

Surprisingly, the man went to his knees, then slowly stood, moving closer to the boy. He pulled away a twig, revealing Eddie's face. The man held out his hand to Eddie, believing him to be hurt.

Abe had had little contact with the Filipino people during his stay in Mindanao. He had read much about them and their history and truly felt sorry for his country's past treatment of their people. In part, he felt good about producing weapons for the Filipinos so they would no longer have to rely on other powers for their own security. He believed the time had come for them to forge their own history instead of always being the pawn of some higher power's struggle.

So, as he reached out his hand, he was reaching in compassion to a people for whom he held great pity. He wanted to talk with them and experience at least some of their culture. He wanted to be able to tell his family about the Filipino people and how they were struggling in a world that recognized only raw power. True to his liberal beliefs, Abe reached his hand toward the young boy, obviously hurt, lying there like a wounded deer maimed by a hunter's bullet. His next poem would be about him, he was sure.

CHAPTER 11

Matt Garrett peered through the scope of his SIG SAUER and tried to assess everything he was watching.

He saw a Japanese man running on a gravel path as if he was doing exercise, which was strange enough. Then he saw the man drop and do some push-ups. Matt watched as a young Filipino soldier approached the Japanese man.

Adjusting his sight ever so slightly, Matt was able to pick out the faces of two well-camouflaged American soldiers.

They must be part of Peterson's team that jumped in last night.

Matt was on ground higher than any of the other participants in this uncoordinated drama, and he could plainly see that the situation was headed for tragedy. The Japanese could be a martial-arts expert. The Filipino could be Abu Sayyaf. The Special Forces soldiers might be wanting to kill anything because of their loss last night. There were multiple combinations and algorithms that could play out, yet none was what he would consider to be positive.

Just when he thought the strange situation could not deteriorate any further, he saw three Asian soldiers running up the path from the east. They were brandishing weapons that looked like small machine guns.

Quickly assessing the situation, he shot the three Japanese guards, who were sprinting toward the man in the orange jumpsuit. His silenced SIG SAUER made no noise at all, and the three men dropped to the ground, dead, though as he swung his weapon's sight back to the American soldiers, he saw them scanning with their own weapons. They had heard or seen something and were spooked.

Matt did what he always believed was best to do in that type of situation; he remained perfectly still. If they saw him, they might shoot him. He presumed he had just saved someone's life ... by taking three. He didn't want to think of the other possibilities, perhaps that the three men he had killed were simply doing rifle physical training and joining their commander on a jog.

No, the men were reacting to something, most likely the Americans who had cut the fence, which was probably wired with sensors. That triggered the response, and the guards were coming to close up the hole in the wire.

Matt reasoned that if that were truly the case, then they might have remote-viewing cameras and monitors around whatever facility the fence was protecting. That caused him to wonder just what the hell was happening there.

Could it be related to the Predators?

Major Ramsey and Sergeant First Class Benson were scanning the far side of the track as they watched the three Asian military men running at full speed suddenly fall as if shot.

"What the hell was that?" Benson asked.

"Those guys were shot," Ramsey said. He moved his scope slowly back and forth, seeing nothing.

Their attention was drawn back to Eddie as he dragged the man in the orange jumpsuit twenty-five meters through the scrub brush. As Ramsey's instincts kicked in, he pulled a roll of tape out of his ruck along with a set of plastic, disposable flexcuffs like those the police use during riots. Quickly, he taped the man's eyes and mouth shut then tightened the handcuff around his wrists. After surveying the situation, they moved quickly along the route back to the base camp, passing through it and stopping some fifty meters to the other side. Benson dropped off, informing the rest of the team what had occurred and that they had five minutes to prepare to move.

Then they walked for what seemed like hours, emerging from the jungle highlands, walking across a low valley plain and reentering another jungle, this time only steeper. They found their way using their night-vision goggles, but the Filipino and the prisoner had none, and the group could only move as fast as the slowest man could struggle blindly through the jungle. Ramsey was surprised at how little resistance the prisoner gave and had cut the flex cuffs for ease of movement.

As they struggled up the steep face of a rock outcropping, the captive grabbed at a rock with his bound hands, then lost his grip, dragging his fingernails along the face as he fell several meters. SFC Jones watched as the darkened figure let out a muffled scream and tumbled into him, knocking him back and down before he had a chance to move. As he fell, his rucksack protected his body, absorbing the force of the impact on both men. He heard the unpleasant sound of metal scraping on rock and silently swore at the prisoner, hoping the radio had not absorbed the impact of the fall.

The team re-formed and helped the captive to the top of the rocks, where one might expect to find an eagle's nest, and set up a new patrol base.

They were high above the coastal town of Baganga, some eight kilometers south of Cateel. Ramsey had decided to stop for the night, what little of it remained.

Ramsey knelt next to Benson.

"Hell of a hump we just did, Major," Benson said.

"You think it was Ron?"

Benson, who was using his knife to cut some thorny vines from his pants, looked at his leader in the moonlit night.

"Had to be somebody. You know anybody else who can shoot like that?"

CHAPTER 12

Matt had made three precision kills with his silenced weapon, then watched the two Americans disappear to the south into the dense jungle with the young Filipino and their hostage.

So Peterson was not alone.

His position afforded him a view of the action that had unfolded beneath him and an unnatural flattened expanse of land to the east, his left. He was well protected by an assortment of large rocks and tall pines. The climb down the back side of the mountain had been less difficult than the climb up the western slope, yet knowing Peterson's body was still up there weighed on him emotionally.

He tried to understand what he had just seen. Obviously, there were survivors from the jump, and they had taken captive a jogger. Three Asian men, who he now realized were Japanese soldiers, had quickly responded to the breaching of the metal fence. As he watched, there were about ten soldiers standing at the location from which the man had been abducted.

One man in particular seemed to be in charge. He was in civilian clothes and wore a pearl-handled revolver on his hip, like a cowboy. An old officer's hat, like MacArthur's, shielded much of his face, making it difficult to ascertain all of his features, but Matt could see that the man in charge was taller than any of the others.

His information on the Predators had led him to believe that China was developing the unmanned aerial vehicles for clandestine use against the United States or its allies. His mission was to find out whether that was true.

Yet, there he was in some uncharted rain forest of a remote, yet strategically vital, Philippine island, and he was watching Japanese soldiers and businessmen move about what appeared to be an old mine.

Knowing he had no chance of catching the Special Forces team that had bolted into the jungle, Matt eased away from his perch and moved to the north, away from the gaggle at the fence.

As he approached the fence on the northeastern side of the compound, Matt saw that there was a sensor wire running through the chain link and every fifty meters or so there was a solar panel and battery pack that powered each sensor. Matt's experience told him that some enterprising villagers had probably toyed around with stealing the batteries for their own purposes, so he continued walking along a minor path that mostly paralleled the fence.

Sure enough, when he reached a spot that afforded him a view, albeit darkened, of Cateel Bay, Matt saw that not only was the battery and solar assembly missing, but there was a small tunneled area beneath the fence. Either an animal had burrowed underneath, or an enterprising villager had evaded the sensors in that fashion.

Matt scraped some loose dirt out of the hole, slid his rucksack underneath, then snaked his way under the fence, the barbs of the chain link scratching at him as he burrowed. Soon he was inside.

He grabbed his rucksack and weapon, continuing downhill until he saw the opening.

Kneeling behind a tree, Matt placed his PVS-18 night-vision monocular to his face and scanned the area like a pirate searching for land. He saw the group rounding the corner about seventy-five meters southeast of his position.

He noticed a rail spur that led to a concrete ramp at the mouth of the complex in the mountain. What looked like an old mine shaft actually was some type of extremely well concealed facility. On the rail spur sat five flatbed cars and four armored vehicles or tanks. The Japanese soldiers seemed to have stopped in the middle of driving what looked like a German Leopard tank onto the last railcar, as the mammoth machine was perched precariously half on the last car and half on the ramp. It seemed to Matt that everyone was moving in the direction of the abduction, so he efficiently moved to the line of railcars and observed closely the tanks, committing to memory every detail possible. Six wheels, the two in the middle almost touching, an armored skirt, and what appeared to be a 120mm main gun.

This is the Japanese Type 90 Main Battle Tank.

He heard a sound less than fifty meters away and looked up. He noticed the taller, pearl-handled-revolver aficionado break away from the gathering and begin walking to the east with two armed personnel.

Interesting.

Matt backed toward the fence, stepping past some generators and telescoping lights like one might see at a Little League facility in the middle of a cornfield in Iowa. As he reached the perimeter fence, Matt followed the pearl-handled-revolver man in parallel and watched as they exited a small gate that was well guarded by at least four soldiers. He had moved along the fence about two hundred meters from where he had started. Not wanting to lose time by heading back to where he had initially gained entrance to the compound, Matt retrieved his Leatherman and cut the fence. He pushed out a small section, scooted through it, then pushed the section back in, as if someone had just cut his way *into* the compound.

A siren immediately began wailing in the background, and searchlights, those telescoping lights, began crisscrossing as if he were a prisoner escaping from Alcatraz. Behind him he heard the harsh commands of a Japanese guard team. His sense was that they had a general idea of his location but did not yet have a bead on him.

With clarity, Matt understood that he was in a tenuous position. The facility behind him, teemed with armed Japanese soldiers, and the Pacific Ocean lay to his front.

The trail on which he ran pushed him in a due easterly direction, and he could at last hear the water of Cateel Bay lapping at the shore. Two shots ricocheted through the leaves above his head. Probing. Spray and pray. They did not have a fix on him yet, he believed.

He reached the beach, kneeling next to some chest-high scrub. Thankfully, he was in superb physical condition, and his breathing remained calm. He smelled the faint odor of dead fish, as if he was near an area where they were either dumped or cleaned. Or both.

Listening, Matt heard the men talking in Japanese.

"I'm getting a report of another break-in."

"Have the defenses go to full alert. We cannot afford a compromise at this point."

"Where are you going?"

"I told you. To refuel and to inspect the fleet. I have already called for another engineer to take Abe's place. I will talk to Talbosa about him. He is not to survive. Clear?"

The conversation continued, but a coughing airplane engine drowned the voices.

Matt looked all around, then into the bay, and for the first time noticed the float plane sitting about ten meters to his front. The tail of the airplane was toward the beach, and the prop wash blew directly onto him.

He looked to the west along the trail he had traveled and saw the faint beam of flashlights sweeping and the disturbing sound of search dogs barking.

Not good.

Operating mostly on instinct, Matt tightened his rucksack on his back and moved parallel with the shoreline until he could enter the water near a grouping of Bangka boats. As he stepped into the bay, he could see the three men handling a small Zodiac, the sound of whose engine further masked his movement.

By then all four turbo propellers of the airplane were spinning loudly. Matt waded behind a Bangka boat in which he had placed his rucksack and rifle. To the naked eye, the boat would appear to be drifting slowly toward the airplane, as Matt's shoulders were just above the level of the warm water, but his head was below the rim of the boat.

As he entered the backwash area of the propellers, he was blasted with salt water and hot air. He grabbed his ruck and rifle and pulled himself up onto the float plane's landing gear well, which on that aircraft, was perpendicular to the fuselage as opposed to underneath it.

He released the Bangka boat, and it blew onto the beach. Matt could still see the Zodiac making its way to the starboard side of the aircraft, so in one deft movement, he leapt inside the port cargo door and rolled to the floor. He brought his weapon up to eye level but only saw the darkened hull of an airplane and an open cockpit door.

In his periphery, he saw the Zodiac approach. In the rear of the plane he found two pallets of combat rations, behind which he hid.

The tall man with the pearl-handled revolver boarded and strode to the cockpit, where he entered and took a seat.

Matt saw the man's head swing around and stare at the rear of the airplane, directly at him. Matt tensed as he watched the Japanese man step out of the cockpit and walk toward him. The man pulled a long knife from a sheath opposite his holster as Matt cradled the SIG SAUER, his trigger finger firmly in place.

The two pallets were about five feet high, filled with tan boxes of rations and other supplies. As Matt pressed his body into the back of the pallet, trying to make himself as small and invisible as possible, he noticed that flexible white binding straps secured each box. He was unable to see the man now, save for the toe of a cowboy boot that was pointing in his direction.

Matt felt the pallet tug and heard a "pop" followed by some rustling noises. Soon the boot toe turned in the opposite direction and he heard both cargo doors close on either side of the airplane.

Confident that the man had not seen him, Matt peered around the corner and saw him stepping into the cockpit holding a combat ration in one hand.

Soon thereafter, they were speeding along the smooth waters of Cateel Bay until they were finally airborne.

To God knows where.

CHAPTER 13

The climb through the treacherous mountains had nearly killed Abe. The only thing keeping him alive, he knew, was his physical-conditioning regimen for the past six months. The same path that had led to his capture had prepared him to survive the kidnapping.

Upon waking, Abe sensed he was still bound and gagged, his back smarting from the fall and the tips of his fingers bloody and sore. He had heard of such Islamic extremists, and how they were capable of such actions, but never expected anything to happen to him. He was sure he could reason with them. A Filipino voice spoke to him in broken English, occasionally mixing in a couple of Japanese words. A hand tore off the gag and placed a cup of water to his lips. Abe thanked the provider, using slightly better English. The Filipino asked him questions, and he responded. Still blindfolded, Abe had the sense that others were around him, listening.

"What you doing here?" the voice asked him.

"I manufacture," he replied. "You Abu Sayyaf?" Abe's weak voice asked.

"Abu Sayyaf! I spit on Abu Sayyaf!" the man said. He sensed the man move, as if to elevate, perhaps preparing to strike him.

"What make?"

Abe told him that they were making helicopters and tanks for the Filipinos so they could achieve independence from foreign powers and fight the insurgency.

"Traitor!" the Filipino screamed, slapping him across the face.

Abe felt others move quietly around his questioner, perhaps pulling him back.

The man regained his composure, though, and continued questioning.

"Japanese?"

"Yes. Japanese," Abe responded.

"Other Japanese with you?" Again Abe responded affirmative.

"Name?"

"Abe. Mister Kanishi Abe," he said slowly.

The questioning continued, and Abe gladly told them everything. He mentioned the number of Japanese in his plant and the number of plants, as well as how long the facility had been operating. One plant produced small arms, such as rifles and pistols, he believed, while his and two others made tanks, infantry fighting vehicles, and attack helicopters. He kept reiterating that the weapons had been ordered by the recognized government of the Philippines. At least that is what Mr. Takishi had told him.

Abe simply did not understand what all of the confusion was about. Needless to say, he was scared. Despite his fear, he realized that his situation was definitely good material for a poem; something to do with the blinded man groping for reason.

The images of his family tumbled through his mind as a wave of sadness settled over him. He was tired, hungry, and had no quarrel with his captors. It would be so simple to let him go. The hand placed a bowl of rice in his lap, and he ate voraciously but awkwardly, with his hands still cuffed.

"Let him eat," a voice said.

"I think he's telling the truth," another spoke.

"Agree, but keep him tied up."

Abe heard the new voices. They were Americans. What were Americans doing kidnapping him from his main battle tank production plant on Mindanao? The Americans, he knew, had authorized and paid for much of the construction.

At least that's what Mr. Takishi had told him.

Believing that they had stumbled onto something significant, Ramsey had Jones set up the satellite communications antenna, so that he could call in the information to Okinawa. They only had one satellite radio remaining, as the other was packed in Ron Peterson's rucksack. Watching Jones play with the antenna brought images of Peterson rushing back through his mind, but he stopped the onslaught, erecting a barrier in his mind, telling himself, *Not now, save it for later.*

"Son of a bitch," Jones said in his distinct Boston accent, toying with the radio and repositioning the antenna. What had been a consistently reliable means of communication failed him for the first time. It was not that he didn't expect it to happen, because it always did; but the timing could not have been worse. Ramsey thought it might be something about their new position, but Jones kept insisting that everything was functioning properly until he remembered that Abe had fallen on him. Quietly he looked at the bound and blindfolded man, wanting to be mad, but knew it was not his fault. "Son of a bitch."

"What do you think it is?" Ramsey asked.

"Don't know. I'm getting power, but I can't reach anybody. Last time I used it was to keep comms with your fox mike when you captured this guy," Jones said, pointing at the captive and referring to standard "frequency modulation" radio communications. With a flip of a switch, the tactical satellite radio was capable of performing routine FM short-distance communications or long-range satellite communications.

"When he fell on me, I landed on my ruck. Sounded like the radio took the blow, but I'm getting a signal. Can't figure it out. Son of a bitch!" Jones exclaimed, pained at the failure of his equipment.

Sending his men to perimeter positions in the triple-canopy jungle, Ramsey began to think of a way to communicate.

There had to be a way.

CHAPTER 14

PALAU, SOUTH PACIFIC OCEAN

Matt was surprised first when he heard the landing gear of the aircraft come down. He was expecting another water landing. Second, he was surprised at how soon the landing gear had been extended—maybe three hours.

The pearl-handled-revolver man had mentioned something about needing to refuel, so Matt surmised that was why they had landed. Then, inspecting "the fleet." What fleet?

During the flight, Matt had begun to have serious reservations about his decision. He was a passionate, driven decision maker, yet a calculating man. Most importantly, perhaps, everyone worked for someone, and he had a handler who was no doubt furious right about now.

For certain, he had little to no chance of making contact after his satellite communications had been disabled. Most likely, his cell phone would not work until he got to Davao City.

But Matt had sensed that they were flying east. They had taken off straight out of the bay, he was sure of that much, and he had felt very little banking in one direction or another until he felt the landing gear deploy.

He gathered himself and his equipment as they were leveling off for the landing, which came suddenly with a loud report and bounce. Obviously the pilot was more adept at water landings than runway approaches.

As the aircraft taxied and began to slow, Matt worked his way toward the cargo door, which he opened and leapt from. He conducted a combat roll as if he were performing a parachute landing fall. The concrete runway smacked his rib cage, and his head bounced slightly off the tarmac.

He stood and quickly assessed his surroundings, as the plane braked about fifty meters away, and began running.

He saw a warehouse, a fuel pump, and what looked like an old dump truck etched against the night sky. There appeared to be a single Gulfstream jet parked on the tarmac at the terminal. He was moving too fast to determine the origin of the Gulfstream, but noticed that on either side of the runway was low brush, such as he had just seen near the beach in the Philippines.

Could they have taken the long way around to Davao? He didn't think so.

Guam? Too far; they could not have made it in under three hours.

Luzon? He didn't believe that option either, as they had not banked hard enough.

He heard a voice call out to him in Japanese.

"Yamete!" *Stop*.

Opening the cargo door while the plane was moving had obviously triggered an alarm in the cockpit, but he had chosen getting out over being cornered in the airplane.

He ran across the runway and threw his bag over the chain-link fence that abutted the length of the airfield. He heard several shots above the din of the propellers, and his luck didn't hold.

As he flipped over the fence, a bullet ricocheted off the top post and grazed his shoulder. A few centimeters to the right, and the lead would have caught him square in the face.

Despite the pain, he kept moving into what he thought looked like scrub oaks. Unfortunately, they weren't large enough to provide cover or sufficiently conceal his movement. Nonetheless, no more shots came close, and he continued to run like a tailback with no blockers, ducking, weaving, spinning, and lunging.

His plan was first to survive ... then cycle back and ask some questions of whomever he found.

He found a dirt road, which he followed to its end, then sprinted into the woods, which were again sparsely populated with scrub oaks. Soon he found himself standing on a blacktop road from which he could see the faint outline of lights to the north. He jogged in the direction of the lights and rounded a bend, stopping when he saw buildings less than a half a kilometer away.

There was something familiar about this place; either that, or he was experiencing déjà vu, which, with his wound clearly more serious than he originally thought, was a possibility. But as he studied the terrain and the buildings, he quickly recognized that he was on the island of Palau, about nine hundred kilometers due east of Mindanao.

Further, he knew that he was on the road to the Airai View Hotel, where American diplomats sometimes lay over on their way to Australia or other Pacific Rim nations. Matt recognized the road and the bright lights from the hotel because he had on occasion used a safe house in the small village near the airport.

He remembered that the contact's name was Pino, and he moved in the direction of the swank resort hotel, despite the fact that his bleeding was worsening, he smelled like a stable hand, looked like an assassin, and clutched the dog tags of a dead American soldier in his right hand.

If he could find Pino, he could make contact with his handler and alert him to everything he had witnessed in Mindanao.

Even though he wasn't exactly sure what he had seen.

CHAPTER 15

As Taiku Takishi stood at the fence line where the stowaway had climbed over, the spot of damp blood he could see on the top rail convinced him that one of the four bullets he had fired had wounded the fleeing man.

Who was it? Was it just some local seeking a better life outside of Cateel Bay, or was the man in some fashion connected to the two security breaches at the plant? Although Takishi's instincts told him that the man was not some ordinary stowaway, he had business to do and time lines to keep.

He retrieved his satellite phone from his pocket and dialed a number.

"Do you have anyone snooping around Mindanao?"

"Well, hello, to you, also," the voice replied.

"Answer my question, please, because we've had two breaches in one day, and I just had an uninvited passenger on my airplane," Takishi said. He turned and watched the refueling truck pull up to his Shin Meiwa. Next to his aircraft he saw two men walking around a U.S. government Gulfstream jet.

"Don't get terse with me, Charlie. We've given you everything you've asked for. That was Matt Garrett gathering frequent flyer miles with you."

Garrett? That's not possible.

"Slippery little bastard," Takishi said. He did a superb job of hiding his surprise … and shock.

"I told you. The real question is, what did he see?"

That was tricky territory for Takishi. First, he didn't know what Garrett had seen, but he had definitely seen something. And if he'd caught sight of, for example, the main battle tanks on the railhead, then there were problems. The Rolling Stones had been led to believe that they had purchased a small-arms-manufacturing facility.

They didn't know that Takishi and Prime Minister Mizuzawa had taken the funds and, with true Japanese efficiency, created the facilities to make tanks and helicopters. That would, Takishi determined, come as a bit of a surprise to his musician buddies.

"All I know is he saw the inside of my airplane, if it was Garrett," Takishi said. *They'll know soon enough what he saw*, he determined.

"Take it however you wish, but we are in the final stages, and we need your action to happen exactly as discussed. Things are still a bit iffy on this end. Momentum seems to be gathering, and unless you are successful, the train might run away, as they say."

"Don't worry about my end of the deal." Takishi laughed. "If Garrett saw anything, he's probably confused as hell anyway. I've got soldiers down there guarding the plant and even a couple of armored vehicles." *Perfect,* Takishi thought.

"Okay, Takishi. Now let's get off this phone. Any further questions?"

"We are getting satisfaction. Good-bye."

Takishi flipped his phone shut and continued to watch the men conducting a preflight inspection of the Gulfstream. It appeared that Keith Richards was on schedule. *But if Matt Garrett was indeed on my airplane, what should I do,* he wondered? *Stay or go? Is Garrett a threat to me?*

Possibly. Do I have anyone on this island who can kill Garrett?

Of course.

Over the course of the past two years, he had worked in clandestine fashion with Keith Richards, the only member of the Rolling Stones to span two administrations. The money had begun flowing nearly a year ago, money Takishi promptly began funneling to Talbosa and his loose band of Muslim insurgents.

Better than Iran-Contra! Takishi thought. *At least the Contras were on the American side.* The Rolling Stones were funding the Abu Sayyaf to start a war in the Philippines so the Americans could fight there instead of in Iraq.

"Makes sense to me." Takishi chuckled.

The smile left his face as he thought of Garrett and whom he needed to call. Yes, he would take his chances and let Keith deal with Garrett while he got on with orchestrating the big picture.

Anyway, perhaps he had mortally wounded Garrett.

CHAPTER 16

Matt knocked on the wood door of the small A-frame house that served as a manager's residence on-site at the Airai View Hotel. He heard heavy footfalls and the sliding of a chain against metal.

A pistol poked through the gap in the door as a voice said, "You rang?"

"Pino, it's Matt Garrett. Put down the pistol."

"I could shoot you and have you stuffed like one of those bears," Pino said, laughing as he opened the door. Matt watched him as he flipped a cell phone shut and stuffed it in his pocket.

"I wouldn't be too comfortable to lie on," Matt said. "And the thought of your fat ass humping some chick on my back makes me want to puke."

"Now that you have exchanged proper bona fides, I will let you in." Pino laughed again. He was a short man, nearly as tall as he was wide. Thick black hair was cut just above his ears, which were small compared to his rotund face. "Cherubic" wasn't necessarily the right word, but it was close enough.

They hugged, and Pino backed away.

"You're shot?"

"Yes. Just a nick, though," Matt said, entering the small residence. "Is the missus home?"

"No, she's working the floor tonight. Do you need a doctor?"

"I might," he said absently, touching his wound. "There are Americans here tonight, right?" He guessed that the Gulfstream was an official U.S. government aircraft. Palau had become a U.S. protectorate after

World War II, and the American government had just signed up for another fifty years of providing for its defense, whatever that might entail.

All Matt had seen were high-ranking government officials using the island and the hotel as a stopover point for long hauls to points west.

"Yes, Rathburn's here. Are you here to see him?"

"Yes," Matt said, searching his mind for the name Rathburn. He thought he might be in the Department of Defense. "I need to see him tonight if possible."

Pino looked at him with suspicious eyes.

"Here, have a seat," the Palauan said. Pino's house was an odd mixture of rattan island furniture, photos of high-ranking U.S. officials hanging on the walls, and furniture that looked as if he had purchased it from a 1970s Sears and Roebuck catalog. Lived in, was how Matt thought of it.

Matt sat in an old corduroy La-Z-Boy recliner while Pino took a bottle of astringent and a damp paper towel to the open wound on Matt's shoulder.

"Son of a bitch." Matt grimaced at the stinging.

"This is more than a graze, Matt. I need to call the U.S. doctor. Is it okay?"

Matt looked at his arm, and said, "Call Rathburn's assistant and get him over here. Then we can talk about the doctor."

Pino looked at Matt.

"You have no idea who Rathburn is, do you?"

"Not a clue. Defense?" Matt offered.

"Yes, and his assistant is a 'she,' not a 'he.'"

"Whatever, I need to talk to her. My comms are broke. I've got some huge shit to give her."

Pino sat across from Matt on the sofa, and said, "I'll call her if you let me get the doctor."

"Okay, whatever. Get the damn doctor. Hang it on your Web site that I'm here. Whatever. Just get me Rathburn or his assistant."

"Hey, douche bag, you came to me for help, remember?"

Matt felt himself fading a bit. Between not sleeping for two full days and the loss of blood, he knew that he needed help.

As his mind spiraled, his last thoughts were that there were others that needed aid more than he; Peterson, for example. While it was too late for the dead Special Forces officer, Matt thought, the rest of his team desperately needed some assistance.

Matt's mind spun into sleep, pulling with it the soft music emanating from Pino's stereo. "I can't get no sat-is-fac-tion ..."

CHAPTER 17

"How long has he been out?" Meredith Morris asked the doctor.

"About an hour," he said. "I gave him four full IVs, cleaned his wound, and pumped some antibiotics in him. That he lasted this long is pretty amazing."

Meredith looked at the doctor, and said, "I've got it from here, thank you."

Understanding his cue to depart, the doctor walked out of Pino's guest bedroom and into the night.

Meredith sat in the chair next to the bed, wondering about this man, whom she had only read about. She looked at her watch; it was past midnight. Pino had summoned her from her suite in the hotel and she had taken nearly an hour to get dressed and walk the half kilometer to the house.

She studied Matt's strong jaw line, tousled brown hair, and rhythmically rising chest. The wound was on his left shoulder just above the clavicle through the trapezoid, she presumed. It appeared to her that the doctor had done a tidy job of patching the bullet hole and that the CIA agent would be okay with some rest.

When Meredith thought she heard Matt mouth a word or two, she leaned forward.

"If I'm dead, are you one of the seventy-two virgins?"

Meredith, momentarily taken aback, laughed, and said, "No, but I am a Virginian."

"Even better," Matt replied. "Are there seven-one others?"

"Yes, but I think I'm quite enough for you right now, Mr. Garrett."

"Well, with a blond Virginian as my gatekeeper, I must be doing something right."

Meredith smiled. "Actually, to be lying here in fat Pino's sweaty bed sheets with your shoulder shot up is not an indicator of your doing something right."

"Ah, man, did you have to put it that way?" Matt chuckled. "I mean, I'm okay with the gunshot wound, but Pino's sweaty sheets, who knows what lurks beneath?"

Matt opened his eyes again and, though a bit hazy, saw a young Meg Ryan facsimile staring back at him. She was wearing a blue cotton shirt and light blue denim jeans.

Apparently Meredith saw him appraising her attire and said, "You woke me from a restful sleep. You okay to talk?"

"I need to talk," Matt said, sitting up. "But I want to get out of this bed first."

Pino entered the room, carrying a large pitcher of water.

"Hey, bro, doctor said no getting up. Just no wet dreams in the sheets, okay?"

"Pino, these sheets are so stiff and nasty I could use them as a body armor," Matt countered.

"Listen, brother, I washed those sheets two months ago. They are fine."

"I'm getting up," Matt said.

And he did. He sat up and collected his thoughts, then fished a clean Underarmour T-shirt from his bag. As he wrestled it over his head, Meredith held one sleeve for him. Grimacing, he pushed his arm through the hole, then stood and walked from the guest room into the family room, where he sat back in the recliner.

He watched Meredith follow him. She had a nice figure and was at least five and half feet tall. *Very attractive,* he thought. It had been a month or two since he'd seen a real, live American beauty up close. Sure, he loved Asian women, but there was no replacement for a girl-next-door American knockout such as was standing in front of him right now.

"What is it you need to talk about?" Meredith asked. "And why are you here?"

"Can we go for a walk?" Matt said. He knew that Pino was on the payroll of the Agency and other departments within the U.S. government, but still he preferred to keep his information held within as tight a circle as possible.

As they were stepping out of the door, Matt looked over his shoulder at Pino and asked, "Since when do you listen to the Rolling Stones?"

Pino looked at Matt, curious, "Talking about, bro?"

"'Satisfaction.' I remember hearing that song when I passed out."

Pino looked at Matt a moment, then laughed loudly. "Whoa, buddy. Must be from your puberty days. I wasn't playing no music. Now get out of here."

Matt shrugged, and soon they were walking the trail she had followed from the hotel to Pino's cottage. Vault lights were located every ten meters or so, illuminating the flagstone path.

"I need to see your credentials, first," Matt said. The doctor had given him enough Percocet that the pain was numbed, but not so much that he couldn't think straight.

"Sure," Meredith said. She pulled out a circular ring with about five different identification badges on it. Matt flipped through them. One was for the Pentagon, another for the State Department, a third was for the White House situation room, and a fourth was for the Agency.

"What's this one?" Matt asked of the fifth.

"Pentagon Athletic Club. Is that the one you need to see?" She smiled.

"Just checking to make sure you're in shape." He handed the credentials back to her. "If indeed you are the first of seventy-two Virginians, then I'm assuming there was some type of competition."

"Pretty sure of ourselves, aren't we?"

Matt ignored the rebuke and asked, "Clearance?"

"Top secret, special compartmented information."

She seemed to know the right combinations of words, and the pictures on the identification tags certainly looked like her.

"Okay, I've been working a project down in the Philippines," he started. Then he told her the entire story about the *Shimpu* , the contact's getting shot, his handler having him jump in to the plane crash, and what he had seen in Cateel.

By the time he was done, they were at the main hotel and had taken a seat by the dimly lit pool area.

"We need to get somebody to Mindanao quickly to help those guys and recover Peterson's body," Matt emphasized. "And the tanks. What the hell could they be doing with tanks on Mindanao?"

"I'll let Secretary Rathburn know immediately and call back to the Pentagon," Meredith said, worry etched across her forehead.

Matt had lain back on the poolside recliner, exhaustion getting the better of him again. He watched cars over the bluff crawl along the coast road. When he saw a small sports car snake around the corner, he thought of his fifteen-year-old Porsche 944, an outdated sports car that he purchased at the same junkyard in which he found his pitching machine. Having played shortstop on the University of Virginia baseball team, Matt often swatted away his demons in the solitude of his makeshift batting cage in his Loudoun County home. Given his career, his love life was less than he had actually hoped for, the multiple "friends with benefits" opportunities out there notwithstanding. Sometimes reluctantly, Matt always rejected FWB offers because women to him were more than a quick fix. His last serious relationship was a two-year college girlfriend and the ensuing two years after graduation as she moved to New York City for a high-profile accountant's job. For Kari Jackson, the love had faded with the distance. Her beauty and brains had vaulted her into a different, more elevated, social circle, something which Matt could not or perhaps cared not to provide. Time and distance had sawed at their connection from the other end, then there was nothing.

Though on his short break between Afghanistan and China/Philippines, Matt had received a message from Kari on his home phone.

It had started, "Hi Matt, this is Kari, and I just miss …"

He didn't know any more of what she said because he had punched erase and gone out to his batting cage and rifled nearly a hundred fastballs traveling about ninety miles an hour. The blisters on his hands had started bleeding against the stained athletic tape wrapped around the grip area of his Pete Rose thirty-four-inch bat. Better to have bleeding blisters than to revisit four years of a slowly dying relationship.

That was Matt. All or nothing. Either you had him or you didn't. Either he was committed or he wasn't. And while he understood shades of gray just fine, his personal moral guideposts prevented him from operating in that fashion. He could tell a straight-faced lie to a source he was trying to turn, but deceitfulness in his personal life was out of the question.

Matt's mind spiraled and followed a path toward that fateful day only a few months ago.

Why, he wondered. *We had them in our sights.* His relentless, haunting conflict over the missed opportunities to kill Al Qaeda senior leadership was overcome by pure physics. His body shut down, but not before a thought scrolled through his swooning mind: *Every time I'm close, I'm moved.*

Matt drifted off to sleep as Meredith sat there, her arms crossed, wondering how the hell she was going to handle everything she had heard tonight … and she meant *everything*.

And how her report would be received.

CHAPTER 18

ORANGE COUNTY, VIRGINIA

Secretary of Defense Robert Stone looked at his friend as they relaxed in his Orange County, Virginia home. He contemplated what he had set in motion as the backdrop of the war in Afghanistan played out on the nightly news. Bin Laden's trail had gone cold and the country seemed to be on the bullet train to Iraq.

As he had watched and listened to the administration quickly move their focus from Islamic extremism to ousting Saddam Hussein so soon after 9-11, he had gathered three other men to rapidly develop a scheme to counter the movement into Iraq. Given his surname and his penchant for classic rock music, he had labeled their group "The Rolling Stones," choosing for himself the nom de guerre of Mick Jagger.

His assistant secretary of defense for international security, Bart Rathburn, had latched onto the name of guitar ace Keith Richards. Japanese businessman and former Naicho operative, Taiku Takishi, had been summoned and handed the cover of drummer Charlie Watts.

Stone looked across at Ronnie Wood, whose participation in the scheme was the ultimate high-risk gamble, given his exalted government position. The men had made a pact to use only their rocker aliases when communicating, but all realized the importance of keeping Wood's name a secret forever, like buried pirate treasure never intended to be found.

What the four men had in common was a desire to keep America focused on the root causes of 9-11 and its associated enemies. This was in distinct oppostion to the sleight of hand of the likes of Fox and Diamond, who were using the attacks on America as a causus belli in Iraq.

With Rathburn in Palau and Takishi already on the ground in the Philippines, Stone was confident that the plan was off to a good start. He puffed on his cigar, looking at Ronnie Wood sitting across from him as the floor-to-ceiling windows provided a view of rolling terrain that somewhere on the horizon gave way to James Madison's Montpelier.

Ronnie Wood returned Stone's gaze as if he was awaiting a status report. The tune "Wild Horses" played in the background, the real Mick Jagger belting out "... *couldn't drag me away*"

They each took a sip of a local Merlot from Donna Kendall Farms, the best winery in Virginia. A bowl of venison jerky sat on the mahogany Queen Elizabeth table between their two burgundy leather chairs that were canted inward at 45 degree angles. They faced a stone hearth fireplace, handcrafted with rocks from the Rappahannock River. A musket hung on brass hooks above the mantel. A bugle and powderhorn adorned either side of the cavernous firepit, hanging like Christmas stockings. Stone broke the silence.

"Charlie seemed to take the news of Garrett's presence in stride, no?"

"A little too cool for school," Wood said.

"Takishi's good. Bart vouches for him," Jagger said.

Wood stared at Jagger.

"Hope you don't slip up when talking about me," Wood said, always concerned about his role in the conspiracy.

Jagger paused.

"Sorry. It's the wine."

Wood nodded. He was a born skeptic. He had to be, given his business.

"Was always skeptical about bnringing in Charlie Watts," Wood said.

"Needed him. No doubt about it. Where would we be without him." Jagger had recovered from his faux pas.

"Keith has a handle on it, I'm sure," Wood said, unconvincingly.

Jagger paused, considered the comment and then decided upon a new line of discussion.

"So the first few riffs have been pretty good, so far, no?" he said to Wood.

"Well, it's really your tune now, isn't it, Mick? I've played my chords, and we've got Matt Garrett right where we want him," Wood said.

"True, true," Jagger noted. He swirled the merlot as he stared through the windows of his Orange County estate. Two bay windows framed the fireplace, giving him a view of the distant Blue Ridge Mountains. Dozens of ash, oak, and birch trees dominated his prominent grounds, their branches crisscrossing like the fingers of a child watching a horror flick.

"Just a brief conversation with Keith and, I mean, wow, this guy is perfect. He's all pissed off about being pulled out of Pakistan …"

"He was close, you know," Jagger said. "And I would know."

"That you would," Wood agreed.

"And just to be clear, we pulled him out why?"

"You know damned well why we did it. We needed the flexibility. Plus, I had to do it. Fox has me by the balls. There was no option for me."

"But perhaps for the nation?" Jagger challenged. "There was a better option."

"Well, it was just one move," Wood said. "Besides, don't you think this continuous thread of insecurity has given us some wiggle room, so to speak? I mean, if we had crushed Al Qaeda, would we be able to use the notion of a global threat for our purposes in the Philippines right now? It preserves our flexibility."

"Yes, but it is this same strategic flexibility that has allowed the notion of invading Iraq to gather momentum. One move always leads to another. For every action, there is a reaction, and so on," Jagger said. "For example, Garrett is pissed off now, which turns out to be a good thing. But tomorrow, who knows? Thankfully, Keith's got him."

The two men were able to enjoy their conversation in the relative security and comfort of Jagger's country estate thanks to the security details that both men were accorded because of their government positions.

"Yes, a good thing," Wood said. "Keith will get him up to Manila and feed him back into this thing. You get his reports?"

"Yes, got them all. Not sure what to make of the Japanese tanks he reported. Charlie says that it was just his security. What do you think? I mean we only paid for small arms right? For the insurgents. We didn't sell enough Predators to finance tank production."

"Two things," Wood noted. "First, they may have gotten the money from somewhere else. Second, what the hell do they need tanks for?"

"I don't know, but here's how we'll proceed. We need to keep the manufacturing bit secret. We don't want to focus any unneeded attention there, like satellites and so on. We'll do a press conference saying that we've started diplomatic, informational, military, and economic initiatives in the Philippines. It's the Asian arm of Operation Enduring Freedom.

We'll call it OEF-P as opposed to OEF-A for Afghanistan."

"That's good. We need to get some media coverage of this thing, connect it to Al Qaeda, and show how the real threat is reaching all the way into the Pacific," Wood said. "The eastern anchor of Bin Laden's Caliphate."

"That's right," Jagger agreed. "Plus, turbulence for the Asian markets would not be good for our economy. Not to mention China, North Korea, and Taiwan in that general vicinity. It's a freaking powder keg."

"All that combined should make the case that Iraq is a red herring," Wood said.

"Oh yeah, and we can't forget to mention that we had some soldiers killed there," Jagger said.

"Yeah, almost forgot," Wood agreed. "Peterson, right?"

"Think so. Might be Patterson. Anyway, what do we do with Garrett?" Jagger asked.

"I think we blow his cover."

"While he's there?" Jagger asked. And answered, "Great idea. He will go ballistic and go public and the media will make him a hero. More importantly, it will add the extra bit of pressure so that they'll be stymied."

"We hope," Wood added. "I'm not completely comfortable with the blown-cover deal. He could wind up dead."

"That's okay," Jagger said. "That works for us, too. A dead Matt Garrett becomes a martyr for the cause. Woe is us. We pulled out of Afghanistan too early. Al Qaeda got away. We found them again in the Philippines. Now we've revealed the identity of our number one Al Qaeda hunter, blowing his cover and getting him killed." Jagger theatrically waved his hands as he talked, as if he were rolling out one point after another.

"Hmm. I like it. Makes you wonder where the real conspiracy is," Wood said, tapping his lip with his finger. He crossed his legs and sat back, sipping his Syrah and popping a bite of venison jerky into his mouth. Then he laughed at a thought he had. "This provides the perfect counterweight to Fox and his band of idiots, and I'm sure we can work it so that Garrett's outing stems from something bold and audacious."

"Good. We need the flexibility to pin all of this on him if it goes south," Jagger said, concluding the point. "Okay, so our next move is to get some forces flowing to the Philippines and, as you say, that's my tune. So, I've got that ammo detail thing I mentioned that is about to kick off. They'll be leaving shortly under the guise of OEF-P," Jagger said. "I'll do a press conference tomorrow and announce Patterson was killed, express our sorrow, the usual tap dance. Hold him up as a hero, and he's our game changer. If Garrett is killed, then I think that seals it."

"I'm getting satisfaction." Wood smiled.

"Well, you know, it's only rock and roll." Jagger smiled in return.

"And we like it," they said in unison.

CHAPTER 19

PENTAGON, WASHINGTON, DC

Media pundit and leading neo-conservative Dick Diamond checked his Blackberry, shielding it from Saul Fox' view as he nodded with approval and pulled out a checklist written on a pad of yellow legal paper. He sat in the chair facing Fox, the deputy secretary of defense. A large, framed, oval world map hung on the wall behind Fox's desk. The desktop was cluttered with stacks of papers and books, much the way a college professor's might be. Puccini's "Nessun Dorma" played softly in the background. *Turandot* was Diamond's favorite opera.

The two men smiled at each other and held their right hands up simultaneously as if swearing one another in for a court appearance. Then Fox and Diamond performed a maneuver with their hands, a secret hand shake of sorts, nodded and began their discussion of what they called "conditions setting."

If there was a counterpoint to the Rolling Stones, Fox and Diamond were it. Diamond was tall, soft and plump, and had a bad hair transplant, making his scalp look like something akin to a Chia Pet. Fox was an elfish man with a bald pate. Secretly toiling away with Central Command, they had built their own intelligence apparatus and were building the case for the Iraq War. The opera playing in the background served to underscore how very different they were from the clandestine Rolling Stones. Fox and Diamond were in the engine room of the train, shovels in hand, pouring giant heaps of coal into the combustion chamber. Speed was increasing. The Iraq war was looming nearer and nearer on the horizon, like a shimmering oasis. Their path was clear and, like a locomotive, they were going to blow through anything that got in their way.

"The checklist. Al Haideri?" Diamond said. He was referring to the Iraqi Saeed al Haideri from Kurdistan, who claimed he could vouch for Saddam's massive forbidden weapons stockpile.

Fox looked at his friend and said, "Check. We've got him teamed up with our perception manager, Randall. They're working his story. He's solid."

Diamond's pencil scratched at the paper as he made a checkmark. "Solid," he whispered. Then he asked, "Yellow cake?"

"The Italians guarantee that Saddam is getting it from Niger." Fox smiled.

"Wonderful," Diamond agreed, then paused. "Ah, our Italian connection. Perfect."

"*Perfecto,* I believe, is the proper term." Fox laughed.

"Metal tubes?"

"Some *New York Times* reporters are working leads there. They look solid," Fox said.

"Solid," Diamond echoed as he put another check mark on the paper. "And if not, we can send them some, right?"

Fox looked over his glasses at Diamond and stared at him a moment. He broke into a broad grin and pointed at him.

"You're such a kidder, Dick. You know we did that last year before we even had jobs here."

"Just checking to make sure you're awake, Saul. Okay, Chalabi?"

"As solid as they come." Fox smiled. "The future of Iraq. He will mobilize the Iraqis and unify them."

"Unify," Diamond agreed, nodding.

"Listen, Dick. This is going to happen." Fox reached his hands toward his chest as if he were an actor about to belt out a Broadway tune and said, "I can feel it in here. We've been talking about this for years. We're perfectly positioned. Nine-eleven is tailor-made for our purposes. The window is open, as if we opened it ourselves."

"As if." Diamond smiled.

Fox looked at Diamond with a knowing grin. "Well, maybe it was a bit more aggressive than we imagined, but it's all about effect, you know."

"Nine-eleven gives us unlimited opportunities."

"That's right. Anything less than what happened might not have opened the aperture enough," Fox said, then stopped abruptly, his face growing pensive.

"Looks like we're getting there." Diamond put his pad down and looked at Fox, who was lying back in his chair with his hands laced behind his head. "Thinking?"

"Just wondering where this bullshit in the Philippines came from," Fox said.

"Could it be Stone and his gang? I was wondering the same thing. It's as if it appeared magically out of nowhere," Diamond agreed.

"Isn't that the Lucky Charms commercial?" Fox said seriously as he leaned forward in his chair.

"No, that's 'They're Magically Delicious,'" Diamond corrected.

Fox snapped his fingers. "Thought I had one there. Man."

"It was a good try," Diamond offered, and pursed his lips as if to lament Fox's near miss at trivia.

"Anyway, back to the Philippines. Someone's working it, I think, to try to stall our movement toward Iraq. They'll make some tenuous connection to Al Qaeda in Afghanistan and Pakistan and say it's an infestation everywhere. Blah, blah, blah. We've got to knock that bullshit right between the eyes every time it comes up. The road to Iraq should be a Montana autobahn not an Arkansas back road."

Diamond thought about Fox's comment a minute. "You're good, Saul. I'm so glad we're friends."

Fox leaned forward and looked at Diamond's round face, one he found appealing despite its shape.

"*We're* good, Dick. We're good. Just remember that."

"I will. And we will knock this bullshit between the eyes. I mean we've got so many people lining up for our course of action anyway. The snowball is rolling downhill. It's almost as if nothing can stop it. This is our idea. We are at the cusp of tectonic change in world history."

"At the cusp," Fox said. "You know, Dick, life is about ideas and eternal fame. Look at us." He waved his hand between them. "We're wealthy beyond imagination. We have incredible power. What else is there beyond having our ideas endure throughout history like Marx or Einstein or Jefferson?"

"Nietzsche's Will to Power," Diamond offered.

"Indeed, the Beast with Red Cheeks. Fame, legacy, eternal recognition are all awaiting us." Fox smiled. "They will call us the 'Brothers of Babylon.'"

"Statues, perhaps?"

"Perhaps. We *will* walk down the streets of Baghdad with rose petals thrown at our feet like ice skaters finishing an Olympic performance."

"Rose petals," Diamond affirmed.

"This will be the time of awakening. Stay the course, and we'll be famous."

"Famous," Diamond repeated, and checked his pad with the scratch of his pencil.

CHAPTER 20

PENTAGON, WASHINGTON, DC

Secretary of Defense Robert Stone stood at the podium in the Pentagon press room. The round Department of Defense symbol hung on the laminated wood of the lectern and another one hung behind Stone on the wall. In case the camera was going in for a close-up, there would be no confusion.

"I've received many questions from the media in the last day or so about some things occurring in the Philippines as well as from Operation Anaconda and other action in Afghanistan. So I'll offer a few observations about the war in Afghanistan, which is going extremely well, by the way, then outline our global effort, which is also taking shape particularly well in the Philippines, our next front."

He had wisely started by asserting that the only reason he was giving a press conference that day was because the media had asked for it. He was there by their choice, not his. Stone spoke without notes or a written script. In that fashion he drove his public-affairs officers crazy. But there was no way that they could know what he was talking about because they weren't privy to the information. Sure, he let them build some talking points, and sometimes he read the work that his staff prepared for him, but usually what he said was what the Rolling Stones had agreed upon.

Takishi, Rathburn, and "Ronnie Wood" had elected him as the leader of their group. He was the one with the vision, and it had been his desire to use more force in Afghanistan, yet Fox had presented him with some documents that were more powerful to him than kryptonite was to Superman. Essentially, he was a bought man. His options were to either lose his job, career, and reputation in one fell swoop, or to be Fox's pawn.

He'd accepted duties as the pawn in late 2001 but quickly tired of Fox's manipulations. He pulled together Rathburn and Takishi, two Harvard Business School classmates, explained the situation to them, and they agreed he was screwed.

But they proposed an option. Actually, it was Takishi's idea. Japan had a few mineral and manufacturing plants on Mindanao and in a few months, if not weeks, they could retool those structures to produce some small arms. Takishi had the contacts that could feed the weapons to the insurgents, who would overthrow the government of the Philippines and voilà, America would have to manage an insurgency in the South Pacific as opposed to a full-scale, bloody, intractable situation in the Middle East. Further, the enemy in the Philippines would be the Abu Sayyaf, an Al Qaeda chain, of sorts. It would fit nicely with the overall theme of their plan, their musical score.

"We have good intelligence that Abu Sayyaf in the Philippines is a major threat not only to our close ally, the Philippine government, but also the shipping lanes, and by extension, the Pacific Rim region. While Iraq is still in the picture, we are becoming increasingly concerned with the information we are getting from our JUSMAG, the Joint United States Military Advisory Group, in the Philippines. And I regret to inform the American people that a Special Forces soldier was killed in combat in the Philippines recently. We will release his name pending notification of the next of kin."

Reporters' hands shot into the air followed by their incessant howls of wanting to know a name or why they weren't informed of the military operation. Chaos reigned briefly until Stone called on a reporter with whom he had a brief conversation prior to the press conference. The question was a plant.

"Mr. Secretary, so to make sure I understand what you are saying, can you tell me what the U.S. defense priority is right now? Is it Afghanistan? Iraq? Philippines? Where are our vital interests?"

"That's a great question, Mark," Stone said, grimacing, but not too much. His public- affairs officer had told him to be pleasantly present. Not sad, but a tad mournful. Just there. Friendly, but concerned. "Our priority is to crush Islamic extremism wherever we find it and to counter the proliferation of weapons of mass destruction. That remains our priority, and what I'm telling you is that's exactly what we're doing. Operation Enduring Freedom-Philippines is our Pacific front in this war."

Stone saw his public-affairs officer cringe when he used the term "front," but it was deliberate on Stone's part. He wanted to alert the world that he had started another front.

A shapely blonde from the back of the room raised her hand and shouted, "Do we have enough force to do all of this?"

Stone lifted his hand to his face as if in a salute, peering over the throng of reporters, trying to see who had just spoken.

"Oh ... hi, Betsy. Of course that is a primary concern of ours. We, in fact, are trying to determine right now how best to apply the force we have and where."

How's that for saying nothing? Stone smiled.

On cue, a staffer handed him a note and his public-affairs officer, Johnny Smithwick, replaced him at the podium to handle any further questions.

Of course, the note merely said, "Time to go."

And it *was* time to go. He walked into the National Military Command Center and called the Pacific Command Admiral in charge.

"Have you deployed that rifle company to Subic Bay to guard the ammunition stockpile yet, and are they prepared for further combat operations?"

Phase II: Brothers in Arms

CHAPTER 21

SCHOFIELD BARRACKS, ISLAND OF OAHU, HAWAII

"Blow me, McAllister," Captain Zachary Garrett said to his close friend, Captain Bob McAllister.

"I don't have time to form a search party," McAllister shot back in his Boston accent.

The two company commanders sat in squeaky gray chairs in Zachary's office on Schofield Barracks, an Army base in the middle of the island of Oahu.

"I'll give you a lead—start searching near my ankle."

"Listen, Zach, all I'm asking for is an introduction," McAllister said.

"Yeah, right. You'll follow that up with a dinner at a cheesy restaurant, or worse, the O-Club, some drinks to loosen her up, then a quick slam at your place."

McAllister looked confused, waiting for Zachary to continue. "So what's your point?"

"That's exactly my point. I've only been close with Riley a short while, she's an admiral's daughter, and you want me to introduce you to her sister just so you can pounce on her—forget it."

"Look, I saw this girl—she's gorgeous. She is the future Mrs. Robert M. McAllister—"

"Please—a fate worse than death. I'll buy her a one-way plane ticket to the mainland."

"I can't quit thinking about her. She's in my every thought," McAllister said with mock theatrics, his Boston accent sounding almost like a Cagney impression. "This morning at PT doing push-ups—"

"Forget it."

"Come on. What do I have to do?" McAllister asked. Zachary noticed that perhaps he was serious, despite the joking. The two men were dressed in Army combat uniforms and had their feet up on Zach's desk. They could see the Waianae Mountain Range through Zach's window.

"Promise me you will not touch her on the first date," Zachary said.

"Promise," McAllister agreed, "But what if she goes for the big guy herself?"

"Forget it—"

"Okay. Okay. I understand. We can double-date—"

"Yeah right, so Riley can see what kind of morons I hang out with."

"The best kind." McAllister laughed. "Call her now, hero, or I'll tell Riley how you let Ballantine get away."

Zachary studied his close friend and laughed. He knew all along he would set them up but couldn't pass up an opportunity to give McAllister some grief. McAllister's mention of Jacques Ballantine referred to Zach's lieutenancy in the first Gulf War, Desert Storm, where he had personally captured the Tawakalna Division commander, Ballantine. After spiriting him to the Division rear, Zach had learned that the fabled commander had been released in a prisoner exchange shortly after the cease-fire.

"I'll call her tonight, now beat it."

"No, I'll let *her* do that." McAllister laughed, stepping out of Zachary's office. He successfully dodged the brass paperweight that flew past his head and struck the orderly-room wall.

"Get out of here!" Zachary yelled.

"Call me tonight," McAllister said as he walked across the lanai and into the Hawaiian afternoon heat.

Zachary and his company had been back in garrison nearly a week after an arduous field-training exercise and relaxing company party at the beach. Even though he had no family on the islands—he was divorced—it was nice to be able to enjoy "the Rock," as he called the island of Oahu. Zachary was a little over six feet, with dark brown hair. Despite the square jaw and green eyes, when his tan was deep, the locals sometimes confused him with one of their own. Regardless, he associated well with the native Hawaiians when many of his peers could not make that connection.

He was a few years older than most of his fellow company commanders because he had taken a break in service. Graduating from West Point in 1989, he saw combat duty in early 1991, fighting with the 101st Airborne Division in Operation Desert Storm. After a few years of peacekeeping duty in the mid 1990s, Zachary took a slot in the Army reserves and pursued some civilian interests. He had nabbed a master's degree in business from the University of Virginia, then had tried his hand at farming on the family property just north of Charlottesville. With no combat in the offing, Zachary had resigned himself to life on the farm.

The Army had already cost him a marriage. Glancing at the photo of his daughter sitting on his desk, Zach recalled how he had completely focused on hanging on to the thread of a relationship with her when one day, she just quit communicating. His efforts toward Amanda had been so all-encompassing that they had prevented Zachary from developing any meaningful adult relationships. Then, on the way out of his divorce hearing, he had met a child psychiatrist from Atlanta, Riley Dwyer, who was now coming to visit Zach in Hawaii for a week.

"Coming to see me or Diamond Head?" he had asked, smiling into the phone.

"You have rattlesnakes, there?" Riley asked in mock horror.

"Those are diamondbacks—wait a minute."

"Gosh," Riley joked. "I had no idea Hawaii was so dangerous."

"Just get your pretty face over here." He laughed. "It's been a while."

"It has at that," she whispered into the phone.

And it had been a few months since he had spent any time with Riley. Nine-eleven had occurred, and Zach was on the phone to the Army Personnel Command immediately. The assignment officer opened the gate for Zachary, given his outstanding record in combat and the fact that he had continued to drill with the reserves. The Army brought him back on the active rolls as a captain, which was fine with him. It meant he would have a second chance at a company command.

Not only had he been assigned to company command, but that assignment was in Hawaii's Twenty-fifth Infantry Division, the quick-response force for the Pacific region. While initially disappointed that he had not drawn what he considered a more prestigious unit such as the 82nd Airborne Division, he was nonetheless satisfied to be back in a combat unit when it looked like there was some fighting to do. Besides, Zach considered as he kicked his feet onto his desk, with combat in Afghanistan or even Iraq as a possibility, he would surely get back into the fight soon. Operation Anaconda was still wrapping up, only whetting his appetite.

Sitting at his desk, he opened and read the most recent letter from his sister, Karen. The glint from his West Point class ring caught his eye as he read that his brother Matt was off on another assignment somewhere in Asia, she wasn't sure where, and Matt certainly couldn't say. He smiled warmly, thinking of him and the great times they had growing up on the farm hunting and fishing.

The phone rang and he heard the CQ answer the phone in typical fashion, "B Company, Thirtieth Infantry, this line is unsecured, how may I help you, sir?"

Momentarily, the soldier in charge of quarters knocked on his door.

"Sir, the battalion commander wants to see you in his office ASAP."

"Look, Jackson, if I get relieved, you can be in charge," Zachary joked.

Jackson was a new recruit and pumped his chest out proudly, saying, "Can do, sir!"

"I bet." Zachary laughed.

He made the short walk to the commander's building. The Hawaiian afternoon sun hung over the jagged green Waianaes. He stopped at the battalion adjutant's desk to try to discern as to why the old man wanted to see him. Glenn Bush, the adjutant, was talking on the phone while sitting at his desk, which was positioned in an office just outside the battalion commander's door.

"Hey, Glenn, what's up?" Zachary said, ignoring the fact that Glenn was on the phone. Glenn held up a hand while he finished his conversation. Zachary liked Glenn, who had a reputation as someone who hustled to get the job done, and as a staff officer who supported the company commanders regardless of the circumstances.

Hanging up the phone, Glenn stood up, leaned toward Zachary, and said in a low voice, "I don't know, but the brigade commander called five minutes ago with a blue-flash message. I answered the phone, heard someone say 'blue flash,' and immediately buzzed the old man. Not a minute later, he told me to get you up here right away."

That was good news to Zachary. Blue flashes meant real missions. Real missions meant high morale for his troops. In the post-9-11 world, everyone was seeking to fight the enemy. With that thought, he knocked on the commander's door and entered the spacious office.

Lieutenant Colonel Kevin Buck was a young battalion commander. The division commander had frocked him from major to lieutenant colonel, meaning he wore the insignia but didn't get paid for the rank yet.

Buck was a short man, only about five foot six. He had his black hair neatly cropped around his ears, but did not wear a high-and-tight-style crew cut. He had a youthful face that belied his thirty-six years. He wore freshly pressed army combat uniforms to work every day and possessed all of the requisite badges an infantryman should have: airborne, Ranger, air assault, and the expert infantryman's badge. Buck had missed the action in Panama and Desert Storm like so many of his peers, who were in jobs classified as "away from troops." Accordingly, Zach knew that Buck was slightly jealous of the combat infantryman's badge and right shoulder 101st Airborne Division patch that he wore, signifying his service during Desert Storm. Additionally, Zach was just a few years older than the "fast mover" battalion commander, making their relationship a tad awkward for Buck. Zach was fine with it; perhaps even enjoyed pushing the commander's buttons a bit.

He stood in front of Buck's desk and was always mildly surprised at his height. He reported to the battalion commander and assumed a relaxed position of parade rest. The office was situated at the corner of the quad that housed the battalion's troops. As such, he had almost a panoramic view of Waipahu. The commander had decorated his office with the customary plaques, mementos, and pictures of him with VIPs, as so many officers tend to do.

"Zachary," the commander said, standing from behind his desk, "we got a blue-flash message from brigade for you to deploy to the Philippines in twenty-four hours."

Zachary let the statement hang in the air briefly, expecting Buck to follow up with further instructions. He realized that there was an Al Qaeda splinter group in the Philippines and wondered if his mission somehow involved the Abu Sayyaf. He also knew that the Department of Defense had closed Clark Air Base and Subic Bay in the mid-nineties.

"That's good news, sir," Zachary reacted. "Do we have any word on the mission?"

"You'll get a full mission statement at the N+2 meeting." "N" stood for "notification." So, Zachary knew he would receive his mission in two hours. "You understand that this is a company deployment?" the commander continued.

"Yes, sir. We're the quick-reaction force this week for the battalion, so all of my men are within two hours' return time," Zachary said, looking at his watch. He cursed beneath his breath as he remembered that the first sergeant had just released them for the day. It was 1700 hours.

"Good. Get back to your unit and start the alert. The bitch of it is that Division's known about this for nearly a week. Would have been nice to know. The embassy knows you're coming though. I'll have a staff meeting set up for you in two hours to determine initial requirements and where your unit stands as far as processing for overseas movement."

"Thanks, sir," Zachary said, snapping a quick salute, turning an about face, and exiting the commander's office before anymore discussion could take place. *A week? What kind of bullshit is that*, Zach wondered.

He spoke briefly to Glenn, asking him to prepare processing packets for three of his men. Zachary knew that he had three new soldiers enter his unit since he had last processed his company for deployment. Glenn said he would get right on it. Zachary then walked quickly down the steps from the headquarters area into the service road that formed a track on the interior of the quad.

As he walked, he simmered over the fact that Division had held the information, but set aside his anger and made a mental checklist of things to do. They had to be wheels up in less than twenty-four hours. It was a test of his unit's preparedness; there would not be time to go back and fix things that were broke, either systemic or mechanical. It was basically a come-as-you-are operation.

Reaching his company area, he summoned the first sergeant and the executive officer. First Lieutenant Marcus Rockingham, "Rock," and First Sergeant Isaiah Washington quickly arrived at the commander's office, sensing something was happening. Zach closed the door behind the two men and spoke without emotion.

"Good news, guys. We've got a blue-flash mission to the Philippines. We have to be wheels up in twenty-four hours. Top," he said, looking at Washington, "I want you to activate the alert roster. The message is SOP. Just have the CQ say, 'this is a blue-flash message—report to the unit immediately.' Write it down for him so he doesn't mess it up." The XO and 1SG were frantically writing on hand-size notebooks that Zachary required every soldier to carry.

"XO, I want you to activate the N-hour checklist, ensuring we make all of the proper reports to headquarters. Don't fudge the numbers, just give the staff the facts. This is no time to try to cover up mistakes. The earlier we identify deficiencies, the better chance we have of making them up before we fly. First Sergeant, as the troops begin to come in, I want them to line their gear up outside in formation and start drawing weapons, night sights, binoculars, and so on. Everything goes, guys. We don't have any idea what type of mission this is, or how long we will be staying. I'll be in my office getting my personal gear straight for the first fifteen minutes. Then I'll be periodically checking company operations and hounding the battalion staff for information.

"It's now 1705. I have a meeting at 1900 with battalion. I want a quick meeting with you two and the platoon leaders at 1845. At that time everyone should be here, and I want a written, but concise, listing of the number of personnel missing, any problem areas, and issues for deployment. The first thing I can think of right off the bat is that we need maps of the Philippines. Any questions?"

The two simply nodded, salivating to get the train rolling. Both the XO and first sergeant were task-oriented in their own right. Rockingham was a VMI graduate who had starred as a tailback on the football team. He looked every bit the part. Washington had served as a Ranger platoon sergeant during several combat missions and knew how to soldier. They were warriors in the finest tradition.

"That's all," Zachary said.

Zach turned to his wall locker, retrieved his duffel bag and rucksack, then walked outside. He placed his gear on top of the letters CO. As commanding officer, he was leading by example by having his equipment ready first.

As he was reentering the headquarters, he saw that the arms room was already open. He walked up to the split door, the top half of which was open, and said to Private Smith, the arms-room chief, "Hey, Smitty, need my M4 and nine mil."

As Captain Garrett signed for his weapons, an ominous feeling settled over him. He pulled back the charging handle of his M4, looked in the chamber, then slammed the bolt shut.

As he reentered his office, the sound of soldiers dropping their gear in formation resonated throughout the quad.

CHAPTER 22

SUBIC BAY, LUZON ISLAND, PHILIPPINES

The loud hum of the four propellers had kept Zachary awake for most of the flight. With the rush of the rapid deployment behind him, he could contemplate what lay ahead. Bound to his nylon-strapped seat, bouncing with the C-130 as it fought the Pacific trade winds over the Luzon Strait and racing toward the forgotten islands of Asia, Captain Garrett mentally ticked items off his checklist.

He had nearly forgotten to give Riley's number to Bob McAllister; or perhaps he just loathed doing so. Regardless, his friend said he would "square them away" when they arrived. Whatever that meant.

They were to make two refueling stops, one each at Wake Island and Guam, then land at an old airstrip on the Subic Bay Naval Base. Zachary had been keeping up on developments in the Philippines and knew that there was an Al Qaeda offshoot called Abu Sayyaf, which operated in the island chain. They were closely linked with the New People's Army, or NPA, many of whose members had seamlessly merged with Abu Sayyaf. As global insurgencies went, Zach surmised, these splinter groups probably wanted to coalesce and tap into bin Laden's funding stream. He did wish that the intelligence officer had given him a decent update because it wasn't clear to him whether the locus of the insurgency was on the main island of Luzon, or in the southern island of Mindanao. Furthermore, they had received precious little in the way of maps.

Looking at his soldiers, the weight of his responsibility settled over him with a discernible subtlety. There would be no one to check his decisions or give advice. It was a commander's dream, yet he felt a bit like he did in his old West Point collegiate wrestling days, when it was him out there to succeed or fail ... in front of everyone.

Amidst his tumbling thoughts of isolation and responsibility, it occurred to him that a West Point classmate of his, Major Chuck Ramsey, led a Special Forces A team based out of Fort Magsaysay in the Philippines, and thought perhaps he could catch up with him if time permitted.

As the aircraft began to descend, Zachary figured they were getting close. He unfastened his seat belt and stood to look out of the window. Sure enough, he could see bright city lights below. It was an enchanting sight, reminiscent of flying into Honolulu International Airport and seeing the bright yellow lights twinkle from below. The song "Honolulu City Lights" played briefly in his mind until the aircraft took a sharp dive. The movement threw Zachary back against the stanchion supporting the webbing. He held on to the red strapping tightly. It seemed that they were almost in a delta dive, in which a free-fall parachutist tucks his body to achieve maximum aerodynamics.

Suddenly the aircraft leveled with a jerk, and Zachary could see out of the window that they were no more than 200 meters off the ground. The plane then banked sharply, turning its wings almost perpendicular to the ground. By now, all of the troops were awake and wondering what in the hell was happening. The aircraft shot up into a steep pitch and banked hard to the right, pinning Zachary against the frame. As soon as he could, Zachary sat down again and refastened his seat belt. The aircraft reverberated as the pilot was obviously stressing it beyond its design capacity. Another steep drop made Zachary's stomach fly up into his throat. The subsequent leveling slammed it back down into his stomach. Zachary smiled grimly and shook his head at First Sergeant Washington, who seemed to be enjoying the ride. The plane's turbo propellers whined and craned, trying to carve into the night air and defy gravity.

Zachary's silent thought was a humorous one, not reflected on his furrowed brow. He envisioned the C-130 in the middle of a Blue Angels or Thunderbirds aerial show. Perhaps the pilot was a frustrated fighter jock. He did not care as long as all the wheels touched the ground safely.

The aircraft jolted, causing a loud bang underneath, and Zachary could hear the familiar sound of all of the engines going into reverse. More jolts followed until the plane rolled to a hot landing, using nearly the entire runway. Regardless, they were on the ground safely. One of the pilots came into the back of the aircraft wearing night-vision goggles, smiling broadly. It suddenly occurred to Zachary that they had been doing nap of the earth, or NOE, flying where the pilots follow the contours of the ground. If the pilot used night-vision goggles, the technique was especially dangerous. *Well,* Zachary thought, looking at the pilot with a wide grin, *half of my troops puked in the back of your airplane, so we're even.*

The ramp dropped, giving way to an eerie darkness as a blast of warm, sticky air rushed into the hull of the plane. The men poured into the dark expanses of the runway and surrounding scrub grass. Zachary, Rockingham, and Washington were immediately making things happen. The airfield was deserted except for the two C-130s, a forklift, and a lone white Chevy Blazer with U.S. government markings on it. Inside the Blazer, Zachary presumed, was his contact. The forklift was to unload the pallets of duffel bags.

Meanwhile, the troops had taken up security around the airfield. Each platoon leader had a green metal can full of 5.56mm ammunition locked and stored in his rucksack only to be issued on the personal direction of the commander. Those were the rules of engagement that had been wired from the JUSMAG to the Twenty-fifth Division headquarters. Zachary was not happy with it and had every intention of distributing the ammunition once he got settled.

He walked over to the vehicle to meet his contact, his boots cracking the crusty shell of dried lava from the Mount Pinatubo eruption several years earlier. He had never seen anyone play it so close to the vest, thinking the guy would at least come and talk to him. Looking through the window from a distance, he saw a lone man wearing Army battle dress uniform. On the dashboard was his black beret with the silver oak leaf cluster indicating that he was a lieutenant colonel. Beret meant one thing to Zach; that the U.S. military in the Philippines was in administrative mode rather than combat focused.

Zachary walked around to the driver's side to talk to the man, who had not yet looked at him. In fact, the colonel was motionless. The closer he came to the window he instinctively began to raise his M4. Something was definitely wrong. The colonel was leaning against the door, and as Zachary began to reach for the door handle to open it, a hand grabbed his arm and pulled him away.

"Sir, don't touch that," Washington said, urgently, pulling his captain away from the vehicle and turning his glistening black face from side to side. He saw for the first time the bullet hole in the center of the colonel's forehead.

"See these wires, sir?" Washington said, pointing through the windshield at a taut silver wire connected to a small credit-card-like object that was clamped between the teeth of a metal clothespin. Zach got it immediately. Open the door, the wire pulls the card out, and the clothespin snaps shut, completing the electrical circuit, which would then trigger whatever explosives had been assembled. Someone had shot the man, then rigged the Blazer with explosives. "Jackson from First Platoon had a report of a local running fast along the other end of the runway. I got suspicious and came over here and saw this shit. Improvised explosive device—IED. Sir, this is some spooky shit," Washington said.

Zach took control immediately. "Might be remote-controlled as well, so let's move out. Top, find someone who can run a forklift. I'll come back over here with our engineer after we've secured the perimeter. You can get the forklift moving the pallets to those buildings back that way." He pointed in the direction of some white barracks huts about three kilometers across the runway. There were a few operational streetlights around them, and he figured that would be the safest place for the equipment in the interim.

As they jogged away from the vehicle, Zach continued. "Have the loadmaster roll the pallets off the planes now and tell the troops to make sure they have all their crap off the aircraft because I'm sending them away from here. Then we will cover the airfield until we can secure the buildings over there. Get the ammo issued out immediately and put out a net call for everyone to stay away from the Blazer."

Zachary quickly pulled his night-vision goggles out of his rucksack, snapped them onto his helmet mount, and flicked the metal ON switch. It was a deep black night with ample starlight to give the goggles adequate illumination. As Zachary scanned

his surroundings, he came to the grim conclusion
that his troops were in a valley. There was high
ground to his north, east, and west. Obviously, the
water must be to the south.

He heard the pallets slide off the back ramps.
Zachary explained to the pilots that it was not safe
for an airplane in that location. They agreed and said
that they still had enough fuel to make it to Andersen
Air Force Base on Guam. Zachary thanked the pilots
for their concurrence, because he felt the aircraft
would only make them a bigger target.

The equipment was unloaded, the forklift had
safely cranked, and Slick, the commander's radio
operator, handed him the radio handset, saying,
"Let's get down to business, sir."

With that, Zachary began controlling the
movement of his platoons, leaving Kurtz's platoon to
cover to the north, while Taylor's platoon provided
flank security to the east. The XO led the
headquarters platoon, while the first sergeant floated
between platoons, keeping the men alert. Second
Platoon led the way for the company as it followed
the beacon of the streetlights. The Air Force
crewmen did a good job of turning the aircraft.

As they were maneuvering the ancient beasts,
images of the disaster in Iran at Desert One popped
into Zachary's mind. He had mixed emotions as he
watched them quickly turn, bump along the runway
noisily, then float into the silent night sky. In a sense,
he wished that he and his men could be flying away
with them. On the other hand, he had a mission to
do, and the soldier in him thrived on situations like
these. With the deafening roar of the two aircraft
gone, the silence was enhanced. Ears rang, unable to
hear the more subtle noises.

The three-kilometer walk was uneventful, which
Zachary attributed to the unit's good security during
the move. They found four white Quonset huts

unlocked and ready for their occupancy, with metal-frame beds, mattresses, and sheets laid out. A row of three streetlights illuminated the buildings. Zachary had the sapper inspect the buildings for bombs or other booby traps as he searched the area.

To Zachary, they seemed positioned in the middle of a desolate wasteland. By now, he could see Subic Bay to their south. It was not far away, maybe another three hundred meters. But other than a pier to the south, the barracks were not remotely close to anything that resembled a naval base. Walking with Slick to the pier, he saw what appeared to be a more complete facility across the water. Mists of salt water stung his eyes, and he returned to his company and decided to move them another two hundred meters to the west, away from the buildings. *They're magnets, those buildings.* The base was a ghost town, complete with tumbleweed rolling through the spotlights of the streetlamps like lost children searching their way home.

At that moment, Zach reaffirmed every commander's mantra. *All my men are coming home.*

CHAPTER 23

Zachary had his company form the standard triangular patrol base. It was the most secure position for his troops. He did not trust the buildings, yet. The night was strangely silent except the low muffled sound of crates opening, 5.56mm ammunition speed loaders zipping the rounds into magazines, and the assorted metallic clicks and clanks of equipment distribution and inspection.

He probably could have reached the embassy from Subic Naval Base using standard frequency modu-lation communications, but he wanted to test the Single Channel Anti-jam Man Portable (SCAMP) radio and saw this as the perfect opportunity. Slick knelt on the hard-packed dirt and popped open a white metal suitcase about the size of a gym bag. It weighed thirty pounds altogether. One half of the suitcase lid separated from the other and served as the radar dish. It was square and pivoted on a metal frame with four legs that angled out from each corner of the chassis. The other half of the suitcase contained the voice and data sending units. The SCAMP operated on extremely high frequency (EHF), using the Military Strategic, Tactical, and Relay Satellite Communications System (MILSTAR). A satellite positioned somewhere over the Pacific Ocean would receive the message and relay it to the receiving station.

Zachary tucked his map into the cargo pocket of his pants while Slick performed the standard RTO habit of blowing into the mouthpiece after turning on the transmitter. He heard nothing come back to him in the earpiece, but delivered the handset to the captain anyway.

"JUSMAG, this is Bravo six," Zach said.

They waited in the darkness as his men either slept or pulled security. He had one patrol, led by Second Lieutenant Mike Kurtz, the Second Platoon Leader operating under the call sign "White six," clearing the perimeter two hundred meters to the west.

"JUSMAG, this is Bravo six, we have crossed phase-line October and are awaiting further instructions. Your liaison element was incapable of communicating with us, and we had enemy contact on the objective. Request immediate link up, over." JUSMAG was an adjunct to the U.S. embassy in Manila. A small military team coordinated all Department of Defense activities within the country, and Zach had been instructed to contact the JUSMAG immediately upon arrival.

"Bravo six, this is JUSMAG, I'm the only one awake here at the moment. I will inform the colonel as soon as possible, over."

"Listen, this situation is not normal and requires immediate notification of your leader, over." Zachary was getting angry. *No one is awake? What kind of excuse is that? I'll bet that lieutenant colonel with a bullet in his head wasn't awake either.*

Zachary's feeling about the mission did not improve when the voice came back, "Bravo six, this is JUSMAG. Your instructions are to continue with the mission, over."

"Continue with what mission, over?"

"Wait one." After a minute or two pause a different, harsher voice came on the line, "Bravo six, this is JUSMAG six, what seems to be the problem?"

Finally , Zachary thought, *someone with authority.* The six suffix was the designator for the commander, so he knew the voice belonged to someone in charge.

"Your liaison was incapacitated prior to our arrival. We need link-up with a member of your team for further instructions."

"Incapacitated in what way?"

"Your man was shot through the forehead before we got here," Zachary said, violating what he considered to be operational security. There was a long period of silence.

"What is your status?"

"We have secured our equipment and moved across phase-line October, awaiting further instructions."

"Roger, I'll be at your location ASAP. Anything else?"

"Negative, over."

Zachary and Slick looked at each other, wondering how long ASAP would be. A warm, moist wind pushed across their faces. Slick left the SCAMP operational as Zachary slipped on his night-vision goggles to get a glimpse of his unit's security. From one knee, he could see all three platoons, tightly joined in a triangular formation. It was a bit close together for his liking, but considering the circumstances, and the fact that he had three new platoon leaders, he was satisfied. The sun would rise shortly, giving him a clearer vision of what looked to him to be a wasteland of hardstand surrounded by high-rising hills on three sides and water on the fourth.

Too vulnerable.

As the morning sun crested the eastern mountains, scattering its rays through the jagged peaks, Zachary slept sitting on his rear end, leaning against his rucksack. He was tired and floated in and out of a dream state, vivid images of his parents' farm in Stanardsville dancing through his mind.

CHAPTER 24

"Sir?" Slick said. "Sir, there's a helicopter coming in."

Zachary pulled out of his dream slowly. It had been a rough two days for him, ever since the alert notification back in Hawaii. The only sleep he had managed was a shaky three hours on the airplane. The rest of the time he had spent making plans, reassuring soldiers, and thinking about his family. His mind rose out of the dream like a fighter pilot pulling out of a dive, spinning rapidly across the Blue Ridge, the continental United States, Hawaii, and landing with a thud in the Philippines. He rubbed his eyes and, in the wafting heat of the morning, looked at Slick, who was pointing at a UH-60 Black Hawk helicopter flaring as it was about to land.

A portly man in solid green jungle fatigues stepped out of the aircraft, holding his flop hat in one hand. His pistol holster slapped his thigh as he ran from under the prop wash. Zachary looked at his watch. 0830. *So, ASAP meant three hours.*

Lieutenant Colonel Fraley, miffed that some of Zachary's soldiers had challenged him before he could enter the perimeter, stood before Zachary in anticipation of something. Like two men squared off on a short distance duel, it finally occurred to him that Fraley was awaiting a salute.

Sure, give this dude a sniper check. Zachary smiled, then snapped a sharp salute. The overweight lieutenant colonel performed a sloppy half-salute. Zach smirked and considered it the lieutenant

colonel's good fortune that none of his men had shot
him as he blew into their perimeter. He was
doubtless a garrison officer. He had a thick, bushy
mustache that hung over teeth stained from smoking,
and his hair, while balding, was long by Army
standards.

Earlier, Second Lieutenant Andy Taylor's First
Platoon, going by the call sign "Red six," had moved
back to the airstrip where the colonel had been shot
to secure the body they had left behind. Taylor had
radioed back that the vehicle and the body were
nowhere to be found.

"Whaddya mean you don't have the body?"
Fraley lashed out at Zachary in the middle of his
company perimeter, troops watching.

"Sir, the vehicle was rigged with explosives. My
immediate concern was for the safety of my troops,"
Zachary responded with authority.

"You ever think he might still be alive!?" Fraley
barked, his mustache catching spittle as he talked.
Zachary looked awkwardly at the man, then his own
soldiers, who were hovering around the two men and
staring at the ground. He had always followed the
leadership maxim to "praise in public and punish in
private."

"And who the hell do you think you are sending
those two airplanes away—they were supposed to
backhaul some equipment."

Zachary felt less bad about that, figuring he
might have saved the government two airplanes. But
the dead colonel was another matter. He was sure
that man had a family somewhere and would at least
want a proper burial for him.

However, he took consolation in the fact that he
still had all of his troops, and remained poised
despite Fraley's ranting.

"I'm calling your division commander and telling him not to send another hothead commander

in charge of a ragtag unit to my islands," Fraley said, launching rockets of spit at Zachary.

"Sir, any intel you think you can give us in light of what happened last night?" Zachary asked, ignoring the rebuke.

"Your clearance ain't high enough, son. Now move your shit into those buildings, lock up your ammo, and don't breathe unless I tell you to," Fraley ordered. "The ammo's over there, and the boat will be here tomorrow to pick it up. Not hard, Captain."

"Sir—"

"At ease, soldier. Come down here itching for a fight, are ya?" Fraley said. "Well, you just better back off it, son, and do exactly what I tell you to do. Are you sure you saw a dead body, I'm beginning to wonder—"

"Yes, sir. I'm positive. I've stood here and listened to you rag me out in front of my troops, but I will not allow you to question my integrity," Gar-rett shot back.

Fraley did not budge.

"Listen here, Captain. This ain't no game, and you ain't in charge. I'll have your ass locked up for insubordination next time you talk to me like that."

Zach stared at the overweight and unprofessional officer. It was easy. He decided to employ the method of voluntary disobedience; in short, he would do exactly the opposite of what the colonel had told him not to do.

As Fraley remounted the Black Hawk, Slick looked at the commander, holding the radio handset in one hand and his M4 in the other, saying, "Boy, what an asshole."

Fraley's head turned, as if he heard Slick.

"You said it, my friend," Zachary said to Slick, who knelt back down and continued to monitor the SCAMP, his FM radio, and the phone line that he had run to each platoon command post.

Zachary watched as the Black Hawk pulled away from the ground, sucking twigs and dirt into the air and spitting them back down upon his troops as the pilot flew low over his company perimeter, blowing hot dirt onto the men.

"Go to hell," Zachary said under his breath, watching the aircraft fly away. Slick looked up at his commander and smiled, as did some of the other headquarters platoon troops who had overheard the ass chewing. Nobody gave their commander shit and got away with it. They were sure of that.

He called his platoon leaders and platoon sergeants in. This was a time for both commissioned and noncommissioned officers to receive the word straight from the commander. He briefed them on exactly what had transpired between him and the colonel. They shook their heads and offered words of support to the commander, which he quickly hushed.

"Here's the deal. We will only rotate one platoon at a time into the barracks. The other two will dig fighting positions and defend the primary avenues of approach into your area of operations. Headquarters, you'll set up in one of the buildings also, but we will change barracks every night to avoid presenting a stationary target. If we have to, we'll even pilfer the ammunition stockpile. If you haven't already done so, I want leaders to distribute all of the ammunition we brought to every soldier. I'm talking everything we've got," Zachary directed.

As the commander talked, the group coalesced. They became more cohesive as a result of the simple altercation between an outsider and their commander. In all, Zachary figured, things had actually worked out for the best.

"Platoon leaders, you need to sight weapons and give me your sector sketches so I can develop a company fire plan. We want aggressive patrolling within the confines of the base and you have my order to take suspicious personnel captive for tactical questioning." He did not know if his directive was within the rules of engagement, but he did not want strays roaming around the vacant, windswept base.

Zachary finished the meeting by saying, "As long as we are in this ghost town, B Company is the sheriff." His leaders smiled and crowed with a few "hooahs," the standard infantry signal of approval. One of the troops even barked out the name "Garrett's Gulch," which would stick. They had to call their new home something.

His briefing had been more like a halftime pep talk at a football game. Indeed, Zachary recognized that part of his job was to motivate these people.

Quickly, they moved out to perform their missions. They checked ammunition, dug foxholes, and determined the location of their machine guns.

Zachary stood in the middle of the activity in the same fashion that a head football coach directs a practice session. In his mind, he gauged his playing field and assessed his position's strengths and vulnerabilities.

With sudden clarity, he realized this was an away game.

CHAPTER 25

PALAU, PACIFIC OCEAN

Matt bolted upright in the bed and was momentarily confused by his surroundings. He was in a plush hotel room, swaddled in thousand-count Egyptian cotton sheets, and resting on a bed that seemed to swallow him. In addition, there was the blond woman again, hovering over him.

"My Virginian," he said, turning and looking at her. She was dressed in a turquoise business suit and had obviously been in some professional environment.

"Time to go," she said curtly, stuffing her Blackberry into her purse.

"Did you file my report?"

She looked away, then back at him. "I did, with Rathburn, who called back."

"So, can you give me a status of what's happening in Mindanao?"

"We'll do that in the car. The secretary wants you to fly to Manila with him. It's a short trip, and you can update him on everything during the flight."

"Manila?" Matt was thinking out loud as opposed to questioning her directly. That would put him in the thick of things, he realized. He would get back to his assigned country and could perhaps pick up the trail of the Predators again. On that thought, he asked Meredith, "Any status on the Japanese float plane?"

"It departed quickly after refueling. It hasn't been sighted since," Meredith replied.

"Anyone check the refueling logs?"

"Let's go," Meredith said impatiently. "You've been out of it a day now, so you should be well enough rested to make a short plane flight."

"Who are you, Florence Nightingale?" Matt laughed. It was a defensive mechanism for him. An attractive woman was in his hotel room, and he had the distinct impression that she was bothered by something. "By the way, how did I get naked?"

Again she averted her eyes. "Pino undressed you … and I'm not sure what else he did."

"Not again. C'mon," Matt said, standing and wincing at the pain. She was flashing a movie-star smile back at him, chuckling a bit.

"Thought that might get you moving. Here's a bio on Rathburn. You two will be going to Manila, then you'll be further assigned from there. We talked to your agency."

"Further assigned?"

"I assumed you would have a better feel than I for what that meant," she said, smiling.

He looked at his shoulder, which in all honesty felt okay.

"You really don't remember, do you?"

"Remember what?"

"It's just as well," she said. "Ten minutes. Be dressed and downstairs."

"Okay. One question?"

"One."

"Are you going to Manila?"

Meredith walked to the window, which provided an expansive view of the Pacific. Closer in were palm trees and beautiful horseshoe beaches that appeared as a series of semicircles beneath the bluffs.

"No. I have to get back to DC. I was the advance team for Mr. Rathburn's Asia trip. I have briefed him on everything he needs to know, the trip is set, and I'm heading back."

"Don't sound too happy about it," Matt said.

"How would you like to be the expert on the region and get punted by a bunch of women?"

"Women?"

She turned and looked at him.

"You ever hear of the Defense Advisory Committee on Women in the Service? DACOWITS?"

"I'm not even going there with that acronym. And no," Matt said, pulling his washed and pressed cargo pants over his legs.

"They are going with Mr. Rathburn to Manila, Okinawa, South Korea, and Hawaii on the way back in order to assess the status of women in the military."

"You're a chick, why can't you do that?" Matt was pulling his shirt over his bare chest, but needed some help with the shoulder.

Meredith walked over, lifted the shirt, and slid it over his arm so that Matt didn't have to raise it above shoulder level. He felt her place her soft hand on the small of his back as she used her other hand to manipulate the shirt.

"We talked, didn't we?" Matt asked.

Meredith moved around to his front once her chore was complete.

"Yes. You were doped up, but we talked," she said.

"That's about the only way to get me to talk. Did we watch Oprah, too?"

Meredith laughed. "No, but you told me about your brother Zachary and how much you love him and your sister, Karen."

Matt shrugged. "As long as I'm not remembering stuff, you're in my room watching me get dressed. How was I?"

"I'm not smoking a cigarette, am I?"

"Ouch."

"Actually, I was unaware that you were naked, but time is of the essence here, and you didn't respond to two phone calls and five minutes of knocking on the door."

"So a little Givenchy did the trick?"

"Works every time." She smiled, picked up his rucksack, and said, "C'mon. We've got an assistant secretary of defense waiting on us."

"Who gives a shit?" Matt said. "That's just some dude who sucked up to the right guy at the right time. Give me a minute to do some personal hygiene here."

Matt did his business in the bathroom, brushed his teeth with the gratis incidentals that he guessed always came with thousand-dollar-a-night rooms. He studied his four days of growth and decided not to shave. If he was riding shotgun with a defense department assistant something or other, he wanted to look either like security or galley help.

As he exited the bathroom, Meredith turned and began walking at a fast clip along the hallway. They took the elevator down to the lobby and immediately walked out and got into one of two waiting Suburbans.

"He in the other one?"

"Yes. Now I'm warning you that he's got a bit of a temper."

"That doesn't bother me," Matt said, a confused look on his face.

"Then what does?"

"That you're not going."

Matt's compliment seemed to stagger her for a moment, but she regained her composure, and said, "Thank you. I wish I was going, too. I've not been to Manila or Okinawa, though I've been to Korea."

"I just think you're hot." Matt smiled. He followed up his awkward comment with, "Do me a favor. When you get to DC, if you have the chance, tell my sister I said 'Hi' and that I'm okay. She worries, and sometimes I'm not as good as I should be about keeping up. Mom and Dad are getting up there, you know, and she's trying to hold everything together." He pressed a phone number into one of Meredith's hands.

Meredith looked at him, then at her hand, and said, "I will."

"But before you do that," he said, looking at her, "take these and make sure his family knows he died a hero, and I want you to close the loop on where his teammates are and that they're okay."

Matt placed Peterson's dog tags into her other outstretched palm as they bounced along in the back of the Suburban. Her eyes dropped to the two metal strips with Peterson's name and other identifying information. He closed her hand around them and held it.

"I can joke around with the best of them," he said. "But I never forget my mission."

CHAPTER 26

As the plane taxied along the Palau International Airport runway, Matt's thoughts reflected back to his foggy day with Meredith. He honestly couldn't recall much about their conversation, though much of it had occurred poolside, where he remembered falling asleep. How he had gotten the room, or even to the room, was anyone's guess.

He was facing the rear of the airplane and seated across from Assistant Secretary of Defense Rathburn. The U.S. Air Force Gulfstream 5 jet ambled along the runway and lifted slowly off the ground, then banked hard to the right, turning from south to west to northwest as it climbed to altitude.

Matt had actually been mistaken for security by one of the female officers belonging to the advisory committee that Meredith had mentioned. She had handed him a bag to carry as she ascended the steps to the aircraft. Once he saw she was inside the airplane, Matt walked over to a local, who was toying with the auxiliary power unit for the Gulfstream, and said, "On behalf of the President of the United States, please accept this as a small token of appreciation for all that you do for us."

The man smiled back at him with what teeth he had left in his mouth, took the shopping bag, and nodded. For all Matt knew he had just given the man a bagful of thongs, which he was sure would be put to good use. He smiled at the image of returning to Palau and all of the ground maintenance crew wearing thongs around their heads like surgical masks.

Secretary Rathburn and Matt sat on opposite sides of a foldout table in the forward cabin. The female delegation was in the aft cabin, which was separated by a pocket door. Rathburn placed a small personal digital assistant into his briefcase, leaned back, and slid the door shut, saying, "Bunch of women," as if he disagreed with their presence. Matt got the distinct opposite impression as he observed the few minutes of interaction between Rathburn and one woman in particular. His ever-churning mind began to wonder if Meredith's simmering rage wasn't jealousy as opposed to professional displeasure.

"Meredith told me your story. Fascinating," Rathburn said.

Matt couldn't see what was so fascinating about a dead American and chaos in Mindanao, so he didn't take the bait and remained silent.

After a moment Rathburn continued staring at him and said, "She also told me you were a tough nut. I'm assuming her assessment is based on reading your dossier as opposed to personal knowledge."

Matt didn't exactly like where the conversation was headed. He believed he was going to get an update on the *Shimpu*, the situation in Mindanao, and the float plane that had both carried him to safety and deposited him in the lap of a mystery.

"A little of both, I guess," he said in reply to Rathburn's comment, which elicited a raised eyebrow from the political appointee.

"Why don't you tell me what you saw in Mindanao, Matt?"

"Sir, I quite frankly thought I was getting an update from you," Matt replied. "I gave a big dump of information to Meredith, and now I'm your hostage on an airplane headed to Manila. What do we know about Mindanao?"

"We can always open the door and let you out, you know." Rathburn smiled. Matt looked through the gray morning at the dark ocean ten kilometers below and said, "Give me a parachute and I'm out of here."

Rathburn paused and said, "We're not sure what's happening in Mindanao. We got the report of the two Philippine C-130s shot down and were unaware that any Americans were on either of them until we got your confirmation from the Agency. I think this was a bit of the left hand not knowing what the right hand was doing."

"How do you mean?"

"There weren't supposed to be any Americans in Mindanao," Rathburn said flatly, and left it at that. Something registered in Matt's mind that Rathburn was wrestling with something, perhaps a decision he had to make. Or one he had already made.

"Well, as long as we're on this bus to Abilene in Iraq, what difference does it make?" Matt posed the rhetorical question to flesh out his own instincts that Rathburn was doing mental gymnastics, to determine in which camp he might reside, if any. Maybe it was just the fact that Rathburn was sitting here with his manicured fingernails, well-coiffed hair, pinpoint cotton shirt, and silk tie while across from him sat Matt in his nondescript dark shirt and olive cargo pants, muscles pushing at the seams of his sleeves, four days of growth on his face, and a bullet wound in his shoulder. Personally, he felt Saddam needed to go, but was struggling with his own failure to kill Al Qaeda senior leadership in Pakistan when he had them in his sights. *Every time I'm close, I'm moved.*

Some might be intimidated by the fact that Matt's reputation within the Agency was legendary, and Rathburn paid homage to Matt's repute by saying, "Pretty ballsy move going into Pakistan last December. Many of us were cheering you on."

Many of us? Why not everyone? Matt wondered.

"I've got a saying," Matt commented. "When you're right, don't worry about it."

"Your conscience is indeed clear, but you're rightness landed you in the Philippines. What do you make of that?"

"I go where they send me. But I still don't understand why they stopped me," Matt said, looking over his wounded shoulder through the oval window. The ocean passed silently beneath them.

"Ever think it might be this Iraq thing? We are, as you say, on a runaway train," Rathburn said.

"I said bus to Abilene," Matt corrected. To Matt, words meant exactly what they were intended to mean. There were no slip-ups, and there were no coincidences, especially with a man of Rathburn's relative import. *He* had said "runaway train." Was that an unintended look into Rathburn's psyche and what he truly believed? Matt's "bus to Abilene" comment was a reference to the group-think mentality that takes hold when gathering momentum effortlessly silences dissent.

"Same difference. I'm concerned about something you told Meredith," Rathburn said. "Something about Japanese soldiers on Mindanao. Can you tell me more?"

Had the situation been reversed, with Matt as the senior defense official, he would have asked first about Ron Peterson, then about the Special Forces team and the young Filipino, then about the *Shimpu* or the abduction of the Japanese man. Sure, the presence of Japanese soldiers on Mindanao was curious, but a man had to have his priorities.

And he presumed Rathburn did.

"They were guarding something. It was a facility with civilians. It's something they are trying to hide. I told it all to Meredith," Matt said.

"Why would the Japanese government have soldiers in Mindanao?" Matt wasn't sure if Rathburn was asking him or talking to himself, so he remained silent for a moment.

Indeed why? And more importantly, why was that Rathburn's primary concern?

CHAPTER 27

Silence usually begets someone else's opening his or her mouth, and Rathburn did not disappoint Matt when he said, "You know, Ambassador Kaitachi came over the other day to talk to the secretary. Something about China-Taiwan. Wants us to put some eyes up there."

As he was thinking, Matt swirled his Diet Coke, which had been delivered by a young airman.

"Doesn't really make sense."

"I know."

Rathburn was a tall, handsome man with a shock of grey hair on either side of his balding head. His beak nose and marble eyes gave him the appearance of a hawk. He was generally respected in the defense community. And he leveled those hawkish eyes on Matt.

"Ever hear of *Bridges to Babylon*?"

Matt shrugged. He faintly recalled a movie, he thought. "Film?"

"Stones. Where have you been? Their last album of the nineties," Rathburn chided.

Confused, Matt hunched his shoulders, and said, "So?"

"We're on that bridge now, and it's a one-way road to Iraq. China-Taiwan won't get any traction."

"We could always back up," Matt said.

"Ever try to back your way out of a traffic jam?"

"This isn't I-395, sir. It isn't that hard," Matt said.

Rathburn stared at him for a long moment, as if

he was considering saying something. Matt noticed his countenance actually become softer, less tense, the way a patient might look before finally talking about that one issue to his therapist. Matt thought he might actually hear the man say something he meant.

Just as quickly, though, Rathburn's face tightened again as he instead asked, "What do you know about Japan?"

Back to Japan again. Matt wondered why. "Not really my specialty. Philippines, Korea, China, and missing Predators; those are my fields." Matt took a sip of his Coke and ate some peanuts, consciously not bringing up Afghanistan and Pakistan again.

"We're on this airplane together for the next few hours. We'll land at about eight in the morning. My sleep cycle is all screwed up, and you seem like a knowledgeable guy. So, humor me and tell me what you know about Japan," Rathburn said with an edge in his voice.

"On one condition. Can you guarantee me that my report on Mindanao has been filed and someone is working that intelligence?"

"Guaranteed," Rathburn said, slapping his palm on the table.

Matt racked his brain and lined up some points to make for the man, searching for a logic flow.

"Okay, Japan. Like a country report that might lead to clues as to why they have soldiers in Mindanao?"

Rathburn nodded.

Matt ran a hand down his face, stalling for time, but finally started talking. "Okay, not sure if this is what you want, but, I'll free-associate. Stop me if it's not what you're looking for."

Rathburn nodded again, and assured him, "Don't worry, I will. I don't suffer fools or bullshit, which is why you're still sitting here with me and not in that viper's nest back there." He pointed over his shoulder at the aft cabin, where the faint cackle of feminine laughter could be heard.

Matt smiled thinly and said, "Well, for example, Japan has what we call a population inversion. They have more old people than young people, and the gap is growing. Meanwhile, they've got this economy that needs X number of people to keep it running. Today, their unemployment rate is just over one percent. So, we've got a labor shortage in the world's fastest-growing economy. What are they going to do, farm out their jobs and markets to other countries that need the work? Takishi did just that last year with the China agreement."

"Why not? We do it with Mexico *and* China?" Rathburn said. The political appointee hid his sudden alarm that Matt knew his friend's name. *How does he know who Takishi is?*

"Yes, sir, we do it because it makes short-term economic sense in our almost purely capitalist system. To the Japanese, who have more of a state-directed capitalism and a circular vision of life instead of the Western linear view, to seek labor outside of the country would be anathema; which makes Takishi's move so ... interesting. For them it is like exporting their success while devaluing their own net worth. You're right, in many cases the U.S. has done exactly that with the call centers in India and Pakistan, for example."

Rathburn nodded.

"So then, add that to the fact that we have gotten protectionist and practically reduced their markets by 10 percent in the last year. The European Community has done the same thing, and they've only started. Nearly 60 percent of Japanese exports head either to the EC countries or the U.S. Chop that number in half and Japan loses one-third of its trade. We've already decided that they can't sustain their economy with current labor projections. So that's two strikes against their economy already. Remember, the Japanese have staked their entire future on their economic prowess. So in a sense, their security environment revolves first around the economy, then goes to the basics of the vulnerability of their geographic positioning."

The plane ran into a brief period of turbulence. Matt looked up at the ceiling of the airplane, sensing the motion with his body. Convinced it was nothing unusual, he looked back at Rathburn and proceeded.

"Now we've almost got something to think about," Matt said, grabbing the matchbook out of the glass ashtray on the table. The flimsy white cardboard book had the Department of Defense symbol on it, an eagle with its head turned and claws holding three arrows. He pushed up his shirtsleeves over his thick forearms and decided how to demonstrate his newfound logic.

"This represents the labor shortage," he said sliding the matchstick across the table toward Rathburn. "This is the fall in trade from U.S. and EC protectionism." He dropped both sticks into the ashtray.

"Now let's talk energy policy. Japan has reduced its dependence on foreign oil much better than most other countries by pursuing alternative means of energy. They've got everything ranging from geothermal to windmills to nuclear power. They have big plans to build twenty or so more new nuclear plants, adding to the fifty they already have. But every time a shovel hits the ground, students and radicals are protesting and blocking construction. Imagine how we'd feel with sixty nuclear plants in California."

"Not a bad idea." Rathburn smiled, the first indication of connection.

"Agreed." Matt smiled in return. "The point is that they have no oil or natural gas deposits, and they cannot expect their energy needs to keep pace with their economic expansion. So there's another match. In fact, I'll give that issue two matches," he said, tossing a third and a fourth stick to the pile with a confident flick of the wrist.

"We've already mentioned that the U.S. is almost solely focused on the Middle East, reducing its security presence in the Pacific Rim. This has a proportional effect on Japan's perception of its own security. The more we pull back," he said emphatically, "the more insecure they feel. More sulfur." He dropped a fifth match into the ashtray.

"Now we can count, if you want to, all of the intangible and esoteric stuff like the fact that they are a strictly closed Confucian society with almost a purely homogenous people. Confucianism operates on three levels. First, Confucian societies have a strong sense of identity with their heritage and ancestry. Second, Confucianism breeds a sense of exclusivity. That is, it produces the closed Japanese society that only someone born in Japan to a Japanese family can belong to. In essence, very racist. Third, Confucianism stresses that the family is the critical unit of a society and that government should simply be an extension of that family. This reinforces the exclusivity of the society and also produces a we-they type of mentality. That equals nationalism. Another match.

"They've been putting up with our bullshit since the end of World War II. Americans wrote their constitution and set up their government. We have a base or two on their land. While ninety nine percent of American troops are the best our nation has to offer, there's always that one percent of bad apples who have committed crimes against the Japanese. I think there was a rape in Okinawa not too long ago. So, the wounded pride of having to kowtow to the Americans and the distorted perception created by the few bad apples calls for a seventh match." It fell from his fingers, landing in the ashtray.

"Taiwan was formerly called Formosa before it was anted to China in the post–World War II settlement. It had belonged to the Japanese for fifty years before that. They bargained with the Russians for the Kuriles to their north. Imagine how they feel about something like Formosa to their south. Territorial claims," he said bluntly, dramatically dropping an eighth match into the pile.

"So we've got a Japan poised for economic downturn, minus its former security umbrella, with no real threat from Russia, and with some territorial disputes. Its traditional enemies are challenging Japan on the economic level. Korea's pursuit of markets is very aggressive, and China is the eight-hundred-pound gorilla about to rip free from its chains. Sir, economic competition is just another form of warfare, only on a lower level. Competition is competition. So, traditional enemies and an unwillingness to mediate historical differences calls for another match."

Matt looked at Rathburn whose eyes were fixed on his. He seemed uncomfortable, almost nervous.

"Then, there is the idea of *Henka*. It's a Japanese process of accepting new, radically different positions. Simply put, it formalizes new decisions that are dramatic departures from old positions. It allows them to change their minds without having to explain why. It's a Japanese social tradition. It allows them to completely shift social or personal direction without any forewarning. That accounts for the ease with which they moved from a militaristic society to a democratic one. Similarly, it accounts for the shift from a Samurai society to the Tokugawa era."

Matt looked at Rathburn, and said, "Governments can 'do' Henka and people can 'do' Henka. The only constant in Henka is that it always serves the common Japanese good."

He dropped the last match. The sticks crossed in

the ashtray, looking like a pile of bones.

"So that is ten, I believe. The only question is, Will there be a spark? Or is it already smoldering and we just don't see it," he asked himself, thinking, then pulling a match out of the book and striking it. The flame burned eerily bright in the darkened cabin of the aircraft as he held the match above the ashtray.

"Do they seek to shed the implications that Western thought set their society on the correct path?"

"Thought you didn't know anything?"

"I know some stuff," Matt said.

"How does that square with Kaitachi's Taiwan-China issue?"

"I don't know, sir. Let me ask you, what do you make of all of this? And why did you ask me about Japan instead of my real areas of expertise?"

Rathburn looked away. "The ambassador's visit just didn't make sense to me."

The plane droned along, and Matt dropped the lit match into the ashtray.

The matches ignited simultaneously, burning a fluorescent white, then fading to orange. Both men fixed their gaze on the flame.

"Something about a fire makes you stare at it," Rathburn said.

"Agreed."

The plane etched a trace across the sky, arching toward the Philippines where a government delegation, and God knows what else, would meet them.

As Matt drifted to sleep, a thought nibbled at his mind, spiraling into the black void that brought rest. What was it? There, he had it for a moment.

Something about watching fires.

rime Minister Kirusu Mizuzawa sat in
ie *Kantei*, the Japanese equivalent of the
. Upon becoming prime minister two
e had decorated his workplace with
res and mementoes he had acquired
is distinguished military and political

s first actions as prime minister was to
) the map of Japan a large map of
a. Sitting at his desk, he could look up
ur major islands of Japan in large scale,
ie Pacific Rim from the northeastern
er to central Australia. Centrally locat-
Philippine Islands. Just to the north of
ies was the island of Formosa, or
had circled Taiwan and the Philippines
lighter and put a question mark next to

and walked around the front of his
against it. He was a short man in his
. His face was wrinkled like that of a
-Pei. His eyes peeked from between two
his wizened face. He kept his black hair
e to his head with a crew cut. A scar
erican bayonet during the Great Pacific
ss the top of his right forearm. It had
operly and curved outward in grotesque

CHAPTER 28

GEORGETOWN, WASHINGTON, DC

Dick Diamond stood at the window of Saul Fox's Georgetown townhouse reading his Blackberry. Looking up, he could see the Potomac, some stores along M Street, and a glimpse of the Kennedy Center. It was, after all, prime real estate. He had turned up Puccini again, Calaf's voice belting out, *"Ma il mio mistero è chiuso in me, il nome mio nessun saprà."* But my secret is hidden within me. None will know my name!

Diamond pocketed his digital assistant and ran a well-manicured hand along the revolver he had purchased, then walked to the bed and fitted the weapon between the mattress and box spring. He stepped back, assessed its positioning, and made an adjustment. Then he sat on the bed, leaned back a bit, and let his arm fall naturally along the mattress. He felt around and determined the pistol needed to be moved about six inches toward the headboard and a few inches toward the edge. His considerable weight had crushed the mattress into the pistol, making retrieval at the right moment awkward, if not impossible.

And that would not be good.

He removed the pistol and awkwardly stuffed it in his coat pocket, confident that he could place it properly when necessary and have it … available.

As soon as his hand left his jacket, Saul Fox came walking into the bedroom, wearing a white robe that had the letters SF stenciled on the left breast pocket in gold thread—real gold.

"Dick, we need to talk about this Philippine thing," Fox said.

"That's why I'm here, isn't it?"

"Yes, yes, I presume so," Fox agreed. He sat on a chaise and the robe fell away, exposing a short, bare leg.

Diamond sat in a cherry Thonet No. 14 chair made of six pieces of steamed and bent cane wood. It was nearly a hundred years old, and Diamond thought he was going to break the chair as his large derriere pressed into the antique.

"You know Takishi, right?" Fox asked.

Diamond hesitated, not wanting to answer right away. "Yes, of course. He's a big wheel in Japan, and he was a student at Harvard B School when I was teaching at the JFK School. Quite popular, bright mind, very … Japanese."

"Good. Good," Fox said. He pulled the robe over his leg and rubbed his face with an open palm as if to test his shave.

"How so?"

"I'm thinking about everything we're hearing. We've got one dead guy in the Philippines. Patterson, something like that. Matt Garrett was supposedly roaming around down there from the CIA. Stone had his press conference, and now we've got an infantry company going there."

"Still all very manageable within the big picture. I mean an A team and a rifle company, that's not much more than we let Stone send to Afghanistan."

Fox smiled, then his expression changed as he sat up. "I know. That's sort of my point. Our entire plan was to let Nine-eleven happen, however that was going to play out, then use it as a window of opportunity for our own purposes; to achieve lasting fame. Brilliant."

"Yes, but are ⟨...⟩ window?" Diamon⟨...⟩ "That's what ⟨...⟩ about."

Japanese⟨...⟩ his office in⟨...⟩ White Ho⟨...⟩ years ago,⟨...⟩ various pi⟨...⟩ throughou⟨...⟩ careers.

One o⟨...⟩ place nex⟨...⟩ Southeast⟨...⟩ and see th⟨...⟩ as well a⟨...⟩ Chinese⟨...⟩ ed were⟨...⟩ the Phil⟨...⟩ Taiwan.⟨...⟩ with red⟨...⟩ Indonesi⟨...⟩

He s⟨...⟩ desk, lea⟨...⟩ mid-sev⟨...⟩ Chinese⟨...⟩ coin slo⟨...⟩ cropped⟨...⟩ from a⟨...⟩ War ra⟨...⟩ not hea⟨...⟩ fashion⟨...⟩

He took his suit jacket off and placed it over the back of his chair. He then slipped on his black samurai robe and walked through the open glass doors behind his desk. The night air was cool and heavy, settling upon Mizuzawa in wavy mists. Stepping with a bare foot past a decorative rock, he strode onto the bridge that spanned the dark koi pond. He watched the large orange and white fish smack at the water's surface and swim lazily in another direction. A small pagoda faced him on the other side of the pond.

His robe flowing with his gait, he strode slowly around the carefully trimmed hedges in the garden. He stopped and raised his arms, palms stretched outward, then slowly brought them down, beginning a jujitsu ritual of relaxation. He performed several maneuvers, eyes closed, as he felt the enemy surrounding him.

An unarmed method of defense, jujitsu was designed to throw the opponent off-balance through movement and deception. Karate differed in that it focused on the accurate application of well-timed blows to the opponent. Mizuzawa moved in rhythmic harmony, clearing his mind for the monumental decisions that lay ahead. His process of Henka had been gradual, but he felt that he had a consensus within the administration and that they were convinced of the course he had chosen.

In the courtyard stood a bronze statue of Confucius. He relied on Confucian ideology as his spiritual guide and, more than ever, needed reassurance that he was embarking on the correct path. He looked at the painting and bowed. Kneeling on a red satin pillow, he closed his eyes and prayed silently. He asked for the wisdom to do what was correct for Japan and the courage to act on the wisdom. He felt that Confucius was listening and continued to ask for the right and proper guidance. He asked for forgiveness in advance should he fail.

It was a prayer he had been making daily for two years, ever since he launched compartmentalized sectors of his government on the mission that would elevate Japan's security resources to the same level as its economic and political resources. Under his direction, Japan would be a true superpower.

His society had suffered the humiliation of Western dominance long enough. With America so fully engaged in the Global War on Terror, he sensed a rare geopolitical opportunity. He saw America losing its hegemonic control as it got further sucked into the twirling vortex of Muslim extremism. Assuredly, there would be missteps, and Japan needed to be prepared to capitalize on those as they occurred. Similarly, China and North Korea loomed just over the horizon, and Mizuzawa had suffered the last embarrassment of a missile shot across his land from China or North Korea.

Mizuzawa believed that with political systems in turmoil, economic systems would soon follow. With a reduction in Japanese exports to those economic systems, the Japanese economy would wither. Such a path would add insult to injury. Western domination, followed by Japanese decline, would be unacceptable. Preemptive measures to ensure Japanese security, Mizuzawa assured himself, were in order.

Mizuzawa finished his prayer and stood, feeling relaxed and confident.

He sat upon a pillow, overlooking the pond. Doing so, he thought back to his childhood. He remembered being fifteen years old when he heard that the Japanese attack on Pearl Harbor had been an unqualified success. He had swelled with pride in his family and his nation. He had asked his father if he could serve in the armed forces like his two brothers. His father gave him permission, telling him he needed to fight for his country. He saw limited action on Okinawa and watched Americans kill his

CHAPTER 28

GEORGETOWN, WASHINGTON, DC

Dick Diamond stood at the window of Saul Fox's Georgetown townhouse reading his Blackberry. Looking up, he could see the Potomac, some stores along M Street, and a glimpse of the Kennedy Center. It was, after all, prime real estate. He had turned up Puccini again, Calaf's voice belting out, *"Ma il mio mistero è chiuso in me, il nome mio nessun saprà."* But my secret is hidden within me. None will know my name!

Diamond pocketed his digital assistant and ran a well-manicured hand along the revolver he had purchased, then walked to the bed and fitted the weapon between the mattress and box spring. He stepped back, assessed its positioning, and made an adjustment. Then he sat on the bed, leaned back a bit, and let his arm fall naturally along the mattress. He felt around and determined the pistol needed to be moved about six inches toward the headboard and a few inches toward the edge. His considerable weight had crushed the mattress into the pistol, making retrieval at the right moment awkward, if not impossible.

And that would not be good.

He removed the pistol and awkwardly stuffed it in his coat pocket, confident that he could place it properly when necessary and have it … available.

As soon as his hand left his jacket, Saul Fox came walking into the bedroom, wearing a white robe that had the letters SF stenciled on the left breast pocket in gold thread—real gold.

"Dick, we need to talk about this Philippine thing," Fox said.

"That's why I'm here, isn't it?"

"Yes, yes, I presume so," Fox agreed. He sat on a chaise and the robe fell away, exposing a short, bare leg.

Diamond sat in a cherry Thonet No. 14 chair made of six pieces of steamed and bent cane wood. It was nearly a hundred years old, and Diamond thought he was going to break the chair as his large derriere pressed into the antique.

"You know Takishi, right?" Fox asked.

Diamond hesitated, not wanting to answer right away. "Yes, of course. He's a big wheel in Japan, and he was a student at Harvard B School when I was teaching at the JFK School. Quite popular, bright mind, very … Japanese."

"Good. Good," Fox said. He pulled the robe over his leg and rubbed his face with an open palm as if to test his shave.

"How so?"

"I'm thinking about everything we're hearing. We've got one dead guy in the Philippines. Patterson, something like that. Matt Garrett was supposedly roaming around down there from the CIA. Stone had his press conference, and now we've got an infantry company going there."

"Still all very manageable within the big picture. I mean an A team and a rifle company, that's not much more than we let Stone send to Afghanistan."

Fox smiled, then his expression changed as he sat up. "I know. That's sort of my point. Our entire plan was to let Nine-eleven happen, however that was going to play out, then use it as a window of opportunity for our own purposes; to achieve lasting fame. Brilliant."

"Yes, but are we the only ones looking in the window?" Diamond asked, getting Fox's point.

"That's what I want you to talk to Takishi about."

CHAPTER 29

TOKYO, JAPAN

Japanese Prime Minister Kirusu Mizuzawa sat in his office in the *Kantei*, the Japanese equivalent of the White House. Upon becoming prime minister two years ago, he had decorated his workplace with various pictures and mementoes he had acquired throughout his distinguished military and political careers.

One of his first actions as prime minister was to place next to the map of Japan a large map of Southeast Asia. Sitting at his desk, he could look up and see the four major islands of Japan in large scale, as well as the Pacific Rim from the northeastern Chinese border to central Australia. Centrally located were the Philippine Islands. Just to the north of the Philippines was the island of Formosa, or Taiwan. He had circled Taiwan and the Philippines with red highlighter and put a question mark next to Indonesia.

He stood and walked around the front of his desk, leaning against it. He was a short man in his mid-seventies. His face was wrinkled like that of a Chinese Shar-Pei. His eyes peeked from between two coin slots in his wizened face. He kept his black hair cropped close to his head with a crew cut. A scar from an American bayonet during the Great Pacific War ran across the top of his right forearm. It had not healed properly and curved outward in grotesque fashion.

He took his suit jacket off and placed it over the back of his chair. He then slipped on his black samurai robe and walked through the open glass doors behind his desk. The night air was cool and heavy, settling upon Mizuzawa in wavy mists. Stepping with a bare foot past a decorative rock, he strode onto the bridge that spanned the dark koi pond. He watched the large orange and white fish smack at the water's surface and swim lazily in another direction. A small pagoda faced him on the other side of the pond.

His robe flowing with his gait, he strode slowly around the carefully trimmed hedges in the garden. He stopped and raised his arms, palms stretched outward, then slowly brought them down, beginning a jujitsu ritual of relaxation. He performed several maneuvers, eyes closed, as he felt the enemy surrounding him.

An unarmed method of defense, jujitsu was designed to throw the opponent off-balance through movement and deception. Karate differed in that it focused on the accurate application of well-timed blows to the opponent. Mizuzawa moved in rhythmic harmony, clearing his mind for the monumental decisions that lay ahead. His process of Henka had been gradual, but he felt that he had a consensus within the administration and that they were convinced of the course he had chosen.

In the courtyard stood a bronze statue of Confucius. He relied on Confucian ideology as his spiritual guide and, more than ever, needed reassurance that he was embarking on the correct path. He looked at the painting and bowed. Kneeling on a red satin pillow, he closed his eyes and prayed silently. He asked for the wisdom to do what was correct for Japan and the courage to act on the wisdom. He felt that Confucius was listening and continued to ask for the right and proper guidance. He asked for forgiveness in advance should he fail.

It was a prayer he had been making daily for two years, ever since he launched compartmentalized sectors of his government on the mission that would elevate Japan's security resources to the same level as its economic and political resources. Under his direction, Japan would be a true superpower.

His society had suffered the humiliation of Western dominance long enough. With America so fully engaged in the Global War on Terror, he sensed a rare geopolitical opportunity. He saw America losing its hegemonic control as it got further sucked into the twirling vortex of Muslim extremism. Assuredly, there would be missteps, and Japan needed to be prepared to capitalize on those as they occurred. Similarly, China and North Korea loomed just over the horizon, and Mizuzawa had suffered the last embarrassment of a missile shot across his land from China or North Korea.

Mizuzawa believed that with political systems in turmoil, economic systems would soon follow. With a reduction in Japanese exports to those economic systems, the Japanese economy would wither. Such a path would add insult to injury. Western domination, followed by Japanese decline, would be unacceptable. Preemptive measures to ensure Japanese security, Mizuzawa assured himself, were in order.

Mizuzawa finished his prayer and stood, feeling relaxed and confident.

He sat upon a pillow, overlooking the pond. Doing so, he thought back to his childhood. He remembered being fifteen years old when he heard that the Japanese attack on Pearl Harbor had been an unqualified success. He had swelled with pride in his family and his nation. He had asked his father if he could serve in the armed forces like his two brothers. His father gave him permission, telling him he needed to fight for his country. He saw limited action on Okinawa and watched Americans kill his two brothers in the battle.

He winced as he remembered being nineteen years old and hearing of the atomic bombs dropped at Hiroshima and Nagasaki. Why had the Americans dropped the bombs only on the Asian race? Could they not bear to destroy their own precious European culture with the same devastation that they wreaked on the diminutive yellow people?

He had read Truman's memoirs with disgust. Despite those lies, he was convinced the bomb was available for use on the Germans but saved for the Japanese. Why did the Americans not lock up the immigrant Germans when they joined the war in Europe? But they felt at liberty to shame and humiliate the Japanese immigrants who had, for whatever reason, searched for a new life in America. Worse, it took them fifty years to give those innocent Japanese bystanders the proper recompense for their losses. Most were dead, anyway. Why had America denied the Japanese immigration rights? Mizuzawa worked himself into a rage, clenching his fists. *Americans—self-righteous bastards!*

Mizuzawa believed that the Japanese people owed the Americans nothing. The United States had defeated his country in battle and occupied his people's land to shape Japan in the Western image. *No more,* Mizuzawa thought to himself, *no more.*

Yes, the Japanese Empire would once again rise from the sea, not like some hideous monster, spraying foam and seawater in all directions, but like the benevolent vessel that she was, sifting through the fog of the post-9-11 world order and aiding the sinking ships around her.

He was at peace, sitting cross-legged on the bridge, suspended above the water. With his eyes shut, another Sun Tzu maxim rolled through his mind.

Draw them in with the prospect of gain, take them by confusion.

CHAPTER 30

SUBIC BAY, LUZON ISLAND, PHILIPPINES

Juan Ayala stuffed his cell phone into his pocket. Talbosa, his mentor, had given him the word to execute his mission. Ayala had made two subsequent calls: one to his assault element at Manila International Airport and one to his support team leader at the naval base, where he was located as well. Ayala was about half a kilometer from the team that would create the diversion before he personally led the attack on the American position.

As he cleaned the Shansi pistol that he had carried with him through ten years of the revolution, he smiled thinly at the opportunity to kill more Americans. Only twenty-two, he remembered receiving the Chinese mock up of the broom-handled Mauser C96 semi-automatic pistol from an Abu Sayyaf veteran when he was a twelve-year-old boy living in the wastelands of Olongapo, a city of brothels just outside Subic Bay Naval Base.

He carried four ten-round stripper clips of .45-caliber ammunition for the thirty-centimeter-long pistol with attachable buttstock, the broom handle, which allowed Ayala to shoulder-fire the weapon or use it in pistol-grip mode. It had served him well on the stupid American sitting alone in his truck on the naval base. That had almost been too easy. He had asked the man for a cigarette.

"Hey, Joe, any smoke?" he had said to the man sitting in the white SUV. The man, with his elbow propped on the frame of the open window, had not been alarmed at the sight of the short brown man with a deep scar running from his right ear to his chin. The fool had shut off the ignition and reached into his pockets, acting without hesitation.

Images of ten-year-old Filipino girls who had turned to whoring for the American sailors had sprung through Ayala's mind. From less than a meter away, without hesitation or remorse, he had leveled the pistol and pulled the trigger. One shot was all he had required. The .45 caliber bullet had struck the *Yanqui* in the forehead, just above the nose, causing bright red blood to spray outward and onto the windshield of the Blazer.

Surprising to Ayala, the man's forehead had remained largely intact. The bigger hole had been to the back of his head, where the exit wound had removed a quarter of his cranium. Ayala had then taken his roll of M186 demolition charge and taped pieces in strategic locations on the vehicle. The M186 consisted of pentaerythrite tetranitrate (PETN), a highly sensitive and powerful explosive that he had acquired from the last ammunition raid they had conducted at the naval base. He had rigged the blasting caps so that they would ignite when the driver-side door was opened and a metal clothes pin snapped shut, completing an electrical circuit to the vehicle battery. Proud of his work, he had then faded into the darkness moments before two airplanes landed not a half kilometer away from his latest victory for the cause.

Watching as soldiers disembarked from the aircraft and moved aggressively to the outer reaches of the runway, he had padded into the night, having accomplished his mission.

Killing Americans or high-ranking Filipino government officials had become his specialty in the Abu Sayyaf organization. He had organized his own sparrow squad, and like policemen writing tickets, they were expected to reach a weekly quota of either assassinations or intelligence gathering. On that night, he had done both by himself. For that, he was awarded a command in the final coup.

Now, two days later, at 0400 hours, he slid the pistol into the attachable wooden shoulder stock, a unique feature of this weapon, wrapped it in plastic with the .45 caliber ammo, and jammed the deadly ensemble into his backpack. He leaned over, grabbed his Chinese Type 68 assault rifle, and looked at the seventy-five men he commanded, all huddled tightly in the dark, steamy jungle just northwest of Subic Bay Naval Base. They carried a mixture of Type 68s, a Chinese version of the Russian AK-47, M16s, and AK-47s. Through years of pilferage from U.S. ammunition storage locations, and their own resupply efforts, they had accumulated a healthy stockpile of contraband. They had 5.56mm and 7.62mm ammunition, explosives, mortar rounds, and light antitank weapons. Ayala's men had three 81mm mortars they had stolen from the Army of the Philippines over two years ago.

Working with Talbosa's guidance, Ayala knew the airport raid he would direct at 0500 hours would be coordinated with similar attacks across the islands. An air traffic controller friend had given him a tip that an American government airplane was scheduled to arrive that morning. Destroying it and killing the passengers would reap huge financial gains for the movement.

The Abu Sayyaf network had issued broad guidance and, through the Internet, the small cells scattered across the Philippine Islands had developed the plan to overthrow the central government. Ayala's mission involved capturing the airport and the ammunition that had been unloaded from the American barge yesterday.

His plan was to have the mortar teams lob rounds
away from the ammunition dump, drawing the
American unit away from the real target. Then he
would sweep from the west into the rear of the
American position, shooting and killing them all.

CHAPTER 31

Zachary Garrett walked the company's defensive positions wearing his night-vision goggles. His men were alert and wide-eyed, having learned of the American ruthlessly shot through the forehead two days ago.

The ammunition was stacked on a pier to the south of the white barracks. The navy ship had been delayed a few days, a major at the embassy told him, even though the ultimate destination of the ammunition was Afghanistan, where combat was raging.

Doesn't make sense, Zachary thought to himself.

He had stuck with his original plan to use two platoons for perimeter defense and let one platoon "relax" in the barracks every twelve hours. The constant movement was designed to confuse any enemy that might want to target them or the ammunition and had worked so far. He looked at his watch, popped a cracker from an MRE into his mouth, and continued to survey both his position and the defensive array of his company. It was 0415 hours. The sun would soon rise, and he would want to be on full alert when it did so because "that's when the bad guys always attack," as the saying went. He furrowed his brow.

Taylor's platoon was defending the eastern approach to the base. They had developed a good defense in depth that protected the main mounted avenue of approach into their position. The Olongapo gate had a four-lane road going through it that the enemy could use to make a mounted assault. Taylor had positioned his three squads of eleven men throughout the depth of the road as it led to the dock area, and they had constructed an elaborate barrier plan to prevent car bombs and such from splitting their defenses. He was nearly five hundred meters from the command post. Stan Barker's Third Platoon, "Blue six," was to the north, covering the route that they had taken from the airfield that first night. His right flank was tied in with Taylor's left flank, and they had mutually supporting lines of fire. His sector sketch back in the command post (CP) reflected the array. Barker's men would intercept anyone coming out of the valley along the runway.

He was accepting risk in the west along the waterfront. Zachary felt that Barker's left flank could accurately observe any movement into that area and reposition to defend against any attack from the docks. Success would depend upon Barker's initiative, something that concerned Zachary.

Zachary had one squad of the reserve platoon guarding the stockpile of ammunition. That foggy morning, Kurtz's men were in the barracks, most sleeping soundly. Their primary mission was to act as the company reserve, a sort of quick-reaction force. Zachary had them sleep with their boots and uniforms on, so that the only thing they would have to do was grab their weapons, which were in their cots with them, and move to the location he ordered them to. The CP was also in that area, so they could pass the word quickly.

He walked, kicking at the dirt and dried lava that would soon be hot dust in the raging Philippine sun. He had worked on several flex plans in his mind. With no vehicles to move his troops, they would have to run if they were to get into alternate positions to handle other avenues of approach.

Sampaloc Point, a high volcanic rise, guarded the

mouth of the bay and dominated the Western terrain just outside the base. Beneath the jagged, cross-compartmentalized feature was a barren flatland that gave way to the hardstand upon which they currently operated.

Zachary had worked on several contingency plans, none of which seemed sufficient. He was yearning for information. He turned and watched the fog tumble off the soundless bay, lifting and separating in the light breeze.

His mind shifted back to the problem at hand. Regardless of the embassy's insistence that "there is no threat," he did not want some assassin's bullet to find any of his soldiers. If he had to attack the place, Zachary thought, he would try to fix the two forward platoons with a base of fire, then descend from the mountains, through the valley by the airstrip, and sweep the built-up area, using the Quonset huts for protection.

He was primarily concerned with his own ammunition situation. Each man had just one thirty round magazine of 5.56mm ammunition. Each squad's automatic weapon had one box of three hundred rounds, and each M203 grenade launcher had only two high-explosive rounds and five white-phosphorous smoke rounds.

Arriving back at the CP Quonset hut, he stood outside and looked over at the men faithfully protecting the ammunition, not walking a standard to-and-from guard rotation, but from the prone or one knee, observing with night-vision goggles. They were nearly two hundred meters away, but he could see their images burned black in his own goggles.

Zachary sat on his rucksack and removed his goggles. The perimeter was good, but something still gnawed at the back of his mind.

What am I missing? he wondered.

CHAPTER 32

The three explosions seemed farther off than they really were. The sound came from the east, and Private First Class Teller, a backup radio operator from Kurtz' platoon, was immediately taking a phone report from Lieutenant Taylor that their positions were taking mortar fire.

"Sir! Captain Garrett! Wake up!" Teller screamed. The rest of the Quonset hut was empty. Lieutenant Kurtz had quietly taken his men to the quick-reaction force position to the western edge of the hut, sort of an "on-deck circle" for the reserve force. There, they waited on one knee to begin a stand-to patrol assigned to them by Captain Garrett. Their route was to take them to the left flank of Barker's platoon.

The mortars came raining onto Taylor's position near the front gate about a kilometer away as Kurtz and his men were preparing to begin the patrol.

"What the hell was that?" Zachary said, already waking as Teller shook his shoulder. In no time, Slick was standing near the communications center ready to take over the radio duties.

"Mortars, sir! First Platoon's taking mortar fire!" Zachary was on his feet, lacing his arms through his outer tactical vest with small-arms protective inserts, or body armor, and grabbing the field phone, cranking its handle. A soldier from First Platoon answered, then put Taylor on the line.

"Sitrep?" Zachary said.

"Sir, we've got mortar rounds coming down all around us!"

"Anybody hurt?"

"Negative."

"See any enemy coming at you?" Zachary hated to use the word "enemy" because he could not define it. What was he expecting Taylor to see? They had received no intelligence from the embassy.

"Nothing, sir. Just sheaths of three mortars coming—"

Zachary heard a solitary loud bang near the hut. The phone line was dead. Either Taylor had been hit or a mortar round had impacted directly on the underground cable, severing it. Hoping for the latter, he reached for the FM radio handset. Looking at Slick, he said, "Call our friend at the embassy and tell him we're receiving mortar fire."

Hundreds of thoughts were tumbling through his mind. He needed to sort them and remain calm. It could just be a scare tactic. After all, Taylor said the rounds were not hurting his position.

Another stray landed just to the north of the CP. A spray of dirt, gravel, and shrapnel pinged against the thin steel wall of the hut.

"Net call, over," he said into the black microphone. His three lieutenants responded immediately by acknowledging they were listening.

"This is Bravo six. Red element is receiving mortar fire. I want every man in a foxhole and behind a weapon. Assume a ground assault will follow. Take full defensive measures to protect your men. I'm moving to Red six's position now, over," Zachary said. Taylor's platoon was First Platoon, and their call sign was "red." Kurtz was second; "white." Barker was third; "blue."

Zach's voice had an edge to it, yet he managed to sound confident and collected. Jogging out of the Quonset hut, he looked for Slick, his primary radio operator, saw him working the SCAMP, and instead told Teller to strap the radio onto his back and follow him. Teller gladly accepted the mission, grabbing the radio and his M4. Zachary first ran over to Kurtz, who was only thirty meters away, having had his men spread out and move into the prone position. The lieutenant had acted exactly as he had trained him.

"Mike, I want you to take your men and move about two hundred meters to the west. Have them put their goggles on and watch that area from Barker's left flank to the tit," he said, pointing at the volcanic shape to the rear of their position.

"You can array your men any way you want. I would prefer some depth, but you're still my reaction force, and you'll need to have a tight string on your guys in case I need you."

"Yes, sir," Kurtz said, a big wad of chewing tobacco stuffed in the side of his mouth looking like a large tumor beneath his cheek. He spit half saliva and half tobacco onto the ground. Not having had a chance to shave that morning, his face was ragged with stubble growth. He had rolled his combat uniform sleeves a quarter of the way up each arm, so his huge, bulking forearms strained the material.

He looked at the captain with steely gray eyes and said, "No sweat." He rounded his men up and made a plan as the captain ran to Taylor's position, holding the radio handset in his hand, with Teller running behind him tethered like a leashed dog.

Kurtz used a portion of a weapons-cleaning rod to sketch a plan in the dirt quickly. He drew a picture with the water in the south, the "tit" in the west, the airfield and mountains beyond in the north, and the barracks behind them.

"Look here, men," he said over the booming sound of mortars exploding to the east. "I want first squad to hold down the right flank by linking up with First Platoon's left flank and angling back toward the barracks, kind of from northwest to southeast. Make sure you tie in with First Platoon, though. I don't want a gap in the line. Second squad, you move to the edge of the water about two hundred meters up and angle back to the barracks as well." He drew two lines, one for each squad, forming a neat V, with the base meeting near the barracks area. Meanwhile, the mortars continued to pound the First Platoon's area.

"This will be our engagement area," he explained, circling the area between the V. To avoid fratricide, I want everyone to pop an IR chemlight right now and stick it under your camouflage band on the back of your helmet." The soldiers began to shuffle and dig the small plastic devices out of their rucks.

"There's not much cover out there. Find what you can and make the best use of it. I want you guys to call me when you're in position and set up. Also, I want all of you to lock a full magazine in your weapons right now." They did so, the process creating several loud metallic noises as the soldiers slapped the magazines to ensure they were properly seated.

"Third squad, I want you to jump down on the pier and guard against any kind of water assault. Since it's least likely, you'll probably be reacting to something else, so keep your guys in tight. But first, I want you to cover the other squads as they move," he said, echoing the commander's words. "I'm gonna give y'all five minutes to get in position, then come check your lines. Now get moving and kick ass," he said. The squad leaders huddled briefly with their squads, laid out a movement technique, and drifted into the darkness.

"Sir," Slick yelled to Lieutenant Kurtz from the CP, sticking his head out of the door frame, "CO wants me to cut these lights, so find your stuff. It's gonna get real dark."

"Got ya," Kurtz said, grabbing his ruck off the ground and hooking it onto his back. With his rifle in one hand and the ruck hanging loosely over his shoulder, Kurtz moved with his radio operator and platoon sergeant to a position behind some old tires that had been left by the Navy. It was a good position for Kurtz to get prepared to control the battle.

He had a distinct sense, though, that he was short on time.

CHAPTER 33

Ayala's men moved swiftly through the night. They scampered single file along one of the ravines cut into the side of the old volcano. The men wore a variety of uniforms, mostly whatever they had worn to their lousy jobs the day before. Most of them had cinched red bandannas around their foreheads and carried old Chinese assault rifles or Japanese-manufactured M16s from the Mindanao plant. They were grateful to the Japanese for giving them the opportunity to achieve victory.

On the minds of every soldier were the oppressive Americans and how their own actions that night would allow them to form an Islamic nation and also grant them freedom from imperialism, feudalism, and capitalism. Although they weren't quite sure what that meant, it sure made a good rallying cry.

They ran in synch, as if someone were calling cadence. At the front was Ayala directing his men with hand and arm signals. The mortars continued a slow but steady harassment of the eastern flank. He knew they would soon exhaust their entire allotment for the operation. Resources were scarce, and the Japanese had told them they did not have the capability to develop mortar rounds for them, having been out of the arms-production business for over fifty years.

Pouring from the ravine, they could see the lights around the Americans' command area. About a hundred meters toward the water, he could see the large ammunition pile waiting for him and his soldiers. *Once again, the Americans have underestimated us*, he said to himself.

Suddenly, the lights went out, causing Ayala a momentary blackout. He had been focusing on the yellow-and-white haze, and his pupils were too constricted to gather enough of the surrounding starlight to let him see. Seconds later, the world came into focus again, like turning on an old television set.

After a brief pause, he motioned his men forward through the high scrub. Reaching the fence that surrounded the base, they quickly cut through it in five locations, using large bolt cutters. The men scurried beneath the fence, some ripping their clothes. One had a piece of the fence snap back and tear into his eye. He let out a short scream, but stopped when he realized the pain was insignificant compared to the suffering the imperialists had wrought on his country for decades. One band of men broke off to the south to move along the pier and approach the ammunition from that direction. Another band moved toward where the lights had shone only minutes ago.

Ayala lowered his head and sprinted toward the American positions.

CHAPTER 34

Captain Garrett reached Taylor's platoon about the time the mortar firing slowed, finally grinding to a halt.

"Sitrep?" Zachary asked, lying behind Taylor's fighting position, looking down into the bunker beneath the plywood and sandbags that were the overhead cover. He could hear one soldier screaming loudly and saw through his night-vision goggles the blackened figures of two soldiers running to the wounded soldier's fighting position.

"That's Sergeant Cartwright, sir. He received a direct hit on his bunker. I've checked him. Pretty bad leg wound. The medic's with him right now. Do we have any kind of medevac support or anything?" Taylor said in a hurried and nervous voice.

"I've got Slick calling the embassy right now. We'll get a medevac here ASAP. You stay here and command your platoon while I go check on Cartwright."

"Yes, sir," Taylor said, eyes darting back and forth in the darkness. The thick haze of gunpowder was a phantom wafting through the air, devilishly grinning at the young lieutenant. *So you thought you wanted to be a soldier*, he could hear it saying. *Welcome to the real world.*

Zachary told Teller to call back to Slick and have him contact the embassy and order a dust-off immediately. One of the few morsels Fraley had thrown Zachary's way was medical support.

He then high-crawled to Sergeant Cartwright's

position. The screaming served as an audible beacon in the darkness. The fighting position had been reduced to rubble, splintered plywood, and dirt. The medic had pulled the squad leader from his foxhole and placed a dressing over his upper thigh area.

"You gonna be all right, man," he heard the medic saying, confidently. "Nothin' but a little cut. Old doc here fix you right up." The screaming continued into an otherwise momentarily, yet dangerously, silent night as the mortars failed to repeat their previously voluminous fire.

"Hey, Wheels," the captain said, referring to one of his best squad leaders. Cartwright was exceptionally fast, having made it to the last cut for the Washington Redskins and losing out to another wide receiver. Captain Garrett laid a hand on his soldier's knee and could feel it trembling. Zachary looked at the medic, whose face he could see in the moonlight. The medic looked at the captain with reassuring eyes, indicating that he really would be fine with some proper medical attention, that his words to Cartwright were not just shock prevention.

"That you, sir?" Wheels said, comforted by the sound of his commander's voice. His voice was raspy, punctuated by rapid breathing. Sometimes all a soldier needed to hear was the calm and reassuring voice of his commander. Surely the commander knew things that he did not, and if the captain was in control, then the situation must be under control.

"Yeah, Wheels, it's me. Doc says you'll be fine," he said, glad that Cartwright had recognized him. It was a good sign that he was not going into shock. Still, it was unnerving for Zachary to see one of his own soldiers writhing on the hard-packed dirt.

"You believe him, sir?" Cartwright asked, half-joking, looking at the commander with white eyes illuminated by the contrast to his black skin.

"Yeah, Doc gave me a behind-the-scenes thumbs-up. Only a scratch," he said, personally inspecting the bandage and acknowledging the fact that everyone knew the game. The medics were trained to reassure the wounded no matter what their condition. "I'm gonna check on the rest of the company. We've called the embassy for a medevac, and they should be here shortly. Doc, stay with him until the helicopter gets here." The medic nodded.

"Sir," Cartwright said, before Zachary could stand up, "thanks for being here." Zachary slapped Cartwright on the shoulder, noticing the medic starting to elevate the leg to slow the blood flow, and ran back to Taylor's foxhole. When he updated Taylor on Cartwright's condition, the lieutenant stared blankly and nodded with a glazed look in his eyes, as if some part of his brain had been fried momentarily.

Zachary wanted to talk to him, but did not have time as he heard the first gunshots ring out in the western part of his sector.

I know those sounds too well. He grabbed Teller by the shirt collar the way a football coach snags a player's face mask before sending him into the game, and they ran toward the fight.

CHAPTER 35

Meanwhile, through his night-vision goggles, Kurtz could see some black figures scurrying across the open ground. He made a quick radio check with Barker to see if he had any men moving in that direction. He did not. He had tried to call the commander, but got an urgent radio message from Staff Sergeant Nichols, his second squad leader, that they had nearly thirty enemy personnel moving in their direction. Before he could respond, the advancing Filipinos noticed second squad moving into position and began firing from the hip as they continued to run.

Nichols's men eluded the first salvo of bullets, kicking up dirt around them and zinging overhead. With the goggles, the Americans had the advantage, and the Filipino fire remained glued to the south, where they had seconds earlier spied the soldiers running for cover.

"If you can acquire the enemy, open fire," Kurtz said, making a decision on the spot, not having time to consult the commander.

The exhilaration surprised him. He was in complete control and could sense the enemy movement like a blind man can feel his way around a familiar room. So far, he had planned accurately. They seemed to be coming directly into his engagement area, where first and second squads could simultaneously destroy them. He remembered his reserve, guarding the ammunition and the approach along the pier, considering whether he had any mission for them. Deciding against moving them, he heard the first burst from a squad automatic weapon sing through the night air and echo down the valley with resoluteness. Bright muzzle flashes appeared from both first and second squads, orange tracers dancing low through the darkness, sometimes ricocheting and careening magnificently upward to the heavens. The tracers converged and crossed paths, creating a surreal X like a neon sign flashing in the night.

He watched through his goggles and listened to the radio for sitreps. There was no need to bother his squad leaders, who were busy conducting the fight. He could see two of his squads lying in the prone behind whatever cover they could find in the hardstand, some using old railroad ties, others lying behind discarded appliances such as refrigerators and washing machines.

The fight raged, M4s popping softly but consistently producing a cadenced rate of fire, indicative of good fire discipline, countered by the intermittent distinctive cracking of AK-47s. Kurtz was astonished at his own clarity of mind. He was in a chess match that he knew he was going to win. It was only a matter of time. The son of a bitch had already made one move to which he had accurately responded. *What's next asshole?* Kurtz said beneath his breath, trying to outthink his adversary. The ammo. It had to be the ammo.

"Red six, this is red three, over," Staff Sergeant Quinones said urgently into the radio.

"Go," Kurtz responded to his third squad leader.

"We've picked up about thirty enemy moving directly toward us along the pier."

"Roger, can you defend from where you are?"

"We're really too close together. This pier's only about fifty meters wide, then it drops into the water."

"Roger. Leave one fire team on the pier behind some cover. Remember that they can't see you. Move the other team near the back to my location by the tire pile. You stay with the pier team, and I'll take charge of your other team," Kurtz commanded with crispness.

"Roger. Happening now, out," Quinones said.

"Red six, this is red two, over."

"Send it," Kurtz said, his eyes fixed on the dark horizon to the west.

"Fifteen enemy soldiers wounded or killed, two Enemy Prisoners of War, continuing to observe, over."

"Roger, red one, status?" Kurtz said to his first squad leader.

"Seventeen enemy dead, five EPWs, continuing to observe, over."

"Roger, break," he said, releasing the handset momentarily, and he was back to Quinones, who had called in the advancing enemy element. "Red three, sitrep?"

"Roger. Enemy still advancing. About two hundred meters out," Quinones whispered.

"Sitrep, Mike," Captain Garrett said, sliding into position behind the tire pile. Teller was still tethered to him, and Zach was glad that the young man was in good physical condition. Able to listen to all of the action on the radio, Zachary had personally inspected the positions of all three platoons and decided to command from Kurtz's position, where the largest threat seemed to be.

"Sir, we've got some enemy bearing down on Quinones's men on the pier. I've got him with one fire team ready to open up any second. I'm gonna send the other five-man team into their flank about two hundred meters up to keep them from getting in behind second squad."

"Need First or Third Platoons to do anything?"

Zachary asked, unable to envision a mission for either of them worth risking the integrity of the company position.

"Not right now, sir. We've got it," Kurtz said confidently, spitting some chaw over his knee. He looked through his goggles in the direction of the pier about three hundred meters away. It had all come together for him. It was easier than Ranger school or any field-training exercise. Sure, the training had prepared him, but this was something inside of him, something tangible that he could connect with. He knew exactly what to do, like playing a game and being the only one who knew the rules.

"Contact!" Quinones's voice blurted into the radio, as Taylor and Kurtz heard two audible clicking noises and shortly thereafter two successive explosions. Quinones had let them get within a hundred meters, then opened fire with two high-explosive grenades from the M203 grenade launchers, followed by the squad automatic weapon, which raked the expanse of the pier.

CHAPTER 36

Ayala had never seen anything like it. A withering cross fire had decimated his force heading directly toward the white buildings. Luckily, at the last moment he had joined the smaller group moving along the pier.

It seemed clear sailing, as they less than quietly padded along wooden ties next to the choppy bay. His plan had worked, though, as the Americans were so fixated on his larger force that they had neglected the obscure pier. Looking to his south, he saw Subic Bay, a mixing bowl of windswept water perhaps reflective of the murderous activities ashore. To his left was a five-and-a-half-meter iron retaining wall supported by I-beams that abutted the pier. The top of the wall was even with the ground. He was looking at the outline of the ammunition stockpile, above his eye level about two hundred meters away when an explosion propelled him into the water, momentarily knocking him unconscious.

The Abu Sayyaf charge continued along the pier into a hail of bullets that cut them down three and four at a time. Tracers screamed at them like lighted arrows, too often finding their targets. The muzzle flashes came from behind the I-beams along the retaining wall, the bullets ripping open the attackers' flesh. There was no place for them to hide, as they were advancing along a bowling alley into a curtain of steel. Their determination was solid, though, like that of a weary marathoner nearing the finish line but about to collapse. The Americans had whittled the advance down to four wounded insurgents, refusing to surrender, yet unable to see the six-member team that had selectively and completely destroyed their flanking effort. The moaning and dead rebel bodies lay strewn over a one-hundred-meter swath along the pier.

Suddenly the night carried nothing but the reverberating echo of gunshots and the howling of dying men.

Ayala floated beneath the surface of the water, then bobbed back up, coughing and wheezing for air. His rifle had dropped like a rock into the deep expanse of the bay. It was all he could do to stay afloat, as he was a non-swimmer, fighting against the saturated weight of his clothes and backpack. Flailing his arms, reaching for anything that would support his weight, he found purchase beneath the pier on a long pipe that carried water to several points along the dock. Grasping the five-centimeter-wide tubing, he rested. After catching his breath, he listened to the diminishing battle above. From his position, it had a distant quality, the sound dampened by the wood and steel pier above him. He could see through the slats in the wood, catching a glimpse of an American tracer etching an orange trail in strobelike fashion as it flew above the pier. He lifted one hand to the strap of his backpack, which met his touch with the reassuring knowledge of his Shansi tucked securely inside. Then he pressed on, shuffling hand over hand along the water pipe, his buoyancy in the water making the process remark-ably easy.

The shooting ceased, distant echoes galloping through the low valleys to the west and north. His plan had not failed, however, as he was still alive and could take the Americans himself. He had thirty-two rounds of ammunition. He vowed to kill that many with his pistol. The rest would surrender, he was sure. He struggled beneath the pier, observed by huge rats pecking and scratching along the concrete to his left. He had seen them before. For a child growing up in the slums of Olongapo, rats were like pets.

The waterline was about a meter below the level of the pier, yet the depth was seven meters directly beneath him. Hand over hand he shuffled along, making progress until he could hear the voices of Americans talking quietly. Perspiration beginning to bead on his forehead, he slowed so that his wake was an unnoticeable ripple, passing the voices above him. Making his way to the end of the pier, he located a steel cable hanging from the concrete wall that marked the end of the dock. Grabbing it, he pulled himself out of the water and was dismayed at his own weight and that of his drenched clothing once the water was no longer supporting him. He momentarily lost his grip, then tightened his fist around the cable, grabbing into some frayed wires that dug deeply into the bone of his right hand. He wanted to scream, but refused. His pain would go away; the suffering of his people at the hands of the Americans would not. He bit his lower lip with force, causing streams of warm, red blood to trickle down his chin and drop into the water like drips from a leaking faucet.

Pushing on, he laid an arm on the pier, his hand pulsing with pain. Putting pressure against his elbow, he flung his right leg on the pier and rolled onto the level surface. Quickly, he looked and saw a ladder that led to ground level and his eventual victory over the Americans.

CHAPTER 37

The entire engagement had taken only twenty minutes since the first mortars landed. At 0520 hours, it would be another twenty minutes until the sun provided enough daylight for them to assess accurately what they had accomplished. What would have been a beautiful sunrise amidst the pleasant music of the adjacent jungle was transformed into a barbaric scene of death, accompanied by the howls of wounded men.

"Red three, status?"

"This is red three. We're counting bodies right now. We do need a medic. Say again, we do need a medic!"

"Roger, he's on the way with a two-man security team," Kurtz said, motioning to his platoon medic and two members of the fire team that Quinones had sent to Kurtz's location.

"We've got all our personnel, but one has been hit in the neck. Say again, one hit in the neck! Currently holding position with four EPWs. We are low on ammo, but are redistributing right now."

"Roger. Good job. I'm sending your other three men to pick up those EPWs now. Continue to consolidate and redistribute," Kurtz said. Captain Garrett and Mike Kurtz sat, mentally exhausted, leaning against the pile of tires. Their exhaustion was paradoxical. As the battle progressed, each leader realized that control of the fight tended to decentralize to the lower level. Zachary had initially felt foolish, running back and forth between positions, but he reminded himself that he had to be at the critical point of the battle.

He had managed to change positions as needed. Plus, it was his plan that had earned what seemed like a victory for his company. Zachary knew in his heart that it was the hard training that had allowed them to survive this first battle. Both he and Kurtz had watched, as tracers bounced wildly over the bay like some macabre fireworks display. He watched Kurtz, wide-eyed and alert, like a wildcat, waiting for the next intruder into his den.

"We will hold in position for now," Garrett said.

Captain Garrett conducted a communications check with all of his platoons. The only real casualty was Sergeant Cartwright with the gash in his leg. The soldier in Quinones's squad had merely burned his face firing left-handed from behind an I-beam on the pier. The M4 was designed for right-handed shooters with the casing ejector port on the right side of the weapon. A white-hot metal casing had flown from the port, smacking the soldier in the face and searing his neck as it came to rest beneath the collar of his body armor. In the excitement of the moment, he had thought he was hit. Zachary was thankful and had personally inspected that soldier as well.

He had told his platoons to conduct ammunition redistribution and accountability of personnel. No one was missing, but Kurtz's platoon was critically short on ammunition. Zachary had Taylor send a squad with some of his platoon's ammunition to the tire stack, where he gave it to Sergeant First Class McDonell, Kurtz's platoon sergeant. McDonell then rapidly redistributed the ammunition. All of the platoons held their positions and watched into the surreal green world of the night-vision goggles.

The embassy had radioed with some good news

and some bad news. The good news was that the medical evacuation helicopter was on its way to pick up Sergeant Cartwright. The bad news was that the attack on Subic was just a small part of an island-wide Abu Sayyaf attempt to seize power. They had a doctor in the embassy who could examine Cartwright, but they believed that they were in imminent danger of being attacked. Zach told Fraley simply to get the helicopter to him ASAP, that he had a man dying. He knew he had leverage over the colonel and used the man's guilt to force a decision that a day ago he would not have made.

He spoke briefly with Slick and told him to continue to monitor the SCAMP radio. Calling on Barker's platoon, he asked them to establish a landing zone using red VS-17 panels to signify that the landing was an emergency. The helicopter could not get between the maze of dormant electrical wires that hung above Taylor's platoon. Cartwright's squad members constructed a field-expedient litter using a poncho and two-by-fours to carry him to a secure position behind Barker's lines. Near Cartwright's position, Barker's men were establishing the landing zone. Zachary had asked all of the platoon leaders to leave their platoon sergeants in charge and meet him at the tire pile immediately for a quick intelligence update and review of the action.

The sun had risen far enough above the horizon across the island of Luzon to scatter the darkness, casting a gray shade. When Kurtz took off his goggles, he could see dark humps lying on the hardstand about two hundred meters from the tire pile, where first and second squads had executed a perfect L-shaped ambush. Some of the bodies were moving, some were crying out in anguish, yelping as much in their mortal pain as they were bemoaning their complete defeat. The thick smell of spent powder hung in the air like a fog, waiting for the sun to burn it, and the memories of a horrible night, away.

Zachary walked toward the ammunition pile, faithfully guarded by Quinones's squad, then looked over the bulkhead down onto the pier, where he saw Quinones and his men still oriented to the west, ever vigilant. The darkened lumps of bodies were scattered along the pier, across its width.

Zachary returned to the tire pile, the de facto command post, with ever-growing numbers of soldiers gathering there. Some of the headquarters troops, who had remained in the barracks to monitor radios and react to emergencies, came out, looking in amazement at their company's baptism of fire. The platoon leaders had arrived, kneeling next to each other, comparing notes. As Zachary approached, he made it a point to look at Taylor's eyes to see what was there. They all stood as the commander and the tethered Teller approached. Taylor returned Zach's gaze with the reassurance that he had the mettle for this business and the understanding that he had matured immensely in the last hour.

Taylor was the tallest of the lieutenants, but Kurtz's sheer breadth made him seem larger. Barker was a rather short and slight officer, but large in heart. *He performed well,* Zachary thought. *He did not overreact and secured the flank.* Barker's red hair and boyish looks stood in stark contrast to Kurtz's partially unshaven face and Taylor's ruggedness. The three lieutenants stood next to each other, waiting for the commander.

"Take a knee guys," Zachary said. The lieutenants obeyed, forming a semicircle around the captain, who was still standing. First Sergeant Washington scattered the onlookers, telling them to assist their platoon sergeants in detainee control and collection of enemy dead. Zachary began to talk, saying he wanted to gather them and very quickly determine what adjustments they needed to make in case of another attack. The first thing he could think of was that they needed to break into the ammunition dump because he was certain they were nearly out of everything.

Teller, Slick's backup on the radio, looked up at the UH-60 helicopter, its rotor blades beating against the sky like drumsticks. The noise caused everyone except Kurtz to look skyward at the Black Hawk helicopter with the big red cross painted on its side. It was the medevac for Cartwright. Kurtz, however, was consumed in his own thoughts, staring blankly at the ammunition stockpile near the water.

Always shoot the two men nearest the radio, Ayala said to himself. His hand was bleeding profusely despite the white dirt caking inside his palm. His black hair hung in strands over his forehead. He had taken his bandanna and wrapped it around his wounded hand so that he could begin to eliminate the Americans, one by one.

Ayala low-crawled along the barracks building adjacent to the command post and edged his scarred face around the corner. It was just light enough for him to see the ammunition pile about fifty meters to his left and a grouping of Americans kneeling around some old tires. He heard the helicopter fly overhead and used the cover of its roar as an opportunity to extract the Shansi from his backpack. He attached the shoulder stock and fed one ten-round clip into the box magazine. He saw them looking up at the black helicopter and decided the movement could wait no longer. He painfully clutched his pistol, seated it in his shoulder, and began to rise. Moving first to a crouch, then to a low duckwalk, he began walking faster and faster in their direction, completely undetected.

His men had performed beautifully, Kurtz was thinking to himself, fixated in a blank stare in the direction of the ammunition pile. The noise from the helicopter would soon subside and they would get on with business. He was just glad that none of his men had to take that ride. In his periphery, he noticed one of the troops seemed to be walking toward them as the curtain of night gave way to a blue-gray shade. It was still not completely light, and—*the platoons are continuing the mission—and why does he not have a helmet—and why is he starting to run at us with a rifle in his hand?!* The thoughts tumbled through his mind with increasing momentum, each successive notion unable to completely express itself before the next came barging forward. His first instinct was to grab the commander.

Get the radio first. He was only thirty meters away. Ayala stopped, as he saw one of the men begin to rise. His world moved in slow motion. He aimed the front inverted V and V-notched tangent rear sites at the American with the radio. He squeezed the trigger and actually saw the large .45 caliber bullet fly from the barrel, striking him in the back of the neck, causing his head to jerk violently backward and his arms to outstretch as if to break his fall. The second round bored through the radio, scattering shrapnel in all directions.

Kurtz grabbed his captain as he heard the first shot thud into Teller's neck, causing streams of bright red blood to spray onto Lieutenant Barker, who by then was moving as well. With his uniform sleeve shredded and his forearm bleeding, Kurtz thought the second bullet had hit him. Regardless, he pulled Captain Garrett to the ground, trying to shield him with his body, but to no avail. The third shot ripped through the captain's scalp, tearing his Kevlar helmet from his head. Kurtz dropped the captain, rolled away from the tires with his M4, and leveled the weapon at the insurgent.

The third shot must hit the man standing next to the radio. One down, thirty-one to go, Ayala thought, walking, then stopping to fire, then walking again. Success once again, as the third bullet tore the skull off its victim. Then he saw the American rolling to his left with a weapon. *Fourth bullet is for him*, Ayala said to himself. Always counting ammunition, the cause needed all it could get. He aimed and felt his own blood pump from his chest as his shot flew silently, but wildly into the air. "Yes," he whispered, "they must take many shots to kill me." He felt the other shots impacting on his body like small-fisted punches in a street fight. He watched his world collect before him and gather into a twisting cloud. Faintly, he could hear his deflating lungs wetly sucking for wind.

"Die, sumbitch," Kurtz yelled with the most emotion he had shown since the deployment. He released on the rebel a violent and pent-up force that nothing could stop. Pumping six shots into the persistent little man with the odd-looking pistol-rifle, Kurtz charged him. The man had fallen to his knees with his pistol cocked limply in a raised hand, trying to hang on, trying to secure one more victory. Kurtz took his M4 and jarred the man's yellow teeth loose with a slashing rip of the butt stock against his face. Then he felt hands on him, all over him, pulling him away.

Meanwhile, Taylor moved fast. He called for the

medics, who came running. He had Barker call his platoon sergeant and tell him to hold the medevac. Then he checked Teller, who was obviously dead, his head precariously connected to the rest of his body by half of a neck. As he lay on the dirt with his vacant eyes open, a picture of his pregnant wife and two-year-old child peered up at Taylor from beneath his camouflage band. Tears welled in Taylor's eyes, but there was no time for grieving.

Taylor held Captain Garrett, propping his head in his lap. He was still alive. The bullet had not entered the brain, but he was bleeding heavily.

Doc Gore, an enlisted medic, quickly took control, checking for cranium penetration. Good news, there was none. He whipped a bottle of Betadine out of his kit bag and poured it liberally on the captain's wound. It was only a graze, but a deep one. Then he pulled the captain's first-aid gauze from his pouch and placed pressure on the wound, wrapping the loose ends around Garrett's head. He told Lieutenant Taylor to take off the captain's boots so that he could check for any paralysis that might have been caused by the force of the bullet's pulling the captain's helmet off. With the commander unconscious, though, he was unable to proceed. He wrapped him in a space blanket, silver on one side to attract and retain heat, and green on the other side because it was Army equipment.

Taylor responded to the medic's next request for a sheet of plywood, which some of the headquarters troops brought to the scene. With Taylor's help, Doc Gore slid his commander's limp, but living, body onto the plywood and tightened tie-down straps across him. From there a group of almost too many volunteers carefully walked the three hundred meters to the helicopter. It was out of their hands now.

The helicopter took off. There was no need wasting precious time with Teller. He was dead, and to load him on the aircraft would have taken another five minutes—time enough to kill the commander or Sergeant Cartwright.

Taylor organized the troops quickly, ordering them back to their battle positions. One hundred percent security, he told them. Once the dust settled from the departing helicopter, having billowed in small puffs above the ground, he walked to where his longtime best friend, Mike Kurtz, sat against the white sheet metal of the Quonset hut whence the attacker had come.

Taylor sat next to him, pausing, then said, "He's still alive."

Kurtz looked up and gave Andy a blank stare that made commentary on so many things, his pain, his sorrow, and his guilt for not moving the commander sooner. He wanted to reset the clock and do it again, like in training or at the hundreds of football practices that he and Andy had suffered through. He was hurting, and his friend knew it.

"Mike," Andy said, barely controlling his emotion, "he'd be dead if it wasn't for you."

Kurtz, the senior lieutenant, with Rockingham having been ordered by Colonel Fraley to go to Manila the day before, simply said, "Let's go to full defense and be prepared for another attack."

CHAPTER 38

MANILA INTERNATIONAL AIRPORT, PHILIPPINES

Matt felt the Gulfstream make a bumpy landing along the concrete runway of Manila International Airport. He looked at the stiff windsock, which was pointing directly at the landing strip, indicating strong crosswinds from Manila Bay.

Jack Sturgeon, the pilot, rolled the craft to a stop on the tarmac. Sturgeon had briefly come back and introduced himself to Matt and Rathburn, having them both sign a logbook that he kept for his daughter and wife in California. Matt simply inscribed, "I know you're proud of your dad—Matt."

Matt felt Sturgeon pull the airplane to a stop. He looked through the oval window and saw that the morning was still a dark gray. The flashing red and orange wing lights pumped like strobes.

Grabbing his rucksack and SIG SAUER, Matt followed Rathburn and Sturgeon down the steps. He awkwardly lifted the ruck with his good arm, though he was surprised at how much better he felt after nearly two days of rest. The Percocet and antibiotics were doing their jobs.

"Leave that here until we get past the formalities," Rathburn directed, pointing at the rifle.

"Never more than an arm's length away from my weapon, sir," Matt countered.

"I don't want it visible, so hide it in your ruck. We're not at war here, for God's sakes."

"Excuse me. We just had an American soldier killed in a shoot-down of two C-130s."

"That was an accident. Now do as I say," Rathburn demanded.

Matt looked at Rathburn for a long moment and stuffed the weapon into his ruck. They deplaned and walked toward the terminal building.

Matt noticed his shoulder was beginning to bite him a bit and decided he needed a Percocet, but opted for a Motrin. He walked into the latrine of the terminal and cupped some water into his hand to swallow the horse pill.

The advisory committee remained on the airplane for the moment. Rathburn was a bit miffed that there was no delegation to meet him. He wandered around the empty terminal, looking for the red carpet, Matt presumed. Meanwhile, Sturgeon needed to file a flight plan for the next leg of his trip to Okinawa.

They all looked curiously at one another, thinking they heard the soft, but rapid, sound of distant gunfire.

Growing concerned with the rising noise of gunfire toward the inner city, Rathburn picked up a phone to call the embassy. Matt extracted his weapon from his rucksack as the three men stood near a service entrance that led through two glass doors onto the airport tarmac. A long, dark hallway went in the opposite direction, toward the baggage-handling area.

"What do you make of all that gunfire?" Rathburn asked Matt.

"Sounds like a combat zone," Matt said, stepping outside with his weapon at the ready.

"Up in the tower I could see Army trucks going everywhere. Green and orange tracers too."

The staccato sounds of small-arms fire continued, growing louder. Suddenly Matt thought about the women on the airplane and that he should probably have them join the men in the terminal. Best to keep everyone together.

As Matt jogged back on to the runway, he watched as a colorful truck with several hood ornaments drove along the runway and stopped less than fifty meters from their airplane.

Three men poured from the back of the red truck and set up RPG launchers on their shoulders, aiming them at the Gulfstream. Standing on the tarmac, screaming, "No!" Matt leveled his weapon on the gunners as three rocket-propelled grenades left smoking vapor trails flying from their launchers and impacted into a wing and the side of the airplane.

The fuel tank in the wing exploded with a bright orange fury that immediately began to spew flames and black smoke skyward. On either side of the wing, the grenades pierced the thin sheet metal and exploded beyond their impact points inside the passenger cabin. Matt knelt as he fired into the attackers. The heat from the fireballs that erupted pushed him back and, as he turned, he thought he could see people, women, running desperately down the aisle. Their movement was visible through the elongated series of windows as in some B movie as they tried to escape what was now a blazing inferno. Moments later, the aircraft exploded in an enormous eruption, billowing black smoke.

Matt sensed someone behind him, spun to his left, and swept his rearward attacker's feet off the ground. In a swift movement, he punched the small man in the stomach hard while grabbing the pistol with another hand. He noticed a knife moving to his side as he turned the pistol into the face of his initial attacker and shot him point-blank.

Sidestepping the lame thrust of a second attacker, Matt spun the now-dead rebel who had been holding the pistol into the path of the next insurgent.

"Hey, Joe, put down the pistol, no?"

"No," Matt said, then stopped when he realized what had occurred.

Two insurgents were holding Rathburn and Sturgeon by the neck, with knives pressing into their carotid arteries.

"Drop the gun, or we kill these Joes."

Matt sized up his predicament. He could really care less about Rathburn, a Beltway lightweight, but he presumed the man had a family. Sturgeon did have a family and actually seemed like a decent guy. Matt eyed a total of four Filipinos, Abu Sayyaf, he assumed. Two were holding Rathburn and Sturgeon. One was talking to him from the same vicinity near the door to the terminal, and one was standing near him with a knife and pistol aimed at him.

Really, he thought, *I could make quick work of these clowns if they didn't have knives ready to slice through Rathburn's and Sturgeon's necks.*

"Let them go, and I'll drop the weapon," Matt directed.

"You think we stupid, Joe?"

"My name's not Joe, dipshit, now let them go," Matt ordered again.

"Okay, watch this, Joe," the man holding Sturgeon commanded as he removed the knife from Sturgeon's neck and lifted it high.

Before he brought it down, Matt fired a single bullet into the man's head. Sturgeon quickly lifted the arm of the man holding Rathburn, hoping to use the surprise that Matt had created to their advantage. It worked.

Another shot, and Matt had killed the insurgent who had been holding Rathburn.

As he turned toward the attacker closest to him, a shot rang out from the distance, felling the man. Quickly, though, Matt realized that the bullet was intended for him and not the insurgent as two truckloads of wild-eyed rebels poured from the backs of Jeepneys.

Matt lifted his hands, as did Rathburn and Sturgeon when they saw the M4s and AK-47s aimed at them. Soon, several insurgents were upon them, pushing them onto the concrete and taping their eyes and mouths shut along with tying kite string around their hands and feet.

"How's this, Joe?" the Filipino said just before ramming the sharp toe of a boot into Matt's rib cage. He heard an audible pop and felt a deep pain in his ribs. Immediately he knew he had at least two broken ribs and possibly a bruised lung. Another kick in the same location made him sure about the lung; he could only pray it was not punctured. He could sense people walking quickly all around him. He heard many loud shouts on the tarmac, men he presumed celebrating their wily destruction of an airplane and the deaths of some American women.

The kicking had stopped, but the concrete ground pressed against his bruised side, making his breathing difficult. When he tried to roll over to his left side, his shoulder screamed with pain and a hand grabbed a clump of his hair as a foot slammed down on his neck. Feeling the steel of a weapon against his temple, Matt heard a voice say, "I kill you, Joe."

The man seemed happy that he was in control. Matt knew intuitively that it was the voice of an Abu Sayyaf rebel. When they spoke Tagalog among one another, he was certain of it.

"What do we do with the Yankees? Kill them?"

"Magsaysay. Kill one by one. Get information, put on television. Use reporter's equipment."

Matt listened to this exchange. He knew Fort Magsaysay was in the central highlands of Luzon Province, about a four-hour drive from Manila, on a good day.

The rebels walked the men toward the airplane. Matt could feel the heat licking his face, making him sweat in the already-boiling morning. Their captors forced them to lie down in the bed of a truck. Matt surmised that it was the same truck that had escorted the rebels who had attacked the airplane.

The searing pain in Matt's shoulder never dulled as he began calculating how he was going to kill his captors.

The one time I hang out with a bureaucrat and this happens, Matt steamed. He closed his eyes and endured the long, bumpy ride.

CHAPTER 39

U.S. EMBASSY, MANILA, PHILIPPINES

The blades from the medevac UH-60 rapped against the humid morning air, the aircraft hovering above the landing pad of the U.S. embassy in Manila. The landing area was a white concrete slab atop the three-story redbrick building surrounded by black wrought-iron-gated fences.

The embassy was in the heart of Manila on Roxas Boulevard and had a sweeping view of the horseshoe-shaped Manila Bay to its west, across Roxas. Palm trees lined the bay, obviously planted and not growing wild, framing the beach and water like a portrait.

Two marines guarded the front door, which was nearly fifty meters beyond a high brick wall with a black iron gate that prevented locals from gaining access to the compound. The Joint U.S. Military Advisory Group had a skeletal team of ten military personnel assigned: Fraley, two Marine Corps guards, an Army major, a doctor, and the medevac crew. The ambassador was in charge of these men who all contributed to the overall effort on what was called the country team.

Inside the embassy was an operations center where the country team had two satellite-capable radio systems. Maps of the major islands hung on the walls, plotting movements of Abu Sayyaf units and hot spots of activity.

As Major Hewit and Lieutenant Rockingham

stood atop the embassy roof and watched the medevac helicopter hovering above the landing pad, Hewit wondered where they had gone wrong. A firefight at Subic Bay, fighting in the streets, and they could not contact Major Ramsey's Special Forces team.

The Black Hawk prop wash created a cool wind atop the JUSMAG roof in the early morning haze. It was an ominous sight to Hewit and a fearsome one to Rockingham, the soldiers running low beneath the chopping blades of the helicopter, carrying a wounded comrade.

Rockingham recognized immediately that the four soldiers carried a piece of plywood with a man lying on it. He ran out to help them, then stopped and nearly gagged when he saw Captain Garrett. He was filthy, his face streaked with matted blood and caked with white dirt. His uniform showed white salt stains where he had sweat through them. A bandage was tied neatly around his head, obviously protecting a wound. He was unconscious—or dead.

Rockingham shuddered.

Major Hewit noticed that the concerned look on the faces of the soldiers showed a deep amount of admiration and respect for the man that they carried. They all searched for the doctor with anxious eyes.

Hewit had summoned the country team physician, an Air Force doctor named Colonel (Retired) Anthony Mosconi, who had stayed in country after Clark Air Base closed. His wife was Filipino, and he preferred to stay in her country as long as feasible. The doctor had a room in the JUSMAG headquarters dedicated to the general practice of caring for the embassy and JUSMAG staffs on a one-day-a-week basis. It had been a while since he had done any combat triage or surgery, but he remembered it well and hoped he would not have to make any tough decisions.

The decision was easy. One of the patients was ambulatory, walking with a crutch provided by the medevac pilot. He had a leg injury, but a quick inspection showed the medic had done a professional job of cleaning and dressing the wound. Turning his attention to the man on the plywood, he saw captain's bars on the soldier's uniform.

Must be the commander. Poor guys—eight thousand kilometers away from home, and their commander gets shot.

He shined a small flashlight into the captain's eyes while the four enlisted soldiers waited close by, hoping, praying for good news.

"Fix him, Doc. I don't care what it takes, fix him," said Sergeant Spencer, a tall black squad leader in Barker's platoon. The doctor looked somberly at Spencer's serious face and moist eyes.

Looking over the doctor's shoulder, Rockingham felt guilty that he had missed the action with his company. Rock was incensed that Fraley had forced him into the situation, but Captain Garrett had told him not to fight it, and to get back as quickly as he could.

"Maybe you'll be able to get some intel," Zachary had said.

Rockingham talked with the four soldiers about the night's activity, but they were seemingly incapable of communication as they watched the doctor work on their commander in the brightly lit room that seemed more like an office-made-operating room than a genuine doctor's workplace.

CHAPTER 40

"What's your name, son?" the voice asked. This was another dream, he was sure. He was inside of a dirty Coke bottle, trying to look out beyond the dusty glass. There were people standing above him, but their faces were large, then small, then large again as he rolled inside the bottle. Voices. He heard voices trying to talk to him. It was his brother Matt, calling his name. He could not see him, though, only hear a voice. The voice again, calling, pleading for him to come. Then he saw Kurtz rising from his crouch, yelling at him, grabbing his arm and pulling. He heard the voice again, calling a name. The voice. He must remember the voice. If he could only hang on, he could pull himself out of the bottle and find the troubled voice.

"What's your name?"

The doctor broke an ampoule of ammonia inhalant open beneath Zachary Garrett's nose, causing his face to wrinkle. That was a good sign, the troops realized as they watched, peering intently down upon their leader. The doctor had taken off the bandage and handed it to Sergeant Spencer, revealing a long, jagged wound that ran a thirteen-centimeter course above his left ear. The doctor surmised that the wound was more ugly than severe, and concluded that the impact of the helmet being ripped from his head must have knocked him unconscious. *Must have been one hell of a big bullet!*

As Colonel Mosconi poked and prodded Captain Garrett, Fraley came rambling down the dimly lit hall, rays of sunlight jumping from each office doorway and highlighting Fraley's cumbersome gait. Rockingham spotted him and angrily moved to meet Fraley in the hallway.

"You, fat son of a bitch!" Rockingham screamed at Fraley, whose eyes bulged wide as Rockingham grabbed him by the lapels and slammed him against the porcelain tile wall in the corridor.

"Get your hands off me, Lieutenant!" Fraley snapped back, his voice muffled by the shirt gathered around his mouth.

"You listen to me," Rockingham said, grabbing with one hand the bloodstained dressing from Sergeant Spencer, who looked on in amazement.

"You're gonna fry for this, Lieutenant, you hear me," Fraley said, sounding like he had a harelip.

"You see this," he said, holding the bloody dressing, "you did this." He had lowered his voice, sounding calmer. Although Fraley was large, he was no match for Rockingham's powerful frame as Rock lowered the man to the floor.

"I want you to have our blood on your face," he said, wiping the bloodstained bandage across Fraley's cheeks, "because you've already got it on your hands."

Fraley quickly picked himself off the floor, brushing his green jungle fatigues, and screamed, "MPs!" Then he added, "Listen here, I'm calling your division commander to tell him to throw your ass in the brig at Pearl Harbor so little boys can screw you up your black ass."

"Like hell you are," Sergeant Spencer said, moving in front of Rockingham. Spencer, taller than Rockingham, looked to Fraley like an aboriginal warrior.

"Stay out of this, Spence," Rockingham said, "this is between me and Fraley." Spencer moved out of the way, giving Rockingham a supportive glance.

"You've got to get past me first," Rockingham said. He was angry. Mostly he was mad about the abuse they had been taking from Fraley. But part of his rage was that he had not been with his company when they needed him.

"Back off, sir," Spencer said, placing a hand on Rockingham's chest. "This guy ain't shit. He's already pissed his pants. Let him go do whatever he's got to do. We've got four eyewitnesses here that heard him threaten you and say you had a black ass. Now, really, what's he gonna do?"

Rockingham backed off, glaring at Fraley with catlike eyes. True to Spencer's prediction, Fraley turned and walked toward the back door, in the direction of his quarters.

The doctor heard the commotion in the hallway, but knowing it centered on Fraley and that the men had been in a firefight all morning, he let it ride, as did Major Hewit, standing by his side. At one time or another, they had all wanted to do and say the things that Lieutenant Rockingham had. Hewit watched out of the corner of his eye as the two scuffled and wondered if it could get much worse.

"Zachary Garrett. My name's Zachary Garrett."

The troops snapped their heads back, watching as their commander awoke.

"Zachary," the doctor said, "how old are you?"

"Thirty-six," Garrett said, weakly, eyes trying to open, but mostly fluttering.

"Good. What is your job?"

"Commander. Commander of the best troops in the Army."

With the last comment, the soldiers knew their commander was going to be fine. They let out a collective "hooah" and gathered around him, where he still lay on the plywood.

"Not so fast, guys," the doctor said, equally happy that Garrett was coherent. "Zachary, I'm taking off your boot and socks, can you feel any-thing?"

The pregnant pause seemed eternal, casting a dreadful silence over the room. "Zachary?" the doctor asked again, this time pricking his foot with the top of his pen.

"I feel something, Doc," Zachary said hazily, "but I'm not sure." The doctor loosened the strap around Zachary's leg that had been securing him to the plywood. "Maybe this will help," the doctor said, massaging his leg, then returning to the chore of stabbing his foot.

"Oh yeah," Zachary said, to a collective sigh of relief.

"The combination of a pinched nerve and the tight strap deadened your senses down there. I think basically all we've got here is a decent head wound that'll heal nicely and a concussion that we can't do anything about except keep you awake for the next few hours."

No problem, Zachary thought, *I've got a ton of stuff to do*.

"Hey, XO, good to see you. Sure could have used you this morning," Zachary said at the first sight of him since he had left with Fraley. Then he realized his comment was like salt in an open wound for the XO.

"Don't remind me, sir," Rockingham said, looking at the floor.

"Don't feel bad. Your lieutenants did great. So did the rest of the company. You should have seen Quinones and Kurtz," Zachary said, shaking his head in disbelief, then stopping at the pain. It was some consolation to Rockingham that the lieutenants had performed well. Being the senior lieutenant in the company, he had taken the three "newbies" under his wing and personally guided them through the nuances of junior officership. But still, he felt remorse for not being at his commander's side during the attack.

The doctor cleaned and dressed the wound on Zachary's head after shaving the left side of his scalp. "Might as well get the other side while you're at it," he joked to the doctor, who laughed and complied with Zachary's request. After that, he worked on Sergeant Cartwright's leg, a more complicated wound than he had originally thought. Nonetheless, he thoroughly cleaned the deep cut, put in a few stitches, and properly bandaged it. Digging through a cabinet full of pharmaceuticals, he gave each of the wounded soldiers a full bottle of antibiotics.

After about an hour, the delegation was prepared to return to what the troops had already affectionately labeled "Garrett's Gulch."

Captain Garrett, the XO, Sergeant Spencer, Sergeant Cartwright, and the other three soldiers collected their personal gear and weapons and began to make their way up the stairs to the helicopter. They straggled, with the healthy soldiers helping the wounded, all with thankful expressions on their faces. It could have been a scene out of the *Red Badge of Courage,* the wounded men limping slowly, arms wrapped around the healthy ones. Uniforms ripped and shredded in places, bloodstained.

They heard a commotion toward the front of the building, followed by several shots fired. Having had their fill for the day, they continued up the stairs, finally reaching the roof, where the medevac helicopter started its engine with the high-pitched whine of the turbines, blades turning slowly and awkwardly at first, then beating and chopping to full speed. The body of the aircraft fought the tremensdous torque and bounced on its wheels.

As they left the air-conditioned building, the Philippine sun blasted their faces with moist heat. Out of instinct, they all checked their canteens. The group hobbled toward the helicopter.

The gunshots grew louder. Automatic-weapons

fire. The helicopter pilot was waving his arm at them, beckoning them forward. As the intensity of firing grew, three men and two women came running toward the helicopter from the embassy side of the compound, about one hundred meters from their position by the embassy.

The fleeing men and women were dressed in business suits and dresses that did not facilitate a rapid escape. The door swung open wide again, this time spewing Filipino rebels with blue and red bandannas. They knelt to fire at the fleeing American diplomats without noticing the straggling American soldiers.

"Spence, you go left, I'll go right," Rockingham said, grabbing one soldier, leaving the other two for Sergeant Spencer, who moved rapidly around the hovering aircraft. The pilot looked nervously at the armed Filipinos and had a moral decision to make. Did he save his own hide, or did he try to save them all? His hand started to pull back on the cyclic and collective controls, then released as he reasoned otherwise.

The five American civilians were running toward Sergeant Spencer's team near the rear of the aircraft. Spencer waved his arms rapidly at the group, most of whom were too scared to notice the whirring, invisible tail rotor of the UH-60. They could not hear Spencer's cries of warning above the gunfire and chopping of the helicopter.

"Get down! Watch out!" Spencer yelled as he watched a young blonde sprint toward them, eyes wide and hair tumbling across her face just enough to distort the fact that she was headed directly into the path of the rotor.

The ambassador realized his secretary's mistake and reached toward her, straining to grasp her as a hail of bullets chewed the cement behind him. Spencer watched as the young woman's face splattered against the aircraft and parts of her arms and torso were tossed about the landing pad, looking like some grisly artwork display.

The ambassador rolled underneath the blades, and the rest of his team avoided them as well. They joined Sergeant Spencer's team of three soldiers as they rounded the aircraft. Spencer told the civilians to get down on the cement when he heard the XO's rifle open fire. The five insurgents were caught by surprise, reeling under the withering fire brought forth by the XO's two-man team and Sergeant Spencer's team from the opposite side of the helicopter.

Meanwhile, Captain Garrett helped Sergeant Cartwright onto the helicopter, then pulled out his 9mm Beretta. Noticing the civilians, he hurried them next to Cartwright in time to turn around and see the door open from the JUSMAG section of the compound. It was Fraley.

"They got Doc and Hewit!" he screamed above the roar of the UH-60 blades as he ran from the door. Zachary, his back to the helicopter, saw three rebels spring from the doorway, chasing Fraley. It was Zachary who had the moral decision.

He was a decent man, so there was no real hesitation. He crouched in a good firing position and fired past Fraley's wide eyes at the three insurgents. Fraley rambled past Zachary and joined the increasing population on the helicopter. Zachary fired without hesitation, first selecting a target, then squeezing the trigger. He killed the rebels, who, like their countrymen across the heliport, were surprised by the armed opposition on the roof.

The soldiers quickly boarded the helicopter, their weight exceeding the load limit of the aircraft. The pilot gingerly adjusted the controls so the aircraft slowly lifted off the heliport, obviously straining under the excessive weight. He pitched the nose forward and climbed slowly into the air.

The door from the JUSMAG opened with a slam. Colonel Mosconi, the Air Force doctor, fell forward onto the hot cement. He was bleeding badly from his left shoulder and held a pistol in his right hand. He crawled on all fours, craning his neck to see the helicopter. The cement burned his hands and the pistol smashed his fingers each time he slapped his hand forward to move another centimeter toward the helicopter.

"Cover me!" Rockingham yelled, jumping from the barely airborne aircraft.

Fraley reached across the aircraft, grabbing Rockingham, and screamed, "No! Leave him, or we'll never make it!"

Rockingham punched Fraley in the face, smashing his nose and knocking him out.

Sprinting to Mosconi, the XO slid under him and lifted him into a fireman's carry, feeling Mosconi's blood oozing down his back. He took long, heavy steps back toward the aircraft, as more rebels began spilling onto the rooftop. Flipping Mosconi onto the commander's lap, Rockingham winced in pain as the Black Hawk pulled away. He held on to a metal tube that served as a seat frame, his legs hanging out of the aircraft.

Zachary had both arms around Mosconi, who lay unconscious and maybe dead. With one hand, he grabbed Rockingham's arm to give him support.

Rockingham looked at him with the blank eyes of a wounded deer. He knew then that the XO had been hit in the back with a bullet. Bullets zipped past and into the frame of the laboring aircraft. Sergeant Spencer grabbed Rockingham's other arm. Soon, both arms went limp, and Rockingham's eyes retreated into a world where there would be no pain. His body became deadweight against the pull of Zachary and Spencer.

With sudden alarm and shock, they realized their friend was dead. Hanging on, Spencer and Garrett looked at each other, trying to hold back their emotions. But they were only human.

Uncertainly, the pilot banked the machine hard to the left, diving below the level of the building to avoid the fire, and sped low along Roxas Boulevard with too much weight and too little time. They headed to the only safe place for an American in the Philippines—Garrett's Gulch.

CHAPTER 41

MINDANAO ISLAND, PHILIPPINES

Chuck Ramsey and his Special Forces team had been on the run for four days. The steep, jagged mountains had proved both a blessing and an enemy. Even these hardened men were having problems sustaining the rate of march necessary to elude Talbosa's Abu Sayyaf cell.

Ramsey stopped and looked down into the steep ravine. *Can we make it?* A few days ago, he would not have doubted it. Today, his men standing in single file behind him, panting, he was unsure.

"Take five, men," Ramsey told them. Despite their exhaustion, they moved to either side of their route and turned outward, each man taking a knee. They pulled their canteens out of their pouches and drank heavily. Every man was dehydrated. The heat had intensified during the last four days. The only respite was a gully washer, as Ramsey had called it. The near-monsoon-level rains had drenched his team and the Japanese man for hours, making them cold and miserable through the night. But the next day had brought forth the same burning, searing sun, and soon they were longing for the cool rain again. They needed water badly.

Ramsey knew he had to find a river for his men to refill their canteens. They still had plenty of water purification tablets to make the river water acceptable. More importantly, though, they needed to find a way to establish communications. He felt like he was carrying a deep secret that the world needed to know. He had the key to something, he was not quite sure what. While he had grown to tolerate Abe, he seriously doubted the man's story. Although it was plausible that the United States would be rearming the Armed Forces of the Philippines, he doubted that they would fund Japanese factories to do so. He had to make contact with somebody who could relay the message.

Anybody!

Kneeling on both knees, he leaned back, stretching his weary back muscles. His sixty-pound ruck was beginning to feel like an appendage to his body. He didn't bother to take it off. To put the weight back on again would somehow be demoralizing.

He gazed over some scrub. The ravine was about a sixty-degree drop with no trails. High tropical trees gave way to dense undergrowth and rocks. The terrain pitched deep into a narrow bottom that ran east toward the ocean.

Ramsey grabbed his two-quart canteen and took a long pull. The water was warm. *Must be a hundred degrees out here.* He was right. As he drank, he could feel his body rehydrate. Immediately his pores spewed forth sweat in an attempt to cool his scorching skin, only to have the beaming sun lick the moisture away.

Looking over his shoulder, he saw Benson turning his canteen up to the Japanese man's mouth. Water spilled over the edges of his dry, chapped lips as he gulped. Earlier, he had his men remove the tape from Abe's eyes and mouth. It only made sense. He was a healthy, but gentle man. He would do them no harm and would not last a day in the jungle if he escaped.

Abe's story was unbelievable. Ramsey asked him repeatedly if they really were manufacturing tanks and helicopters in the plant. He always responded that they were indeed. Abe insisted that the American government was footing the bill, as they had done for Japan's defense needs for so many years.

But the rub, according to Abe—an obviously bright man—was that America was doing this because they needed help in the Global War on Terror and wanted Japan to maintain stronger defenses. To Ramsey, it made no sense. Tanks and helicopters were not the best tools of the trade in fighting an idea such as radical Islam. The question Ramsey considered was, Why would the Japanese be building and stockpiling weapons on Mindanao?

In the Philippines?

Ramsey looked at Abe, kneeling in the thick jungle vines, looking exhausted with his eyes fixed on the ground at his feet. He had kind eyes and a smooth face. His hands were not the hands of a warrior. Rather, they were soft and delicate like those of a lawyer or executive. Ramsey had made him burn the orange jump suit and given him one of his own extra uniforms. It was a bit large, but served the purpose. Abe, in his running shoes and camouflaged jungle fatigues, reminded him of a soldier with some sort of foot ailment who had received a "no physical training profile" from the doctor. But Abe had proven to be in excellent condition. His stamina was lacking, but he could keep up with the group.

From the rear of the patrol, Benson came slithering through the elephant grass quickly. He carried a concerned look in his eyes.

"Sir, we've got movement to our rear," he said. Immediately, the team fanned into an L-shaped ambush, with Ramsey at the corner so he could control any engagement. Crouching low in the two-meter-high elephant grass, he could still see nearly a hundred meters along the path they had bored through the dense rain forest.

He saw it. There was movement toward them, following the trail they had inadvertently made. Ramsey could see no one but Eddie, who was kneeling and watching next to him. He peered through his binoculars, seeing only the undergrowth move. As his rising adrenaline level made his stomach twist into a knot, he felt a dry copper taste in the back of his mouth. He was tired. He was hungry. Perversely, he thought of all of the Vietnam movies he had seen in which soldiers shot at water buffalo thinking they were enemy. While he did not expect any water buffalo that high in the rain forest, nothing could really have surprised him.

Eddie motioned to him for the binoculars. He had grown quite confident and comfortable with the group. He wanted to make a contribution and had done so on many occasions. While Chuck still painfully mourned the loss of his best friend, Ron Peterson, he was glad that Eddie had happened along. He handed the glasses to Eddie, who placed them to his eyes.

The standard plan for a hasty ambush was first to try to avoid detection. Chuck figured they would use silenced weapons to the fullest extent possible to avoid further detection. His least preferred option was a conventional, loud ambush. For sure, the patrol would be lethally compromised.

Chuck handled his father's Navy SEAL "hush puppy" with ease, rolling it back in forth in his hand, venting some nervous tension. The Smith and Wesson Model 39 pistol was modified with a noise suppressor. Used by the SEALs in Vietnam to kill sentries and guard dogs, the weapon's range was limited to 100 meters. But it was quiet.

The back of his throat was dusty. *Is it the Abu Sayyaf? They've been following us for days. Must be them. How many?* Silently, he wished for a water buffalo instead of what he thought was coming.

"Mamanua," Eddie whispered, looking through the binos. Ramsey gave him a puzzled look. "Here," he said, leaning over and pointing nearly eighty meters from their position. They were directly in the middle of the ambush cross fire, whoever they were. Moving his pistol to his left hand, Ramsey lifted the binos to his camouflaged face.

"What the—"

"Mamanua," Eddie whispered again, covering Ramsey's mouth. Three Mamanua tribal natives were stalking through the rain forest hunting wild pigs or monkeys. They were dark-skinned and wore colorful beaded skirts and necklaces. Each held a spear at shoulder level, ready to release on his prey. The natives were Negritos, black people who had immigrated from Malay to the Philippine Islands centuries ago, the first inhabitants of the archipelago. The Philippine government designated land, primarily rain forests not targeted for clear cutting, in which the tribal groups could operate with impunity. Such jungle woodlands were enclaves in time where progress had made no inroads.

The black tribesmen stalked carefully, one foot over the next, sensing something. Fifty meters. Could his men hold their fire? Ramsey looked at Eddie, who shook his head as if to say, "They are best left alone." The lead Mamanuan looked through the bushes at him and raised his spear, preparing to hurl it forward. The others watched, lowering their spears.

He rifled the spear into the bush, not twenty meters from Ramsey's crouched position. Ramsey closed his eyes, fearing that they had gotten one of his men. He heard a high-pitched yelping sound and saw the spear dancing in the tall grass. The natives hurried forward. Ramsey raised his "hush puppy," prepared to engage. He felt Eddie lay his small, brown hand on his arm, holding him back.

The short black men, skin dry and whitish from the dust and heat, leaned over their prey, a wild boar, and quickly tied its feet together with hemp. They carried the black pig in the opposite direction, slung over their shoulders on a spear. As they were leaving, the lead native stopped, turned his head, stared directly into the bushes at Eddie and Chuck. He saw them, held the eye contact for a brief, knowing moment, then disappeared into the lush jungle.

Chuck lowered his pistol, comprehending that two cultures had just passed in the yellow-white Philippine sun. They had no interest in him, nor he they. Each had stared at the other, seeing a warrior of a different era. They were but mild curiosities to one another, each like a snake, harmless if unprovoked. Chuck saw in the man's black face a sense of satisfaction and contentment. It was something more than just capturing dinner for his tribesmen. The look was the clear countenance of a simple life. Removed from the trials of government and international concerns, the Negrito seemed content with his lot. The Filipinos and peoples of other developing countries Chuck had served in, countries that had been touched by the prospects of unrealized modernization, seemed angry and hateful toward foreigners and one another.

Deciding he would contemplate the significance of his visual interchange with the Mamanuan tribesman later, he turned to more immediate problems.

CHAPTER 42

Ramsey's most dominant thought was that in six more hours the helicopters would come. They could survive that long, for sure. He had to maneuver his team to the north of Cateel City, where the beach was wide and uninhabited. All around him, the sheer cliffs either dropped sharply into the water or gave way to beaches. The mountains reminded him of the Na Pali coast off the island of Kauai in Hawaii.

He motioned to his men to get moving with a pump of his clenched fist.

Looking to the east, he saw the ocean. Near the shore, the water was a tropical turquoise shade. Farther out, he could see a coral reef where waves tumbled harmlessly. Beyond the reef, the sea turned a deep, mystic blue. He knew the Philippine Trough was out there, reaching almost thirteen thousand meters into the core of the earth. *What a world,* he thought. Primitive tribesmen, deep oceans, tropical rain forests. The beach was as white as sugar, much like those in the Florida panhandle.

He looked grimly again at the difficult terrain that lay ahead. He knew that Talbosa's men were only about an hour behind them. Every time his team moved, the Filipinos seemed to pick up on the scent. Only when they went into hiding did it seem as though they were secure. More than once, they had doubled back on their trail, setting up ambushes but not executing them. They were clearly outnumbered.

He flipped his compass open, aiming it toward

the small village nearly six kilometers away and seemingly another atmosphere below.

That's got to be Cateel!

He snapped his wrist, closing the compass lid, and placed it in its pouch. Another drink of water and he would be ready. He sucked from the canteen, draining it, then stood.

From his vantage, everything was downhill. It was just a matter of how steep. Taking the point on this patrol, unusual for a team leader, he inched his way down the ravine. His footing was tenuous at best as he slipped on the damp deadfall and rocky dirt. The rainy season had not officially begun yet, but enough precipitation had fallen to make the rain forest dense with high timber, wild coffee bushes, rubber plants, and an assortment of other tropical shrubs. Huge leaves from elephant plants slapped him in the face as he let the weight of his ruck force him down. Frequently he would turn his back to protect his face, holding on to plant roots above his head, a tactic he had been taught to avoid in Ranger school. But, thankfully the sadistic Ranger instructors had not yet thought of including a brigade of Abu Sayyaf rebels as a motivational tool in Ranger training.

The tactical satellite radio was another issue that he could not shake from his mind. *What was wrong with it?* They had checked repeatedly to make sure that they had the proper angle to the satellite. He even had Ralph Jones, the best communications sergeant in the Army, take the service panel off the radio to see if anything looked awry. Nothing did, to him. They had no other radio or batteries to test the radio against. Major Ramsey had never been so frustrated in his life.

He had little time to think of such matters, however, as he reached an impasse. He had led the group nearly all of the way down the ravine. But the last fifty-five meters were comprised of sheer rock cliffs that dropped directly into a swiftly moving mountain stream. The sloping terrain had forced him continuously to the east, off his azimuth, trapping his team on an outcropping of rocks. To double back might lead him into his pursuers. To walk the ledge south would be too dangerous. To climb the rocks to the north would be suicide. There was only one option.

Chuck halted the patrol. They took a knee, each facing outward again, except the last man, who faced to the rear. He whipped out his smokeless tobacco, smacked the can, and placed a wad in his mouth. Time to think. He pulled a forty-five-meter nylon military rope from his rucksack. Benson moved forward as all good assistant patrol leaders do when the patrol halts. He dropped his ruck as well, snatched a similar coiled rope from his pack, and began backward-feeding it to the ground, checking it for frays. Benson passed the word back to his men to begin securing their "Swiss seats" and snap links. Each man carried a four-meter sling rope that he wrapped around his waist and ran through his crotch to form a seat. Placing a ten-centimeter snap link through where the two ropes met near the belt buckle, the soldier had a seat by which he could rappel down a rope.

Chuck found a thick mahogany tree and hugged it, lifting his feet off the ground and leaning back toward the rock cliff. The tree was sturdy, with green leaves and healthy bark. It would suffice as an anchor point. He tied a round turn knot with two half hitches, snugging the hitches tight against the tree. Using only one rope, he placed the other in his pack. Benson grabbed a third rope, which Randy Tuttle had carried, and stuffed it into his pack. If the first rope did not reach all the way down, then Benson could hammer some pitons into the rock facing and make another anchor point. Ramsey knelt and placed

two burlap sacks between the rope and the rock ledge
to prevent fraying. Benson would go first, Chuck
would go last. He gave an extra sling rope to Eddie,
who knew how to rappel. Abe was another issue.

Each man was already carrying roughly seventy
pounds apiece and could not afford to add another
160 pounds with Abe. Chuck tied the seat around
him and gave him a quick class on the techniques,
knowing full well that he would falter.

He knew he had no time for real instruction. He
acted as rappel master, hooking in all of the soldiers
and having Abe watch them lean singly over the cliff
with their hands in their backs, braking their
movement. As soon as each solider felt comfortable,
he would extend his right hand at a forty-five-degree
angle from his side, locking the right elbow, while
simultaneously pushing off the rock facing. The
green berets bounded their way quickly to the
bottom of the ravine. The significant stretch factor in
the rope allowed each soldier's weight to land him
gently in the waist-deep stream. Releasing the rope
would cause it to bounce crazily back to several
meters above the water. The soldiers moved slowly
down the stream, filling their canteens and
conducting reconnaissance, while those remaining
atop the cliff provided overwatch from above.

Eddie flew down the rope, showing off the fact
that he was a prestigious Filipino Scout Ranger.
Admittedly, he was an expert in jungle and
mountain warfare techniques, and the team had
grown fond of him. One evening, he had killed a
wild boar. Before cooking it, he had cut the pig's
throat and drained the blood into a tin canteen cup
that most soldiers used for drinking coffee and
cleaning their razor; or both. In one of the few
lighthearted moments, Eddie had taken the cup to
each of the green berets, saying it was a Filipino
Ranger tradition to drink pig's blood with his

fellow warriors. What had been a suspicious team initially, readily came to agree that they saw Eddie in a different light. Ramsey and his team were always game for new traditions and delighted in the ceremony. Each man took a mouthful of the blood under Eddie's watchful eyes. He gave a yellow-toothed smile every time he saw one of his new teammates swallow, then grimace at the realization at what he had just done. When Major Ramsey took his drink, Eddie saw him chewing as he swallowed.

"Ah. Blood clot, major. That means you special," Eddie said with a huge grin. The team had laughed and rapidly returned to business.

Eddie slid down the rope, jumped into the water, and took up the number eight position in the patrol. Two more of the team bounced down the rock face, and it was Abe's turn.

"You can do this," Chuck said with conviction. He knelt before Abe, pulled the rope toward the anchor point, and looped it twice through Abe's snap link. The extra friction should make him go slower. Chuck placed his gloved hand on the running end of the rope, then slammed it in Abe's back.

"That stays there until I tell you different." He then placed Abe in a good position from which to rappel and slowly pushed him over the rock ledge. Abe's eyes were wide with fear. Leaning back over a fifty-five-meter cliff was as unnerving experience as any non-climber could have. He went to one knee shaking his head with rocks sliding out from under his feet, almost causing him to slide down the rope.

"No. No." Abe said, looking down. He was ashamed. Ramsey had an idea. He quickly took the second rope out of his ruck and tied it in similar fashion around another tree less than two meters above the first anchor point. He would go down the rope next to Abe, coaching him all the way. Abe was reassured, but still not confident.

He said, "If you do not do this, you will die." The grim look on Ramsey's face told Abe that he had better collect the courage to back over the ledge. With his eyes closed, he inched back.

"Look at me," Ramsey said, already forming an L with his body hanging over the cliff. The rope was taut, scraping bark from the tree as he wiggled his body into position. He leaned and rocked against the rope, giving Abe confidence. Abe slid over the edge, with his knees scraping the face of the cliff. Exasperated, he looked at the brave major. Realizing he was over the cliff, and had not fallen, he smiled weakly. He could do it. Finally, he inched his way down, walking backward. Ramsey led the way. He preferred to rappel quickly, reducing the amount of time on the rope, but understood his primary purpose was to reassure Abe. They reached the bottom, slid into the refreshing mountain stream, and rejoiced that they had made it safely. Abe bowed respectfully to Ramsey, standing waist deep in rushing water. Ramsey inclined his bearded face downward, accepting the compliment.

Standing in the cool water, Ramsey realized there was nothing he could do about the ropes. He would have to leave them as a major clue for the Abu Sayyaf. He just hoped that he and his men would not swing from them anytime soon. On that thought, he motioned to Abe to walk east and join the rear of the patrol, which had already started moving and clearing.

They had all filled their canteens and soaked their overheated bodies in the stream. The stream led to the northeast of Cateel City and eventually gave way to a flat area almost seventy-five meters above sea level with an excellent view of the landing zone for the helicopters. *Only two more hours*, Chuck thought. *Two hours.*

CHAPTER 43

Major Ramsey's men climbed out of the stream and formed a tight perimeter, sensing that they might get out of this situation after all. They drank heavily from their canteens again and again until their urine was clear. They had been in the high mountain region, nearly out of water, and urinating the color of legal paper: a sure sign of dehydration. Their new base camp was in a stand of tall mountain pines. The underbrush was relatively sparse.

Give the old tacsat one more try.

Jones took a knee in the middle of the patrol base beneath some tall pines. Ramsey and Abe watched as he dropped his ruck and flipped a switch on the radio. He popped the radial antenna out of his pocket and spread its arms so that it looked like the skeleton of an umbrella. He set an azimuth on his compass and found the direction to "bird 65," the satellite they had been told to use. It hovered somewhere between the Philippines and Hawaii. All he needed was to aim the antenna in the proper direction, and the radio should work.

Still nothing. Ramsey looked skyward in frustration to see the hot wind blow through the tall pines. He could hear the peaceful lap of waves on the coral reef some six hundred meters away. His frustration was mounting. Normally he could control himself, but not that day.

Ramsey furrowed his brow, wanting to kick somebody or something, when Abe said, "May I 'ook?"

His L was silent. Abe moved to one knee and looked at the radio stuffed into the rucksack for carrying purposes.

"Can we take out?" Abe asked Jones, motioning with his hands.

"You get take out at Chinese restaurants, man. You can't fix that thing—" Jones said, just as frustrated as his commander.

"Let him look," Ramsey interrupted. Jones pulled the radio out of his ruck, a chore in itself. Laying it on the ground, he said, "Here," and walked away.

"Have any, uh—" He did not know the word. He was motioning with his hand, turning it left and right.

"Screwdriver? You want a freaking screwdriver so you can rip my shit apart?" Jones said, angrily pulling his flop hat off and slapping his thigh with it. "No way, sir," he said, looking at the major. Jones was protective of his radio, embarrassed enough that it, and he, had failed them. He would be damned if he was going to let some foreigner play with it.

"Do it, Jonesy," Ramsey ordered, spitting into the ground, resting his arms on his ammunition pouches. Begrudgingly, Jones obeyed his commander and handed Abe a jeweler's screwdriver set.

Abe proceeded to dismantle the radio. He had seen many like it.

"This have line of sight and satellite?" Abe asked, almost impossible to understand.

"Yes, it does," Ramsey said, walking over to where Abe was seated and had essentially disassembled the radio into several pieces. Worried, he sat in front of Abe and watched. Looking at the circuit board, Abe began nodding. He looked back at the front panel of the radio, which had a variety of switches: the frequency dials, voice and data receivers, satellite offset switch, volume and squelch dials, antenna nodes, and encrypting port. In the bottom left-hand corner of the front panel, he played with the switch that read "off-sat-los." As he turned the switch back and forth, he watched the transistor gate on the circuit board. Nothing was happening.

"Find problem," Abe said, flatly.

"What?" Jones screamed, scampering back to where Abe was sitting.

"Show me," Chuck said, highly interested.

"This switch. Control megahertz. You not get enough megahertz. When I move switch, transistor gate stay on line of sight. Not go to satellite."

"I'll be damned," Jones said. "He's right. You need twenty-five megs to go satcom, and you only get four megs with the line-of-sight mode. I was on line of sight to keep comms with you guys when you found *him*," he said, looking at Ramsey and pointing at Abe. "Then my shit caught the impact when he fell on me that night. I'll be damned," Jones said, unsure now how to treat Abe.

"Can you fix it?" Ramsey asked.

"Maybe," Abe said. He would need a thin piece of wire, some solder, and something that would burn hot.

"Where's McGyver when you need him," Jones said, referring to the TV hero who always knew what chemicals he needed to get the perfect reaction.

Ramsey collected a small propane tank from Sid Bullings, a medic. He used it to heat his instruments. Jones carried both wire and solder in his communications-repair kit. Abe worked on the radio for about thirty minutes. The propane tank made him sweat profusely. The noonday sun baked him and the rest of the team. The potential good news spread around the team, and all were hopeful.

"I solder into satcom position only," Abe said. "No way to fix for both."

"That's fine," Chuck said, anxious to give it a try. Abe pieced the radio together with skill. No small bits were left when he was finished, as had not been the case when he put his daughter's new bicycle together before he left for Mindanao.

Yes, Abe thought, if he could only see his daughters again. He absently patted the photograph that he had transferred from his white smock to his orange running suit, then to his first Army uniform. With quiet aplomb he stood, holding his hands out toward the radio, then softly patting his thighs and walking to where he could see the ocean, framed by two coconut trees. He pulled the picture of his family, which showed his wife in the middle and his girls on either side, out of his pocket. He no longer cared about his Ph.D. in engineering or his tremendous success as an auto executive or the fact that he had been handpicked to lead a government production team in the Philippines. He would gladly trade all of that for the freedom to go home. Somehow. Some way. There must be a way. He held the picture at eye level, the clear waters of Cateel Bay framing it. A hot, salty wind blew at his hair and stung a cut on his face. He licked his chapped lips and tasted a salty tear that had strolled along his cheek. He was surrounded, but lonely. The only thing that mattered to him was getting back to his family. He did not care how.

"We're getting a signal," Jones said, excitedly. He had reloaded the encryption variable, turned on the power, aimed the antenna, and seen the red light indicate that he was reaching the satellite.

Chuck picked up the black microphone. Looking at his watch, he saw there was only one hour until the helicopters were to arrive. He hoped they would be there.

CHAPTER 44

Commander Talbosa moved to the front of the column. They had followed the rugged trail blazed by the enemy. He still figured them to be the elite Filipino Scout Rangers. They were certainly the best that he had ever dealt with.

He inspected the two ropes, which dropped over a steep cliff into the Cateel River. He knew the area very well. The Japanese manufacturing plant was nearby, and his men had patrolled the entire area during the rapid construction of the facility. Additionally, he was to link up with Takishi in less than a day in Cateel Bay to fly to Manila and assume control of the entire operation. As it stood, his handheld satellite communications had been sufficient to monitor activities that his years of preparation and rehearsal had allowed to occur with precision. There were other insurgent groups, such as the New People's Army (NPA), that were vying for control, and Talbosa chose to ally with Takishi, keep a low profile, then emerge as the conquering leader with Takishi's backing.

Still, a part of him simply loved the hunt, and so here he was.

He was close. He could smell them. One chewed tobacco, he knew. At several vacant base camps he'd found bits of smokeless tobacco, decidedly not a Filipino habit. Some Filipinos use smokeless tobacco, but it was more of a—yes—an American habit.

Talbosa thought, kneeling next to the ropes.

Could it be? Good, new ropes. A fresh tin of good

smokeless tobacco. Could it be Americans? Could it be Garrett?

Takishi had told him to kill Matt Garrett, but he had seen no indication of the man. Perhaps he was so good that he was never seen. Maybe there was an American or Australian advisor with the Scout Rangers. The sight of blood some fifty meters behind the ropes confused him. Had one of the Rangers been hurt? Was it food they had killed? He was unable to decide.

There were only two places they could have been going, either to the beach or to the top of the mountain. The terrain to the north was much too severe, and he knew they were tired. He had kept them on the run. They would not have rappelled down the ropes if they wanted to go up the mountains. They had followed the stream east, toward the beach.

"Come, men. There is an easy way," he said. He had one of his men untie the ropes and coil them. The cause needed all of the material it could get. Doubling back and breaking bush for nearly two hundred meters, Talbosa led his men to a path that followed the spine of a ridge down into Cateel City. "We will move along the ridge and find them on either side, waiting for something. They came here with a purpose."

Pulling off his bush hat, he ran a long-fingered hand through his sweating, greasy hair. Talbosa was tall for a Filipino, nearly six feet. He was a strong man with a probing intellect. In another country, perhaps he would have been a doctor or college professor. But this was his destiny. His people needed him. Three hundred men followed single file as they walked the southern spine of the ridge that led toward Cateel City. Mostly animals used the path to wander down from the rain forest and gain access to the river below.

Talbosa stopped and looked upon the ocean. He was nearly 750 meters above sea level and five kilometers away from the city. Looking skyward, he caught the image of a Philippine eagle silhouetted by the sun, wings spread, casting a large X onto the trail. In its talons, the eagle had a dead monkey it had just captured. Talbosa smiled, watching the "monkey eater" flap, then soar, heading for its nest. To his left was the huge ravine that Ramsey's team had rappelled. To his right was a dense rain forest. As the trees thinned, the elephant grass took over.

Talbosa reorganized his men, warning them to prepare for an ambush. The enemy was near. He had one company in the lead, walking softly but not without noise. The remaining two companies followed him down the path, which widened as the rain forest gave way to grass.

Talbosa followed a young fighter not a day over fifteen. As they walked in the sweltering morning heat, he recalled his earlier days with the movement. He yearned for the day when the children of the Philippines could lay down their weapons and pick up schoolbooks to learn. He had read hundreds of books during his lifetime: the Koran, the Bible, Weber, Marx, Rousseau, Jefferson, Mao Zedong, Sun Tzu, and many others hoping to understand the world beyond. He knew there were points of view other than his. He also knew that the Philippines would never prosper so long as the imperialistic powers maintained control of the country. They had to achieve their independence through whatever form of government. In the early nineties, the Islamic movement seemed to gain traction, providing an opening. Abu Sayyaf had splintered from the bungling New People's Army, and Talbosa had seen an opportunity.

Like the Muslims in the Balkans, Talbosa had chosen to adopt a practical, almost Clausewitzian approach to warfare, meaning it was simply a furtherance of political endeavors. Talbosa's fight was not for Bin Laden, but for his people, a means to an end.

Walking down the path in his sweat-stained khaki-brown uniform, Talbosa wiped the moisture from his dark forehead. *So much hatred and violence. So many children dying. We can be free. We can have a better life.*

CHAPTER 45

"Any station, this is Bushmaster six, over," Major Ramsey said into the black microphone. He waited and still got no response. He had been trying for over fifteen minutes to contact either the embassy or his group in Okinawa. He was sure the radio was working. Where could they be? He had Jones check the encrypting codes. The frequencies were correct, and he was using the proper call signs. In the past, he had been able to reach Okinawa, but today was getting no response.

"Which bird are we using, Jonesy?"

"Bird sixty-five," Jones responded, looking at the sky as if he could read a bumper number on the satellite.

"How about bird sixty-four, can we try that?" Ramsey asked.

"We can try anything once," Jones said, picking up the small antenna dish and aiming its skeletal frame to the southeast toward New Guinea. "If we get anybody, it won't be our headquarters. Bird sixty-four can't reach Okinawa. Something about the horizon. It might be able to redirect our signal to another satellite, but I don't know how we could do that." Satellite 64 covered the Indonesia, Australia, and New Zealand area, lying somewhat low on the horizon. Its farthest reach north without retransmission was the Philippines. In a southerly direction it transmitted to the Antarctic teams that were stationed there doing ecological work.

"Well, I just want to get our message to somebody who speaks English, so they can relay it to some authority in our government. Japanese making tanks in the Philippines would make a stir somewhere, I'm sure," Ramsey said.

Jones chuckled. "Yeah, especially the Philippines. Okay. Try it now."

"Any station this net, this is Bushmaster six, over." He paused. Nothing.

"Any station this net, this is Bushmaster six, over." Again nothing. He knew he was using secure voice communications and unless people had the same nonlinear, algorithmic encrypting variable set in their radio's microprocessor, they would not be able to hear him. The variables were randomly configured and contained in small, handheld devices that interfaced with the communications equipment. In essence, they disguised and protected an otherwise-naked transmission that would normally be free for intercept from anyone using the same frequency bandwidth. The satellite radio had a port on the front panel where Jones had "re-keyed" the tacsat. He was sure that no one in New Guinea or Australia had their variable.

"Bushmaster six, this is Bravo six romeo, over," a voice responded. Ramsey scrambled to his knees, grabbing the handset. Jones pumped his fist next to his ribs in silent hope that it was someone who could help them.

"This is Bushmaster six, who are you and what is your location?"

"Stand by. Authenticate Alpha Mike, over." That was a good sign, Ramsey thought, as Jones spooled up his digital encryption device. The two letters A and M had a corresponding response that only someone using the handheld encryption device could locate. They had to be Americans.

"I authenticate Romeo, break," Ramsey said as Jones had indicated, "authenticate Foxtrot Lima, over." It was customary to authenticate in both directions of the conversation so that each party could be reasonably assured that they were speaking with an authorized user. A brief pause ensued. Ramsey was hopeful, though. *Finally, wherever these guys are, I'm giving them the scoop.* He could unload his burden. He had felt a bit like the Navy lieutenant commander that had seen the radar images of the Japanese fleet bearing down on Hawaii from the north on that dreadful day in December 1941. He had the answer, but could get it to nobody. The answer to what, he was unsure.

"I authenticate Sierra, over."

"This is Bushmaster six. What is your unit and location?" Ramsey asked, doubtful that the young RTO would give him the information.

"Look at the bravo designator in your encrypting device." Jones was listening and promptly scrolled through his digital display and found the letter B, which for that day indicated a company from the Twenty-fifth Infantry Division. Whoever these guys are, he thought, their radio guys go by the book. *That's good. I'm in touch with a squared-away unit.*

Jones showed him the Twenty-fifth Infantry Division codes that Major Hewit of the embassy had placed in their encryption device. "We're talking to Hawaii?" Jones asked incredulously. "If we can talk to them, we can reach Okinawa, can't we." Ramsey thought for a moment, rubbing what was now becoming a beard on his chin. He held a camouflaged mechanical pencil in one hand. *Think, Chuck, think.*

"No. These guys are that ammo detail at Subic. Remember my bud, Zach Garrett, that I mentioned?" Ramsey said. He remembered walking out of the embassy before their mission to Mindanao and seeing a calendar that showed one company arriving to guard some ammo that was being transferred to another ship. The manifest had listed Captain Zach Garrett as the leader.

"Okay, I've got your unit, and I think I know your location. I am friendly. Look at Bushmaster in your device. That's me. I need to talk to your commander. I have some important information, over," Chuck said.

The voice came back. "Wait, over."

Ramsey waited among the tall trees and elephant grass. The stream that had been their path was fifty meters to his south. He could see his men, one about every fifty meters, in a circular perimeter, constantly vigilant, but very tired. Their worn senses were not as keen. He could feel the anticipation of the helicopters surge through him, washing away the dikes of caution that normally prevented emotions from interfering with the mission at hand. They had been peaking for four days. Constantly on the run, never a restful moment. It was the time, the body was saying. It had to be immediately. *I can't go much farther without rest and sleep and good food.*

Waiting for the response. Waiting. Special Forces soldiers were always waiting for support from someone else who probably did not understand their precarious situation.

"Bushmaster six, this is Bravo six, over."

The voice was crisp with authority and impatience … and familiar.

"This is Bushmaster six," Ramsey blurted, anxious. "Listen, we know each other. You are the unit that came here for ammo detail. You don't have to answer, but you know who I am, classmate. We are on another island and are supposed to have helicopters pick us up in about twenty minutes. But we lost contact with everybody because of a radio glitch and now we can't seem to get anybody but you. I have some important information. Prepare to copy, over," Ramsey said, rapidly.

"This is Bravo six. You're right about who we are. I know the voice, but give me a minute. Anyway, you're not going to get anybody else on the radio. The Abu Sayyaf launched a major attack today. I've already had my XO and another soldier killed in action. The Abu Sayyaf took the embassy, and they looked like they had the Presidential Palace when we flew over it. We're stranded ourselves. I've got some embassy pukes and a colonel in my base camp. We've called back to our headquarters. They're working on the situation. Plus, I doubt you'll get any helicopters. The enemy is everywhere. Send your message, over," said Captain Garrett, trying to narrow down his list of West Point classmates who might be leading troops in the Philippines.

Simply put, he had been shocked by the loss of Rockingham and had no time for any bullshit. He wanted to kill every last insurgent son of a bitch. He had his men put camouflage paint on their faces and hands, and told them that they were leaving Garrett's Gulch to move into the jungles above Subic. He had read about the Marines in Beirut, and his position was very similar. Low ground, surrounded by high ground on three sides. Too vulnerable. Something inside of him took over, something dark and dangerous. He would not rest until the loss of his soldiers had been avenged.

Ramsey leaned back on the heels of his green and black jungle boots and tried to comprehend what his classmate had just told him. Two dead. That makes three American soldiers killed in the Philippines in the past week. *What the hell is going on? The war is in the Middle East, Afghanistan and probably soon to be Iraq.* No helicopters. He momentarily forgot his message and asked, "Do you have any transportation?"

"Roger. We've got one Black Hawk with a quarter tank of fuel. I doubt he can reach you, over."

"I know he can't. Can you get fuel from anywhere?" Ramsey knew the Black Hawk to have a range of over 950 kilometers. Their position was roughly 725 kilometers from Subic Bay. The helicopter could pick them up, but not make it all the way back without refueling somewhere.

"We'll try. What's your location?"

"Mindanao. We're near a place called Cateel City. If he can just fly above the shore north of Cateel City, we'll guide him to our location."

"I'll talk to the pilot and see what he says. Christ, what are you doing in Mindanao?" Zachary asked.

"Zach, this is Chuck," Ramsey said, hesitating before he played the card and violated operational security over the radio.

The first bullet hit Jones in the right shoulder, knocking him back against a tall pine. The second pierced his neck, spraying red blood onto the bark. He stood for a second, wide-eyed, then said in his Boston accent, "Bastards." His back sliding down the tree, he died.

Ramsey saw Jones get hit before he heard the gunshot. Soon his team was returning fire. They had been surprised, totally. The enemy fire was coming from across the ravine. Ramsey's battle-hardened mind went into gear immediately. *At least they have to cross the river to maneuver against me. That may save us.*

Then he remembered. The message. *I've got to get the message to Bravo six—Zachary Garrett.* He knew he was carrying the glass slipper. These rebels would not have been hot on his trail if the Japanese man had not been right about what he had said.

A bullet blew the bark off the tree next to his head, spraying chips of wood into his eyes. Temporarily blinded, he crouched low and made the decision that he had to be alive to send the message, and he needed radio equipment as well. He picked up the radio and antenna, and moved behind a tree. The enemy was obviously trying to knock out his communications equipment as the concentration of fire seemed greatest near him. But then again, it always seemed that way in a firefight. He grabbed his ruck and stuffed the radio and antenna inside. He had eaten all of his chow and had plenty of room for the comms equipment. Another bullet stuck in the wood next to his ear. They seemed to be everywhere.

He could see Benson and Eddie returning fire with vigor. Abe lay frozen next to him. The other men had coalesced into groups that could conduct independent fire and maneuver.

He grabbed Abe, laid him next to his rucksack, and told him not to move. The volume of fire was unlike any he had ever heard before. Grabbing his M4, he moved north and linked up with Sid Bullings. They moved along the ravine, out of the hail of bullets. He could see enemy soldiers across the river, looking as if they were going to cross at any moment. It would be a long process on their part, getting down the steep bank and back up the far side. Looking back at his men, conducting fire and maneuver, he saw Benson and Lonnie White running down the line, doing something he could not quite identify.

He flipped his M4 selector switch to semi-automatic. He had eight thirty-round magazines. Bullings was his security man. He looked through his telescopic sight and could see his weapon's noise suppressor with his open left eye. They took cover behind a rock, and Ramsey began to fire single shots that left the muzzle of his weapon silently and violently struck their targets.

He watched as a subsonic round struck an unsuspecting enemy, tumbling through his body like a bowling pin, ripping his insides to shreds. The lower-than-usual velocity gave the round a chance for more destruction once it struck its target. He picked another target, then a third.

Suddenly, the enemy rose en masse. There were more than two hundred. At least there had been. His team was holding them off momentarily. But they stood, like some confederate charge in the American Civil War, screaming and climbing down the near side of the ravine. Hand over hand, they scaled down the rocks and would have to do the same coming up the other side.

Ramsey continued to fire, killing every man he shot.

He looked along the ravine. The enemy fell into the increasingly red waters below. Benson had ignited a series of claymore mines, killing at least sixty who had tried to enter the ravine. Ramsey saw a man with an Australian bush hat running up and down the line, screaming loudly. He laid the sight on his head, but the man kept moving through the elephant grass, never presenting a stationary target. He fired.

Missed.

CHAPTER 46

Talbosa turned and looked, but did not see who had shot at him, feeling only the jet wash of the errant shot and listening as the bullet whacked its way through the jungle canopy. He was now certain that it was either Australians or Americans his men were fighting. He hoped they were Americans. *We will be like Vietnam*, Talbosa thought. *We will have started a war with the Americans and will destroy the most powerful country in the world!*

But he was trying to get the confusion under control. He had ordered his men to open fire once they made contact. His point man had misunderstood the directive and fired when he saw the enemy across the ravine. Talbosa would have preferred to circle around and come at them from the north, driving them into the ravine to their deaths.

He had issued instructions to kill the Japanese man as well. Takishi had told him that Abe might inform the world that the Japanese were making weapons for Abu Sayyaf's use, and that would effectively cut off their supply. He could not have that. Running through the elephant grass, avoiding bullets that whizzed around him, he began to get control of his men. He pulled them back, having them cease fire, or at least cover their retreat. They would stop and move into Cateel City, then move north of the river, swinging wide, and slam into the enemy.

The firing stopped. Ramsey continued to pick off retreating soldiers with his deadly accuracy. The team kept up its volume of fire into the elephant grass until they could see no more enemy soldiers. Each man knew that the Abu Sayyaf would come again and that they would need their ammunition. They were also equally aware that there were no helicopters coming to save them.

He organized his team quickly. Moving back to his rucksack, he looked down at Abe, who was shivering. He had pissed his pants and probably defecated, or so it smelled. Snatching Abe by the arm, Ramsey rallied his team, and they moved. Benson slung Jones's body over his rucksack, adding another 150 pounds to his load. He would switch often, but it would slow their move considerably. When they found a safe place, they could bury his body, write down the grid coordinates, discreetly mark the location, and return another day for their fallen comrade.

Ramsey walked hurriedly through the increasingly dense jungle. He looked over his shoulder and saw Benson struggling with Jones. His mind filled with rage. First Peterson killed, and now Jones. He took both deaths personally. When they come again, they will come from the northeast. *We will be ready to kill every last son of a bitch.*

Like a zephyr, Major Ramsey and his beleaguered A team vanished to the northwest.

CHAPTER 47

SUBIC BAY, LUZON ISLAND, PHILIPPINES

Ramsey. That was Chuck Ramsey.

Captain Zachary Garrett looked at the microphone. He had heard a shot and knew immediately that his classmate and his soldiers were in trouble.

But so was he.

As night fell on this incredible day, he rallied his men, as Chuck Ramsey had gathered his. The division commander, General Zater, had personally spoken to him on the radio, telling him that they were sending assistance immediately. He gave Zachary the authority to do whatever he felt necessary to further protect the lives of his men. When Zachary tried to brief him on the plan, the general cut him off, saying, "I have confidence in you. Don't risk compromising your plan. We've been watching CNN all day. You're the one who's been squeezing the trigger." The general's confidence in him had made him feel good momentarily, but then the weight of his burden sank in even further.

The Navy supply ship was not due in until tomorrow, but he was not going to wait for it. Another night in the same location would surely make his company an easy target. They could be attacked from practically all directions, and they had little cover from indirect fire. Sure, their ticket to safety would be the ship, but waiting for it might be their ticket home—maybe in body bags. Zachary had his men pilfer the ammunition stockpile, then had his forklift driver dump the rest off the pier and into the water. He would be damned if he was going to let American ammunition kill his men. They gathered claymore mines, JAVELIN medium anti-armor missiles, all of the 5.56mm ammunition they could carry, smoke grenades, high-explosive grenades, tear gas, star clusters, parachute flares, trip wires, antitank weapons and 60mm mortar rounds, even though they had not deployed with any mortars.

After gathering the ammunition and waiting for nightfall, his platoons spread into a large formation of successive Vs with the point of the Vs aiming in their direction of travel. Each man wearing night-vision goggles, they walked slowly at first, then more steadily as they once again became familiar with moving at night.

He had placed the bodies of Teller and Rock-ingham in body bags, one of those items in the supply room he'd never planned on using. Then he had Sergeant Spencer's squad load the bodies on the helicopter. He gave grid coordinates to the helicopter pilot and told him to meet his company there after doing some false insertions in other places. They were only moving about five kilometers, but the terrain was eminently more defensible than the valley where the naval base was situated. Zachary had his men lock their duffel bags in one of the Quonset huts, expecting they would never see the clothes or *Playboy* magazines again.

He made the civilians walk, despite much protest. Fraley and the ambassador had argued, but Zachary was in no mood for their bullshit. Zachary sat the ambassador down and told him that he was the commander of the unit, and he was more than welcome to stay there.

"You guys hosed me over, and you hosed over Chuck Ramsey, who is fighting for his life, I'm sure,"

Zach had said.

He wanted nothing to do with the ambassador, the other civilians, and especially Fraley.

"Either you let me make the decisions," Zachary said, "or you can go hump yourself. And the way I see it, if you can't help Ramsey, you can't help me. And that makes you useless." With that, he walked out of the white Quonset hut near the tire pile, threw his ruck on, and led his men into the jungle that rose above Subic Bay. *We will be safer there.*

As they walked, a sliver of the moon smiled wickedly at them from above.

Phase III: The Beltway Shuffle

CHAPTER 48

PENTAGON, WASHINGTON, DC

Colonel Lionel Thompson ran from the National Military Command Center, through a small tunnel of a hallway into the Pentagon E-ring, and burst into the secretary of defense's outer office. The administrative aide stood immediately. Thompson convinced her that he had to talk to the secretary in person and privately immediately. Stone was standing at the door.

"What seems to be the problem, Lionel?" Stone asked his assistant. Thompson was a "fast mover" in the Army and had been assigned as an aide to the secretary of defense. An armor officer, he hated the Pentagon duty but knew that it would add that much more grease to an already-oiled career.

"Sir, we've just gotten word there's been a revolution in the Philippines."

"Come in," he said, putting his arm around Lionel. "What are you telling me? Wait just a second." He picked up his phone, buzzed Fox, and said, "You might want to get in here."

In less than a minute, both Diamond and Fox appeared from a side door into Stone's office. Wordless, they sat in the two leather high-backed chairs as if they were spectators at the theater.

"Sir. Gentlemen," Thompson said, looking at Stone, then at Fox and Diamond. "The Abu Sayyaf rose up across the islands to overthrow the government. It appears they were successful. They

have control of the Presidential Palace and the
television and radio stations. President Cordero is
now in jail. The news on our side is worse, however."
Stone's eyes cut sharply upward.

"Sir. First off, Assistant Secretary Rathburn and a
CIA operator, Matt Garrett, have been taken
hostage, along with one of the pilots."

"Christ," Stone said, sliding into his chair and
placing his face in his hands. He was sitting at his
desk and looked out the window. "What else?"

"It gets worse, sir. A stinger missile or some
rocket-propelled grenades hit the DC Guard
Gulfstream. It blew up, with …"—he hesitated,
almost unable to say it—"with the DACOWITS
committee on it."

Stone looked at Thompson. He had known
almost every one of the women on the committee.
All of them were women who had fought the barriers
of discrimination and had been representing their
country on a mission to help improve the lot of
women in the military. Their loss was unfathomable
to him. "Say what?"

"Yes, sir. There's more." Thompson knew that
bad news was unlike wine, in that it got worse with
age. There was no way to soften the blow of the
news. He just had to say it. He looked down at his
Army trousers, hanging perfectly atop his shoes. His
light green shirt conformed to his muscular frame.
His eyes searched Stone's to determine when he was
ready for the next salvo. It was never easy being the
messenger, who usually got shot, but he had learned
to recognize when to talk and when to let the
moment happen. Stone looked up at him from
behind his glasses.

"The embassy has been overrun. Abu Sayyaf
insurgents killed five of our people there, four
military and one civilian."

Stone grimaced. "Berryman?"

"Sir, Ambassador Berryman flew to safety on the medical evacuation helicopter with four other embassy personnel and two officers from the embassy. We have an infantry rifle company at Subic doing an ammunition guard mission, and apparently they had some men at the embassy being treated for wounds from the attack on their position this morning."

"What?" Fox said loudly from behind Thompson.

"Yes, sir. About eighty insurgents stormed the ammunition location. The company performed well, though, killing seventy and taking ten prisoners. We, um …"—it was hard to say. Thompson had never been in combat, something he was concerned about, but still, to lose a soldier, anybody's solider, was painful—"We lost two soldiers in the fight. One enlisted man was killed at Subic, and an officer, a lieutenant, was killed at the embassy. He jumped off the helicopter and saved the embassy doctor. When he was getting back on, he was shot in the back."

"What the hell are you telling me, Lionel?" Stone screamed, standing up. "Just what in the hell is going on? There's no war in the Philippines! We're fighting in Afghanistan and getting ready to fight in Iraq! This isn't part of the plan!" He cadenced his words, as if Thompson could not understand him. He picked up a glass paperweight with a picture of a bear inside, a gift from a Korean diplomat, and chucked it at the wall.

Thompson was beginning to feel uncomfortable, but he could handle it. He'd never been in a worse situation, but had seen far greater displays of emotion from battalion and brigade commanders over far pettier issues.

"Sir," he said, "there's one more item of information you need."

"What's that, the Abu Sayyaf now has Chinese nukes aimed at us?" he said angrily, firing another shot at the messenger.

"No sir. The ambassador sent a Special Forces team into Mindanao a few days ago. Some Filipino helicopters were supposed to pick them up today, but obviously they did not. No one has heard from the team for four days."

"How did all of this happen, Lionel? Tell me. How did we let this happen?"

"Sir. I just got off the phone with the Pacific Command intelligence guys. They said that a week ago they got the order from us to collect intelligence in the East China Sea. They've been focused like a laser beam on China and Taiwan."

Stone looked **at him** with a dumbfounded expression. He remembered his promise to the Japanese ambassador. And he remembered thinking, *Yeah, that should work.*

"Get me Chairman Sewell," Stone said flatly, reaching for his phone. He dialed and told his wife that he was going to be working late. Waiting for the chairman, he thought to himself: *Bobby old boy, you deserve an Oscar. The Rolling Stones would be proud.*

Fox and Diamond began to shift uncomfortably in their chairs. Fox was dressed in a dark blue suit with a gray silk shirt, while Diamond was wearing a dark gray suit with a blue silk shirt. *Photonegatives,* Stone thought.

"Who authorized all those troop movements to the Philippines?" Fox asked, standing in front of Stone's desk.

"That is depleting our focus on Iraq. Jeopardizing the mission," Diamond said.

"Yes, jeopardizing the mission," Fox added.

"This is a one hand doesn't know what the other is doing thing. I can guarantee it," Stone said angrily.

"We need to get both hands out front where we can see them," Fox said. He held his hands in front of him to emphasize his point.

"Both hands," Diamond added, doing the same as Fox.

To Stone, both men looked like mimes pressing their hands against invisible walls. "Don't worry, guys, it's under control. I've got Central Command bringing me the plan this week."

"We might have to go this spring. Just do it," Fox said. "Get in front of this developing Pacific thing."

"We don't have the munitions," Stone said. "We can't get there from here."

"What we lack in armament we will more than compensate for by surprise," Diamond countered.

"Why are we arguing about this? We all agree on the strategy," Stone said.

"Do we, Bob?"

Stone assessed the two men, still sitting in their chairs. They had just heard that American lives were lost in the Philippines and they knew damn well that the fight in Afghanistan was a slow-motion strategic nightmare.

While the soldiers on the ground were performing magnificently, Stone knew that the strategic window to crush Al Qaeda had slammed shut as the enemy senior leaders escaped through the rugged Hindu Kush. Stone's position all along had been now that 9-11 had occurred, the nation should use the event as a rallying cry to attack Islamic fundamentalism everywhere. Hence, the gambit in the Philippines. It had everything to do with putting pressure on the global extremist network. The threat was so obvious to him. Stone wondered how Fox and Diamond could blindly sit there and ignore the evidence: that Iraq, while important, needed to wait.

"We do. Now if you'll excuse me, I've work to do."

Diamond and Fox followed one another out, and Stone shut the door behind them.

Walking to his desk, he picked up his phone, thinking, *the glider is aloft. Let the winds of chance buffet it and pray for a soft landing.* He dialed Rathburn's number, and frowned when he didn't receive an answer. He was certain the hostage thing was an elaborate plan that Rathburn had hatched. An improvisation, for sure, but a delicious one nonetheless. *Matt Garrett, our number one operator, is a hostage!* Not to worry though. Stone left a message:

"This is Mick leaving a message for Keith. It appears we have satisfaction. Good job. Ring me back straightaway. Cheers."

CHAPTER 49

Stone sat at the head of the table as the usual group shuffled into the conference room on the E-ring in the Pentagon. The chairman of the Joint Chiefs of Staff, each of the service chiefs of staff, the director of the Central Intelligence Agency, and various other high-level political appointees gathered as they feverishly worked through the night on a response.

Stone shook his head at the first slide, which determined that the first priority was to save American lives. The next slide showed actions that had been taken to date.

On Stone's order, Special Operations Command had alerted the Ranger battalion dedicated to quick-reaction force duty, which was the second battalion stationed in Fort Lewis, Washington. C-17 Globemasters were flying into McChord Air Force Base next to Fort Lewis. Likewise, he alerted other elite forces located in Fort Bragg, North Carolina. He gave the Twenty-fifth Infantry Division in Hawaii a warning order to have a brigade combat team ready for deployment in less than twenty-four hours.

Again, on Stone's order, the Air Force chief of staff had alerted the fighter squadron at Andersen Air Force Base in Guam. They were put on strip alert, as there was no clear mission, yet. He ordered the movement of cargo aircraft to bases along the West Coast.

The commandant of the Marine Corps, General

Rolfing, gave the marines in Okinawa the mission to be on their vessels in less than twelve hours, steaming south to a position to be determined. The key was to get them moving. And they would be soon. While Stone also approved this order, Rolfing would have done it anyway. The Marines always marched to the sound of the guns.

The chief of Naval Operations made the critical decision to halt the movement of the supply ship that was a day's steaming time from Subic Bay. If he let it continue, the soldiers might be able to use it for a way out, but it would also be too lucrative a target. It was doubtful, if the insurgents now controlled the small Philippine navy, that the ship could get in unescorted as was initially planned. At Stone's direction, he also put the Fifth Fleet on alert.

The men sat in the "tank," a secret briefing room near the chairman's office in the Pentagon. Available to them was every type of sophisticated communications and monitoring system in the world: secure telephones, secure radios, secure satellite radios, huge television screens that monitored CNN and could pick up foreign stations, and satellite downlinks. The chairman sat in the middle of one of the long sides of the mahogany table. The chiefs of staff surrounded him on either side. Seated across from him was Stone, who spoke first.

"Gentlemen, we have a serious situation on our hands. It is a situation that has gotten out of hand very rapidly. We must get a handle on it ASAP, develop a strategy to recommend to the president, then be able effectively to execute it better than we— well never mind. We need to fix it. I'm pretty sure we don't have a plan for this, so let's figure out how to extract ourselves from it and drive on," Stone said somewhat incoherently.

Chairman Sewell, Stone's military counterpart,

leaned forward and laid out the situation as he saw it. He was an Army four-star general who had risen through the ranks from private. He had attended the University of North Carolina on a ROTC scholarship, where he played right tackle on the football team and had earned the Hughes award for the top ROTC candidate of his year. He had large arms that strained the material of his uniform, looking somewhat awkward. He had gone completely bald, with only gray stubble on each side to remind him that he had ever possessed hair. His face was round, and his jowls hung low like a bulldog's. He had diagonal eyebrows that converged near the bridge of his nose, giving him a sinister look.

He believed strongly in protecting his war fighters and wanted some quick, decisive action to get his young troops out of harm's way. But he knew it would not be that easy.

"The first thing we have to keep in mind is that we have a few personnel that we know of in captivity, Secretary Rathburn, Matt Garrett, and the pilot. Anything we do must be tempered with the realization that it might backfire against them—"

"As far as I'm concerned, that's a primary consideration, but again, it can't be a massive operation," Stone interrupted. *Could Keith Richards really be a hostage?*

"Right," Sewell continued, cutting an annoyed glance at the SecDef. "We've got an A team on Mindanao that's probably about out of gas. They were supposed to be picked up near the City of Cateel yesterday, 1600 Philippine time." As he talked, a lieutenant colonel pointed to a huge map of the Philippines, showing the town of Cateel.

"We've also got a light infantry rifle company at Subic Bay. We think the commander has moved. It was probably a smart idea; we'll see. So basically, we've got three groups of people we have to get, and we don't have any real idea where any of them are. My first inclination is to let Special Ops prepare for the extraction of the hostages. We should be able to get a fix on their location in a couple of days—"

"Couple of days?" Stone questioned.

"Sir, we cannot go get people if we don't know where they are. It's that simple," Sewell shot back, looking Stone directly in his eyes. Stone looked away. *All part of the act.*

"Fred, how soon can you have an expeditionary brigade under way from Okinawa?" he asked General Fred Rolfing, the first black commandant of the Marine Corps. Rolfing looked like a Marine. His hair was cropped tightly to his dark skin. He had a thick, square jaw that sported an eight-centimeter scar he had received in hand-to-hand combat in Vietnam.

"Twelve hours," he said, without flinching. A Marine expeditionary brigade (MEB) included an air attack team, a regimental landing group, and its own organic service support group. It was a completely self-sufficient battle group capable of conducting sustained operations. The Marine aircraft group of the MEB included twenty AV-8B Harrier fighter aircraft, twenty-four F/A-18 fighter aircraft, and over seventy cargo helicopters. The ground element consisted of seventeen tanks and three infantry battalions. The entire MEB nearly had the firepower equivalent of an Army infantry division. "But it will take away from our Iraq prep. Those guys are getting under way for the Middle East."

Stone thought that was a good comment. Iraq prep. It was all about Iraq prep, wasn't it?

He looked at Dick Diamond and Saul Fox. With every mention of this unit or that unit being possibly diverted away from "Iraq prep," both Diamond and Fox appeared visibly to take a body blow, like a fastball to the stomach.

To avoiding protesting too much, Stone let Sewell take the lead.

"So our first move is to get people ready. Tad, you've got the Rangers ready go right now, correct?" Sewell asked. General Tad Murphy was the new Special Operations commander. He had been in the position for less than a year and had established himself well. But he knew a simple Ranger mission would not get the job done. Nor would a Marine expeditionary brigade. They needed some good intelligence and they needed to be able to talk to someone in authority, whoever it might be.

"Yes, sir. But let me say something," Murphy said. The others looked at him. It was nearly 0300 hours, and everyone was tired. No one was in the mood for any pontificating.

"Sir," he said looking at Stone, "I have to say that this looks like the next front in the GWOT. This Iraq thing will take hundreds of thousands of soldiers to do it right, so we will have to determine what the main effort is," Murphy continued.

Fox coughed, "That's preposterous, General."

Stone rubbed his face. *Hmm, how to play this one? Side with my deputy or encourage the counterplan?* Stone was reveling in the discourse and determined he should remain consistent.

"Let me make one thing clear, everyone. Iraq is a go. So we have to plan around it. Anyone who can't live with that can go find another job," Stone said.

Two Oscars in one day, Stone thought. *Iraq is a go! Genius.* By so strongly arguing for the affirmative, a simple debating technique, he was certain that someone would begin to harden their position against going to Iraq, the counterplan. If that failed, well, Wood and Watts, the bass and lead guitarists, would certainly come to the rescue.

And the real problem, Stone thought, was that the best way to kill a venomous snake was to cut off its head. By shifting focus to Iraq, Stone believed America's hand was releasing the viselike grip on the neck of the viper and sliding along the scaly abdomen, opening the possibility for another fanged attack.

But thankfully, the Rolling Stones had a solution for this little problem, and it hadn't cost the American taxpayer a dime.

Better than Iran-Contra!

CHAPTER 50

GREENE COUNTY, VIRGINIA

Karen Garrett, Matt's and Zachary's sister, had been calling the Department of Defense, the Central Intelligence Agency, and her congressman for the last twenty-four hours, but only ran into the usual bureaucratic nightmare. Nobody could tell her the location of either of her brothers. Not only because they did not know, but also because everything was "classified."

Angry and frustrated, she had not slept for almost two days. Their mother had passed away, and the funeral was scheduled for that day. They really could not put it off any longer. She reported to her father, almost shamefully, that nobody could locate his two sons. Her father looked away, sad. "Bring the boys home," was all he said, then walked away.

Karen turned her coffee cup in her hand, looking out the window, recalling the events of the past few days. With the help of the bourbon, she had not cried, but her eyes remained moist, ready to gush whenever the switch flipped. She watched curiously as a sedan pitched and rocked, slowly making its way to the house. By then she could see some writing on the door of the car.

Usually, uninvited visitors in that part of the country did not bring good news. Had she paid the taxes this month, she wondered? Was she behind on her fertilizer payments? As the car parked in the gravel lot to the front of the wooden porch, she read the words: U.S. GOVERNMENT on its side. The car stopped, and she watched the blond woman step out of the driver's seat. She was wearing a nice blue dress with high heels. Karen checked her own visage in the hallway mirror as she stood. Trademark ponytail yanked into a knot revealing a fresh, sans-makeup look.

The funeral was not for another two hours. What could she be doing here? And who was she? She let the woman knock on the door.

Walking to the door, she pondered what bad news the woman would bring. Her mother was dead, her father was ill, and she had been in her room crying for two days. Where she got her strength, she did not know. But it seemed to grow with each passing moment. For some reason she knew she could hold on. Opening the door, she stared at the mountains behind the woman's pale hair.

She could feel their strength building inside her, as if her mother's passing had left something tangible in her character; another I-beam. She would need it.

"Hi. I'm Meredith," she said, seeing Karen in person for the first time. "You must be Karen." Meredith looked at Karen's clean face, so fresh and pure. Her eyes were penetrating, like they knew what she was thinking.

"That's right," Karen said, blankly, not making a connection. She held the door open with one hand, her body blocking the entrance to the wooden foyer.

"Karen, may I come in for a second? I've driven down from DC."

"No. Let's sit on the porch," she said, closing the door behind her, as if to protect what remained of her family from the intruder. The porch was a typical farmhouse addition. The roof hung over a high wooden structure that had old metal chairs that would rock if one leaned back in them hard enough. The red bricks from the house were stained with red clay. She let the screen door slam behind her and walked over to a metal chair, taking a seat.

"I'm sorry, Meredith, did you say?" She cupped her hands on her knees. "The funeral's not for another two hours—"

"I'm so sorry for the loss of your mother," Meredith responded, covering her mouth with her hands. She had been traveling for the past two days on her return from Palau. A secretary had told her that Matt's mother had died and that a woman was trying to get in touch with him for the funeral.

Her first stop, though, had been at the home of Chief Warrant Officer Ron Peterson outside of Seattle, Washington. She accompanied the casualty-assistance team on their grim notification duties and passed Ron's identification tags to his wife, as she had promised Matt. Now, having just arrived on the East Coast, Meredith was exhausted, but decided to travel to the farm, two hours away, immediately, and inform the Garrett family of the situation.

"Karen. I have some information on Matt and Zachary," Meredith started.

"Yes," Karen said, eyes darting up quickly, "tell me."

"Both of your brothers are in the Philippines. We have communications with Zachary, who is in the jungle with his company. They have been fighting, but he is fine. Matt," she sighed, "Matt …" She hesitated again.

"What's happened to him?" Karen screamed as she stood and approached Meredith dangerously.

"Karen, Matt's been taken hostage by some Filipino rebels," she said, finally.

"Oh my God. Oh my God," she screamed. "My family. What's happening to my family?" Meredith stood and hugged her, dropping her purse on the wooden porch. Karen was limp in her arms and actually pushing away from the bearer of bad news.

Meredith's clutch was too tight, though, and they both were crying.

"We'll get him back. He's special, I know." Karen hugged Meredith back, more from lack of strength than for any other reason. The dam of stoicism burst under the relentless pressure. Even the bourbon couldn't help. The news had sapped her strength the way the sun sucked the life from a man stranded in the desert. She felt isolated, with nowhere to turn, so she held on to Meredith for no particular reason. She could not show her father such emotions. She had to be strong for him.

But her father watched from the field. He saw the two hugging on the porch and had heard her scream. Once again, he dropped his hoe, took a knee, and grabbed a fistful of dirt, squeezing tightly, trying to wrench one more drop of good fortune. He knew that something was badly wrong and only wanted to make it right. His family had toiled hard for decades. They had served their country better than most.

Looking at the loose, red dirt in his hand, he prayed for the safe return of his boys. "Bring the boys home," he said, loudly and with passion. "Bring the boys home!" he screamed at the heavens, arms stretched high reaching toward the God he knew and loved.

Karen retrieved her father, and they moved inside to the parlor, as they still called it in the Garrett house. Karen had started to fix coffee, but Meredith quickly took over, floating around the kitchen as if she had lived there forever. Soon she came out with a tray of coffee and hot tea. The Garrett family drank heartily, warming their dank spirits. Meredith repeated the story, this time with less emotion on both sides. She said that the Departments of State and Defense were doing everything they could to get a handle on the situation. Meredith tried to be positive, talking up the actions of Zachary's

company. Word had gotten back to the Defense
Department that he and his soldiers had acted
bravely, she told them.

"I expected nothing less," Mr. Garrett said,
proudly.

Then Meredith told them about the airplane and
how lucky Matt was to be alive. She choked on her
words when she said it, but she was looking for
something positive. It had backfired, though, only
serving to underscore the gravity of the situation.

Meredith stayed with the family that day,
attending the funeral and meeting many of the fine
people of Stanardsville, who had always relied so
heavily on Karen and the rest of the Garrett family.
They reminded her so much of her own family and
friends from her part of Virginia. The accent was the
same: Elizabethan English. They all pronounced
their "ou" words with the same throaty mountain
drawl. The "u" was never silent. "House" became a
two-syllable word, stressing the long "u."

It seemed that everyone from town came to the
funeral. The Reverend Early arrived beforehand and
consoled Karen and her father. He delivered a warm
and powerful eulogy, describing their mother as a
woman of the soil. Recalling her family tradition
throughout the county, he quoted from Romans 11:
"If the root is holy, so are the branches."

"Elizabeth Garrett was a loving and caring
person," he had said. "Someone who would give a
stranger water if he was thirsty, someone who would
feed a starving man, someone who provided for her
family without complaint. She was holy, and her life
produced three holy "branches," two of which are
not here. She was a rock, and the Blue Ridge formed
around her; indeed this community formed around
her. And now she returns to the soil that sustained
her, the dirt she had tilled and caressed."

They attended church that afternoon, as well. It

was a small brick structure. The four of them were the only ones there. They sat in a row and prayed for Zachary and Matt and all of the other soldiers in the Philippines as well as those deployed in Kuwait and Afghanistan. It was hard, but they all had faith. Then Meredith helped cook for all of the well-wishers who stayed after the funeral and visited with the family. Many people stayed late into the evening, and she enjoyed the company, but the pall of Matt's and Zachary's absences hung over the room like a deadly fog. No one could concentrate.

After the mourners departed, Meredith went out to her car and changed back into the pair of sandals she had driven down in. There were cups and dishes everywhere, and Karen looked at Meredith, noting her change in footwear, and plopped onto the sofa.

"Thanks, Meredith. You didn't have to do all of this."

"Why don't you just go to bed," Meredith said, holding an armful of plates.

"No. Just leave it. I'll get it later. I think I'm gonna go sit on the porch for a while," Karen said in an exhausted voice.

"Okay But I want to help, so just accept the fact that I'm gonna do this," Meredith said. Karen looked at her and smiled for the first time in days. There was nothing self-serving about Meredith. She was all give and no take. She was just like Karen. Karen walked up the stairs, then came back down.

"Here," she said, tossing Meredith a pair of blue jeans and an old flannel shirt. "You'll be more comfortable in these."

"Thank you, Lord," Meredith said, looking skyward. "My first prayer of the day has been answered." The two women laughed, but it was a fleeting moment, gone like a rabbit into the bush. Nonetheless, Meredith changed into the more comfortable clothes, noticing that they fit rather well.

Karen walked onto the porch and sat on the steps while Meredith busily cleaned the rest of the dishes. When Meredith was done putting them away, she walked into the cool mountain air, letting the screen door slam against the door frame. Karen looked up.

"Sorry," Meredith said.

"No bother. Daddy's a sound sleeper," Karen replied. Meredith sat on the steps next to Karen. Two women cut from the same cloth. Neither knew the depths of the Depression or world wars that their parents had experienced, but they recognized that life was polarizing. They maintained a source and sense of idealism, the lure of the majestic Blue Ridge, while having the grit to perform the tasks at hand. They were driven by lofty ideals but not stymied by the idealism.

"What're you thinking about?" Meredith asked. She could see lights in the small town of Stanardsville about a mile to the south.

"I want my brothers back," she said softly, her voice floating into the night. Crickets chimed rhythmically. Two bullfrogs barked at each other in the pond.

"I want them back too," Meredith said, quietly. She had known Matt for one day, had never met Zachary and yet, strangely, she felt bonded to them. She found Matt to be one of the most interesting people she had met, and she wasn't sure why. Perhaps there was a bit of electricity there when he had woken up and asked her if she was one of the virgins. She smiled at the thought.

They watched the stars blink at them from the heavens and hoped that the Man in charge up there would be good to them. They believed in so many things. They had faith in God. They believed in their country, and they believed that people were basically good.

"Thanks for all your help today. You really made a difference during a difficult time," Karen said. After a pause, she said, "You see that light just beneath the moon?"

Meredith looked, and said, "I think so."

"It's blinking, sort of."

"Yeah. I see it," Meredith said, leaning over to gain Karen's perspective, her hair falling across Karen's shoulder.

"I read somewhere, can't remember now, that you could see satellites in the sky. Never believed it, but that doesn't look like a star, and it sure isn't an airplane," Karen said. Meredith didn't respond. She just watched the dark sky flutter with millions of lights. She looked at Karen, still fixed on the bright moving object. Meredith felt a kinship to her. She was drawn to her strength. A man and a set of circumstances had brought them together.

"You can sleep in Matt's old room," Karen said. "You shouldn't drive back tonight. His old twin bed is still in there."

"Thanks. That's sweet," Meredith said, smiling and remembering her and Matt's goofy conversation in Palau. It was unusual because Matt had been on heavy doses of morphine and Percocet. Rathburn had briefly joined them poolside and was playing the Rolling Stones' "Beast of Burden" on his iPod loud enough for them to hear.

"You, okay?" Karen asked.

"Just thinking of Matt for some reason," Meredith said.

"He's like that, Matt is. Whatever you do, don't get hooked on him, he's trouble."

Meredith smiled. She could see that in him, but there was something …

"Thanks for the clothes," she said, as they both stood and walked up the stairs. They hugged one another before retiring to their separate rooms.

Meredith was lost in her thoughts, and Karen just needed to sleep.

Sitting on Matt's old bed, she studied the room. Half of it had an angled ceiling from the A-frame. The other half was flat. Pictures of Zachary and Matt hung on the knotty pine wall. Other than the bed with cowboy-and-Indian sheets, there were three boxes in the room. They stood stacked on the tongue-in-groove floor. She stood and looked in the top box, pulling back the cardboard flap. She saw a manila folder inside, labeled: WHAT IS GOING ON?!

She took the folder and sat back on the bed, opening it. Several pages of yellow legal paper were folded so they would fit in the undersized folder. Beneath them was a stapled packet of about fifteen pages, once again labeled: WHAT IS GOING ON. Though this time there was no question mark or exclamation point. "Huh," she said to herself as she began reading.

Iraq and Afghanistan … I just don't understand. We had just commandeered several mules from a local farmer and took the path just north of Torkum gate. We knew we were in Pakistan, but we had a solid lead on two specific persons of interest, shall we say. Then I've got the shot. Then someone is screaming at me denying my kill chain. Next thing we know a JDAM lands closer to us than to the AQ and we get the call on sat phone ordering us to turn around and come back. Less than two days later my team is in Iraq, and I'm on my way to the U.S. for a makeover to chase some phantom Predators in China. What the hell is going on?

My thought is that these political appointees have their head so far up their asses they can't see straight. We've got a clear mission in Afghanistan. With no forces to block the passes, though, as we requested, well, the big fish have trickled away downstream. This is personal for me, and it's personal for the country. The one time the nation has asked for a head on a platter and we can't deliver. Bin Laden and his cronies dealt us a sucker punch and we must destroy them.

Where will this lead? There's no question about the rightness of killing Saddam, but it's a tougher problem than anyone can imagine. Hell, give me the mission and I'll go do it. There is no question that a democratic Iraq may be a game-changing entity in the Middle East. Who wouldn't want that? But is it feasible? They should take a look at the Balkans and all the warring factions there to see what might be in store for a fractured Iraq. Post–Cold War Yugoslavia is a good model to think about, but Iraq will be far more kinetic. One thing is for certain; we are treating Afghanistan and Al Qaeda as an economy of force mission. Maybe that's the right thing to do, but I can't see how.

Even more, what happens if we get locked into major combat in Iraq and another country becomes a sudden threat? We will be caught flat-footed, for sure. Take a look at any of the regional contingencies: China-Taiwan; North Korea-South Korea; Iran-any neighbor; Russia-Georgia or any of its breakaway republics and there are other possibilities. The world is short on resources and long on demand. Water and oil will drive the next decade's social and economic policies. What happens if a nation decides it must act for survival despite its impact on economies around its region or around the globe?

Meredith dropped the paper in her lap and put her fingers to her temples. *My God, what is he saying?*

She read on. Matt delineated several Pacific Rim regional threats, but drifted back to Islamic radicalism. He highlighted the Abu Sayyaf insurgent factions that were struggling for help, ripe for outside support. While philosophically aligned with Bin

Laden, the Abu Sayyaf's need for resources outstripped Al Qaeda's ability to provide, Matt argued.

She felt close to Matt reading his paper. Obvious to her, these were just thoughts typed into a computer through stream of consciousness. She closed the folder and sat still, looking through the window into the night. She turned off the light, still thinking, and let the darkness settle over her like a blanket.

As she drifted off to sleep, in her mind a hawk circled, looking for prey. As her thinking processes shut down, there it was. Its talons clutched the rabbit, and her subconscious thought: *It cannot be possible.*

CHAPTER 51

The following morning, Meredith ate the good breakfast that Karen made for her, after which she printed out a MapQuest set of directions to the University of Virginia library. She sped down Route 29 into the heart of Charlottesville and found the library after a few wrong turns.

Once she was parked and now in range of a decent cell tower, Meredith powered up her Blackberry, read her messages, and stared at the library for a minute.

Energized, she barged in, showing the monitor her Department of Defense badge and asked if there was an office with a fax machine. Getting a good look at the blonde official, the student manager gladly let her use the librarian's office. Meredith threw off her coat, still wearing Karen's jeans and flannel shirt. She then walked quickly to the reference and periodical sections, spending nearly thirty minutes collecting country reports and studies on Japan and the Philippines. Then she punched up Google and she found the British "Economist Intelligence Unit" country reports to be the most insightful and comprehensive.

She spun the mouse until the Japanese trade figures appeared. When she had read Matt's monograph, she had not thought of the Philippines as an actor, but as a target. It was resource rich but infrastructure poor. It was a rabbit with no hole to hide.

And Japan was a potential hawk. Circling, starving, resource-poor Japan; its wings spread high into the stratosphere of advanced nations, yet it had little bounty within its own territory.

She studied the figures. Trade was declining with Europe and the U.S. Next, she looked at the demographics. There would be a manpower shortage in Japan in a couple of years. She looked at the energy reports. Japan's coal production had fallen, and its alternative sources program had reached the point of diminishing returns. Gas prices were already exorbitant across the country. She read the EIU report that asserted that Prime Minister Mizuzawa was tiring of American claims of unfair play. Could she have stumbled onto something?

She searched the documents, looking for a link between Japan and the Philippines. The revolution had happened, she knew that. She also knew that about two years ago, the Abu Sayyaf had announced their alignment with Al Qaeda, hoping to reach into Bin Laden's deep pockets. She turned away from the computer and reached under the stack of books and papers, grabbing country reports from two years back. Tucking her hair behind both ears, she dug in. She read agricultural reports, manufacturing reports, trade figures, imports, exports. Nothing seemed unusual.

Then she saw it.

Buried in a "Recent Developments" paragraph of the two-year-old EIU report, she found the sentence, "Surprisingly, Japan has invested in construction on the island of Mindanao in the Philippines. That the Japanese would construct mines and mineral-gathering facilities on the island, which is riddled with Al Qaeda sympathizers, demonstrates the desperate lengths to which they will go to secure resources for their economy."

That was the link, but what did it mean? Maybe they were just getting resources. *Think, Meredith, think.* She stared at the wall, searching her mind for a clue. How would they transport the stuff? On ships. What kind of ships?

She picked up the phone and called her office in the Pentagon. Mark Russell, a young intern, answered the phone. Perfect.

"Mark. Listen. I want you to go to the guys at the Philippine desk and get reports for all shipping activity out of Mindanao. I need you to fax it to me in ten minutes," Meredith demanded. She gave him the number.

"Okay. But they're pretty busy with this current sit—"

"Listen!" she said loudly, "this current situation may be bigger than we think. Now do it. And tell them that Stone wants it."

"Yes, ma'am." She hung up the phone. It was not a total lie. If she could prove a link between Japan and the Philippines, she would try to brief Stone that afternoon. The implications of fighting an insurgency, if that was what her country was going to do, would be vastly different if Japan was supporting the rebels for their own purposes. How had they gotten all the new weapons? How had they grown so fast in the past two years?

Five minutes later, the fax machine jumped to life and began to spit out pages with the past year's worth of shipping data from Davao City and Polomoloc, the two major port cities on Mindanao. She stacked them on the desk, cluttered with open books turned upside down to mark pages.

It was monotonous, looking at the figures of ships and their names and the cargo that they hauled. The only Japanese ships she could identify that went into either port were some taking in consumer goods for the Filipinos, several ships carrying timber back to Japan, and ten oil tankers. Oil tankers? She checked the oil export figures for the Philippines. *They don't export oil to Japan!*

She called Mark back and asked him for some tracking data on the ten Japanese oil tankers that had left Davao City in the past six months. Once again the fax machine whirred to life.

Those ships never off-loaded any cargo in Japan! They entered Davao City empty and left with their hulls deep in the water, the reports read. It looked like a routine oil pickup. While there might be oil reserves in Mindanao, the Philippine government had not invested any infrastructure in either finding or pumping the oil.

By a process of elimination, she came to the conclusion that there were ten, possibly eleven, Japanese ships somewhere in the Pacific with something other than oil as cargo. She also surmised that whatever the Japanese had constructed, they were not gathering minerals. The mineral export-and-import data remained the same after the Japanese did the construction in Mindanao.

She also noticed that the EIU reported that Japanese defense spending remained the same as a percentage of gross national product. But, she noticed that overall government spending had increased without accounting for the rise anywhere in any other line item.

Convinced something was amiss, she gathered her faxes, purse, and coat, and sped out the door.

CHAPTER 52

PENTAGON, WASHINGTON, DC

Secretary Stone pulled a rumpled pack of Camels from his top desk drawer and shook it until two cigarettes revealed their crushed filters. He had been smoking like a fiend since the beginning of the crisis. Grabbing one butt with his large, fleshy fingers, Stone stuffed the white stick in his mouth and lit it with a shaky hand.

Coughing smoke, he said, "It's a different world, this post-Nine-eleven thing, you know?"

"Yes, I know," Kaitachi responded, watching the smoke billow from Stone's rotund face. "But we need your help. Not only with the Philippines, and the China situation, as you might suspect, but with Korea as well—"

"What the hell does Korea have to do with this?" Stone retorted, the cigarette jumping wildly in his mouth.

"The North is playing with nuclear weapons and, we believe, is trafficking nuclear materials. How would it look for North Korea to be passing nuclear weapons to our enemies? And with Islamic fundamentalism threatening our sea-lanes, we now feel threats on all of our borders, so to speak," Kaitachi said.

Stone looked at the other man, Takishi. *This should be good!*

"Mister Secretary, on behalf of Prime Minister Mizuzawa, I must also convey our deep concerns over the situation in Korea. He believes, rightfully so, that both countries on the Korean peninsula pose a significant threat to Japan. And we both know that we can have no satisfaction that way," Takishi said.

Diamond and Fox listened intently as Stone entertained the Japanese delegation. Fox's years as an academic had prepared him for his vaunted position as the Deputy Secretary. That morning he sat quietly in Stone's office, listening to a new Japanese argue about issues in the Pacific.

Diamond and Fox were beyond concerned. With the nagging issue in the Pacific, their theories and musings about Iraq might not come to fruition, their quest for eternal fame left unrealized.

"What are you talking about?" Stone responded. "We're all part of the United Nations. We won't let that happen anymore. Even with everything going on in Iraq and Afghanistan, we won't let it happen, I'm telling you." As Stone spoke, Kaitachi and Takishi looked at each other with reassuring eyes.

"One final protest over Korea—"

"Why the hell are you so concerned about Korea all of a sudden?" Stone demanded, his chin rattling around his neck and growing red where his shirt collar chafed. He looked at Diamond and Fox and shook his head. "Can you believe these guys?"

"It is not a new concern of ours, and we have reason to believe China may be orchestrating the events," Takishi said. He crossed his long legs as he spoke and used his hands to animate his point.

"The Japanese people are beginning to feel increasingly threatened and confined. Almost surrounded, you might say. Without your help, we feel the region may grow unstable," Takishi continued, doing nothing more than creating white noise. This scene was all being orchestrated by the dumb-as-a-fox Stone.

Stone lit another cigarette and thought for a

moment, then said, "Look, we've got hostages to get out of the Philippines, then we're off to Iraq. We don't have time to worry about some back-burner problem of yours."

"We can help with your hostage situation," Takishi said. Kaitachi let the Prime Minister's representative continue. "We have established contact with Commander Talbosa, the senior Abu Sayyaf commander, and can arrange for all Western and freedom-seeking peoples to depart the country by way of Subic Bay Naval Base."

Stone leaned forward, acting almost jubilant, as if the albatross that had nested on his neck had flown out of the window and across the brown waters of the Potomac.

"Are you serious? Why the hell didn't you mention that first?" Stone said, smiling.

"This would be huge," Fox said, entering the conversation for the first time.

"Timely," Diamond concurred.

"Yes, timely," Fox added.

Takishi and Kaitachi exchanged knowing glances; their approach was having the proper effect.

"Wait," Stone said, sitting back in his leather chair, suspecting something. "What's it going to cost us? What's the trade-off?"

"Talbosa simply wants a guarantee of no American intervention in exchange for allowing anyone who wants to leave the country. He sees this as a domestic situation and claims there is no threat to United States' interests. Of course, we have tacked on our interest in the shipping lanes to the negotiations," Takishi said.

"That sounds too easy," Stone said. He was really thinking: *That's not part of the script. American intervention is the entire purpose, you moron, Charlie Watts.*

"It may be. We are still highly concerned about

our shipping lanes, and as I mentioned earlier, all of the other threats we perceive," Takishi said, increasing the level of static.

"Yeah, okay," Stone responded, confused. "One thing at a time." *Is Watts double-crossing me?*

"Of course. We need to close the deal with Talbosa, secretly. Give us a day, then you will need to start sending airplanes into Subic Bay and arranging for the withdrawal of your people. Talbosa has indicated he will give you two days," Takishi said.

"Two days!" Stone shouted.

"Talbosa was adamant. He will not reconsider. Better two days than none," Takishi said flatly.

Kaitachi and Takishi stood, straightened their pants and coats, and bowed slightly toward Stone, who crushed a smoking butt into the ashtray and followed the two men to the door.

"At a later time, we will discuss our concerns about Korea and China," Kaitachi said as the two men walked past the administrative assistant and a disheveled-looking blonde clutching a stack of papers and books to her breast.

"Well, I don't know what to tell you about Korea. They are our allies and yours too, I might add. I mean we all want satisfaction, don't we?" he said, looking at Takishi

"That we do," Takishi replied. "But we all have our beasts of burden."

The two men departed, and Stone reentered his office as Fox commented, "I think we can see our way through this, Bob. We get the hostages back and evacuate the Philippines, then we continue to steam toward Iraq. We can't let Saddam think that we are weak. Plus, Talbosa's demand gets us off the hook. We'd love to send in more troops, but hey, we can't." Fox mocked himself, shrugging his shoulders as if he were helpless.

Stone looked at the diminutive man and said, "You know, Saul, I think you're right. I just hope this thing in the Philippines doesn't get any worse."

Diamond leveled his judgmental eyes upon Stone and asked, "Are we protesting too much, Bob?"

"Why are you saying this to me?"

"We just believe that this situation in the Philippines seems a bit, how shall we say …" Diamond said, looking at Fox, who finished the sentence for him, "… contrived."

"Well, call whoever contrived it and tell him to turn it off, so I can get some sleep at night," Stone retorted angrily.

Diamond and Fox stood in unison and began to exit through the side door into Fox's office. Diamond stopped, turned around, and said, "What is it that gathers no moss?"

Stone watched the two men depart and stood there dumbfounded.

Had he been compromised? Or was Diamond picking up on his code with Takishi and simply toying with him? Possibly warning him?

His intercom buzzed, and his secretary said, "Sir, I think you'll want to see Miss Morris."

CHAPTER 53

The secretary of defense's administrative assistant, whom Meredith knew, looked at her with a raised eyebrow as the two Japanese men exited. She was holding her materials in one hand, her coat and purse in the other. She looked quite the country bumpkin, she knew, in the blue jeans and flannel shirt. She looked up and saw Stone open his office door.

Two Japanese men stepped out, smiled, and gave her an awkward glance. The three men shook hands, and the two Japanese departed. One of the men looked at Meredith lustfully, his eyes undressing her with the evil look of a hyena sensing carrion.

She heard an awkward exchange about getting satisfaction and beasts of burden and watched the SecDef reenter his office.

"Sir, I just need a couple of minutes about Secretary Rathburn," she said.

He held up a hand and closed his door behind him. She turned to Latisha White, the secretary, and mouthed the word, "Please."

"You come dressed like that, it must be important," Latisha said. She buzzed the secretary, and a few minutes later he reappeared, asking, "You are?"

"I'm Mr. Rathburn's assistant, Meredith Morris. I need to talk to you." The urgency in her voice convinced Stone to give her a standing audience just inside his closed door. "Sir, I think we've got a concern over this entire revolution—" she was nervous. Her words were not working.

"Of course we're concerned. Now if you'll let me get on with the business of resolving this crisis—"

"No. Please. I've done some research. I think Japan is behind this whole thing. They're providing weapons—"

"What!" Stone screamed. He had enough. "I'll have you know that the Japanese ambassador just came in here and offered to solve the entire affair for us in the next two days without firing a shot."

She was confused. Why would they do that? There had to be a motive. They would never offer to do such a thing. It was unprecedented.

"It's a trick!" she said, holding up her hand.

"Get out!" he exclaimed, but then held her shoulder and said, "Wait."

He walked over to the intercom and said to Latisha, "I'll be receiving a briefing from Ms. Morris for the next fifteen minutes. Can you please hold all calls and readjust my schedule accordingly. He looked at Meredith and hissed with a sideways glance, "First, I want to know about Keith, uh, Secretary Rathburn. When did you last see him?"

Keith? Meredith wondered. *Rathburn's first name is Bart.*

"Sir, I put him on the Gulfstream in Palau hours before they landed in Manila. I should have been on that plane but the DACOWITS group trumped me." Her voice trailed off as she considered the possibility that she could have been killed in Manila.

"So, we don't know for sure that he's captured," Stone said.

"I think that's established, sir. The rebels have contacted us with demands. We've seen grainy photos taken with cell phones. I think it's true."

She watched Stone consider her comments and nod, indicating she should continue. So, she proceeded to give Stone her analysis and the reasoning behind it. Stone admitted that she had uncovered something, but he was so confused by Takishi's visit that he was having a hard time meshing Meredith's bold analysis with what he actually knew.

"There certainly seem to be some inconsistencies, but why would they offer to resolve the issue for us?" he asked.

"How did he say he was going to do it?" she countered.

"He said they could deal with Commander Talbosa and get our people out of there. If he can do it, I don't care what he's got up his sleeve," Stone said, flatly.

"Unless it's nuclear weapons," she replied, trying to scare him. He stared at her.

"Not possible," he said. "Their constitution prevents any production of nuclear or offensive weapons. I'm sure it's just a snafu in the shipping log."

Frustrated, she dropped her head on his conference table and stretched her fingers out as if to choke somebody.

"Do we know for a fact what's on those ships?"

"I don't need to know. The Japanese have been a good and faithful ally for almost sixty years," he said.

"Because they needed us," she replied. "Before that, Americans were dying because they bombed the hell out of Pearl Harbor with no warning. Can't you see it?"

She slammed her fist into his conference table.

"It's the perfect crime. They start the revolution. Then they ask us to back down while they handle it. Next thing you know, they own the Philippines." She had not come to that conclusion until then. It was so obvious, though. Especially after reading Matt's paper, it all made sense.

"That's preposterous," Stone said. As the notion

took hold, however, Stone thought, *Holy shit.*

"Sir, you okay?"

"Anything else, Meredith?" Stone asked without emotion.

"No, sir," she said, looking away and grabbing her materials. She walked out of the office and passed Latisha, whom she thanked.

Meredith trudged to her office, where she thanked Mark for his quick response earlier that afternoon. The office was a zoo, everybody working hard on the crisis. She guessed that it was good news if the Japanese ambassador could get the Americans out of the Philippines. Then the U.S. could wash its hands of the entire ordeal.

But she knew nothing was ever that simple.

CHAPTER 54

Meredith walked into Rathburn's office and sat down at his desk. There was the usual assortment of photos of the political appointee with various administration dignitaries as well as foreign leaders.

She picked up one framed picture of Rathburn with his wife and two boys. They were leaning together, all dressed in white, with the chrome stanchion of a sailboat behind them. The smooth waters reflected in the picture made her believe that the photo had probably been taken while they were sailing on the Chesapeake Bay.

She sighed and twirled around in the chair, looking through the yellowish tinted window.

She thought about Japan, the Philippines, Iraq, and Afghanistan. What did they all have in common?

Nothing. *So separate them,* she thought to herself. *First came Afghanistan, and now this weird, almost myopic drive to get into Iraq. The country wants to kick some ass, so they look primed for a good ass kicking,* she thought. *Not enough juice to squeeze out of Afghanistan to satiate the appetite.*

"Enough for what?" she whispered.

And now there is this Philippine revolution, uprising really. So, where did that come from? Did our intelligence not see this coming?

She remembered her discussion with Matt and everything he had told her about Japanese soldiers on the island of Mindanao. She coupled that information with her newfound intelligence about the ten missing ships.

Something was out there floating around, and she thought she had it nailed. Japan was going to be the aggressor somewhere, and the Philippines made sense to her.

But why would they start a war just so they could fight it? How could they be that confident that America would not intervene in a significant way?

Unless they had assurances.

She tapped her finger against her lip, thinking. Chess moves. Everything was choreographed, orchestrated, she determined.

But who was doing it?

Everyone knew that that troll Fox and self-aggrandizing Diamond were poking and prodding their way to get everyone hooked into Iraq. There was no question about their intentions.

But was there a countermovement? Were there people in the U.S. government who believed that going into Iraq was *off the mark*?

She knew that Stone had neoconservative leanings but was very much his own man when it came to decision making. Meredith also knew that she couldn't pretend to know the Byzantine machinations of decision making within the Pentagon or even the White House.

Yet, she did understand that sometimes frenzy and momentum became currents too swift to fight lest you drown trying to swim against the tide. *And so perhaps,* she thought, tapping her lip, *just perhaps there were some folks trying to do what they considered to be a good deed.*

Stop a war in Iraq by starting one in the Philippines.

The more she thought about it, the more sense it made.

CHAPTER 55

Meredith waited until everyone had departed for the day, walked through the outer cubicles and offices one time, then reentered Rathburn's office.

Dead men tell no lies, she thought. Meredith immediately scolded herself. *He's not dead.*

Yet.

She tried to stop herself, but couldn't prevent the sinking feeling that her boss was either dead or about to be killed.

She wandered around Rathburn's E-ring lair, where he had worked for the past three months as the newly appointed assistant secretary of defense for international affairs. Typically an impotent position, Rathburn had seemed unusually powerful and connected in his beginning days with the Department of Defense.

What were his connections? she wondered. He had been a professor at Georgetown University's National Security Studies Program and was woven tightly with the party leadership that had risen to power. What gave him that link?

Meredith, just over thirty, had always wondered how powerful men achieved their status. There were worlds that she could simply not imagine, and even the idea of taking a simple trip to Palau with Rathburn had excited her beyond belief. To approach the source of importance and authority was akin to discovering truth. It was, she thought, like reaching out with her hand to touch Mother Teresa. Would some of the goodness rub off? Could she wave her hands over the wafting fumes of power, inhaling them, and experience the sensation herself? Achieve the status?

Rathburn had somehow drunk the elixir and one morning found himself in position to influence world events via his connection to the secretary of defense.

She picked up a football signed by all of the Washington Redskins. Next to it was a large machete given to him by a Gurkha soldier in Nepal. Other mementoes were scattered on several bookshelves and display tables.

She studied the diplomas on the wall for the first time as she spun the football in her hands the way a wide receiver might as he shot the breeze with the quarterback. She had seen the diplomas before, of course, but had never really read them. Rathburn had earned a Harvard undergraduate degree with a major in economics; a Harvard MBA; and a Princeton Ph.D. in political economy. *Interesting,* she thought. *Mostly a finance background.*

I guess that is what makes the world turn, she mused.

She sat at his computer and contemplated what she was about to do. Meredith had thought at length that day after her meeting with Stone. She had gone for a run around the Washington Monument from the Pentagon and during that exercise she began thinking about the comments she'd heard from the Japanese man leaving Stone's office. The Japanese emissary had spoken in perfect English, as if *he* had attended Harvard.

What was the reference to "Beasts of Burden?" Sure, she knew it was a famous *Rolling Stones'* song, but could it have been something else? Then, Stone's preceding comment about getting satisfaction on one hand seemed innocuous enough, while on the other hand, when coupled with the "Beasts of Burden" comment, could have been some kind of code.

Speaking of codes, she thought, she pulled out the three-by-five card she'd had the computer technician give her months ago. Rathburn was always forgetting his password and finally the overworked twenty-two-year-old jotted on the card the secret and regular computer code words for access to Rathburn's computer.

"Don't tell anyone. I'll deny it," he had said, winked at her, tugged on his earlobe, and departed.

As they had before when Rathburn had called for help, the passwords worked, and she was into both his unclassified and classified hard drives.

She first checked his Internet browser cache to see what kind of Web sites he surfed. She found Google, Yahoo!, MSNBC, and the garden variety of other URLs. Nothing unusual, she determined.

Then she clicked on history and was interested to see that Rathburn had never cleared his history file. She was able to view his activity from three months before, when he assumed the job. She spent some time perusing the Web sites that he had visited; again, nothing unusual. He apparently had a G-mail account and a Yahoo! e-mail account.

She tried to find the user names of those accounts, but everything came up with the blank sign-in screen. If he had been logged in, the browser had ultimately logged him out for inactivity. She then opened his Outlook work e-mail account, scanned through those, and again saw nothing that would raise a red flag.

She clicked on MY PICTURES and saw nothing, then clicked on the TRASH BIN and found one deleted photo.

It was a photo of four men, one of whom she presumed was Rathburn, all standing with arms laced around their buddies' shoulders. She did a double-take as each man was wearing a Halloween mask. She immediately recognized Mick Jagger and thought she could tell which one was Keith Richards, but she wasn't enough of a *Rolling Stones* enthusiast to remember the other two members of the band. There was a big tongue and lips superimposed on the photo, and she remembered that to be the logo on one of the *Stones*' albums. *Sticky Fingers* maybe? Maybe not.

Huh, she thought.

She switched the Cybex Switchview box to the classified computer, which could not access the Internet but could access a Secret domain. There wasn't much there, some routine e-mails on Outlook.

She closed the dialogue boxes and opened the MY COMPUTER icon. She saw the common O: drive, where they shared office files and such, which she opened. Scanning through those there was nothing she either hadn't seen or hadn't put in there herself during her duties as his special assistant.

She closed the O: drive and studied the open MY COMPUTER box and looked at all of the network drives. Again, nothing out of the ordinary. No references to the *Rolling Stones* or Keith or "Beasts of Burden." Just the one photo, but what did that mean?

Frustrated and beginning to feel foolish, she stood, grabbed the football she had initially picked up, and began to put it back in the orange placekicker's tee from which she had lifted the pigskin.

Her eye caught something in the center of the tee. She studied it more closely and saw that there was a small tear in the middle where the ball would rest on its pointed end. She touched it and determined that the tear was actually a tab, like a battery compartment cover. Meredith pulled at the tab and peeled back the soft orange material.

In the bottom of the well of the tee was a small thumb drive.

Huh, she thought.

Meredith flipped over the tee and a SanDisk 1-gig removable drive tumbled onto the desk. She sat back down and picked up the drive, which was indeed about the size of her thumb.

She removed the plastic tip and inserted it into the computer. A moment later a dialogue box appeared asking her if she wanted to open a file.

"Of course," she whispered.

She clicked on the box and a series of tan manila folders appeared on the screen. They were, in order:

PRED-CHINA.

AIG.

MICK JAGGER.

CHARLIE WATTS

RONNIE WOOD.

None of the folders would open though, as they were all password-protected.

Fearing locking the drive from errant attempts to enter a password, she closed all the dialogue boxes, clicked on the icon to eject the thumb drive, then removed the device from the computer.

Meredith pocketed the drive, pushed the orange plastic back into the tee, replaced the football on the tee, then dusted off everything she had touched.

After shutting down both computers, she walked out of the office. Stepping through the darkened halls of the E-ring after most of the Pentagon work force had already departed, Meredith stopped and turned. What had she heard?

There was a noise coming from directly across Rathburn's office. Then she saw it. A stairwell door closed just as she looked farther down the hallway.

Creepy, she thought, and quickened her pace.

As she finally reached the dark South Pentagon Parking Lot, she shook off the creepiness and wondered: *Why wasn't Keith Richards, the second most famous Rolling Stone of them all, on that list?*

But she thought she knew why. She picked up her pace, looking over her shoulder as she unlocked her car, and said to herself, "I'm getting some satisfaction."

CHAPTER 56

MINDANAO ISLAND, PHILIPPINES

Talbosa removed his Australian bush hat, stained with sweat and dirt, as he lifted his knife. He focused on the cobra no less than two meters away, apparently oblivious to his presence. He flipped the knife with a snap of his wrist, and the large blade pierced the back of the cobra's neck, pinning it to the ground beneath. The snake's body coiled and uncoiled, flipping violently until Takishi stepped on the heel of the knife and severed the snake's head.

He felt his phone buzz as he retrieved his knife. He placed it back in the sheath and held the phone to his ear.

"You fool, why did you have to attack the Americans?" Takishi shouted. Of course, he was speaking about the defense delegation at Manila's airport. Talbosa looked over Cateel Bay, its turquoise hue calming the man who had been chasing this elusive band of Rangers and perhaps even Takishi's Matt Garrett, if such a man even existed. Talbosa was nonplussed at Takishi's ranting. He knew that he had deviated from the plan, which called for no attacks on Americans or any NATO allies.

"This is my country, Takishi. Don't tell me what I can and cannot do. We have suffered for nearly a century from the imperialism of the United States and your country as well. So don't tell me how to run a revolution," Talbosa said calmly into the satellite phone Takishi had provided him.

"We had a deal," Takishi said. "We produce the weapons for you, and you do not kill Americans." Takishi spoke from the luxurious confines of a Japanese government Gulfstream executive jet settling into its final approach into Tokyo where he would shift venues to his Shin Meiwa. He needed to give Bob Stone the personal reassurance so that he did not deviate from their plan. He believed he had succeeded. The 48-hour diversion had set him back, yet the information gained had been invaluable, and useful. This was the tricky part for Takishi, transitioning from able co-conspirator with the Americans to Machiavellian statesman for his country.

"No. The deal was that you make us weapons, and you get the free extraction of the many minerals in my Mindanao countryside," Talbosa replied, his confidence bolstered by the physical separation. Really, what could Takishi do? He looked at the dead snake and thought: *Sometimes the snake charmer gets bitten*.

"Consider me, then," Takishi said, changing strategy, like a chameleon, "an emissary from Japan. On behalf of the Japanese prime minister, I respectfully request that you set up a release point for all of the American soldiers and citizens. To include the government officials your men have taken hostage."

"What's your interest in this?" Talbosa asked.

In truth, Talbosa needed to establish his presence on Luzon before the NPA beat him to the seat of government. Though the Islamic Jihad recommended small cells fighting under a unified commander's intent, he did not want to be politically outflanked by the NPA. He would soon be in Cateel, and determined at that moment that he might just kill Takishi after arriving in Manila. Doing so would enhance his already impeccable bona fides among the lower class throughout the Philippines.

"We have an interest in maintaining strong ties with the United States for trading purposes, as you will need to do if you ever want to be anything other than a fourth-world country," Takishi said.

Talbosa knew that Takishi's plan was in jeopardy. The loss of Abe had been a blow to the tank plant, and the Luzon faction's capture of the Americans, while not part of the plan, certainly had Takishi bothered.

"Are you so stupid that you cannot see victory?" Takishi asked.

"We have already achieved victory!" Talbosa replied. "We have overrun the U.S. embassy. We own the Presidential Palace. No problems."

"You idiot, you have bitten the tail of a snake. Right now you have a Marine brigade coming down from Okinawa and carrier groups steaming from the Indian Ocean and Hawaii. Their infantry division in Hawaii is scheduled to fly to Guam tomorrow to establish an intermediate staging base. The head of the snake, my fine Filipino friend," he said sarcastically, "is about to give you a fatal strike."

Talbosa leaned against a mahogany tree and sighed. "How do you know all of this?"

"My ambassador was given their entire deployment plan. They're prepared to throw everything they've got at you unless you cough up every American on these islands."

"Then they will leave us alone?"

"Then they will leave you alone."

Talbosa cast his gaze upon Cateel Bay a kilometer and a half below him, its water sparkling like so many diamonds. They had achieved total strategic, operational, and tactical surprise in their attack. Of course, it would not have been possible without the Japanese-produced weapons. Talbosa firmly believed, though, that they did not owe the Japanese anything. He knew that the Luzon cell planned to kill, or had already killed, one of the American hostages for general purposes and were about done with the others. He felt he was making good progress in chasing down the invaders in Mindanao, and he had issued instructions to the Luzon cell to kill the American soldiers at Subic Bay.

You told me to kill Matt Garrett, he wanted to say, but didn't. He sensed that Garrett was at the core of the illusory nature of his prey. And so he remained on the front lines, determined to protect his people of Mindanao and to kill the American spy before relocating to command all of the Philippines.

Talbosa felt an adrenaline rush, then sighed. Their struggle had always been difficult. They had often taken two steps back for every step forward. As much as he wanted to take revenge on the Americans, he decided that Takishi's advice was solid. No, the cause must come before revenge. He would not let his petty emotions stand in the way of freedom for his people. He had to start thinking like a strategic leader, a president, as opposed to an operational military commander.

"Okay, Takishi. I will inform my men that Subic Bay Naval Base is off-limits. The Americans have forty-eight hours to depart. But tell them that I only want noncombat aircraft to come get their people. I am doing this in an exchange for our right to determine our own form of government. If we want to be part of Bin Laden's caliphate, so be it. If I see combat troops or planes, we will shoot them from the sky."

"Of course," Takishi said. "I will pass on the message for you. My plane should be arriving shortly in Cateel to escort you to Manila, so that you can assume the presidency."

"Thank you," Talbosa said.

"And Talbosa, you should talk to your men at Fort Magsaysay. They have succeeded where you failed."

"How's that?"
"They've got Matt Garrett locked in a cell."

CHAPTER 57

Abe was glad that Major Ramsey's team had finally broken contact with the insurgents. It was dark, and they had been on the move for a full night and an entire day, each man taking a turn carrying Jones's body. Abe was glad to contribute and demonstrate strength and character by carrying the dead man once, albeit briefly.

Abe's heart went out to the American men. They were strong and rugged, but he knew they all had families as he did. They were all only doing what their country had asked them to do. He watched their stark faces as they faded into and out of his sight in the moonlit night, silently stalking through the high-mountain rain forest. Their painted faces, streaked with black and green camouflage, reminded him of the Indian warriors he had read about in American history. The men stepped lightly, seeming never to touch the ground. Large green leaves would brush against their faces, leaving the moisture from the dew and rain across their brows. Each man held a weapon, pointed outward. He was impressed at their professionalism and quietly yearned for their, and his, safety. One day he would write a poem about the contrast in their compassion and their duty.

He could sense that the men were scared, but they dared not reveal fear. He was reassured by their compassion for one another and the fact that their leader, Major Ramsey, had brought him into the fold. He sensed that they still did not entirely believe his story about the weapons. To them, it did not compute. To him, it made perfect sense.

Over the past five days he had become drawn to Major Ramsey. Abe found himself respecting the commander's authority and command presence. In his society, it was natural to be drawn to the source of power and obey. He had noticed in Ramsey an ability to remain calm even in the most dangerous situations. To Abe, the more confusing the situation, the more stressful, the more dynamic, the more the major would retreat into his inner sanctum and draw from a deep reservoir of knowledge and power and control.

Like adding ballast to a listing ship/the man in green/leads his men/they the arrow/and he the tip.

He patted his empty pockets for a pen to jot down the thought, then hoped he could remember it.

He had no ideological differences with the men. In fact, he had found himself to be quite similar in character to his captors, who were beginning to accept him. After fixing their radio, a quite simple task, they identified with him. He was of use to a team consisting entirely of useful people. He had been a burden but had become an asset.

In the growing darkness, Abe looked down at his jungle fatigues with the crazy black, green, and brown patterns interwoven in the fabric. He was beginning to be like them, he thought. As they walked, he carefully chose his steps through the dense underbrush to avoid the dreaded black palm plants and any poisonous snakes that might be lurking, as was usually the case. He stepped first with his heel, rolled his foot gently to the side away from the arch, then pushed quietly with his toes.

He still did not carry a weapon but could taste the excitement as they moved like an invisibly connected team through the jungle. Each man knew where the others were, always looking in a full circle. Turning slowly halfway, then back again.

Lifting an arm to quietly push a branch aside. Letting the insects fly about his face. He was learning the discipline of martial arts that he had eschewed as a young man in Japan. So many of his friends had trained in the jujitsu and karate skills, but he had chosen piano lessons and engineering at an early age.

That night, as he moved in synch with the soldiers through the lush green highlands, he felt something instinctual that had never been there before. He had the taste of copper in his mouth. His heart beat fast, but in control. He wanted to be a part of the team.

He watched as Major Ramsey halted the patrol in the darkness. They had doubled back on their trail and were about six and a half kilometers northwest of Cateel. Their initial path was only two hundred meters below the slope they occupied. A rare clearing in the forest connected their current position to the previously traveled path. Abe watched as Ramsey gave instructions to Benson, who quickly went about the business of implementing them. Ramsey then slipped his rucksack off his shoulders, grimacing as he did so, and set up the tactical satellite radio.

"Bravo six, this is Bushmaster six, over," Chuck whispered into the radio. The sun had fallen behind the mountains to his rear. He faced east, peering between two mahogany trees into the clearing. Slipping on his night-vision goggles, he saw Benson directing his men into different positions and tacking what looked like fishing line ankle high to trees near the other side of the clearing. They worked quickly and professionally, knowing exactly what to do, despite their hunger and fatigue. Three days ago they had officially run out of food. Most of the men had conserved their MREs, however, and had lasted up until that point only through Eddie's expert foraging.

"Bushmaster six, this is Bravo six romeo, over," a voice responded. Ramsey sighed with relief. His connection to civilization was intact.

"This is Bushmaster six, get me your zero-six, over." The romeo, the radio operator at the other end, told him to wait. Ramsey looked at Abe, who was watching his team prepare their position. He had gained respect for the man over the past five days. Abe had so willingly given them the information about the weapons-production plants that he believed the man to be telling the truth as he knew it. Abe's help with the radio had been instrumental both in contacting the outside world and maintaining faltering morale in his team.

"This is Bravo six," Captain Garrett's voice came back, "good to hear from you. We've been trying to contact you."

"This is Bushmaster six. Yeah. We have some enemy hot on our trail. We lost another man," Ramsey said.

"Christ. Chuck, this is Zachary," he responded. They were emotionally connected, Garrett and Ramsey, two West Point classmates finally recognizing each other in the midst of an impossible situation. It was only natural that they forgo proper radio procedures and share a moment of friendship. It *was* lonely at the top, and sometimes leaders needed reassurance.

"I know. I'm glad it's you down here. Any luck with that helicopter?" Chuck asked, hopefully.

"He's on the way. He departed our area about an hour ago and will try to island hop and steal gas until he can reach you. We've moved. Like I said before, this whole place is under attack by Abu Sayyaf. We can still hear fighting down in Olongapo. I know you're sucking, man," Zachary said.

"Okay," Chuck said, hopeful. "Any way to predict when he'll be here?"

"Couple of days at the worst. If he's lucky, about twenty-four hours."

"Okay. I think we can hold out. Zachary …"

"Yeah."

"If I don't have a chance later … thanks. I know you could use that Black Hawk. You didn't have to send it."

"I'll see you in a couple of days, and we'll drink a San Miguel and go chase bar girls," Zachary said, Slick looking at him with a smile, hopeful that he could go too.

"Listen, I've got some important intelligence that you need to get to your higher. I can't seem to get bird sixty-five right now, so you have to relay this information, over."

"Send it," Zachary said.

"We have captured a Japanese engineer who has been working in a weapons-production plant on the island of Mindanao for the past six months, break," Chuck said, taking a moment to spit some smokeless tobacco from his bearded lips.

"We found him jogging in an orange running suit. He said that there are four production facilities on Mindanao. Three produce tanks and helicopters and the other produces small arms and ammunition, over."

A long moment of silence ensued. He assumed the commander was copying.

"You gotta be shittin' me," Zachary responded.

"I kid you not. What I need to know is, were there any tanks or helicopters in the Abu Sayyaf attack this morning?"

"None that I saw. We captured about ten enemy, and they all had new M4s and M16s. Hell, we just got those M4s a couple of years ago ourselves," Zachary responded.

"Yeah. I know what you're talking about. Listen, I've got about a battalion of insurgents hot on my ass. Just get that information to your higher headquarters. Then we won't have died in vain over here. Gotta run, out," Ramsey said without emotion.

CHAPTER 58

SUBIC BAY, LUZON ISLAND, PHILIPPINES

Zachary dropped the hand holding the radio handset into his lap and stared into the darkness. His company position was facing west on the slope of the rain forest just north of Subic Bay. The hopelessness of Ramsey's situation perversely gave him optimism. His father had always told him never to feel sorry for himself, because somewhere somebody had it worse than he did.

Immediately, Zachary called the Twenty-fifth Infantry Division (Light) headquarters in Schofield Barracks, Hawaii. He had Slick angle the small SCAMP dish between a saddle in the mountains behind them. He had positive contact with bird 65.

He contacted the headquarters and passed the message to a tired young lieutenant pulling shift duty in the early-morning hours. The International Date Line separated Hawaii and the Philippines, but in reality the time difference was only six hours. For Zachary in the Philippines, it was 2200 hours, yet for the lieutenant in the division operations center, a rather monotonous duty, it was 0400 hours of the same day. The old joke was that someone could fly from Manila to Hawaii and get there before they left.

The lieutenant assured Zachary that he had the message. Zach had asked him to repeat the message, but the lieutenant would not respond. Zachary presumed that he had raced to the division commander with the information.

However, in typical fashion, he had scribbled some shorthand notes, something about finding some old Japanese weapons on a Philippine island. He relayed the message to Captain Garrett's battalion operations center, which was busy preparing for a massive deployment to Guam to begin establishing an intermediate staging base for possible combat operations. The officers and enlisted men of the unit would periodically gather around the television sets in the dayrooms and watch cable news, listening for the latest updates.

Japan had intervened, and it seemed that they were going to be able to get Captain Garrett's company and all of the other Americans out of the Philippines. The only issue remaining concerned fighting the insurgents. The president had not committed himself yet, stating only that he would take whatever action was necessary to protect American lives.

The young private on radio watch in the battalion headquarters took the message from the sleepy division lieutenant. He found the message interesting and took it immediately to Lieutenant Colonel Buck, who was in his office stuffing a sleeping bag in his rucksack.

"Sir, division got a message from Captain Garrett about him finding some Japanese weapons," the private reported. Lieutenant Colonel Buck, looking tired, stared at the private, waiting for the rest of the message.

"So tell me something important. What was it, an old World War II stock or something? Christ, the guy's fighting for his life, and he calls us about old Jap weapons," Buck said, shaking his head. "Thanks, Pitts," he said to the young soldier.

Pitts saluted and went back to his post three offices down in the battalion headquarters. Officers were bustling about, filing deployment reports and coordinating the multitude of staff actions. The communications officer brought a white box into the operations center. "Just signed for this from division," he said, seeming unsure as to its contents. The officer departed without further instructions.

The metal box had a white shoe tag on it that read SCAMP. Pitts being fresh out of communications school from Fort Gordon, Georgia, knew the acronym. It was a satellite radio. During crisis times, new and improved equipment seemed to creep out of the woodwork. Pitts, with nothing better to do, set the SCAMP into operation, and keyed the encryption variable into the encrypting port. He then ran onto the second-floor balcony of the operations center's building and aimed the white metal box at bird 65, as he had been taught in the division communications refresher course.

"Lightning signal, this is Knight six romeo, communications check, over."

"Knight six romeo, this is Lightning signal, keep all communications to a minimum, over," came the lieutenant's sleepy voice. Pitts was proud of himself though. He had set up the complex device with ease. He delighted in the fact that he had done so on his own initiative.

"Pitts, is that you?" a voice came over the radio. Pitts rubbed his shaved head. He recognized the voice. His best friend in basic training had been a young soldier named John Cane. They called him Slick because he considered himself such a ladies' man.

"Pitts?"

"Slick?" he responded, both totally ignoring proper radio communications procedures.

"It is you!" Slick responded. He had been monitoring the radio and could hear Pitts as if he were only a kilometer away.

"Hey. Got your message," Pitts said.

"Yeah. Some pretty wild shit, isn't it? Scary—"

"Get off the net!" The lieutenant's voice overrode their improper conversation. The two privates gave a "roger, out" and each went about his business, Slick listening for word about a hoped for extraction of his company, and Pitts wondering what was scary about finding some old World War II Japanese weapons in the Philippines.

There were probably tons of them everywhere, he figured.

CHAPTER 59

MINDANAO ISLAND, PHILIPPINES

Major Ramsey saw the first man enter the engagement area slowly. He was glad to see them attacking at night. It meant that they still did not know they were fighting Americans. Or if they did, they were stupid. The insurgents, to his knowledge, had no night-vision goggles. Chuck Ramsey's team did. All except Abe. Ramsey had given Jones's goggles to Eddie, who had become an indispensable member of the team now. Eddie held down the pivot position in the L-shaped ambush. He would be firing diagonally across the engagement area.

Looking through his goggles, Ramsey saw three infrared chemical lights glowing softly. Invisible to the naked eye, they were clearly evident through the goggles. The lights were positioned perpendicular to Eddie's line of fire. Benson had tacked the three lights to tall bushes along the main trail cutting across the open field to be used as fire-control measures. When the lead member of the enemy patrol reached the last light, Ramsey would initiate the ambush with a claymore. The other two lights helped divide the engagement area into sectors of fire to avoid redundancy of killing. The five men positioned along the top portion of the L, facing downhill, would fire between the two lights farthest away, almost directly down the hill. The other six men would fire along the slope of the hill, directly across the frontage of Ramsey's position. That would produce an effective cross fire that might, once and for all, get this particular enemy off his ass.

By then a four-man patrol was at the second light, directly in the middle of the engagement area. Ramsey could see a man feeling his way with one hand in the darkness, ensuring no branches or twigs caught his eye. He looked like a blind man, groping his way through an unfamiliar room. Soon, he *would* be blind, Ramsey thought to himself.

Nearly thirty Abu Sayyaf were stacked single file behind the lead team, wandering aimlessly into their sights.

As a precaution, he had sent Abe nearly fifty meters to his north to serve as a listening post on the left flank. He had tied their remaining rope around Abe's waist so that he did not get lost and to serve as a communications device. Two tugs meant enemy soldiers were coming from that direction. Abe had readily accepted the mission, glad he could help. Ramsey, desperately short of personnel, placed complete confidence and faith in him.

Talbosa struggled up the mountain, still reeling from his conversation with Takishi and the fact that the Luzon faction had Garrett. He had unsuccessfully tried to contact the Fort Magsaysay team and vowed to try again in the morning.

Rocks slipped beneath his feet. Branches whipped into his face, unintentionally launched by the man to his front. They had found a trail, which made movement easier and faster. With Takishi's report that Matt Garrett was detained in Luzon, Talbosa's frustration mounted. He found himself thinking less of the enemy and more of a way simply to get to Cateel so he could fly to Manila.

His men had slowed, reaching what seemed like a clearing. The lead company, whittled to only forty rebels, noisily passed back the word to the other two companies of equal size that they would slowly move across the clearing. Talbosa was impatient, frustrated at the elusiveness of the soldiers. Before, he had caught them easily. He knew all of their tactics. They were particularly careless at night, bunching into tight clusters with little to no security. He wanted a quick victory. His brothers in arms had seized control of the government, and he could not even catch a ten-man patrol.

As his first men crossed the clearing, he sensed the second element move along the trail. He had positioned himself at the lead of the second unit and felt the commander brush past him quietly as he watched dark figures drift silently through the night. His frustration was replaced by the exhilaration of watching his men perform. He had read all of the American manuals on patrolling and conventional combat and watched his men execute what he believed to be a perfect danger-area clearing. He thought it was good, too, that his other two battalions had remained north of Davao City. Too many people in the jungle would be difficult to control. His men slid past him in silence as they followed the trail. He was close. He could feel it. Victory would soon be his.

Ramsey had watched the four-man team barely clear the danger area. They had not checked the far side. Looking through his goggles, he saw the lead man of the patrol walk past the third infrared chemical light.

He squeezed the electrical blasting machine, a small, handheld device that generated an electrical pulse via the rapid pumping of a handle that turned a small motor, sending an electrical signal along the wire to ignite the claymore mines.

Nothing happened. He squeezed again. No

response. Groping in the dark, he felt for the firing wires. He found them. Somehow one of the wires had come loose from the post. He awkwardly reinserted the wire, pressing down on the post as if he were inserting a stereo wire into a speaker. The blasting machine tumbled clumsily out of his hands as he watched five men move past the last infrared light. His hand dug into the dirt, snatching the small device. He pumped the blasting machine with two hands cupped around it, forcing it into his chest.

A bright light flashed into the darkness like a single strobe. He had forgotten to look away from the blast, allowing the sudden whiteness to burn out the batteries in his goggles. He was as blind as the rebels, and with the deafening blast he could barely hear.

Nonetheless, his team began firing. All of them had PAQ-4C infrared strobes mounted on their weapons to augment their goggles. Their fire control was rough at first. The men on the right flank started by shooting the lead five men, then turning their rifles on the predetermined sectors. Tracers rocketed downhill and sidehill, most finding their way into the warm bodies of Filipino rebels. Screams of pain sang out in the night, interrupted by the now-cadenced fire of M4s, M203 grenade launchers, shotguns, and sniper rifles.

Because he had lost his night vision, Ramsey could only direct his fire toward the tracers, a default fire-control technique. He hoped that whoever was firing the tracers could see what he was shooting. But he felt stupid, pulling the trigger with no target. Being so low on ammunition, he stopped, deciding wisely to conserve. The withering fire stymied the Filipinos, nonetheless. He could hear men drop, and had yet to see a single shot returned.

Talbosa registered shock as he watched his first company get raked by a screaming hail of bullets. Half of the second company was trapped as well. He had jumped back into the first cut of trees at the sound of the explosion. Popping his head above a rock, he could see the fire outlining the enemy's positions. The tracers were coming from directly up the hill and immediately to their right about 150 meters away.

We can flank them. He tightened down his hat and grabbed a shaking soldier, telling him to get the rest of his company and to follow him.

"Sir, there are only five men left in my company," the soldier said, smelling of urine.

"Then get them!" Talbosa yelled beneath the sound of the raging American rifles.

He had the trail company lay down a base of fire, to imply that they were not moving. Swiftly, he took his five-man team to the north, moving through the rain forest with unexpected ease. *This is brilliant,* he told himself. As they moved, they were clearly out of any danger from the ambush. The firing grew more distant as he led his team behind the enemy's north flank. It seemed surreal, the tracers diving into the ground, sometimes arching eastward toward the ocean. The soft pop of the weapons belied their destructive nature. They made the turn and were moving parallel to the ridge. Talbosa could not believe his good fortune. He was behind the enemy, unimpeded. They moved to set up a position from which to kill them. He decided they would attack silently, using knives to kill each man individually.

Eddie was firing his weapon, looking for more rebels to shoot. As the pivot man in the ambush, his pickings had been particularly good. He fired at will, striking targets easily with the use of his new night-vision sight. He would flip the goggles over his eyes, locate a group of rebels, and train the aiming device on whoever he wanted to shoot. He was removed from the killing almost one hundred meters, not comprehending that he was killing other Filipinos.

But as he felt the knife coming around his neck, he turned and saw a young rebel looking him in the eyes. The darkness accentuated the ferocity of his attacker's piercing gaze. The knife cut deep into Eddie's throat, as he had cut the pig's throat only days ago. The attacker felt resistance at reaching Eddie's windpipe, but pulled the knife through cleanly to the other side.

Eddie looked at his fellow countryman and mouthed, "My brother," then fell forward, his blood gushing onto the rebel's hands. Lying in the tall grass, dying, Eddie watched as the attacker, a boy younger than himself, ran whence he came, disappearing into the woods. *I just wanted a better life for my country*, Eddie thought, his mind spiraling with rapidity. He saw rice paddies outside of Cabanatuan, a small town on Luzon. He saw his mother and father spreading rice to dry on the dirt road. His younger sister played in the dirt beside the thatch hut.

And as he circled above them, they looked skyward, grief-stricken, watching him ascend to another place.

CHAPTER 60

Abe watched with amazement the execution of the ambush. If only he could play a role. He felt his hands reaching for a weapon, pulling an invisible trigger, and delighting in the kill. What kind of transformation was he experiencing? he wondered. Was it something primal?

Suddenly, he heard footsteps in the darkness. The major had told him that no one friendly would be moving unless he saw a green star cluster. None had been fired. Without hesitation, he pulled the rope twice, watching five bodies pass him on either side. One stopped, cocking his head to one side like an alert deer, then proceeded.

Ramsey felt the tug and turned in Abe's direction. He could see dark outlines moving quietly along through the trees, as if they were looking. They passed him. He had not been firing. They had not noticed a muzzle flash from his direction. Then he saw a dark figure stop only three meters away, turning his head slowly in Ramsey's direction.

Chuck leveled his hush-puppy pistol in the man's direction, hoping it was not Abe, and pumped a single, silent shot into the chest of the man, who fell backward into the bushes.

He sensed the others stop and turn. They came back to the shot man and he fired another bullet at a rebel who was bending over to check on the first. Then he sensed at least two had moved to his left, on his downhill side. His position was between two trees. Quickly, he backed away, and the three enemy soldiers converged on one another. One screamed in pain, apparently at a knife wound. The other two leapt directly at him, knocking his pistol to the ground.

Ramsey grabbed his K-Bar knife out of its sheath as he felt the hot steel of an enemy knife pierce his left arm. He screamed in agony, thrusting his knife into the innards of one of the men on top of him, turning the blade back and forth like a fork collecting spaghetti. Pushing away, he saw a man, older than he, wearing a bush hat poised above him ready to end his life.

"Americans?" the voice said.

"Die, scumbag," Ramsey said, trying to throw the man off him with no success. Talbosa held down Ramsey's good arm while his wounded arm lay helpless at his side.

"No, my friend. This is a great victory for my people. We will parade your stinking bodies down Roxas Boulevard. Bin Laden will give us money. America will suffer," Talbosa said, smiling.

Ramsey spit tobacco in his face. Talbosa raised his right arm, the knife silhouetted against the dark sky.

Three shots from the hush-puppy knocked Talbosa off Ramsey. Bursts of machine-gun fire suddenly erupted all around the two men. The tracers and muzzle flashes lit the night sky like strobes. Gaining visual acuity was difficult, and Ramsey sensed that Talbosa was no longer next to him. Staying low to avoid elevating into the cross fire, Ramsey low-crawled through the elephant grass.

Talbosa was gone. Grasping at the grass to his left and right, he touched a foot, then a leg.

The fire abated and Ramsey rose to one knee as Abe helped him to his feet. Looking up, Ramsey saw Abe's face highlighted by the weak moon. He looked at Abe's hand, holding the hush-puppy pistol. With a calm demeanor, Abe looked down at the weapon, then at Ramsey.

"Why this thing make no noise?"

The moment was almost comical. Then Abe moved to one knee and lifted an Australian bush hat from the grass. He held it in his hand without commenting as he stood again.

"That man, with the hat, where did he go?"

Abe and Zach were both without night-vision goggles and therefore could not search the darkness with any advantage.

"Ran. Like the wind. Not find. Need to get you a medic."

The ambush had slowed in intensity, producing an occasional pop from a friendly weapon. No tracers burned in the sky. There was only the collective moan of wounded bodies. Chuck stood eye to eye with Abe, grabbed his pistol, and said, "Thank you." But then he had to kneel again. His wounds were worse perhaps than he had initially believed.

He still had a fight to command, however, and people to protect. He found his rucksack, which had been riddled with bullets. He cringed when he found the radio shattered inside. The green star cluster was still serviceable, though, and he promptly sent it screaming into the air. He handed Abe his rucksack, and said, "Please."

Abe was happy to help. He flipped Ramsey's rucksack onto his back, fitted the Australian bush hat onto his head and started up the mountain.

CHAPTER 61

NEAR FORT MAGSAYSAY, LUZON ISLAND, PHILIPPINES

Matt Garrett looked at Bart Rathburn and Jack Sturgeon. He was thankful that he was practiced enough that he had brought no identification materials and truly looked like a security guard. To his knowledge, none of the rank-and-file insurgents had connected that they had a CIA operative in captivity. They were focused on Rathburn, with all of his important-looking badges. *Sucks to be him,* Matt thought. So far, Matt had not been questioned; nor had any apparent leader presented himself.

Matt was squatting on his haunches in the corner of a dank cellar with adobe walls and a thin green slime of mildew and mold along the dirt floor. So far he had killed one snake and four rats. He should have just let the snake live, he thought; maybe it would have eaten the rats.

Their Filipino captors had stripped them of their weapons, rifles, pistols, and knives, and dumped them unceremoniously into this basement. When they removed their blindfolds and restraints, Matt noticed that there was a large Native-American-looking man sitting in the muck on the far wall. The man opened his half-lidded eyes when the three of them had appeared in his heretofore solitary cell. Just as quickly, he closed them, as if retreating back into some sanctuary.

Matt noticed Rathburn and Sturgeon were visibly shaken, though the pilot seemed like he could handle himself. Rathburn was a different story altogether. The guy was coming unglued, Matt realized. Sturgeon was leaning against one shoulder in the far corner as if he might be twirling a toothpick in his mouth at the local soda fountain. Rathburn was pacing back and forth looking at the floor and muttering to himself like Rain Man.

"Gotta call Mick Jagger. If he can't help, Ronnie Wood is the man. *The man*, you know what I'm saying? This is Mick's doing, I know. You know? If not Mick, then for sure Ronnie. You know what I'm saying?"

Matt walked across the slimy surface and stopped Rathburn by placing a hand on his shoulder. Rathburn spun wildly, which caused Matt to snatch his wrist and hold it.

"Actually, no. I don't know what you're saying," Matt said. He looked at Rathburn's eyes, wild with fright. *Flight-or-fight syndrome*, Matt thought. *This bureaucrat has no fight in him, for sure.*

"Jagger's screwed up somehow. This wasn't part of the plan," he said to Matt, as if Matt should understand exactly what he was saying.

"They took my iPod. I had some Stones," Sturgeon said, providing a bit of levity to the scenario.

"The Stones, man. We are the Rolling Stones, and this thing happened too soon," Rathburn said.

Matt noticed that the political appointee had the thousand-yard stare of a man who knew he was going to die soon. His vacant look indicated a man whose eyes were searching for reason but coming up empty. Imagining the worst and trying to find a plausible scenario to escape the treachery that surely waited, Rathburn was spiraling out of control.

"What the hell are you talking about? You knew about this?" Matt growled.

Rathburn stopped his pacing and stared at Matt, perhaps through him.

"I'm Keith Richards, don't you understand?"

"You're a whack job," Matt replied.

"Hey, Keith, gimme shelter," the large man in the corner said. "Or shut the hell up."

Matt turned to the man who had been silent to that point, looked at him, and watched him stand. He was enormous, probably pushing seven feet, Matt guessed.

"What's your name?" Matt asked, still holding Rathburn's trembling body.

"Rod Stewart," the man said, breaking into a wide grin. Matt noticed his teeth were white and straight, at odds with his disheveled appearance. "Let's have a jam session."

"Don't mock me, asshole," Rathburn said, trying to point but unable to because Matt was restraining him.

"I don't know you, but I will kill you," the stranger said. "But I would be doing you a favor, so I think I'll let these guys do it."

As if on cue, four Abu Sayyaf guards barreled down the steps and opened the door, splashing a rectangular spotlight of sunshine across the floor.

"Hey, Joe. You die," one man said, as three gathered up Rathburn and took him up the stairs.

"We're going to see Jagger, right?" Rathburn shouted. "This is all a ruse. Make it real. No propagandists. It's all real." Then he pointed at Matt, and shouted, "He's the one you're supposed to take! That's Matt Garrett. He's your beast of burden! Let it bleed!"

They listened at the incoherent ramblings as the guards escorted Rathburn out of earshot.

"Looks like some wild horses dragged him away," the man said.

Matt watched the men drag Rathburn up the dusty concrete steps and said in a low whisper, "What the hell was that all about?"

"Sounds like you were supposed to be set up," Sturgeon said.

Matt remained silent, then turned to the large Native American.

"Name?"

"I told you ..."

"Don't even mess with me," Matt said approaching the larger man. He leveled his jade laser like eyes into the man's bloodshot brown pupils.

"You don't scare me. But just so you know, Johnny Barefoot's the name."

"American?"

"Yeah. Was here on assignment."

"You do CNN stuff, right?" Jack Sturgeon asked, moving toward the conversation.

"That's me. Was supposed to cover some deployment of an infantry company from Hawaii to here. CNN was getting all kinds of static from the Department of Defense as to why there were no embeds in the Philippines covering this 'war.'" He made quotations marks around the term "war."

"So they sent one dude?"

"That's right. Not even my thing, you know. I do American West, Native-American issues, casinos, corruption, that kind of thing."

Huh, Matt thought. He turned away and walked toward the door, which he checked. It was secured, as he expected.

Matt's mind spun. *I get pulled out of Pakistan when I'm about to kill Al Qaeda senior leadership. My team is broken up, and I'm sent to China and the Philippines pursuing teaser leads on Predators. I'm told to jump into a plane wreck only to find an American body I wasn't told about. I find Japanese tanks on Mindanao and a Japanese man flying in a float plane to Palau, where, coincidentally, perhaps not, Rathburn is cooling his heels. Then I run across a second-tier journalist who was sent to "embed" with a rifle company in the Philippines, where a Muslim uprising has suddenly taken root. And Rathburn is giving up my name to Abu Sayyaf.*

None of it made sense separately, but there were some threads he could see that created a fabric. With Barefoot standing there, he was reminded of a Bev Doolittle painting *The Haunted Ground.* At first glance, the painting was simply a cowboy atop his steed looking over his shoulder as he fled through an aspen forest pulling his galloping supply horse. When he stared at it long enough, the knotty trees dissolved into an image of three Native-American faces and an eagle watching the intruder.

What was he seeing when he stepped away from the individual threads and put the mosaic together?

As his mind spun to wide field of view, he stopped, like a gear catching.

"Who were you supposed to interview?"

"That's the thing. The company was in a hell of a fight, a couple of guys were killed, and they bugged out to the jungle."

"Who?" Matt asked, approaching Barefoot.

"Some company commander named Captain Zachary Garrett."

CHAPTER 62

SCHOFIELD BARRACKS, ISLAND OF OAHU, HAWAII

Private Pitts had waited an hour after the lieutenant at the division operations center just up the road from his quad on Schofield Barracks, Hawaii, had told him and his good friend, Slick, to get off the radio. They had changed frequencies, and it would be appropriate for him to conduct a communications check with his old buddy. He lifted the black handset to his mouth and spoke.

"Bravo six romeo, this is Knight six romeo, over"

"This is Bravo six romeo, go ahead, over."

Pitts smiled wide as he heard Slick's voice beam down from the satellite. He was amazed, but glad, that they could talk even though they were 8900 kilometers away.

"Sitrep, over." He had heard the battalion commander and operations officer say it often. His intent was to convey to his friend that the conversation would not degenerate to the level it had earlier when the lieutenant at division had admonished them.

"This is Bravo six romeo. Currently holding in position. No enemy contact. Anxiously awaiting your arrival."

"This is Knight six romeo. Roger. Say again SALUTE report given to higher earlier this morning, over," Pitts said. SALUTE was a standard reporting acronym that stood for Size, Activity, Location, Unit, Time, and Equipment. The acronym provided a simple format for reporting enemy dispositions.

As Pitts waited for the response, he realized his exhaustion. He had been awake all night, helping the unit prepare to fly to Guam later that day. Most of the soldiers were already at Hickam Air Force Base near Pearl Harbor preparing to board C-17 aircraft and a variety of commercial charter planes. As members of the communications platoon, they would be the last to travel to the airfield. He saw the battalion adjutant wander aimlessly into his office, obviously tired.

"Hey, Pitts, what's going on?"

"Not much, sir. Got a commo check on our new satcom here with Captain Garrett and the boys."

"No shit?" Captain Glenn Bush responded, awakening. "How're they doing?" The entire battalion wanted desperately to go to the rescue of their isolated comrades.

"Slick says they're holding in position without enemy contact," said Pitts.

"That's good," said Bush, sounding relieved.

"This is Bravo six romeo. I say again last SALUTE. Size: one Japanese executive. Activity: producing weapons for Abu Sayyaf attack to include tanks, helicopters, and small arms. Location: island of Mindanao. Uniform: orange running suit. Time of capture: unknown. Equipment: four large weapons-construction plants. Informant captured by friendly elements operating in the area, over."

Pitts's hand dropped the microphone as if it had suddenly scalded him. Captain Bush looked at Pitts and said, "Is that for real, or just some game you guys are playing?"

Pitts, his mind reeling, looked at the captain.

"Sir, we've got to get this information to division. They think that Bravo Company found some old Japanese weapons from World War II. That division TOC officer must have been asleep to miss that shit."

"You're telling me this is real? Ask him to repeat

it." Bush directed, leaning over the desk and staring at the young private.

"No sir—I mean—sir, I know Slick. He wouldn't bullshit about something like that." Looking at the captain, he said, "We need to find Colonel Buck and let him know."

The two soldiers ran quickly to the commander's office and knocked, then entered. The colonel was working on some last-minute plans before traveling to the airfield. Dressed in his Army combat uniform, he looked worried, almost overwhelmed by the recent developments.

"Sir, Pitts has something he wants to tell you," Bush said, playing adjutant and not stealing the young soldier's thunder. Pitts looked at the captain as if to thank him. He was proud of his discovery. It was like being handed a rock and washing the dirt away to find gold. No one at division had treated the information with any concern.

"Sir, I just set up our SCAMP—uh—it's a new tactical satellite—"

"Get on with it, Pitts, we're leaving soon," Buck said.

"I talked to Bravo Company." The colonel looked surprised. "That spot report about the Japanese weapons I brought into you earlier was bogus."

"I sort of figured that," Buck said.

"It's worse."

Pitts went on to explain the report, and Buck, like Bush, questioned its validity. Pitts's insistence convinced the battalion commander to radio the brigade commander with the information, who promptly located the division chief of staff. The division chief of staff informed the division commander, who asked that the spot report be verified. The division operations center confirmed the spot report with Captain Garrett's company in Luzon. When asked why they had not picked up on the report earlier, the division staff officer blamed the reporting unit for faulty reporting procedures.

The division commander then informed the U.S. Army Forces, Pacific, Commander, who called the Commander Pacific Command, a Navy admiral. The commander then promptly called over a secure red-switch telephone to the chairman, Joint Chiefs of Staff. The CJCS received the message with alarm and skepticism, but nonetheless reported it to the secretary of defense. Stone immediately asked Vice President Hellerman for an audience.

"There has been a new development," he told the seasoned politician. What Stone was really wondering was: *Four plants? There was only supposed to be one. There's just one glider, right?*

As the information ascended from the muddy operating levels into the upper reaches of national strategy, it remained relatively unchanged in content. In fact, the number of plants grew from four up to six, but the message did not change in meaning.

As Matt Garrett wondered if Zachary was alive; as Chuck Ramsey's men clawed their way to safety up the jagged edges of the rain forest; as Zachary Garrett and his men huddled in the highlands above Subic Bay; as Karen Garrett knelt and prayed for her brothers; as Meredith Morris fondled the thumb drive and wondered about the Rolling Stones; and as "Mick Jagger," Robert Stone, played out the possibilities in his mind, the simple endeavors of two privates brought unmistakable clarity to the situation.

CHAPTER 63

PENTAGON, WASHINGTON, DC

Stone placed the secure phone in the cradle and leaned back in his leather chair. *This is good,* he thought. *We're definitely going to have to commit some resources to the Philippines. But what do the Japanese have up their sleeves? Ten ships that young lady mentioned. Four, not one, weapons-manufacturing plants on Mindanao. Keith Richards is possibly dead. Hmm. What kinds of chess moves were being made?*

Fox and Diamond entered the room via the side door. Each man had removed his suit coat and had the sleeves on their respective Egyptian cotton shirts rolled up just below the forearm. *We are working hard,* their appearances screamed.

"This is out of control," Fox said.

"Out of control," Diamond reiterated.

"I'm busy, guys. You *just* may be right," Stone agreed.

"We are getting off track here," Fox said.

"We have some ideas to get back on course," Diamond said.

"I'm thinking we'll have to wait until next year to do Iraq," Stone said.

"That's unacceptable. The window of opportunity is now. The American people want to kick some ass," Fox said.

"And now," Diamond seconded.

Stone, tiring of the tag-team duo, said, "Well, how about we kick some Filipino ass?"

"Not enough targets. We need more targets," Fox said.

"More ass," Diamond added. "The more targets, the more ass we can kick. Who wants to kill a bunch of zipperheads?"

Stone looked at Diamond and gave him a disapproving look for using a derogatory term to describe the Filipino people.

"We don't go to war with the theories we wish we had; we go to war with the theories we've got," Stone said. *That ought to clear it up for these twits.*

Fox and Diamond stopped, looked at one another, and seemed to ponder this pearl of wisdom.

"Yes, but what the hell is in the Philippines?" Fox continued. "I've got CENTCOM's troop list right here. If we keep pouring troops into the Philippines, this plan becomes no good." Fox shook a thick stack of papers at Stone."

"World peace will suffer," Diamond added.

"We need to destroy Iraq so that we can rebuild it as a shining beacon of democracy on a hill in the heart of the Middle East," Fox said.

The two men were machine-gunning Stone. They sensed that they needed to close him the way a real-estate agent gets a skittish buyer to sign the contract.

"Baghdad's in a valley; the Euphrates River Valley. You guys aren't even making any sense. Do you have any idea of what is happening in the world? Democracy in the Middle East is important, but can't we wait a year? Develop a plan, maybe?"

"CIA says it's a slam dunk. We need to go," Fox said.

"What *is* a slam dunk is that Al Qaeda is still on the loose. We've captured or killed a few midlevel functionaries, but the big fish have just changed streams," Stone said.

"Al Qaeda is incapacitated," Fox said.

"Out of commission," Diamond reiterated.

"Is this how you really feel?" Fox asked Stone. "Are you jumping ship?"

Stone sighed. Where were the Rolling Stones when he needed them? One might be dead; another was half a world away. Maybe Ronnie Wood would come to his rescue. He was really the most powerful of them all, but had asked for the Wood pseudonym to further disguise his participation. If Wood was ever found out, well, the whole thing might come tumbling down. That left Stone to carry the weight of the counterplan on his own shoulders.

"You guys are killing me," Stone said, ignoring the question. "I've just ordered a Navy SEAL team to check out the ships the Japanese have supposedly loaded with tanks and helicopters."

"All conventional weapons. Iraq's got nukes," Diamond said. "And, we'll need the SEALS to get into Basra and other port areas immediately."

"Yellow cake, aluminum tubes and rockets," Fox sang.

Stone thought he might hear Fox mutter an "Oh my" à la *The Wizard of Oz*. He turned away and looked out of his window. He could see the Washington Monument standing erect in the middle of the Mall.

Yes, as soon as he could shake his leg loose from these two terriers, he would call Ronnie Wood and talk things through.

Indeed, it was rock and roll, but he sure didn't like it just then.

Stone watched Diamond and Fox depart, then ordered Meredith to report to his office immediately. He was going to see Ronnie Wood, and she could come in handy.

As the last person to see Rathburn alive, Meredith could be valuable to him, Stone figured. First, he didn't know what, if anything, she knew about the Rolling Stones. Second, she would deflect attention from him. He had been concerned lately about being too obvious. And, if nothing else, she was beautiful, and that would cheer him up.

They made the quick trip to the Old Executive Office Building adjacent to the White House. It was an overly ornate structure, almost a medieval eyesore amidst the modern office buildings.

There they met Vice President Hellerman, who deemed it necessary to give the briefing personally to President Davis. He ordered the National Command Authority to convene in the White House Situation Room, a small room with a cherry conference table and a white phone where the president sits.

Eventually, the service chiefs of staff, the CJCS, SecDef, vice president, Central Intelligence Agency director, and Meredith all huddled around the table. The secretary of state was already on his way to Japan to discuss regional security issues and possible economic sanctions against the Philippines.

Meredith was dumbstruck. In her inexpensive dress, not a women's power suit, with a stack of papers and books tucked in her arms, she looked like a schoolgirl. She felt like the country bumpkin that she was. She was clearly much younger than every other person in the room.

They all stood when the president entered, then sat quickly when he waved his hand at the group. The chief executive sat at the head of the table with the vice president on his right and the national security advisor on his left. Stone was next to the vice president and across from Sewell, the CJCS, and Frank Lantini, the CIA director. The chiefs of staff filled the other seats, with Meredith awkwardly positioned at the other end of the table, providing a weak counterbalance to the president, who was opposite her.

"I know almost everybody," President Davis said

in his smooth Southern drawl, looking at Hellerman, who smiled and stood.

"This is Ms. Meredith Morris. She's an analyst, is it, with Bart Rathburn's group?"

Meredith stood, bashfully.

"No, sir. I'm his special assistant. I handle a broad range of issues for Mr. Rathburn."

"I bet," the Air Force chief of staff whispered loud enough for most to hear, prompting a scowl from the president.

"Everybody's got to start somewhere, Ace." The president smiled.

"Okay. Let's proceed. The situation, as my national security advisor has advised me, is this: The Abu Sayyaf has taken control of the Philippines, President Cordero is in jail, Secretary Rathburn and two others are hostages." The president went down the checklist as if he were grocery shopping.

Meredith winced when she heard Matt's name fall into the "others" category.

"We have a Special Forces team on Mindanao and an infantry company on Luzon. We lost fifteen women, some military and some civilian, on an airplane at the Manila International Airport. The Japanese have arranged for us to use Subic Bay Naval Base for the next two days as an airport of debarkation only. No ships, is that correct?"

"Yes, sir," Sewell responded. "That's a good summary. It's also important to let you know that we have developed a joint task force under the command of Admiral Dave Jennings; he's with Pacific Command. Right now he's got the majority of a light infantry brigade and division headquarters in Guam, a Marine expeditionary force moving south from Okinawa through the East China Sea, and a naval carrier group steaming from the Indian Ocean. They should be in the South China Sea in two days. We've got the fighter and bomber wings at Guam on alert.

And, of course, portions of the Ranger regiment are waiting on the airstrip in Guam."

"Okay, but we plan on a simple extraction of our personnel, correct? I mean, we just start flying airplanes in and taking them out. Right?" the president said. "I can see no reason for becoming militarily involved in the Philippines unless we can't get all of our people out. I still want to focus on Iraq and Afghanistan as the main front in the Global War on Terror. I don't want anything to divert our attention there."

Meredith was convinced that he passionately believed what he was saying.

"We want democracy and market systems in the world, but not at the expense of American lives. While we prefer democracy, but communism is no longer our enemy, and last time I checked, these rebels were really communists just trying to hook on to the Muslim thing. So, it's like Cuba suddenly saying, 'Hey, me too.' So, if these communists cum Islamists want to have it, then let's find a way to contain it and get after the real threat."

The president looked around the room and continued, "The point is that we will be able to use other forms of power to influence whatever regime is in control of the Philippines. We should let the Philippines go through the growing pains of revolution, assisting them in ensuring human rights and economic prosperity if possible."

Communism? Meredith was certain everyone in the room was having the same thought. *Where is he getting that from? Sure, they were communists twenty years ago, but Islamic fundamentalism has always been an issue in the Philippines.* Meredith leaned back in her chair as if blown away in slow motion. *And what about the Japan angle? Hasn't anyone mentioned that to the president? If not, I wouldn't want that ass-chewing afterward.*

Sewell looked at Stone, motioning for him to take charge. There was something in the exchange that piqued Meredith's curiosity. *What was it? A knowing look? A familiarity?* After all, they were counterparts. Davis also saw the interchange and asked the secretary of defense to respond.

"Sir, there has been a development that warrants our discussion in this forum. It significantly muddies the waters if our intelligence turns out to be true," Stone explained, looking at Lantini.

"Go ahead," President Davis said, kicking back in his chair with his hands behind his head and briefly resting against the nearby wall that made the room so cramped.

"We just received an intelligence report from the Special Forces team in Mindanao that they captured a Japanese auto executive jogging."

The group chuckled, unaware.

"This executive, it appears, had been in Mindanao for six months"—Stone paused, looking at the rest of the group—"operating a massive assembly line making tanks, armored personnel carriers, helicopters, small arms, and ammunition. The whole operation's been going on nearly two years." Stone stopped, then added the stipulation: "According to the report."

"What!" McNulty, the Air Force chief of staff responded. "That's bullshit!" He had served as the commander of the Thirty-fifth Fighter Wing at Misawa Air Base in Japan.

"All we know is that we got the spot report through about ten different parties," Stone said, "but I brought Meredith here to discuss some of the background and even some of the implications."

"Really, Bob, a secretary? I've heard of sleeping your way to the top, but this is ridiculous," McNulty retorted.

"I resent that," Meredith said, angrily. She stood

amidst the all-male gathering, tucked her hair behind her ears, and glared at the general, who turned red. She did not need his harassment, and she was certainly not there for the prestige or to get a job. She wanted to help. She had the answer and she knew it. President Davis was about to speak, but Meredith began by slapping her notes onto the table.

"Pardon me, Mr. President," she said, the president motioning for her to continue, smiling at her brashness. "But that little spot report confirms what our intelligence has been missing for the past two years." Lantini glared at her as she picked up a stack of papers stapled together and passed them around. "I mean, it's bad enough we get our jockstraps handed to us on Nine-eleven, but it's about to happen again.

"In these packets, you'll see copies of newspaper articles that discuss Japanese mining activities in Mindanao. The next page shows Japanese mining imports remaining the same over the period of alleged activity. The next page shows Japanese oil-tanker activity in the Davao City port. And the last page is a newspaper article concerning an oil find on Palawan Island, Republic of the Philippines."

She tossed another stack at McNulty. "These papers show Japanese economic statistics. Declining population plus declining trade plus declining resources equals declining economy."

With dramatic effect, she said, "When your entire security environment revolves around your economy and your ability simply to buy protection from others, our shift toward the Middle East and a reduction in economic growth combine to form a severe threat to Japan's national security." She paused for a breath and let the men thumb through the packets. When the president finished reading, she continued.

"So what the Japanese have done is to exploit the

Abu Sayyaf revolution. They produced weapons for them, giving them more of a chance to overthrow the government—"

"Missy, why didn't they just attack the Philippines if that's what they want?" McNulty whined.

"General, if you'd ever read Sun Tzu, you would know that the ultimate form of strategy is to win without fighting," she said. Meredith had taken a military theory course as part of her political science curriculum at Virginia Tech and had read Sun Tzu along with Clausewitz's *On War*, which now made a superb doorstop in her closet. "So why not arm the rebels, stage a show of force in the East China Sea, ask the U.S. to watch the pending conflict between China and Taiwan, let the coup happen, then step in with tanks and helicopters to subdue the country?"

Stone thought to himself, *Holy shit. Has she been talking to the Rolling Stones? How much else does she know?*

"Sounds a bit far-fetched to me," Lantini said, looking at Stone. Meredith knew that as CIA director, Lantini, who during his heyday was an impressive college linebacker at Boston College, would feel upstaged by her conclusions based upon simple open source research.

"I don't know," Rolfing, the Marine commandant, replied, "let's hear her out."

"Well, everything I said is true up to the point of what happens after the coup."

"Why would they let Americans be killed. Wouldn't that jeopardize this plan of yours?" McNulty commented dismissively.

"It's not my plan, sir. The Abu Sayyaf, like Al Qaeda, are very decentralized. They probably didn't get the word or just didn't care about hurting Americans. I mean, how many of you knew we had an infantry company in Subic guarding ammo, or a

Special Forces team in Mindanao?" Meredith asked.

Stone wanted to scream: *Know! Hell I sent them there. You're carrying my water and doing great. Keep going!* He glanced at Ronnie Wood, who had a pensive look on his face, and winked.

"You've got a lot to learn about talking to superiors, young lady," the Air Force general said.

"And you've got a lot to learn about listening when you're wrong, sir," Meredith responded, fully expecting to be asked to leave the room. Davis saved her.

"She might be right, you know," the president said, taking control. "We need a way to verify this."

Stone picked up on the cue quickly. "Sir, we've located the ships that Meredith identified as going into the Davao City port and supposedly leaving with oil or minerals. They all are suspiciously anchored just off the Luzon Strait. Talking with Bill here, I thought we'd send some SEALs in to board one of the ships and see what's on them."

"Good idea," Davis responded. "What if Japan really is trying to pull a fast one on us? What do we do? What's our new strategy? How does this compare to the threat of Islamic terrorism and its potential nexus with weapons of mass destruction?"

Meredith leaned forward, thinking President Davis asked a good question. Had the 9-11 attacks opened other seams for Machiavellian statecraft, seams for which they may not be prepared? Meredith believed it all came back to the perennial issues of economics, resources, and culture, exacerbated previously by communism and currently by the threat of Islamic fundamentalism. In the Global War on Terror, allied relationships were shifting, like the earth's tectonic plates, bound to create a rumble, or God forbid, a full-blown quake.

Only things were not so clear, Meredith knew. Officers and statesmen trained in the Cold War era were unsure of how to proceed. She wondered if they could set aside preconceived notions to deal with the obvious, though sudden, threat? It was sounding to her as if Davis was asking the right questions and guiding his foreign policy staff in the proper direction.

And what about Afghanistan, where it all began? That was Matt's issue all along, she remembered.

CHAPTER 64

Secretary Stone had been watching. He looked directly at the president, who was seated next to Vice President Hellerman and Frank Lantini, with Saul Fox and Dick Diamond behind him. Chairman Sewell was next to Lantini and in Stone's line of sight. As Stone looked, he noticed Ronnie Wood return his gaze.

What's he thinking? Stone wondered.

The entire premise had been that the actions in the Philippines had to occur in order to create enough military movement to make rushing into Iraq logistically impossible.

Indeed, the Rolling Stones had released the glider, and it was flying strong, creating the effect. Many were beginning to question the drive to Iraq and whether they needed to forestall the massive military buildup against Saddam Hussein and focus more on the global transnational threat of Al Qaeda.

If the China-Taiwan tension gained more traction, and if the Philippine situation was not resolved in the next couple of days, then the Rolling Stones would have a chance at presenting a *fait accompli* to the neoconservatives without losing their power base, while appearing entirely logical and practical to the American people.

Win-win for everyone. That was always the Rolling Stones' goal.

Restore a patriotic fervor, crush Islamic fundamentalism, and keep the focus on the endgame: a stable, secure, and prosperous America.

Takishi, Charlie Watts, had been a Harvard Business School classmate of Bart Rathburn's. So Takishi was the logical choice as he began negotiating billion-dollar deals with countries such as China. He had the power, as did they all, to start an insurgency in the Philippines, like a brushfire. They wanted just enough to get the attention of the world so they could say, "Look, over there, a fire."

So the question was, how to keep the Philippine insurgency to a manageable level given all that had occurred—a containable insurgency. It appeared that with the deal Takishi had cut, the urgency would subside in a couple of days. That wouldn't be enough to divert attention away from Iraq.

He looked at Dick Diamond and Saul Fox, sitting next to each other, whispering to one another, trading notes. Like puppeteers, they always sat closest to the key decision makers in the room, so their presence could be felt.

He flipped his notebook annoyingly on the table, wishing for a cigarette and gaining a bothered look from President Davis, his friend. So he stopped and looked down. As he stared at his black notebook, he saw a yellow sticker protruding from one of the pages. He opened the book slowly, half-listening to the conversation and saw his pencil scratching from the ambassador's visit yesterday.

The big letters "KOREA" leapt off the page. Yes, he thought. Takishi was sending him a signal that the Rolling Stones needed more fodder to enhance the illusion of chaos in the Pacific. Stone looked up, smiled inwardly, and said, "Korea."

Amazed, everyone turned in Stone's direction.

"Korea. That's it. Korea," he said, shaking his head with the appearance that he had figured it all out.

"How's that?" Sewell asked.

"The ambassador, you know, Kai," he said,

looking at the president, "came over yesterday with an envoy from Mizuzawa."

Lantini shifted in his chair and glared at Stone. *What's he doing?* Lantini thought. *How can Stone be so reckless as to suggest that?*

"Why didn't they ask to see me?" Davis interrupted.

"I don't know," Stone said. "They probably did not want to bother you and were asking for our assistance in the Philippines and Korea. They're worried about China and Taiwan, and now they're getting rumblings from North Korea."

"They really presented that to you as an issue?" the president asked.

"Yes, sir. It makes sense. North Korea keeps shooting missiles over Japan, and China is always testing in Mongolia or somewhere. So I'm thinking the Japanese government developed these weapons to protect themselves from the growing Chinese and North Korean threats. My guess is that they felt like they had to do it in the Philippines to get around their constitution. You know, article seven—"

"Nine," Meredith interrupted and wished she had not. McNulty cut a mean gaze her way. Stone looked confused. *Another Oscar, baby!*

"Anyway. My reasoning," Stone continued, "is that these ships are sort of a floating weapons storage site, you know, prepositioned stuff, ready to react to some threats. Post-Nine-eleven, it might not be such a bad idea. They've got security challenges all around them with China, North Korea, and now this situation in the Philippines. I mean, can we really do it all?" It was a risky strategy, and Fox predictably pounced on the unprotected pawn in the debate.

"Perhaps the flotilla of tanks could be used as a balance of power in the Pacific so that we don't have to commit sizable U.S. forces there, allowing us to proceed with our levelheaded strategy of removing

Saddam Hussein and his weapons of mass destruction from Iraq," Fox explained.

"Balance of power," Diamond added.

"Now that makes sense," McNulty said, finally finding something he wanted to believe.

"So the choice is to deal with the Pacific or invade Iraq? What happened to grand strategy? Why can't we make it an all-inclusive strategy? Take a look at the Islamic terror threat as a multinational threat, much the way we viewed communism, and develop the equivalent of a containment, or destruction, doctrine that informs our decisions?" Diamond continued, then looked at Stone.

Now that made sense, Meredith thought.

"If the choice is between the two," Fox said from his back-row seat, "then there is no question that Iraq, with nuclear potential, must be handled promptly."

Jagger saw that Ronnie Wood was staring at him, wanting him to take the lead and counter Fox.

"Think about how many nukes are in China and North Korea, Saul. There's as much of a terror nexus there as we might find in Iraq," Stone said, picking up the ball for Wood.

"But what we are really talking about is some minor revolution in the Philippines. The China and North Korea arguments just don't hold water."

Everyone looked at President Davis, who said, "Let's give it twenty-four hours and see how this plays out."

Fox slammed back in his chair, his feet dangling above the floor like a schoolchild's.

Still dodging the bullet, Stone thought. *That glider is still hanging in the air, buffeted about a bit, but still hanging, flying, creating events. Real events.*

"Mr. President, I recommend that we keep this all tightly under wraps, which will of course preserve our strategic flexibility," Lantini, the CIA director said.

About time you said something! Stone thought.

"Of course," Davis replied, smiling at his old friend Bob Stone.

Stone rode back to the Pentagon with Meredith at his side, their legs touching in the back of the limousine. He wondered about her personal life. He glanced at her crossed legs, his mind defaulting to the testosterone instinct of forsaking mind over beauty. Silky panty hose covered her slender thighs. She was beautiful, sitting there looking out the window, watching DC bounce by. Maybe she would be drawn to his power. Yes, maybe that would work, he thought, ogling the naked skin above her neckline.

Besides, he was tired of Ronnie Wood and Keith Richards getting all of the chicks.

Phase IV: Winds of Chance

CHAPTER 65

TOKYO, JAPAN

Takishi raised his glass to Mizuzawa's. The expensive crystal chimed like a bell, signaling a new era.

"Wonderful job in Washington," Mizuzawa said, complimenting Takishi on his joint performance with Kaitachi.

"Thank you, sir," Takishi said, feeling vindicated for losing Abe and the killing of the Americans. The plan was proceeding nicely.

"As we anticipated," General Nugama said, also holding a glass of champagne in his hand, "phase one is going smoothly now that we have arranged for the departure of the Americans. Fine job, Takishi." It was a rare compliment from Nugama. They had strategically fooled the Americans. The demonstration in the East China Sea had worked.

The three men stood and talked in Mizuzawa's private garden behind his office. Normally, he did not allow visitors in the area, but it was a special day.

The resurgence of Japan to her rightful place in history had begun. The result of their actions would be no more reliance on the United States for security and no more kowtowing to the American people. The Philippines would provide ample resources for future Japanese domination.

The first order of business was to finish the job in the Philippines. Next would be to bring Taiwan home. What could the Americans do? Economic sanctions would be unrealistic. They would effectively be shutting down one-third of their economy. They would have to continue trading with Japan. Likewise for Europe. No, this was Japan's moment in the sun. She would rise from the seas like King Neptune, pitchfork in hand, almighty and all-powerful.

But it was a good plan. Stone had bought it totally. *First the business about the Chinese and Taiwan. Now we have them thinking about Korea*, Mizuzawa thought to himself.

"Hopefully," Mizuzawa said, smiling, "they will 'turn another satellite' for us." He did his best Robert Stone impersonation. They laughed heartily. Deep and guttural. It was a mean laugh, sinister, low-pitched, and evil.

Their intentions were in sharp contrast to the peaceful surroundings of the garden. The pagoda and bridge rose above them as they stood next to the dark water of the goldfish pond.

"Yes, 'we need you to change your constitution,'" Takishi said. More laughter.

Then they stopped, noticing Mizuzawa's eyes, fixated and burning red-hot. His eyelids wrinkled together, like knife slits in his skin. They watched the hatred and emotion well inside him. He was transforming. The moment had come, and he was remembering Nagasaki and Hiroshima. He was remembering MacArthur and his constitution. He was remembering almost sixty years of American domination and control.

"No more!" he yelled, shocking Takishi and Nugama, causing them to step back. "We shall prevail!" he said in a husky voice. He raised his champagne glass high into the air, framed by the bridge and pagoda. Then he crushed it with his bare hand, squeezing the glass to tiny pieces, gashing his skin. Blood ran down his thick arm as he stared at his associates, standing near him, unsure of what to do.

"We shall prevail!" Takishi barked, following suit.

"We shall prevail!" Nugama yelled, caught up in the emotion of the moment. The two men raised their glasses, crushing them, and grinding the glass into their hands as blood streamed down their arms.

"We shall prevail!" The words echoed in the garden enclave as the three men stared at one another, blood dripping from their hands, shards of glass stinging them all.

Mizuzawa dismissed his two comrades. He would see them later that evening. First, though, he had to prepare for the speech he would give to his faction that night. He would inform them of his growing security concerns. It was all true. Korea was a threat. China was looming larger than ever, hanging its nuclear umbrella over Japan like a dark shadow. Taiwan had armed forces of over half a million people. Russia still leaned on them from the northwest. The least of their worries was the Global War on Terror, but what a wonderful opportunity it presented.

Japan would create its own destiny.

First, he had led them to the slick political takeover of the Philippines. Whether Talbosa realized it or not, he was a bought man. If he refused to play the game, Mizuzawa figured, he could simply impose a military government. But he needed the Philippines to secure an intermediate staging base for his war plans. After securing the Philippines, he would move to encircle Taiwan from both sides. It would be interesting to watch the Chinese reaction to that one. The United States would be caught flat-footed, he knew that for certain. *You think you have problems in the Middle East?*

He sat once again on the bridge, cross-legged, peering down into the dark waters of the pond. His reflection gazed upward into his eyes, spinning his mind into another era. He could see the furrowed brow beneath his short hair. His eyes were mere rips in the cloth of his face.

His thoughts spiraled into the distant past, and he was looking upon Tokyo Bay. He saw the American flotilla moored there, surrounding the USS *Missouri,* on which the infamous defeat of the Imperial Armed Forces had been formalized. It was humiliating. The Americans deliberately carried the limping Japanese Navy into port, as if on a leash, to display their loss to all of Japan. His country had been a bad dog, and America was the master, whipping them in front of the world. He watched as millions of radios across the world broadcast live the disgraceful Japanese surrender.

From above, he could also see the holes in Japanese soil that used to be Nagasaki and Hiroshima. The Americans had claimed they were attacking industrial locations. True, those cities had weapons plants, Mizuzawa saw, but why hadn't the Americans used their new weapons of mass destruction on their European ancestors? Truman's decision, he determined, was a racist one. It was okay to vaporize little yellow people, but *Kami* forbid he should attack his European lineage with the same ferocity.

Mizuzawa felt hatred well inside him. No one could deny him or his country their rightful place in history. They had shown the world that Japan was the most determined, educated, and fastidious race in the world. They could reign supreme over the United States and everybody else. It was their turn.

Yes, it was Japan's turn.

CHAPTER 66

Mizuzawa stood and walked slowly to his office. After washing and picking the glass from his hands, he walked across a courtyard to the ornate Imperial Palace, the residence of the Japanese emperor.

He knocked on the door and opened it without waiting. The emperor stood in the foyer wearing a robe the color of a rusty mauve. It symbolized the rising sun.

Mizuzawa bowed slowly. The emperor returned his bow with a slight nod.

The one concession the United States had made to Japan at the conclusion of the Great Pacific War was to allow the emperor to remain as the head of the Japanese state. Truman had done it from a purely practical standpoint. He had seen the emperor as the one figure most revered in Japanese society, and the one person who could pass the message of utter defeat to the Japanese people. It had worked.

But the emperor served as the single thread to the era of the Japanese warlords. He was a man of direct lineage from some of the most barbaric and courageous warriors in Japanese history. Theirs was a bloodline of savagery. Most other aspects of Japanese culture and society had blended with the dominant Western society.

The Imperial Palace was uniquely Japanese, as was the emperor. Mizuzawa was unsure what the emperor knew about his plans for the future of Japan … and he knew that he had to do something about that.

The emperor, an aging man in his early seventies,

had a peaceful look on his face, one of contentment and solitude. His wife, the empress, had passed away recently, and he was lonely. But he served in his figurehead position well. He held state dinners and entertained guests, a Western tradition, Mizuzawa thought with disgust.

"Greetings, Prime Minister," he said.

"Good afternoon, Your Majesty," Mizuzawa said in response.

The two men walked into the palace along a dark koa wood foyer decorated with paintings of the former emperors. Mizuzawa recognized them all. He noticed with pride the paintings of Prince Ninigi, the grandson of the Sun Goddess Amaterasu Omikami, and Emperor Jimmu, Ninigi's grandson. The oil paintings were cracking with age and in desperate need of restoration.

As is my empire, Mizuzawa thought.

They walked into a small room. It was the emperor's private room for discussing matters of importance. Japanese pine framed a large trophy case that had been built into the wall. Behind the Plexiglas cover to the trophy case were three items. On either side of the trophy case were paintings of the eight gods of heaven and earth, who were viewed by the Japanese as the guarantors of their security.

Mizuzawa and the emperor stood in front of the case, looking at the three sacred treasures, the Mirror, the Jewels, and the Sword.

"What is this matter of importance you bring to me tonight, Prime Minister?" the emperor asked. His wrinkled eyes were drawn and set, as if he were ready to die. His pallid face was in sharp contrast to the rose-colored beauty of his flowing robe.

"Your Majesty," Mizuzawa said, looking at the sad, pale figure, "may I have access to the sacred treasures of Ninigi?"

"Why do you desire this access?" the emperor

asked without suspicion.

"Your Majesty, I have embarked on a long and arduous journey as prime minister. I need to feel the strength of the sword in my hands; I need to fondle the beauty of the jewels against my skin; I need to see the vision of my actions in the mirror," Mizuzawa said, poetically.

"What is this journey?" the emperor asked, sliding open the glass, revealing the three sacred Japanese treasures.

Mizuzawa looked at the items lying harmlessly in the open case. The jewels were curved jade beads nestled against a black velvet bag. The mirror was amazingly simple, yet old. Black and brown spots dotted the glass. Its frame was simple black lacquer.

But the sword. The sword was wide. Its ivory handle gave way to a pristine, curling blade. It was the Kusanagi sword of Japanese legend. Mizuzawa fixated on it, knowing what must be done.

"Your Majesty, I have taken your Japan on a course that will provide for her security for many generations to come," Mizuzawa said, kneeling at the case and running his hand lightly over the jewels. His thick hand brushed the delicate velvet, causing it to wrinkle.

"That is good, Prime Minister. Tell me more."

Mizuzawa shifted his gaze to the mirror. His face looked distorted, evil, reflecting back at him from the antique glass.

"We have begun to build the military again, your Majesty. We will soon attack to regain Formosa," Mizuzawa said. His words hung in the air like smog, polluting the Imperial Palace.

"But for what purposes would you do such a thing?" the emperor asked, slowly. "We are protected by the eight gods of heaven and earth. They shall provide for us."

Fool, Mizuzawa thought.

"Your Majesty," Mizuzawa said, turning his lusting eyes to the huge saber, "we have many concerns." *None of which I expect you to understand.* "Our economy cannot sustain itself forever. Our military is not adequate to defend the homeland against the Korean Peninsula or Chinese nuclear weapons."

"But the United States—"

Fool. Just as I thought. The last tie to our true heritage has been tainted with Western lies.

"—has guaranteed our security. They will come to our aid if it is necessary. I cannot allow your plan," the emperor said, sternly, images of the old warrior bubbling forth in his words.

"Your Majesty," Mizuzawa said, taking his handkerchief out of his pocket and placing it on the pearl handle of the sword, "we must pursue this course. We have no other choice."

"You are wrong—" The emperor's eyes grew wide, bulging outward, as he felt the sword slice through his abdomen.

Mizuzawa had lifted the sword and turned slowly to the emperor, who had been only two steps behind him. He slid the sacred sword into the emperor with a well-trained thrust.

He grabbed the emperor's hands and placed them on the saber's handle, as if he were performing *seppuku,* or *hari-kari.* He guided the old man onto his knees, ensuring he avoided the gathering pool of blood on the floor. He watched as the blood gushed onto the emperor's robe, casting a dark image onto the rust-colored hue that once represented the morning glow of the rising sun.

Its image had changed to something far graver. It was the unsettling darkness of a cold and eerie night, spreading across the robe, engulfing the fabric.

Mizuzawa turned the sword in the emperor's hands. The emperor looked at him and gasped,

"Thank you. Now it is your responsibility." He sucked one last gurgling breath and closed his eyes.

Mizuzawa was momentarily taken aback. *Had he known?*

The emperor's body toppled to the floor, his hands still holding the sacred sword as he died.

Mizuzawa stood above the man. "That's right, old man. It *is* my responsibility. And my reward."

I didn't think you had the stomach for it.

CHAPTER 67

WHITE HOUSE, WASHINGTON, DC

The president sat at his desk in the Oval Office. The camera's huge eye blinked at him as it came to life. He stared into the TelePrompTer and read.

Today I speak to you concerning Operation Enduring Freedom in the Philippines. Some American lives have been lost as they were caught in the cross fire of a revolution in that tormented country. I am sorry. Our nation's heart goes out to the family members of the twenty-two individuals who were killed.

Likewise, Filipino terrorists are still holding three Americans hostage. Thankfully, our gracious allies, the Japanese, have secured the release of the hostages and all other Americans and freedom-seeking individuals who wish to depart the country.

We are conducting an evacuation of all U.S. personnel from the Philippines who wish to depart. Tonight, as I speak to you, American aircraft are soaring to a designated point in the Philippines to pick up our beloved countrymen.

We will not condone attacks against Americans, and we will not tolerate those countries that harbor terrorists. While I firmly believe in the Filipino people's right to determine their own form of government, independent from colonial or superpower influence, we will not stand by while Islamic fundamentalism imposes an oppressive form of government on freedom-loving peoples.

As an initial step in countering the Philippine insurgency, I intend to impose economic sanctions on the country until the insurgents allow the elected government of the Philippines to return to power. I know sanctions at this time are no consolation to the family members of those Americans lost in combat, but it is a moral policy, and a policy that allows us to continue to focus on the United States' vital interests in Afghanistan and Iraq.

God bless our fighting men and women and God bless America.

The camera eye closed. Davis cast a glance to Stone, Lantini, and Sewell, who were standing in the opposite corner of the office. They gave him a thumbs-up sign, approving of his performance. The men shook the president's hand as the camera crew packed up its equipment.

"That should do the trick," Sewell said.

"I hope so," replied Davis, who looked at Stone and shrugged.

On his way out, Sewell pulled his satellite Blackberry from his breast pocket and frowned as he scrolled through his messages.

CHAPTER 68

SUBIC BAY, LUZON ISLAND, PHILIPPINES

Zachary Garrett watched airplane after airplane land, load civilians, and take off into the sky from the very runway that they had used to enter the Philippines. The white Quonset huts were occupied with kitchen facilities and administrative personnel, who seemed to be orchestrating the evacuation of Americans.

Resting his binoculars against the strap around his neck, he pondered why he had earlier received instructions to move to Subic Bay to board an aircraft for Hawaii, only to have that decision overturned by a tacsat message from his division headquarters to freeze in place. Moments later, another message from division informed him to move all civilian, wounded, and deceased personnel to the airfield that evening. He was to do this under the cover of darkness and conduct linkup with a CIA operative named X-Ray, whoever that was, at a specific grid-coordinate location northwest of the airfield just outside the naval base fence. X-Ray would have an infrared strobe light flashing and would use proper bona fides to identify himself.

How refreshing, Zachary thought. X-Ray was to escort the personnel onto the airfield, load them on an aircraft, and send them home. His security platoon, however, was to retreat to his base camp and await further orders.

The flaming sun hung low over the western

horizon, large and distorted, sinking into the ocean.
With it, the ferocious heat simmered ever so slightly.
It was like turning an oven dial from broil to bake;
nonetheless, the relative difference in the heat made
it feel cooler. Zachary looked for the flash of green
light that he had always heard about, but saw none,
as the sun dipped below the horizon on the sea.

In the musty jungle darkness, he watched his men
prepare for the mission. Stan Barker's platoon would
escort the ambassador, his four civilian support staff,
the wounded Sergeant Cartwright, Lieutenant
Colonel Fraley, and the Air Force doctor who had
been severely wounded. Doc Gore, the young
enlisted medic who had so expertly patched Captain
Garrett, had performed field surgery on the doctor.
He removed a bullet from his shoulder using a hot
knife and tweezers, then thoroughly rinsed the
wound with Betadine. But it was the ample supply of
penicillin that the doctor had given Zachary and
Sergeant Cartwright that held the fever and infection
in check. He was ambulatory, and that was all
Zachary cared about. Zachary's wound had begun to
heal nicely. A long scab formed on the left side of his
head, making it uncomfortable to wear his helmet,
but other than that, he was fine.

Barker's men had enough of a problem carrying
the bodies of Rockingham and Teller the three
kilometers to the airfield. The platoon members had
constructed two stretchers using rain ponchos and
ten-centimeter by three-and-a-half-meter mahogany
branches. By snapping two ponchos together, then
folding them, they slid the sturdy branches through
either side. But it was not so much the physical
aspect of carrying their deceased comrades away, but
the mental vision of two of their own, brutally
slaughtered in a war they never expected. Surprised,
shaken, unnerved, his men had handled themselves
exceptionally well. He feared though that their

adrenaline had been blocking their emotions, and soon fear and unrest might set in. He needed to counter that if it occurred.

He watched as Barker slipped past him in the twilight, moving his men and his "cargo" to a rally point. Zachary saw him coordinate with Kurtz, whose lines he would be passing through. Kurtz had marked a single passage lane and designated his best squad leader to serve as the guide through that lane. Each man in Barker's platoon had popped an IR chemical light and placed it in the camouflage band of his Kevlar.

Barker's platoon moved quietly through the center of the patrol base. The other men watched as they saw the civilians, Fraley, Mosconi, and Sergeant Cartwright hobble past. Cartwright made one last plea to the commander to stay, but Garrett told him no. His fever had risen in the last twenty-four hours, and the hot dust always found its way to the most remote parts of the body. Zachary feared infection. He would hate for Cartwright to lose a leg.

Zachary handed the good sergeant two envelopes and told him to get them to the addressees. Cartwright limped back into the growing mob near Kurtz's position. Soldiers were casually hugging and conversing with Cartwright, who was torn between wanting to stay with the unit and wanting the medical attention that he needed.

Then Fraley came forward in the darkness. Zachary could make out his rotund outline carved against the crazy array of the jungle.

"I just want to apologize," Fraley said, his head hanging low. Zach figured that it had finally occurred to him that he was dealing with a professional combat unit. They had saved his life, despite his poor treatment of them. During the night in the jungle, alone, apart from his world of Filipino concubines and whiskey, Zach surmised that fat Fraley had suffered "cold turkey" and got some religion. *Tough shit. That won't bring back Teller or Rockingham.*

He presumed that Fraley had forgotten that regardless of his position or duty, there was always a soldier out there somewhere, on the ground, holding a weapon, looking through the sight, wondering, waiting, hoping, and praying that someone above him had made the correct call. That someone cared.

Fraley had not. He had gone native, so far removed from supervision or the "real" Army, whatever that was. Zach knew that Fraley had believed he could collect a paycheck, have an adult fantasy every night, and laugh all the way to retirement.

But he had been wrong. Zachary looked over Fraley's shoulder as Barker's platoon hoisted the bodies of Rockingham and Teller past him, carrying them into the darkness like a medieval funeral procession. Out of the corner of his eye, he heard Slick mutter, "*Son of a bitch,*" and saw him turn away.

"Don't tell me," Zachary said, staring into Fraley's eyes. Fraley looked away, down toward the ground. "Tell the families of those two men."

With that, Zachary walked away and spit into the ground. No way was he going to ease Fraley's conscience. The whole fiasco might have been avoided had Fraley done his job. But it was too late to think about that.

Barker moved his platoon through the jungle. They had reconnoitered and marked a route to the linkup location during the day. It was a simple matter of following the pre-positioned IR chemical lights.

Barker met with X-Ray, a large man dressed in khaki civilian attire. Barker thought the man looked like a safari hunter, but he had answered the challenge properly and spoke with authority. X-Ray stood at least a foot taller than Barker.

He had a HMMWV with cargo space in the back. The high tarp on the back made it look rather conspicuous, but still concealed the cargo.

"This'll make everybody but the three hostages," the man said. Barker looked at him through his glasses with surprise. "They should be here tomorrow morning."

"What three hostages?" he queried.

"Some guy named Rathbun, a DoD bigwig, and two of his staffers," X-Ray said, intentionally concealing the fact that he knew Matt Garrett was a hostage for fear of compromising his negotiated release. "Terrorists blew up a DoD plane with a bunch of women on it."

"No shit," Barker said, trying to be cool. It was out of character for him, and he seemed awkward saying it.

"You guys did a kick-ass job. That's what the president says anyway," X-Ray told Barker. "Now get out of here." He patted Barker on the shoulder, hopped into the truck, and pulled away, disappearing behind a jagged rise in the extinct volcano.

Barker could not wait to get the message back to his commander. A compliment from the president. That would lift morale. Popping his chest out, he moved his platoon back through Kurtz's lines, conducting the proper far-and-near recognition symbols with the IR flashlight.

"Way to go, Stan," Kurtz said, offering a high five. Barker responded awkwardly, but finally felt as though he had contributed to the operation.

"Sitrep," Garrett said, emerging from the darkness behind Kurtz.

Barker first gave his platoon sergeant instructions to re-form his portion of the patrol base.

"Sir, X-Ray correctly responded to the challenge, and he fit the description you provided. We successfully transferred all personnel and the … uh,"—he found it hard to say, the reality of Rockingham's and Teller's deaths just now sinking in—"along with Rock and Teller, sir."

"Anything else?" Zachary said, picking up on Barker's discomfort.

"Well, sir, X-Ray sent a message from the president."

"As in president of the United States?" Zachary queried.

"Yes, sir," Barker proudly responded as the sole possessor of the information. It occurred to him that knowledge really did equate to power.

"No shit!" Kurtz said with much more authority than Barker could ever dream.

"He said we, and I quote, 'did a kick-ass job.'"

"Son of a bitch," Kurtz said.

"No shit?" Zachary asked.

"No shit, sir," he responded.

Zachary immediately had Taylor and the first sergeant move to the command-post area. The CP was located beside a huge mahogany tree. Slick had set up the SCAMP and aimed its antenna to the northeast. Other communications gear surrounded the tree in a weirdly organized fashion. In the darkness, only the white casing of the SCAMP stood out.

Zachary sat in the dirt, facing his three lieutenants and first sergeant. Slick and a couple of the other headquarters platoon soldiers naturally acted like they had something to do near the meeting and listened intently. There was a certain amount of pride associated with hearing the fresh scoop from the commander before anyone else did. Later, they would be able to take the inevitable rumors back down to ground zero and assert that they "were there."

"Guys, we've lost two of our own. I know nothing will ever bring back Rock or Teller. I was closer to both of those guys than any of you will ever know,"

Zachary began.

A monkey screamed in agreement from high in a tree off in the distance, adding an eerie quality to Zachary's gathering. He noticed the dark outline of Slick's head turn in the direction of the noise, which was followed by another. It sounded like a wounded banshee, lost in the dense jungle.

"It hurt me bad to watch Stan's guys haul their bodies away. The envelopes I gave Sergeant Cartwright were letters of sympathy. I handwrote them today when I knew he was going back. One was to Pat Teller, and the other to Glenda Rockingham." The lieutenants knew both of the wives. Glenda was a major force in the company, organizing events, and Pat had seemed eager to contribute to platoon events even though she was new and pregnant. They were great Americans and had paid the greatest sacrifice—the loss of a loved one in combat.

"I have to tell you, it's the hardest thing I've ever done." It was important for Zachary to share that moment with his men. They needed to understand that he was human and felt the loss. They needed to know that if one of them was killed, he would handle the situation with the same compassion.

"We held off a large, unexpected attack with minimal loss of life. We safely evacuated the frigging ambassador and his staff from the embassy. And now we have successfully put those people plus Cartwright and Rock and Teller onto an airplane to fly home.

"We performed those missions well. In fact, Stan's contact gave us a message from the president that I want you all to convey to your soldiers. I want you to do it personally, walking from position to position.

"The president said, and I quote from Stan, that we 'did a kick-ass job.' We're a good company, probably the best I've ever seen," he said, intentionally mixing his feelings with the president's quote. "But we've got more missions. Probably tough missions. There's a reason we did not fly out on those planes tonight, I guarantee you that.

"Now I want you to go talk to your men. Comfort them. But keep them alert. The fat lady ain't singing, yet. That's all."

The men departed and did as their commander said. After an hour, the word in the company was that the president of the United States had personally called the commander over the tacsat radio and told him that they kicked serious ass, had absolutely the best unit in the Army, and would receive the Presidential Unit Citation when they returned. The United States infantryman was the undisputed master of creating rumors and talking bullshit.

Zachary smiled in the darkness when Slick informed him with a grin of the transformation of "the word," as soldiers commonly referred to commanders' edicts.

He sat near the Mahogany tree, looking west into the ocean 550 meters below their position, pitching his K-Bar knife into the dirt and pulling it out only to toss it down again. He shook his head at the contrast. Only two weeks ago, he had been looking at a similar sight in the Kahuku training area after his platoon leaders had botched a night raid. *They've come a long way. No better test than the real thing.* But he knew with due modesty that it was his training that had molded the lieutenants.

Zachary thought about Glenda Rockingham and Pat Teller and how they might react. They would be crushed, he was sure. On the thought, he pounded the knife into the ground, venting some anger. He wondered if he had failed. Could he have done something different? What if he had not gathered his men on that first morning? What if he had carried his own radio? Then maybe Teller would still be alive.

But he would be the dead one, and where would that have left his men? He reconciled his doubts in his own mind. Still, he thought about Amanda, his daughter, and whether she would ever get to know him outside the image of him created for her by others. What if he were killed? She'd live the rest of her life thinking he had abandoned her. On that note, he simply decided that he would not die there in the Philippines. Exhausted, he lay back in the tall grass and closed his eyes.

His rest was short. Barker reappeared from the darkness. He thought he heard the commander sniff. Strange that he would catch cold in this heat, he said to himself.

"Sir, I forgot to tell you something," Barker said.

"What's that," Zachary responded, wiping his face before he sat up. *Good thing it's dark.*

"X-Ray said that they had extracted all of the Americans except three hostages. Seems the Abu Sayyaf blew up an American plane, but three had already gotten off."

"Oh yeah. Maybe that's our follow-on mission," Zachary said, thinking aloud.

"I never thought of that, sir, but he said they were three Defense guys."

"Department of Defense," Zachary said.

"Some guy named Rathburn and two of his assistants."

"More bureaucrats to save," Zachary grunted.

"Sir! First Platoon says they've got gooks in the wire!" Slick exclaimed, holding the telephone to his ear.

CHAPTER 69

"*What?*" Zachary grabbed his radio handset. Taylor's voice was on the other end, finishing a sentence. *No way, this shit has gone too far.*

"—four to five personnel, over."

"Andy, what's happening?"

"Sir," Taylor said, recognizing his voice, "I've got five personnel to my front signaling my forward observation post with an IR flashlight. My guys challenged them, and they came back with the proper response. But I told them not to let them pass. They're just lying there in the grass."

Zachary's mind raced quickly, making the quantum leap from familial worry to steadfast concern for the men the president had entrusted to him. Had they lost the encryption codes and a radio? No, the first sergeant had done a sensitive-items check earlier. Did he have any patrols out? No. The next patrol didn't go out until midnight. Who could they be? He thought back to his call from the division operations officer. He gave him an exact grid coordinate of his unit's location. Had that transmission been intercepted?

The embassy! The embassy had been taken over by Abu Sayyaf. They had all the call signs and secure-encryption variables. He had Slick call the other two platoons using the field phone. Then he decided to inspect the situation personally.

"Get back to your platoon, go to one hundred percent security," he told Barker, who split like a scared rabbit.

Zachary hurried down the hill the hundred meters to Taylor's position using his night-vision goggles. In the darkness, he passed the clear-cut area where the Black Hawk helicopter had once sat idle.

Moving beyond the clear-cut, he immediately picked up on the lieutenant and his platoon sergeant kneeling next to the platoon CP area. They were wearing their goggles as well.

"Where are they?"

"Down there, sir," Taylor said, pointing to the northwest. Zachary looked and decided to move forward. He walked, high-stepping the roots and bushes that made for tough going. Taylor followed, the platoon sergeant stayed at the CP. Approaching the two soldiers he noticed they were nervous. One had his night-vision laser sight trained on the individuals lying in the grass only ten meters away. The other soldier was scanning for more intruders.

"Sitrep?" Zachary asked, assuming the prone position next to the private.

"Sir, these gooks got our codes. They know our shit," he responded, continuing to look through his sight. Zachary pulled his Beretta pistol out of its holster and went to one knee.

"Carnival!" Zachary yelled across to the group lying in the grass. His goggles picked up five bodies with rucksacks lying side by side.

"Saloon!" a Boston accent responded with the proper password.

Zachary listened carefully to the voice. It was American, he was sure. Not only that, he recognized it.

"McAllister?" Zachary asked.

"Garrett?" the voice responded.

It was too good to be true. Bob McAllister was the A company commander from his battalion.

"Bob McAllister, the dateless wonder?"

"Since you left, not the case my friend. Riley and

her sister say hello," McAllister said, not moving.

"Ease off, guys," Zachary said to the young privates. They did so warily. Their wires were strung tightly. They kept trained eyes on the five men as they passed. Then they saw their commander and Captain McAllister hug each other.

"I never, in my wildest dreams, thought I would be glad to see your ugly ass here," Zachary said.

"Well, you've got a lot more than my ass to deal with. The whole stinkin' battalion just landed about twelve klicks northwest of here. Pave Lows flew us in. I'm the lead. Got any hot chow?" McAllister said.

"Yeah, right. Take out the 'hot' part, and you'd have a good question," Zachary strained.

"Yeah, that's what we've heard. You guys kicked ass, though, man. Whole division's talking about you like you're Rambo or some shit," McAllister said.

McAllister was a ROTC officer, commissioned from the University of Massachusetts. He was cocky but always backed up his bullshit with proper action. He had knotty red hair that sometimes looked too long. Freckles splashed across his face in asymmetrical disarray. He was average height and looked like a ruffian, which he was.

"I'd love to stay and bullshit, but we've got to call back to the Buckster and let him know we found you weenies," McAllister said, kneeling and grabbing his radio microphone from his RTO. He radioed the battalion commander and informed him that he had affected linkup. Buck seemed beside himself in his response, as if he never expected it to happen. He delivered an order to proceed as planned, and McAllister handed the handset back to his radio operator.

"The Buckster, you gotta love him," he said, shaking his head with a huge grin. "Hey," McAllister said, "did you know Riley and her sister each has a mole underneath her left breast. Talk about genetic symmetry—"

"Not a good time for the sex jokes, McAllister. Now move out before we get fired up. This is the real thing, dickhead," Zachary said, half-joking, half-serious.

"Trying to lighten you up a little. You're gonna need it when you find out our next mission. Here," McAllister said, handing him a stack of letters. "She sends her love and misses you." Zachary rifled through the stack; nothing from Amanda.

McAllister patted Zachary on the back, grabbed his radio operator, and moved out.

The news traveled through the company like a lit fuse. After talking with Buck on the radio, Zachary went back to his CP, lay down, and went to sleep. Buck would have a meeting in the morning.

Looking at the letters from Riley, oddly enough, he thought of his brother, Matt, wondering where he could be. *Sure would be nice to get him in here to help us out,* Zach thought to himself.

Where can he be?

The thought slipped away from him though, as he spiraled into a much-needed sleep.

CHAPTER 70

NEAR FORT MAGSAYSAY, LUZON ISLAND, PHILIPPINES

It had been twenty-four hours since Rathburn had been snatched from their cell, and Matt wondered if he would ever see the man again. Maybe Mick Jagger had saved him, who could tell?

"You're sure you never saw Zachary?" Matt said, stepping toward Barefoot.

"Yes, for the tenth time. I got there and the place was vacant. Looked like a hell of a firefight had taken place, though. Spent ammo everywhere. Bloodstains. No bodies. It was weird. I started snooping around the barracks and got waylaid by a bunch of little zipperheads," Barefoot said.

"Roger," Matt replied, dismayed. For twenty-four hours they had tried breaking the door, picking the lock, and screaming to get a guard, but it appeared they were all alone.

"Wait, I hear something," Barefoot said, holding up his hand.

The outer lock rattled, and the door opened, casting a bright yellow sunlit square across the green slime on the floor. Rathburn's body fell with a thud, his head smacking the wet concrete.

Matt slipped behind the door while Barefoot stood in the middle of the small cell. Sturgeon was reaching into his boot for a Velcro-pocketed knife that his captors had overlooked as he squatted in the other corner. They had been over this as many times as Matt had asked Barefoot about Zachary.

"You all go next, Joe. Let's go," a different Filipino voice said.

Matt moved closer to the door, which began to open slowly, casting a brighter spotlight onto Rathburn's body like some eerie floor show.

"Hey, Joe! Time to go!" the eerie voice called out again. Matt saw one shadow fall atop Rathburn's body. Then another. They both appeared to have something in their hands.

The first guard stuck his head around the corner of the door, unable to see in the darkness.

"Hey, Joe!" he screamed. "Where Matt Garrett? You number one customer today!"

Matt stood slowly and rapidly wrapped his belt around the short Filipino's neck, pulling the ends in opposite directions.

An errant shot escaped from the Chinese pistol, ricocheting off the wall and leaving a spark in its trail. The second guard responded immediately, pulling at Matt's arm.

Matt punched the guard in the face and heard the clank of pistol metal striking the floor. Sturgeon moved on cue stood from his crouched position.

Matt snapped the neck of the first guard as Sturgeon leapt across the splash of light that separated him from the fight and drove the knife into the back of the second guard.

The guard, shorter than Matt, turned toward him as Matt pulled the pistol from the man he had just strangled, placed it against the advancing guard's neck, and fired two bullets.

"Let's haul ass," Matt said, looking at the two dead Filipinos lying next to Rathburn's body in the box of light that framed the bodies like a large coffin. He stripped the Filipinos of weapons, handed Jack a Chinese Type 67 pistol, and said, "C'mon" to Barefoot, who followed.

For the first time in days, Matt saw daylight as

they exited the structure. They had been in the basement of a small adobe building. Leaving the cell, they found themselves surrounded by a high wall and a dirt ceiling, as if the cell had been cut into the ground. They were facing a stairwell carved into the dirt that led to the open skies. Matt carefully ascended the steps, then hesitated as the full brightness of the morning sun entered his dilated pupils.

He looked back at Jack, who was holding his own hand, almost doubled over in pain. Matt pulled a rag from his pocket and wrapped it around Jack's hand.

"I don't see anyone, but it's full daylight so we're gonna have to run. There's a truck about twenty meters to the right. It's running for some reason. Our best bet is to get in that mother and go."

Matt stopped as they were nearing the pickup truck and said, "Rathburn. Never leave a fallen comrade." He ran back down the stairwell and reemerged moments later with Rathburn's body slung over his back in a fireman's carry. It was the right thing to do.

"Let's go," Matt said. The three men ran across the hardstand to an olive drab pickup truck. Matt flipped Rathburn's body into the back as Sturgeon opened the passenger door for Barefoot, who slid across the torn cloth bench seat. Matt quickly slammed the automatic gear level into DRIVE and sped along the only road he could see.

The sun was to their backs, so he knew they were heading west if it was morning. To his front was flat or rolling countryside. He passed a series of buildings and saw a sign that read FORT MAGSAYSAY. He sped past a gate onto a cement road that led off the gentle slopes onto a plain. It was an area of rice paddies, some terraced into the hills behind them and others lying low beneath the flat, flooded ground.

"What's all that shit bouncing around in the back

of the truck?" Matt asked, looking in the mirror. Barefoot turned and looked.

"That's my film and commo gear. Remember, I was supposed to do a satellite linkup and conduct a live interview of your brother?"

"Zachary," Matt whispered. "We've got to find my brother."

Matt maneuvered around the patches of drying rice that farmers had laid on the cement road. He felt the noose that had been around his neck since landing in Manila slacken just a bit. .

His new mission: *find Zachary* ... and they could join forces to fight their way out of there.

CHAPTER 71

MANILA, LUZON ISLAND, PHILIPPINES

Takishi rode atop the bridge of the lead ship as it approached the port of Manila. He watched in the darkness as the captain adroitly maneuvered the large commercial tanker alongside the international port just south of the Pasig River delta. The pier was 150 meters wide and 450 meters long.

Looking over his shoulder, he saw the huge rock outcropping of Corregidor Island, which guarded the mouth of Manila Bay. His countrymen had fought valiantly there. There would be no such fight again. American airborne forces would not come descending from the sky as they had almost sixty years ago to secure the mouth of the bay. He saw the second ship steaming past Corregidor and made a mental note that the other two should be docking at Subic about then. He wondered in amazement how his countrymen had developed such an awesome supertanker, and had actually converted ten of them to roll-on-roll-off military transport ships and even an eleventh to—well, he did not want to think about the *Shimpu*.

The *Shimpu* was an entirely different matter altogether.

Mizuzawa had made the decision to launch four ships, each carrying a nine-thousand-man Japanese combined arms division consisting of tank, infantry, and attack helicopter maneuver battalions after Talbosa had failed to cooperate on the three

American hostages. He had planned to introduce force into the island of Luzon at some point in time, mostly for control purposes, but he believed that the situation could get out of hand rapidly if Talbosa turned on them. Control of the Philippines was absolutely vital to the remainder of the plan.

Takishi had flown in his Shin Meiwa to Mindanao to find Commander Talbosa in a small thatch hut in Cateel, recovering from wounds received in combat.

"When you told me about Garrett being in Magsaysay prison, I ordered them all executed," Talbosa had told him. He had been shot and nearly fatally wounded. Only his familiarity with the Cateel area had allowed him to get to the beach, where some of the peasants had provided medical care and escorted him to Takishi's airplane.

Takishi's medical team had patched up Talbosa during the flight, and Takishi had a security team take Talbosa to the Presidential Palace, placing him "in charge."

"You will respond to my every order, do you understand?" Takishi demanded.

Talbosa gave Takishi a long look and nodded. Weak from being wounded, he walked quietly into the Presidential Palace, where he was greeted by fellow warriors, who had executed their portion of the coup expertly.

"I thought I was close to your Matt Garrett until you told me where he was," Talbosa said.

Takishi had looked at the weakened warrior and said, "Slippery son of a bitch." Stone had contacted Takishi too late for either saving Keith Richards, Rathburn, or killing Matt Garrett. Takishi shook his head at the irony. There were minute degrees between life and death. If only he had gotten the word a day or two earlier, he could have saved his friend, Rathburn, and eliminated a major thorn in the side of the Rolling Stones, Matt Garrett. For the first time a jolt of sadness coursed through him as he realized his Harvard classmate, Bart, was dead ... because of him.

After dropping Talbosa in Manila, he had flown to the location of the oil tankers north of Luzon in the Philippine Sea, landing his seaplane amidst the collection of ships. There he boarded the command and control ship, *Ozawa*, and radioed the prime minister with the news about the death of Rathburn.

Mizuzawa reacted sharply, fearing American intervention for the sake of revenge if nothing else. He had been pleased with the American president's speech. They had guessed right. The Americans were focused on Iraq and stymied by an unexpected variable, the Philippines, for which they had no plan.

But protecting American lives was another issue. Would the Americans respond with military force and try to restore the democracy, using the deaths of a dignitary and the women as an excuse? It was possible. He was not willing to take the chance. They had been one step ahead of the Rolling Stones and needed to act before the Americans could foil their gambit.

If they could move immediately, gain a military foothold on Luzon, they would have checkmated the Americans, once again. *They* would appeal to the United Nations for a response to the situation. Mizuzawa knew the United Nations would not do anything about the revolution in the Philippines; they never did anything meaningful anyway.

Takishi felt the ship nudge the side of the cement pier. There was no activity in the large port area. The fighting had served to halt most of the commercial shipping. What was in the docks at the time of the revolution, the peasants had pilfered. The insurgents had not yet organized the Philippine naval vessels, though they had sunk several of the ships during the revolt. A few Corvette attack boats were still operational, yet were of no use to Talbosa until he could train some men how to operate them.

It was all coming together smoothly Takishi thought, and he sent Mick Jagger a text message.

WE ARE ACHIEVING SATISFACTION.

Stone did not need to know just yet that the Japanese were attacking the island of Luzon with the equivalent of four infantry divisions, about the same size force that the U.S. was planning on using in Iraq. Charlie Watts had played his part for the Rolling Stones, but his role had always been a means to an end, and he was going solo.

Takishi's highest priorities were to his country and his prime minister.

While Mick Jagger had the money and the ideas about how to stoke the dying embers of nationalism around the globe in order to crush rampant Islamic fascism, his other contact in the American government was equally influential.

And on *that* thought, he sent a text to that individual:

TANKS ARE ROLLING.

It was fun to be a chess piece *and* control the board. Takishi found it rather easy to out-maneuver the thinly veiled machinations of the Americans.

Momentarily he received a text in return:

BEAUTIFUL.

Then almost immediately after the first he received another:

PERFECT.

He heard the captain tell him they were prepared to unload the ship. He stepped down from the bridge, and heard the first Model 90 tank roar to life.

This will be easy.

CHAPTER 72

PENTAGON, WASHINGTON, DC

It was a close call, letting the Japanese move ships into the harbor.

Sewell looked at Stone. Meredith was sitting next to him. She was distraught, fighting the notion that Matt might be dead and that she might have sent him to his death in that airplane.

They sat in the National Military Command Center. CNN played on a large screen to their front. The Joint Chiefs of Staff flanked them. Each was wearing a headset that tuned him in to the operations of their respective services. In actuality, the commander of Pacific Command in Hawaii was orchestrating the operation through his joint task force commander, Admiral Dave Jennings, who was on the USS *Carl Vinson* command and control ship in the Celebes Sea.

The service secretaries, though, kept the SecDef up to date on force provider movements in order to allow the war fighters to do their job unimpeded.

Frank Lantini was updating them from his CIA office in Langley, Virginia, over video teleconference.

Lantini said, "Two oil tankers have passed Corregidor and are currently unloading tanks, infantry fighting vehicles, attack helicopters, trucks, jeeps, and large numbers of personnel. There appears to be a crew for every weapon system. Two others have entered Subic Bay Naval Base and are conducting similar unloading activities."

"Frank, how did we miss hundreds, if not thousands, of Japanese soldiers getting on these ships in Japan?" Stone asked Lantini.

Lantini stared at the video camera a moment and then said, "Turns out they loaded in Suruga Bay at night. There's a Japanese training area just north of there called Gotenba in the Shizuoka Prefecture. They supposedly had some big exercise there, Yama Sakura, something like that, in January and just kept mobilizing troops in the wake of Nine-eleven under the guise of anti-terror training. We've got information that during that time they infiltrated from the training area onto troop transports that took them out to these ships." He paused a moment, then volleyed back to Stone. "We missed it because we were watching Taiwan and China."

Stone shook his head. *Kaitachi, that bastard.*

"We've got two SEAL teams checking those ships out," General Sewell said, bringing the discussion back to the point. "Both are using SCUBA gear, swimming freely around the ships, inspecting hull dimensions and giving us spot reports on the unloading operations. They're ready to act when we are. The Rangers are ready as well."

General Rolfing, the Marine commandant, said, "Our Marine expeditionary force is now three full brigades and is positioned to the south of Manila Bay, well offshore. They're ready now also."

General McNulty's Ninetieth Fighter Squadron from Guam was on standby alert with F-15s, A-10s, and F-16s. The B-52s from Diego Garcia were also ready.

"Andersen is so packed with aircraft and people, you couldn't land a glider, so let's be reasonable here," McNulty said. "I don't think we can fit any more troops in this corner of the world."

This is exactly what we're looking for, Stone thought. The Army chief of staff, General Wilson, said,

"The lead battalion of the rapid deployment brigade from the Twenty-fifth Infantry Division has landed safely and undetected, we believe, on the island of Luzon, thanks to some Air Force Pave Low helicopters and MC-130 Combat Talons. They have linked up with the company commander there and are prepared to continue operations."

"We're all relieved that the young commander is no longer alone, but what about the absence of the Special Forces team in Mindanao. Any word?" Stone asked.

"They have not communicated for over two days. No change," Sewell said.

"What kind of force are we showing near Korea, Admiral?" Stone asked Admiral Simmons, the Chief of Naval Operations.

"Sir, we've got an entire carrier battle group steaming there now."

"Good. The president has a meeting with the Japanese ambassador in an hour. I'll give him the information."

"What did he say about the hostages?" Murphy asked. Meredith lifted her head.

"They weren't on the last plane. We've checked the three thousand names over and over. Rathbun and the other two aren't on any of the manifests."

"Could they have used other names?" Meredith asked, knowing the answer.

"They could, but probably not. Someone would have recognized them," Stone said.

The evacuation procedures had gone well. No other Americans who wanted to leave the islands were there except the hostages. Many chose to stay for a variety of reasons.

Stone walked with Meredith the short distance back to his office and closed the door behind them.

"Meredith," he began, "I know you're worried about Bart and your friend, Mark—"

"Matt, sir."

"Yes, of course, Matt. Anyway, I've got a meeting tonight at my home in McLean. I need you to come over and assist me with this thing if you're free," Stone said, looking out of his window.

"Well, sure, I guess," said Meredith. After all, how could she say no to the secretary of defense?

CHAPTER 73

"Now, would you accompany me to the president's office again? I must brief him."

"Certainly, sir. Do I need to prepare notes?"

"No. I might need your brain, though. Ready?" he asked.

"Sure," she said, looking down at her dress. She had bought two new dresses since she started reporting to the secretary of defense every day as a special assistant. Her official title was still as Rathburn's assistant, but Stone had elevated her status temporarily for the crisis.

Stone enjoyed rubbing legs with Meredith again in the back of the staff car on the short trip to the White House.

They showed their credentials at the west gate and walked into the national security advisor's office, where President Davis was waiting with Dave Palmer, the NSA, and Frank Lantini. They exchanged pleasantries and Meredith found both Palmer and Lantini to be likable people. Lantini complimented her on her performance a couple of days ago and mentioned that the president was very impressed with her.

"Don't go giving her any ideas, she's mine," Stone remarked.

They all laughed, then got down to business as Secretary of State Jim Fleagles entered the room a minute late.

"The way I see it, we've got to make them show some force. We can't just sink the ships in the ocean," Palmer said, watching Fleagles take a seat.

Stone looked at Meredith.

"I agree," responded Meredith. "The only problem is, how much is enough? If we let too much get on the ground, it will be too hard to fight. If we don't let enough, the attack will appear unprovoked."

"Why *can't* we just sink the ships, Dave?" Davis asked.

"Well, sir, I think the Japanese could claim that they were going to use those weapons, if they ever admitted to owning them, for defensive purposes. They could claim that they were building storage sites. It would make us look bad."

"I just hate to let a war happen," the president said, concerned. "We'll lose American lives. Hell we've already lost over twenty, and maybe the hostages."

"Sir," Meredith interrupted, "I've got a friend who's one of the hostages—"

"I'm so sorry," Davis said.

Meredith looked at the president. Okay, friend might have been a stretch, but she did feel close to Matt, and she was inexplicably worried about him.

"Thank you, the point I want to make is that I believe force is necessary. Think of how many lives it will cost if we don't stop the Japanese. What happens if they seize the Philippines? What kind of message does it send the world if we don't respond?" she said, still uncomfortable asking the president questions. She continued, "The real issue is, how much do we let the world know about?"

"What do you mean?"

"If we can sink the other six ships and blockade Japan from doing much else with their rather large 'self-defense force,' then we might just be able to show a still somewhat weak Japan kind of gone crazy with four divisions. But if the world, especially

China and Korea, find out that they have ten divisions floating in the water with three or four manufacturing plants in Mindanao still cranking tanks out every day, I think we've got a regional conflict beyond anything we could imagine. So the issue is letting them look like the aggressor but limiting what they can fight with."

"I agree," said Lantini. Palmer nodded also.

"Is there any way to negotiate our way out of this thing?" Davis said, turning to Secretary Fleagles.

"Sir, I think we've already been out-negotiated. If they've got four divisions' worth of equipment moving into Manila Bay, in my opinion they've already attacked. They did this whole thing behind our backs, lying to us every step of the way," Fleagles said.

"Still, why can't we just call up the prime minister and tell him not to attack?" the president asked.

"Once again, sir, the Japanese do not appear to be concerned with our response. Mizuzawa wouldn't even see me when I flew out there, so I came straight back. I think they truly believe we will not respond—"

"Then we must make them continue to believe it," Meredith said.

"Right," said Fleagles, unsure of how to treat Meredith. "If we're gonna fight this thing, we need to make up our minds. I'll go negotiate, but they've been bullshittin' us for a couple of years, and as far as I'm concerned, that constitutes breaking diplomatic relations. In effect, sir, they declared war on us when they developed this plan of theirs."

"This thing has the potential to get way out of hand," the president said. "They need to know that I will do whatever is right for the American people, even if that means waiting to deal with Iraq. Okay? That's the plan then. We wait for their attack on the

Philippines to commence, then we sink the six ships in the water as we launch our forces. I assume we've still got the carrier group moving to Korea."

"Yes, sir," Stone responded. "I've got a team working up an assessment of the impact this will have on the Iraq time line also."

"That's fine, but if we get locked down here, I want to do it right," Davis said.

Meredith cocked her head. *Good move,* she thought. It was clear guidance.

A military aide stuck his head in the door and said, "Sir, the Japanese ambassador is here to see you. He's waiting outside the Oval Office."

President Davis looked at the gathering and declared, "Showtime."

He walked past Meredith, caught a whiff of her perfume and wondered if Stone was getting any yet.

CHAPTER 74

WHITE HOUSE, WASHINGTON, DC

Kaitachi was waiting for the president in the anteroom to the Oval Office. He shook hands with the Japanese diplomat and placed an arm around him as they walked in.

"Good afternoon, my fine Japanese friend," the president said.

"Good afternoon, Mr. President," Kaitachi responded with a slight bow.

They walked into the Oval Office. The military aide closed the doors behind them. The president walked to a window and looked at the Washington Monument. The cherry blossoms were in full splendor around the tidal basin. It was a beautiful, tranquil sight. *The trees were a gift in 1912 from the Japanese ambassador's wife,* Davis recalled. *What other gifts are they bearing today?*

"I've considered your plea for a response from us," the president said.

"Oh?" Kaitachi said, sounding surprised.

The president shot his eyes to the side, measuring the inflection in the ambassador's voice.

"Yes," he said, turning and looking at the old man. "We will send a carrier battle group off the coast of Korea and warn them against any aggression."

"That is not necessary," Kaitachi said, backtracking. "We were only hoping for satellite assistance in observing the region."

"Well, why didn't you say so? Now I've moved an

entire carrier group over there."

"You are free to call them back, sir. My intentions were not to have you send forces, simply provide us intelligence in keeping with the spirit of our alliance," Kaitachi said.

I bet that's all you wanted. He's smooth. Very smooth.

"Whatever you say, but it may take some time to get them turned around. How do you guys feel about this situation in the Philippines?" he asked. The president grabbed a handful of peanuts from a bowl on his desk and popped them into his mouth.

"We are still concerned, but now believe that we can handle the threat in a regional sense," Kaitachi said.

"What do you mean?" Davis asked, interested. *Could this be it? Are they finally going to come clean?*

"Through statecraft, we can ensure our sea-lanes are not intercepted. We do not believe the Muslim insurgents, the Abu Sayyaf, will be a large threat to the region, as Bin Laden is to the world. Though we will watch. If it is more of an internal revolution that may, in the long run, improve the condition of the average Filipino, then, naturally, we support such improvement. But the primary reason I am here is to relay to you that my prime minister is very satisfied with your leadership in this crisis."

I bet, you sneaky son of a bitch.

"Well, thank you. Send my regards to Prime Minister Mizuzawa."

"I shall."

"Oh, by the way. My condolences on the death of your emperor. He was a good man," the president said sincerely. He had known Emperor Shigazawa to be a kind and caring person.

"Thank you. I will pass your remarks on to the prime minister."

President Davis watched Ambassador Kaitachi

leave his office, knowing full well that the diplomat was lying. He wanted to stop him and tell him that they knew everything, but that would have been a mistake.

Davis felt confident for the first time in days. He finally had the upper hand.

The president, still seated in his office, was wondering if they might be able to let Japan attack the Philippines, then counter with American force, eschewing the United Nations initially. After which, they could petition the UN for a peacekeeping force and mandatory trade concessions that would regulate trade imbalances. The key was forcing Japan into the "Hitler" aggressor role as America had rightly done, and was doing, with Saddam Hussein. *That shouldn't be too hard.*

President Davis jotted a note on White House stationery, then called his press aide and gave him some instructions regarding packaging his speech to the American people, the one that would inform the world of impending American action in the Philippines.

Not against the Islamic insurgents, but against Japan.

He picked up a remote and turned on the television, flipping through the channels rather quickly, then stopping and backing up. Then forward again. He recognized someone. There it was.

Kaitachi was on television. The president noticed the small C-SPAN symbol in the corner of the screen. Kaitachi was briefing the General Assembly of the United Nations. He raised the volume and listened as the interpreter spoke after Kaitachi talked in his native tongue. The ambassador must have taken the Japanese diplomatic jet to LaGuardia. Door to door from DC to the UN was less than two hours with the efficient transportation that a head of state or ambassador typically commanded.

"I have just received word from Prime Minister Mizuzawa that I am to address the body today concerning the revolution in the Philippines. Also, I briefed the president of the United States this morning on my remarks today."

What the hell is he talking about! The president sat forward in his chair, pressed an intercom button, and screamed into the receiver, "Dave, get in here, now!" The National Security Advisor came running into the oval office and saw the president watching C-SPAN.

"Look at this shit!"

They watched as Kaitachi spoke.

"Today, we have joined alliances with the United States in a dramatic way in this Global War on Terror. The Japanese military has landed on the Philippine Island of Luzon with a small show of force in an effort to ensure that our critical sea-lanes remain open. As you all know, we orchestrated the release of American and freedom-seeking peoples from the Philippines. Regrettably, further negotiations with Commander Talbosa, the so-called Abu Sayyaf leader, have led to his refusal to cooperate and resulted in a serious threat to Japanese sea-lanes and freedom-seeking peoples in the country.

"The barbaric acts of this Islamic ideologue must not go unchecked. His actions threaten the nascent democracies in the region. We have had several discussions with President Davis and his secretary of defense, who have requested assistance regarding this vital matter. I will provide transcripts of these conversations for the media. In effect, we were given the green light by the United States to handle the situation ourselves, and so we have.

"We promise to attempt to crush Islamic

fundamentalism, restore the democratic process to the Philippines, and ensure that our vital sea-lanes remain open. Our only goal is to alleviate the burden and pain of the Filipinos, who will surely suffer under the rule of Sharia law.

"Rest assured, we have no designs beyond protecting the fine people of the Philippines and protecting our vital interests. We want to thank our great allies, the United States, for their advice and assistance in this matter."

Kaitachi finished and walked away from the podium, leaving behind a speechless delegation, U.S. president, and world community.

Palmer snatched the remote and flipped to CNN, which was scrambling with the news. A CNN correspondent was sticking a microphone in his ear, looking at his notes, ready to provide some in-depth analysis.

Palmer shut off the television.

He and Davis looked at one another for a few brief seconds. Japan had surrounded them with bishops, knights, and rooks. The president felt frozen in place. Was America facing a potential checkmate? No, that wasn't possible.

It occurred to him, as it might have occurred to Napoleon that Wellington was indeed on the reverse slope of the hill as his forces impaled themselves on the British lances, that they had been at least one step behind Japan at every juncture.

"Why do I feel like we're standing here holding our jockstraps, Dave?"

Palmer looked uncomfortably at the floor, then leveled his eyes on the president.

"Because we are, sir."

CHAPTER 75

MCLEAN, VIRGINIA

Meredith had raced to her condo five minutes away in Pentagon City, where she was pulling her nylons over her legs and had a hairbrush clutched between her teeth doing the "Superman change," as she called it. It was nearing seven o'clock, and Latisha had called to remind her that Stone was expecting her to arrive at his home for some planning. Latisha had mentioned that they might return to the Pentagon after the secretary had his dinner, depending on developments in the Philippines. She was not thrilled about having to fight DC rush-hour traffic from her Arlington apartment to his McLean mansion.

The television was blasting FoxNews in the background as she stood, yanking the hose up around her waist, then letting her cocktail dress fall to her knees. She stepped to the mirror, sighed, and said, "This will have to do."

She slipped Rathburn's thumb drive into her purse, disappointed that she'd not had much time to truly consider what its contents might be, or might portend.

"Ambassador Kaitachi has just announced that Japan intends to join forces with the United States in the Global War on Terror to, and I quote, 'crush Islamic fundamentalism' in the Philippines …"

She was brushing her hair, then in slow motion she stopped the smooth stroke against her blond locks, staring at the image of the television in the mirror.

"Oh my God," she said.

Her mind raced and locked onto the big picture. Just as the Third Reich had begun with the embarrassment and constraining loss of territory from World War I's Treaty of Versailles, Japan was still smarting from World War II's post conflict occupation and dominance by the Americans. Like an ill patient who has sweat through the sheets shedding a virus, Japan has suffered the alien imposition of Western culture only to come back to their native heritage.

Hitler had started with the Night of the Long Knives, where key German leaders were murdered in order to allow for consolidation of power. *The Japanese Emperor has just committed suicide,* she thought.

Then Hitler got around the German constitution limiting their Army to one hundred thousand soldiers by merging the Army and the Sturmab-teilung, the assault force. *Japan is circumventing their constitution by building tanks and helicopters in the Philippines.*

In 1938, Hitler compelled Austrian Chancellor Kurt von Schuschnigg to capitulate in a bloodless invasion. Then followed Sudetenland, or Czechoslovakia, then Poland and ...

"Oh my God," she said again.

Japan is starting with the Philippines, then going to Taiwan!

How did we miss this?

She jumped in her old Honda Prelude and took the George Washington Parkway from her Pentagon Row apartment onto Dolley Madison and into McLean. She found the address and debated a few minutes whether to pull into the long driveway or park on the street. She looked around and determined that her piece of junk might get towed if she left it on the street. As she pulled into the long driveway, she noticed that it arced in front of the huge colonial mansion. She followed the curve and stopped just beyond the hedgerow that abutted the asphalt.

She stood, grabbed her briefcase and purse, and walked up the steps.

Soaking in the moment, and the environment, the old Virginia Slims commercial rang in her head.

You've come a long way, baby.

CHAPTER 76

Stone swirled his Scotch in his glass and thought about the day. He had met with the Joint Chiefs once again to discuss the announcement of the Japanese ambassador at the United Nations. The media frenzy was predictable but unnerving. War in Afghanistan was raging, and now the Philippines? How were Abu Sayyaf and Al Qaeda linked? Did the Philippines add a Pacific Rim dimension to the Global War on Terror? Did it scuttle the plan for Iraq? How much joint and combined planning had the United States done with the Japanese?

All good questions.

He had given a brief press conference, not wanting to say anything of significance before the president's speech. They had worked hard through the day, and there was little else he could do tonight other than monitor the situation from his home. Besides, he had Meredith coming over for dinner shortly, and with his wife out of town, he thought he might digress from the rapid pace of events for a while. *It's officially a meeting*, he thought to himself.

She smiled at me a lot today. I'm Mick Jagger! Stone muddied his mind with prurient thoughts of Meredith. *She's wearing prettier dresses for me. She wants me, I can tell.*

He sat in his leather recliner in the study of his McLean mansion, which had cost well over two million dollars. It was a large, redbrick, Colonial design. The house was beautiful, with far too many rooms for any two people, and Stone had a servant who lived in separate quarters.

He heard the doorbell ring and listened to the footsteps of Andre, his butler for all practical purposes. He heard the banter of small talk and smiled when he heard Meredith's voice sing sweetly in the large foyer, drifting through the expansive hallways, echoing into the abyss of his depraved mind. *She wants me. Otherwise, she would not have shown.* He had changed into a shirt and sweater with khaki pants. He figured the collegiate look might attract her. The sweater could not hide his protruding gut, though, and the khaki pants did not make him look any taller. In fact, Meredith was a good two inches taller than he was. It made him uncomfortable, and, therefore, he had to conquer her.

"Hello, sir," Meredith said in a cheery voice. She was dressed in a simple blue cocktail dress that plunged moderately low into her bustline.

White pearls lay softly against her bare neck, beckoning to him. Her hair was its usual blond splendor, only frozen into place with hair spray. The dress cut above her panty-hose-covered knees, and angled slightly up on the left side, teasing him. A faint smell of perfume circled him, accelerating his lust.

Her innocent smile and wide blue eyes greeted him, comforting him in his own knowledge that indeed she did want him. *She dressed up just for me.*

"Meredith, you look beautiful. I'm sorry I underdressed. I thought we were just going to go over a few notes. I can go change if you'd like," he said, standing from the chair. *Good move, Mick old boy. Make her the aggressor.*

Andre had floated back to the kitchen with a shit-eating grin on his face. *Boss man be getting some tonight.* After catching sight of Meredith, Andre could not blame him.

"No, no," she said, smiling, and grabbing him by

the arm. She was personable and liked to touch in a social setting. It was her way of communicating.

Touching, already. That's good. Very good.

"I've got the briefcase right here. And after hearing Kaitachi, I think we've got plenty to work on."

"I was just going to have some dinner with Mrs. Stone, but she got called away. Would you like her plate?" Stone said.

"I'm so sorry," Meredith said, again lightly touching his arm. He wanted to reach out and satisfy her on the spot. She obviously wanted him. The dress, the hair, the perfume, the pearls, the face, the smile, the high heels, the touching. Yes, there was no doubt she wanted him.

"Drinks?" Andre asked. He wore a white butler coat and shirt, with black pants and a black bow tie.

"Meredith?" Stone said, smiling, knowing what bounty lay ahead for him. He would savor the moment.

"Whatever you're having, sir," she said, her voice oozing over him, causing his heart to flutter. He blushed.

"Two glasses of champagne, please Andre," he said. "And bring the bottle." Yes, they would drink, loosen inhibitions, and maybe even skip dinner. *I knew it. She's wanted me since day one.*

They sat on the leather sofa and drank champagne. At some point Meredith had gained the courage to grab the remote control and flip the television to CNN, muting the volume so they could talk. She had one eye on the television though. Soon the president would be on.

Andre had served dinner and cleaned up, retiring for the evening to his quarters after bringing a second bottle of champagne. Stone had drunk most of the first bottle, distorting his already skewed perception of the evening. Meredith had successfully nursed two glasses but was feeling the effects of the alcohol. She still preferred beer.

"Ready to get to work, Meredith?" Stone said. He stood and stumbled.

"Don't you want to wait for the president's speech, sir?" Meredith asked seriously.

"No, I've seen a copy. Let's go to the study."

Stone stood, hovering over Meredith as she stared at the television.

CHAPTER 77

For the first time in the evening, Meredith was uncomfortable. She saw a glint in Stone's eyes that sparkled of a hidden agenda. She looked nervously at her attire and suddenly felt guilty for being beautiful.

"C'mon. Let's head to the study, there's a TV in there," he said. She was still wondering how she could have been so stupid. Had she led him on? No, maybe his motives were pure. She had done much for him, and indeed the country, in a behind-the-scenes sort of way over the past week. Perhaps this was Stone's way of saying thank you, by letting some of the help enjoy a small part of his life. She wanted to believe that.

"I haven't read the speech though. I'd like to see it, sir."

"Hell, you wrote part of it," he said. "I gave your report to Palmer. He said there was no use reinventing the wheel and that he'd embellish your comments and give them to the president."

"Well, now I really want to see it," she said, forcing a smile. Yes, she could do this. Delay until he got tired. He was an old man and would probably go limp soon.

She turned up the volume of the television as the camera panned the face of the president. He looked worried and tired.

Stone turned on the stereo, put a CD in the disc changer, and soon the Rolling Stones' "Wild Horses" was belting out of the speakers, nearly overriding the television. Stone played a bit of air guitar, grabbed a mock microphone, and said, "Mick Jagger!"

Then he moved behind the sofa and rested his hands on the leather to either side of Meredith's shoulders. She could feel his hot breath blowing into her hair. "I'm a rock star," he whispered in her ear.

Gross.

"Good evening, my fellow Americans," the president said. "Tonight I speak to you, the nation, and to the entire world concerning the rapidly unfolding events in the Philippines.

"As you all know, earlier today Japan announced her intentions to intervene militarily in the affairs of the Republic of the Philippines. Specifically, they stated that they wished to restore democracy to the freedom-loving people of the Philippines. Such a move is consistent with our desire to maintain dem- ocratic governments around the world, yet it competes with the emerging international consensus of guaranteeing the right to self-determination of individual countries." Meredith smiled. It was her line. Stone had not lied; at least not about using her words for the president's speech. More heavy breathing, though, like an obscene phone call.

"However, we will begin dialogue with the Japanese government to discuss alternatives to the physical military occupation of the Philippines. We believe there are other methods of securing Japan's lines of communication through the South China and Celebes Seas. I ask the international community to be patient with us and with Japan. We will find a solution through statecraft." Meredith wondered why the president would show the glimpse of a smile when he said "through statecraft."

"My message to the American people is, don't be alarmed. The situation is well under control. My message to the people of the Philippines is that we will work to ensure your country is not beholden to the dark vision of Islamic extremism. My message to the world is that we have the lead in this action. Our Japanese allies will work independently, yet we will closely monitor their military action. All freedom-seeking people wish to stem the flow of Islamic fundamentalism and the sinister future it harbors.

"Thank you and God bless America and all freedom-loving people."

Short and way off the point, Meredith surmised.

It said so little, but meant so much. The world would interpret it as meaning Japan's actions were intended to fight Islamic extremism, saving a bit of face for the president and perhaps calming the fears of China, Russia, and Korea. Those nations, at least in the near term, would be reluctant to take any kind of action against Japan. It was crucial to portray Japan as an ally, she had told Stone, thereby negating a knee-jerk response from any one country, lest they have to contend with the American nuclear and conventional arsenal.

"I told you, dearie," Stone said. Meredith looked down and instinctively pulled her skirt toward her knees.

Stone had dimmed the lights during the short speech. It was clear he had not listened. She looked at the second bottle of champagne. He had nearly sucked it dry, and she cringed at the thought of his operating on a bottle and a half of alcohol. She had eluded several college men in similar circumstances, but never did she imagine she would have to pull the plug on the sexual batteries of the secretary of defense.

"The study, darling, or would you prefer to use— stay on the couch?" Stone said.

She sensed he was on testosterone override. The alcohol had flipped a switch in his brain, sending an electrical current to his penis, thereby relinquishing all control to the lower appendage for the time being.

She looked at her watch and said, lamely, "Sir, I

must really be going. You know what they say about wearing out—"

"The sofa?" Stone said, moving around to her front, intercepting her before she could escape. He grabbed her arm and sat next to her. He stared wildly at her breasts, which she instinctively covered.

"Sir!" Meredith said, weakly.

A weak protest. It always means they want it.

"Don't you want to make love to one of the most powerful men in the world, Meredith?" Stone asked, sounding a bit like Jack Nicholson might. His fingers pressed into the flesh of her slender arm. His breath was sour with the musty odor of the cham-pagne fermenting in his belly.

"Sir, really. This is inappropriate," she said, pushing him away and snatching her arm back. She looked at the bruises.

Then leave. Why are you just sitting there? Because you want it. That's why. "You want me, don't you. You've wanted me since you showed up in my office. Now let's get down to business, Meredith. Let's cut to the chase. I'm Mick Jagger," Stone said, hungrily. He pulled at her dress and a naked breast popped out of the fabric.

Yes, that's more like it. I knew you wanted me.

He grabbed her arms and lay on top of her, hiking her dress all the way up to her waist. He looked down at her panty hose and pulled at them with his fingers, wanting to secure his prize. He deserved it, he figured. It had been a hard week at the office.

Meredith, you stupid bitch, why are just taking this? Do something! He's raping you! she thought.

Meredith used her strength to push Stone's heavy body off her and onto the floor. She stood, stepping over him.

"Oh, want to get on top, huh. I should have guessed," Stone said.

She pulled her panty hose up, grabbed her purse,

and tried to run. Stone grabbed at her legs, causing her to fall and strike her forehead on the oak coffee table, leaving a huge gash, which gushed blood onto her face.

"You son of a bitch!" Meredith screamed, running from the study. She bumped into Andre, who had awakened to the commotion, splattering blood onto his white T-shirt.

"He tried to rape me!" she said, running from the house and getting into her car. She sat in the car and cried for a moment.

When she looked up, Stone's face was at the driver's side window.

She locked the doors and cranked the engine. Typically, as in the movies, the car did not start, and the engine kept turning over.

Finally, she floored the gas pedal, flooding the engine. It cranked, pouring white smoke from the exhaust, and she sped away, purposely veering the car into Stone, knocking him on his rear.

He did not care.

She's just playing hard to get. Mick Jagger never gets rejected.

Stone picked himself up, ascended the steps on his porch, and saw a small metal object in the dim light. Wobbling, he bent over and picked up the small device.

"What's this?" he asked himself, his words slurring a bit as he pocketed an object about the size of his thumb.

"Brian Jones," the newest member of the Rolling Stones, had received a call from Ronnie Wood, who was truthfully not too far away. It seemed he needed some assistance. A jam session, so to speak.

"Mick's going a little crazy, and we will need to clean up after him," Ronnie Wood had said.

"Just tell me where. I always have my axe to grind," Brian Jones said.

And so Brian sat in his Buick Electra 225. "Gets about two gallons to the mile," he always remarked to those who ogled the beast. And it was perfect when he wanted to play bumper cars.

He followed her off of Old Dominion onto Swinks Mill, then onto Lewinsville, where she curled onto the I-495 in preparation, he presumed, for entry onto the George Washington Parkway.

Brian Jones looked at his watch: almost 11:00 P.M. He saw the occasional car, but nothing that bothered him. He tailed the slow-moving Prelude at about a quarter mile distance. By the way she was driving, he wasn't concerned about being noticed. She sped up to ninety miles an hour on I-495 and almost missed the entrance to the parkway, but caught it at the last minute, her wheels nearly leaving the pavement.

Mick must have put a good licking on her, he thought.

It was his time to inch closer. They were barreling down the parkway past Turkey Run Park and approaching the exit for Dolley Madison Boulevard. A sharp turn was approaching, which was followed by a bridge.

He was now less than five car lengths behind her and he flashed his bright lights at her, which caused her to speed up, as he had anticipated. Jones believed that Meredith would be fearful that Stone was following her, so he pulled up directly behind her as they were approaching 100 mph on the narrow road.

She accelerated into the turn and the Prelude left the road.

Jones slowed a bit and watched as the car failed to negotiate the turn and flipped onto its side. The low roof crumpled and sparks were flying every-where, then the vehicle skidded off the road, falling thirty feet below into a ditch just before the bridge.

Close enough, Brian Jones thought, so he kept driving.

The Electra didn't have a scratch.

CHAPTER 78

ISLAND OF LUZON, PHILIPPINES

The attack had been successful. Takishi sat atop the turret of a brand-new, Japanese Type 90 tank with its 120mm smoothbore gun.

It seemed they could not miss. They had secured the Presidential Palace early in the operation. He had flown in the Mistubishi AH-X attack helicopter, still in its experimental phase. It had performed beautifully. Hellfire missiles reduced the thin-skinned rebel vehicles to burning hulks in seconds. The captured Scorpion tanks and old American M-113 Armored Personnel Carriers were no match for the new and improved version of the Japanese Imperial Army.

Once in the compound, they had completely destroyed the radio television stations. A holdover from the Marcos era was the fact that the government controlled the only two means of real-time communication to the people. Takishi had them destroyed immediately, preventing incoming or outgoing television or radio reports. Talbosa was most shocked of all to see Takishi enter the presidential grounds with nearly two hundred Japanese infantrymen trotting beside him carrying American M16 rifles. Takishi was wielding his New Nambu revolver, waving it and smiling at Talbosa.

"Let's go, my friend. It is time to move on to another life," Takishi said, pointing the revolver in Talbosa's face.

"What are you doing, you fool?" Talbosa screamed.

"You are the fool, letting us build weapons in your own backyard. You idiot," Takishi laughed.

Talbosa's eyes sank to the ground, as did his hopes for a new Philippines, independent of imperialism. But once again, it appeared that the Japanese would write another chapter in the historical journal of Philippine conquest. First the Spanish, then the Americans, then the Japanese, then the Americans, and now the Japanese again.

"I guess everything does come full cycle," Talbosa said softly, looking at Takishi.

Takishi smiled and nodded, watching as his forces rolled through the streets of Manila amidst an angry mob of people.

Lifting his pearl handled revolver to Talbosa's head, Takishi pulled the trigger from point blank. Talbosa's lifeless body slumped at the front gate of the Presidential Palace. As if to celebrate, the Japanese soldiers shot into the crowd, killing some, quickly dispersing the group that had assembled to protest. The Japanese army had gathered almost two thousand members of Talbosa's Abu Sayyaf and were marching them north past the airport, into the countryside in the direction of Cabanatuan.

The tank treads creaked forward slowly, as if to nudge the stragglers in the group of rebels. Some women and children had accompanied their husbands and fathers for the march north to wherever. They were the fortunate ones, though, as thousands lay dead behind them.

The insurgents had put up a valiant fight but were no match for the sophisticated weaponry of the Japanese. The Japanese fought from the technological comfort of their machines, mowing down the rebels, who would foolishly stand and fire small-arms weapons at them. The insurgents had used most of their antitank and antiaircraft weapons during the initial assault and subsequent mopping-up operations. In fact, they had gotten downright careless with the ammunition, thinking and hoping they would no longer need it.

They had been wrong.

Takishi's plan was to drive the Abu Sayyaf north to Fort Magsaysay where they would lock them in prison facilities, or shoot them, whichever Prime Minister Mizuzawa had decided.

The crowd neared three thousand as the Japanese soldiers would storm a hamlet of thatch huts, find weapons indicating the residents belonged to the Abu Sayyaf, and add them to the group. They walked with bare feet along the white cement road, past their neighbors and friends, some of whom watched the procession, others joining out of defiance. The Filipinos were a proud people, regardless of political orientation. They were tired of foreign domination of their country and would remain defiant to the end.

The large mob was getting hard to control. Takishi's soldiers formed a cordon on either side of the tired, hungry group, walking much faster than the heat of the day allowed for. The pavement was piping hot, burning hardened bare feet at the touch. Pregnant women passed out along the way, dropping to the side, only to be nudged with the pointed tip of a soldier's bayonet. Some lost their babies, others simply did not continue.

None of the group had enough time to secure any food or water for the march, many dropping from heat exhaustion. They had traveled over twenty miles in less than six hours, a brutal pace. Fort Magsaysay was fifty miles north of Manila. They were almost halfway there. Takishi believed they would be able to make it by nightfall.

CHAPTER 79

"Piece of shit," Matt yelled, kicking the truck. It had died on them. Simply died without forewarning. No idiot light came on. No gauge needle pegged out. The truck just crapped out. They had traveled just five miles from their captivity.

"Where the hell are we?" Sturgeon asked, not really expecting an answer.

"We're just outside Cabanatuan. Used to be an Abu Sayyaf stronghold. Still is, I guess," Barefoot told them. He had studied the country. He wanted to break the mold of the idiot, liberal journalist. Unfortunately, he was running for his life and not covering a story.

The morning sun bore down on them like an eighteen-wheeler with high beams. At least they had made it past the sunken rice paddy area. They had hunkered down for the day in a low area about five miles from their former prison cell and had chosen to move at night. The sun was rising, and they needed to find concealment, Matt knew. Now they were standing amidst a desolate expanse of hardpan covered in white dirt with isolated patches of grass shooting through.

Matt spied a small wooded area to the west and said, "We need to do something about Rathburn's body. We need to bury him and somehow mark the spot so one day we can come back for him."

"Yeah. You're right," Sturgeon said.

"There," Matt pointed. There was a small hill with a tight cluster of hardwoods about three hundred meters to their west. The terrain feature contrasted sharply from the indistinct hardpan upon which they stood and the soggy rice paddies behind them. The town of Cabanatuan was less than a mile to the west, interrupted by the clump of trees on a small hill.

"That looks good," Sturgeon said, pointing to the trees.

"Good," Matt said, thinking. "Barefoot, is there any way we could get the place on film, in case, you know"—he paused—"something should happen to us. At least there would be a record of where we buried him."

"Why don't I do a story on this if my batteries work," Barefoot said. Barefoot carried with him a camera with tripod and remote, a satellite antenna, and the four-port uplink that linked the antenna to the camera and processed the information digitally over the computer. The beauty of the system was that it was all entirely battery-operated.

"Yeah. Let's do that, then tell the world where we are. Why didn't you tell us your stuff worked?" Matt asked, hopeful.

"It will only record. I'm sure the rebels pilfered my stuff," Barefoot said. "I'll check it once we get situated."

Two of the men carried the media equipment while a third carried Rathburn's stiff, putrid body across the dusty surface. It was a short walk, but still, they took turns swapping Rathburn's body among themselves. It wasn't so much the weight as it was the smell. Plus, the rigid body was awkward to handle.

They entered the comforting shade of the wooded knoll and disappeared amidst the trees. The mahoganies were tall and dark, blocking the searing, penetrating rays of the sun. Each man had a canteen of water they had found in the back of the truck, curiously, and drank without concern for where the next canteen would come from.

Matt dumped Rathburn's body on the ground. The dirt around the trees was darker and much softer than the crusted hardpan they had traversed. The woods were larger than they initially appeared, running a couple of hundred meters to the west, toward Cabanatuan. He found a tree branch, snapped the twigs away, and whittled the end into a spade with Sturgeon's knife. He tossed the knife to its owner, who did the same.

The two men dug a shallow grave in nearly an hour. They worked feverishly for some unknown reason—they had all the time in the world, but their sense was that Rathburn had been violated and by planting his body in the ground, somehow it would begin the healing process. Perhaps then, his soul could escape the horror of the past few days and ascend to the heavens.

Meanwhile, Barefoot set up his equipment, testing and checking. He was surprised to find everything in working order. He pointed the satellite dish toward the sky until he got a red signal indicator showing that he had linkup with the CNN satellite. Then the signal faded. CNN's satellite, Barefoot believed, was geostationary. So either he had lost the signal or his batteries were weak. Regardless, he pressed on.

Matt and Sturgeon lifted Rathburn's body into the grave and began the burial process. Barefoot popped a blank tape into his camera and began filming. Out of decency, he filmed only the faces of Jack and Matt, working feverishly to bury their fallen comrade. *This will make a great story, maybe even win a Pulitzer.* Barefoot's immediate thoughts were with Rathburn though. He did not know the man, but knew he had probably suffered a terrible death. Worse, his after-death experience had been one of mutilation and agony. *The gods may never take him,* Barefoot thought to himself.

When Rathburn was covered with dirt, Matt took the two field-expedient spades and drove them deep into the ground with a rock, marking the head and foot of the grave. When the June rains came, and all the ground seemed the same, the two branches should still be protruding a foot or so from the earth's surface.

"I would just like to say a few words," Matt said, unaffected by the camera. He stood with the mound of dirt behind him, framed by the two branches. To his rear, the trees thinned, giving way to the hardpan below and the city of Cabanatuan to the west. The cement road was visible in the background as it emerged from some tiny shacks on the edge of the town only two hundred meters from their location.

Sturgeon took a knee in his salt-lined flight suit. He had sweat completely through it digging the grave. Barefoot didn't notice the red light from his satellite transponder, it had come back on. He was transmitting.

Matt was a continuing contrast, like a photo-negative. His khaki shirt was now gray from dirt stains collecting on the wetness of his sweat. His cargo pants were nearly white from the dusty hardpan. Sweat had washed away the film of dirt from his unshaven face, revealing his drawn, hardened features. He had not eaten for two full days and was weak. His hair was matted and unclean. His voice was solid, though, as he spoke.

"Today we mark the death of Mr. Bart Rathburn, the assistant secretary of defense for international security affairs. Two days ago rebels from the Abu Sayyaf kidnapped Mr. Rathburn, myself, Matt Garrett, and Jack Sturgeon, the pilot of the destroyed Department of Defense airplane. We are fortunate enough to have the company of Johnny Barefoot, a

CNN correspondent whom the rebels mistook for a spy. It is a sad day. Bart Rathburn gave his life in the service of his country. The rebels attacked, took us hostage, and for two days we sat in a rat-infested jail cell at a place called Fort Magsaysay near a small town on the island of Luzon called Cabanatuan.

"Bart Rathburn is a man who died before his time and an American hero in his own right. He had resisted in the spirit of the American fighting soldier, but in the end the Abu Sayyaf tortured and killed him.

"I did not know Bart Rathburn well, but his assistant, Meredith Morris, described him as a dedicated family man with a beautiful wife and two boys. We are making this documentary to record the location of his burial in case we do not escape from this conflict."

Curiously, as Matt talked, Barefoot could see through the camera a group of people walking on the road and thought he heard a faint, high-pitched squeak of machinery. Momentarily, he cut the camera to the side of Matt's face and zoomed past the trees onto the edge of the town. He saw about twenty Filipinos dragging in the dirt. Behind them were soldiers wearing dark green, olive drab uniforms, holding weapons and sometimes prodding the stragglers.

Zooming even closer, Matt's voice droned on about Rathburn while Barefoot watched with horror as Japanese soldiers poked and prodded the emerging masses along the road. Another contrast.

Through the zoom lens, Barefoot taped, but actually transmitted to a satellite, images of another era. *This is not possible today,* he thought. He filmed soldiers herding young children onto the hot pavement in the afternoon sun. He saw muzzle flashes of random gunfire that somehow seemed too accurate. He saw tanks and mechanized fighting vehicles rolling

slowly, setting the pace of the march from the rear.
But there was no rear. The fifty-mile march from
Manila had swelled to over six thousand. Mothers and
fathers carrying their children. Some shot through the
backs if they could not keep up.

He watched in horror and zoomed to a full body
view, as a young Filipino male shouted angrily at a
Japanese soldier, who leveled a pistol at the young
man's head and squeezed the trigger. Through the
camera, the execution seemed to have a higher
resolution. The faces of the two men. One angry, the
other cold and expressionless. Simply doing a duty.
Asian faces, one soft, almost European, the other
harsh, brutally so. Their bodies. One brownish, the
other yellow, one lean and malnourished, the other
strong and stocky like a barrel. Their weapons. One
his temperament, the other a Japanese 9mm officer's
pistol.

Matt and Sturgeon snapped their heads when
they heard the gunshot that sounded so close. They
had become accustomed to the random, distant
firing of weapons, but knew this to be something
else.

"Look between the trees," Barefoot said, pointing,
unaware that a young college intern in Atlanta,
Georgia, was watching the scene as he transmitted his
signal to the Syncom 3 satellite, an old coaxial slotted
array communication satellite positioned nineteen
hundred kilometers north of Fiji. Almost forty years
ago, American television companies used the same
satellite to transmit the Olympics from Tokyo.

The young woman was unsure if she was watching
HBO, reality TV, or a broadcaster's transmission.
Thinking she had better check it out, this being her
first day on the job, she asked the Headline News
production manager, Lewis Silver, to take a look at

what was on her screen. He did so gladly, wanting to help the young lass. Carrying a cup of coffee into the room with a bank of television sets, all transmitting different images, he sat down and looked as she pointed. It was early in Georgia, only five o'clock, and Americans were not awake yet. At least most were not.

President Davis looked away from the television screen and at Palmer.

"There it is," Palmer said.

"I agree," Stone said, working off his champagne hangover. Thankfully, Fox and Diamond hadn't been called into the early-morning meeting in the White House.

"There are other options," Lantini protested mildly, drawing a curious stare from Stone.

"We've got to do it," Sewell said, then looked at Stone.

Three to one, Davis thought, then said, "Pull the trigger."

CHAPTER 80

PENTAGON, WASHINGTON, DC

The next morning Saul Fox and Dick Diamond licked their lips as they watched the video of Secretary Stone assaulting Meredith Morris. From a speaker in the corner of the office, Jean Valjean was belting out "Who am I?" from *Les Miserables*.

"We could not have asked for better timing," Fox said.

"Nothing better," Diamond agreed, stuffing his digital assistant into his suit coat pocket.

The two men sat in Fox's office, where they always seemed to be. His was a large square workspace with a huge mahogany desk and matching conference table that jutted off the front of the desk forming a T. The arrangement allowed Fox to sit at his command center while his minions briefed him, talked to him, paid homage, whatever the task. Diamond, however, being as important as Fox, sat in a leather chair to the side of Fox's desk, facing him.

"So let's review the bidding," Fox said.

"Let's," Diamond concurred.

"First, these silly Rolling Stones have been trying to do an amateur diversion in the Pacific to divert attention and forces away from that which will give us lasting fame."

"Do we know who all the members are? Do we need to do anything more regarding the Rolling Stones?"

"Well, Stone is obviously Jagger and Takishi is

one of them. Probably Rathburn also. Then, of course, you know who the fourth is."

"Yes. Mighty surprising, don't you think?" Diamond asked uncomfortably. In fact, he had no idea what Fox was talking about, but decided to play along. *Does he really know?*

"I do, but as long as we can keep him saying publicly that Iraq is a threat, the idea builds a momentum all its own, even if privately he's participating in a scheme to forestall the invasion."

"I just thought, you know, why does he have Stone do his dirty work?"

"You can ask the man," Fox said, indicating he was ready to move on.

"Yes, well, Rathburn is dead, and Takishi is both out of control and under control, if you know what I mean."

"Yes, good find there," Fox agreed.

"So, we have Takishi turn up the volume with his tank divisions and push the administration into negotiating mode. No way in hell is anyone going to want to go against the equivalent of a tank corps in the Philippines."

"What about the soldiers who are there?" Fox asked. "We just leave them, right?"

Diamond chuckled. "Hey, they signed up for it, so they deserve to stay put."

"Yes, agreed. So, I've already denied several troop requests from Pacific Command and am diverting them to Central Command, and if you can kick old Jim Fleagles in the nuts and get him to use some 'statecraft,' well, that would be good."

"I'll call him shortly, just as soon as Stone leaves."

As if on cue, Stone walked into the office. Diamond didn't move, nor did Fox, relegating the senior ranking man to the "minion" table.

"What's up guys? You said you wanted to talk about the situation?" Stone asked.

"Yes," Fox said, picking up the remote and pressing play. "It seems that Mick Jagger is going to be asking, how shall I say it, to 'gimme shelter'?"

The television showed Stone in full color playing the air guitar, then screaming, "Mick Jagger!" Next they watched as Stone slid behind Meredith and kissed her ear.

"Shall I go on?" Fox asked.

"You son of a bitch," Stone said.

"Not nice to talk about my mother that way, Bob," Fox said.

"Not nice at all," Diamond added.

"Now here's what were going to do," Fox related. "State has lead on the Philippines. Defense focuses on Iraq. And while we can push a lot of forces in that direction, they will be a show of force. Nothing will become decisively engaged in the Philippines, and everything that is not already there will keep moving around the Celebes Sea, into the Indian Ocean, and into Kuwait and other parts of the Middle East to begin preparation for the destruction of Iraq."

"You mean Saddam Hussein, right, Saul?" Stone rebuked.

"Whatever," Fox replied.

"What, you think you're the only player with dirt on somebody?"

Fox looked at Diamond, then at Stone and shrugged, as if to say, *Show me what you got.*

"I will show you. I can play this game, too. Have been, you idiots," Stone said, standing.

"Tsk, tsk, Bob," Fox said. "Dick here will put this on his blog site in an hour if I don't have a firm commitment from you on the Iraq plan."

"In thirty minutes, I'll put all the evidence of your short trading in AIG two days before Nine-eleven," Stone said. "You think that won't raise some eyebrows? Okay, so I was trying to get some skank, but at least I didn't bet on the Nine-eleven attacks.

And if you bet on those attacks, guess what, genius, you knew about them. And if you knew about them, you might have been involved in them. Need me to keep going?"

"What evidence do you think you have?" Fox asked, all of a sudden less confident.

"All that I need, and I can see I've got your attention."

"Certainly have mine," Diamond said.

"Well, I believe you were in on that short sale also, no?" Fox smiled.

Stone stood and said, "You know I wasn't. Here's the deal. We will send what we think we need to the Philippines, slip the Iraq war a year to next spring, and develop a better plan."

"That's unsatisfactory," Fox replied.

"That's the deal. I have compelling evidence of your shorting 500,000 shares of AIG two days before Nine-eleven. The insurance company dropped forty points over the next three months. How much is that, Saul? Two hundred million?"

"My name is nowhere on any of those transactions," Fox said, a film of sweat forming on his brow.

"Maybe not, but we've traced it to you. Are you getting satisfaction now?"

"What about the Predator deal? Where did that money go?" Diamond asked, trying to rescue his friend.

"That's classified, Dick, and I'm having your security clearance revoked immediately," Stone said. He stood, walked to the DVD player, pulled the disc out of the machine, snapped it into little pieces, stuffed those into his pocket, and walked to the connecting side door.

Stopping in the doorway, Stone pointed at Fox, and said, "One word of this leaks, the world will know that you are a Nine-eleven coconspirator and that you became rich overnight. How many years do you think you'll get? It won't be much fun being 'inside'; maybe even GTMO? Treason? How's that sound?"

Fox nodded. Diamond looked at Fox, then at Stone.

Stone walked into his office and shut the door.

Phase V: Hard Landing

CHAPTER 81

USS CARL VINSON, CELEBES SEA

Admiral Jennings put the secure red-switch telephone back in its receiver and turned the plastic key that contained a digitized microchip to encode the phone conversation. Chairman Sewell had called him to tell him that the secretary of defense had authorized the plan for major combat operations in Operation Enduring Freedom-Philippines.

In essence, they had already "pulled the trigger." Jennings had, on the order of Sewell and the president, executed the initial phase earlier that morning by sinking the six ships anchored off the Luzon Straits. A Los Angeles-class submarine had systematically eliminated each vessel with a torpedo in the fore and aft hulls. The SEALs had provided critical information regarding hull density of the vessels, and sinking them had been a quite simple operation.

Jennings praised the actions of the submarine commander, realizing it was a "no-brainer" mission. They had been concerned about the modest Japanese submarine force, but intelligence indicated that the entire submarine fleet was operating somewhere between Taiwan and Japan, as was the rest of the Japanese Navy.

The American carrier battle group had stopped in the East China Sea near Okinawa with a threefold purpose. Its primary mission was to isolate all Japanese units from reinforcing the Philippine

Theater of Operations (PTO). A secondary mission was to protect American forces stationed on Okinawa and in American bases on Japan. While the Navy would never admit it, the Japanese could safely assume that some of the ships in the carrier group contained nuclear weapons capable of targeting Japan. The last mission was to act as a deterrent to Chinese and Korean aggression in the area. While they were unprepared to complete that mission, the nuclear card again came into play in a big way.

President Davis had talked to the Korean and Chinese ambassadors, who were noncommittal in their response to him concerning their own security plans.

Then the president had called Mizuzawa and asked him to withdraw his troops from the Philippines. Mizuzawa told him not to waste his efforts, that Japan would rid the Philippines of the Islamic plague spreading across the island and restore the legitimate government of the Philippines.

"You have no right to intervene," he had told the president. "Did we stop you from invading Afghanistan or Iraq or Panama?"

"We have every right to stop you from terrorizing the world again. I won't let it happen," the president had replied to Mizuzawa.

"We're doing nothing more than you've done in the past. You need our help in this Global War on Terror, as you call it."

"We can still negotiate this thing," Davis had said, trying to calm and reassure the minister-run-amuck, as the other two battalions from the Twenty-fifth Infantry Division's light infantry brigade were flying in C-17 aircraft, awaiting the clearance of the runway. And as the two Ranger battalions were jumping into Fort Magsaysay to stop the terror, the Marine expeditionary force sped toward the southwestern coast of Luzon to encircle the advancing Japanese divisions. U.S. Air Force and Navy pilots, as well, began the long and arduous process of fighting American-made, Japanese-flown jets to try to establish air superiority so the ground forces could conduct their business under an umbrella of protection.

Jennings sat in the command-and-control cell of his command ship off the western coast of Luzon, listening to spot reports as they came in from the J-2 (intelligence) and J-3 (operations) officers. There had been no time to establish massive forces as America had done during Operations Desert Shield and Desert Storm. This was a joint contingency operation all the way, not unlike the recent action in Afghanistan. The Rangers had flown in from the Continental United States, the light infantry soldiers from Hawaii, the Marines from Okinawa, the Air Force from Guam and the continental United States, and the Navy from the Indian Ocean and Hawaii. All were supposed to converge on the island of Luzon, like dancing on the head of a pin, and mesh and coordinate and synchronize and come together as if they had practiced it a hundred times the night before.

Of course, they had not. And it did not.

The Rangers had landed and were experiencing heavy resistance from a large armored force, nearly a brigade of two hundred tanks. Caught off guard, and perhaps inserted by a naval commanding officer who did not quite understand their purpose, the Rangers were moving into the jungle, where they were more effective. But their mission had been to secure the prison camps that the ever-faulty intelligence system had declared "lightly defended." Perhaps to a navy officer used to traveling on aircraft carriers, a brigade of tanks was no big deal. But it was devastating to the lightly armed Rangers, as they made their way back across muddy rice paddies and over the gently sloping terrain until they could blend into the jungle.

Lieutenant Colonel Buck's light infantry battalion had the mission of securing the airfield at Subic Bay so the American forces could establish initial lodgments and receive additional forces. An armored brigade guarded that area as well and would be a tough foe for a light infantry brigade.

The Marines had been joined by another two brigades from Okinawa and were operating as an expeditionary force. They had the mission of destroying the two Japanese divisions that were guarding the Presidential Palace and the major financial institutions in the downtown district. Jennings had planned for them to attack from either side of Manila, performing a pincer movement to squeeze the Japanese out of the city and into the countryside, where their tanks would be forced to stay on the roads, providing easy targets for the aircraft.

It was a risky plan, particularly the Ranger action. He hoped they would be safe until he could shake some fighter aircraft loose to start hammering the tanks around Fort Magsaysay. He slowly shook his head, wondering about the Army's light forces.

What use are they? He vowed to get them some air support as soon as they could achieve air superiority.

The Marines had landed in the darkness of the night and were advancing smoothly on either side of Manila Bay with their 25 series Light Armored Vehicles and M1 tanks. The crew-cut marines followed the roads to Manila, peering through their sights like watching television.

Jennings realized that air power was going to have to play the critical role in the highly decen-tralized operation. They needed to destroy the scrappy Japanese Air Force before they could expect to reinforce the infantry on the ground, but the fact of the matter was that two Ranger battalions were already decisively engaged. Had they miscalculated as to how much they needed?

Did they have enough forces, he wondered?

And why had his requests for more troops been denied?

CHAPTER 82

ISLAND OF LUZON, PHILIPPINES

Through the greenish hue of his night-vision goggles, Captain Zachary Garrett could see about thirty tanks from where he was sprawled in the prone position atop a jagged ridge to the west of the airfield—the same direction from which Ayala had attacked his company and ultimately died. The early-morning air was relatively cool and damp with dew, but Zach knew that the steaming heat would quickly arrive with the sun.

The unsuspecting Japanese forces had not secured their rear area very well, unlike Zachary. The tanks he saw were lining up to move out in single file, practically in an administrative mode. He could see short men running about wildly waving their arms as if they were reacting to an emergency. The tanks were only five hundred meters away, and his Javelin tank-killing missiles should destroy them with ease. His company had procured twenty sights and over sixty rounds from the ammunition stockpile. There were more, but his men could not carry all of them.

Still, with his original nine sights from Hawaii, that gave him almost one weapons device per tank. Looking to his left, he saw Barker's platoon lined up along the ridge, his men peering through the thermal sights, waiting for the signal. Taylor's platoon was to the south, beneath the ridge, while Kurtz's men were opposite him on the other side of Barker.

The other three companies from the battalion

were prepared to assault from the North, across the airstrip, toward the pier. Garrett's company was providing supporting fire for the attack. He was glad that he had a support-by-fire mission for a change. His men would welcome the relative safety of covered and concealed fighting positions as opposed to advancing on the enemy again.

Morale had risen significantly when the rest of the battalion had arrived. The men ate the extra rations that had been dumped by helicopter into their position the following morning. Their stomachs full, and their minds rested, they relished the thought of avenging the losses of Teller and Rockingham.

And then there was Matt, his brother. They had received word of the three hostages, and Zach had heard that Matt was one of the detainees. The thought of Matt as a hostage had worn on him, sapping his strength and diverting his attention. But something had transpired in him, temporarily at least, to allow him to command his soldiers. Partly, Zach knew that if anyone could survive in the Philippines, it was his brother. And partly, despite the pain, worry, anxiety, and frustration, he could feel the hand of God inside him, hammering the molten ore of his character and dipping another red-hot rod of support into the reservoir of his strength and pulling it out, steaming and rigid, once again allowing him to be himself.

Matt. Where could Matt be? Is he alive? Bastards! The thought shot through Zachary's mind like the boomerang from hell. In and out, back and forth, ricocheting from side to side, angling to the nether regions of his mind, then soaring to the frontal lobe, striking pain and fear and hate and vengeance into his heart, kick-starting an emotional, instinctive reaction to kill every last Japanese invader. He knew by then that the Japanese were behind the whole fiasco. *Yes, kill them all.*

The radio crackled with a whispering voice making a net call. Zachary acknowledged. He nodded when he heard McAllister's distinctive Boston accent, comforted by his friend's confident cadence. One night over a few beers at the Schofield Barracks O-Club, he and McAllister had waxed philosophical, something most infantry officers avoided. But out of deep respect for one another, they tried to reach out in a manly way. Each wanted the other to know he trusted the other with his life. "If we ever get on the two-way rifle range, old boy," McAllister had said, eyes glassy from alcohol, "I hope to hear your voice come crackling over the radio."

Zachary had looked at McAllister, wanting to say the same thing, sorry he had not used the line first. "Same here, bud. I want you on my flank." The two warriors had stared at each other in a moment of martial kinship, an intangible combat multiplier understood by few.

And there it was. McAllister would not let him down. He knew that much if he knew nothing else. It was a good feeling.

"Cardinal, over."

Cardinal was the code word for commencing the attack. Zachary was to initiate the fires with the Javelin antitank weapons, then lay down a base of small-arms fire to mask the battalion's movement across an essentially open field. Zachary had recommended against going across the airfield, but Buck believed it to be the best route.

As Zachary was about to signal his unit, he heard the unique sound of an M4 weapon falling to the ground. It rattled loudly off the lava rock with the distinctive sounds of plastic and metal crunching. It was a foolish mistake. One of the small, uncontrollable things that happen when there are 115 young men gathered together. Everybody makes mistakes.

Zachary felt his stomach tighten as he saw a Japanese soldier guarding the fence only a hundred meters to his front look up and ready his weapon. Too late, Zachary said to himself, radioing his platoons to commence firing. The word spread quickly to the Javelin antitank gunners, who squeezed the triggers of their command launch units, sending twenty-nine bright flashes arching through the night toward their preplanned targets. Zachary had identified ten tanks for each platoon to destroy to avoid overkill.

The platoon leaders had then divided the tanks by squad for the same reason. The squad leaders had done likewise.

Zachary had grabbed his M4 and leveled it at the Japanese guard who had reacted to the falling weapon. Looking through his goggles and following the infrared aiming light onto the man's chest, he squeezed the trigger three times and watched him kick backward with each impact. It made him feel good, but he wanted more.

Seconds later, many of the tanks exploded into bright fireballs, some with turrets tipping loose. In the confusion, it was difficult to determine how many they had destroyed, but they suddenly found themselves under fire from somewhere. Large-caliber bullets were impacting all around them.

The sound of helicopter blades in the distance sent a chill up Zachary's spine. Japanese attack helicopters were engaging them at night. The very technology that the United States had developed and employed in their state-of-the-art equipment had been cloned to the Japanese, who were at the moment using it to kill American soldiers.

That was no Abu Sayyaf unit with rented small arms.

"Net call, get your men down, engage all heli-copters if you can acquire," Zachary said into the company radio net. Then he switched to the battalion net.

"Knight six, this is Bravo six," he said loudly into the radio handset. Bullets were raining down on his position with heightened ferocity, streaming from behind the white huts with precision.

"This is Knight six," Buck's nervous voice came back over the radio.

"Roger. We have destroyed over twenty enemy vehicles, but are receiving helicopter small-arms fire from the barracks vicinity, over."

"Roger, good job, over."

Dirt kicked into Zachary's eyes as a 30mm chaingun round impacted less than two feet away.

Zachary, crouching low in a ravine, looked at his microphone and rolled his eyes. He was not looking for praise, but wanted to warn the battalion commander that they needed to wait until he could engage the helicopters and the rest of the tanks before he moved the battalion.

Too late.

Through his goggles, the green landscape showed hundreds of small black dots moving rapidly on foot across the airfield.

The suppressive fires lessened on Zachary's position, and to his disgust, he saw orange tracers, enemy orange tracers, raking the airfield, causing the black dots to fall to the ground.

"Engage all helicopters!" Zachary screamed into the microphone, reissuing his earlier order.

On that order, he saw no less than fifteen missiles soar through the air, resulting in a fireball at the end of each smoke-filled path. The trails of spent gunpowder etched white lines in the darkness of the night, crisscrossing and merging like some crazy traffic pattern.

Then Zachary heard helicopters behind him.

They're everywhere!

He turned and saw four to his right flank and noticed his antitank gunners whipping around to engage them.

He could make out two hellfire missile racks on either side and the two Hydra 70 rocket pods balancing the stubbed wings. Beneath the belly of the ship was the 30mm chain gun, hanging low. He watched as a hellfire let loose from its rack and scorched a hot path into an enemy tank that had turned on his position. The two turbines rode high in the back near the tail rotor, making the craft look like a hovering wasp.

They're friendlies!

Too late.

He watched in horror as a young private first class gunner followed his commander's orders to "engage all helicopters."

"Cease fire! Cease fire!" Zachary yelled into the radio to no avail.

The Javelin missile screamed upward in a flash and impacted with a silent thud into the Apache helicopter, jarring it from its aerial fighting position. The helicopter shuddered once, then began to lose altitude rapidly. He heard the engines quit and watched as the pilot turned his head frantically to see what had hit him.

Fortunately, the gunner that had fired was within the sixty-five-meter arming zone for the missile. Outside of sixty-five meters, and the missile would have armed and exploded into the helicopter, vaporizing the two-man crew.

The pilot auto-rotated the main blade and achieved what his aviator buddies called a "hard landing." The tail boom split in two, sending the tail rotor whipping through the Japanese positions like a circular saw blade. Eventually the fuselage of the helicopter stopped spinning and Zachary sent a squad from Kurtz's platoon—SSG Quinones, who had acted so brilliantly during the defense of the pier—to gather up the copter crew, if they survived, and reel them back to safety.

"Bravo six, this is Alpha six, over!" came McAllister's voice.

"This is Bravo six, go, over," Zachary replied.

"The old man's gone to yellow brick. I'm in charge of the maneuver element now until I can talk to his second-in-command."

Buck's dead? This can't be happening!

Zachary had no great affection for Buck, but he was a nice guy. The man had a wife and four sons. *Now what?*

"This is Knight five, copied last message, moving into position now."

Knight five was the battalion executive officer, who was second-in-command during the maneuver phase. The battalion operations officer was positioned with Zachary's unit and was responsible for controlling the supporting fires. With Buck dead, Major Kooseman stepped into the saddle to gather in the reins of a horse that could quickly get out of control.

Zachary watched through his goggles as the remainder of the battalion performed fire and maneuver across the airfield, through the high brush and into the Quonset hut area, where his company had defended only days earlier. He thought he could see McAllister with three radio operators hovering around him and wanted to tell him to be careful, that someone might come surging from the water with a pistol in hand trying to kill him. He rubbed the clotted scar above his left ear as he gave the order for his men to lift their fires.

The bulk of the Japanese helicopter force had reacted to the Marine landings on either side of Manila Bay, allowing Buck's battalion to seize the critical airfield at Subic Bay. They needed to secure the area quickly, call the C-17s circling in the sky, and prepare to defend against a heavy counterattack.

As quick as it had begun, the battalion's first battle had tapered off. Casualties had been heavy on the airfield, as Japanese AH-X 30mm chain guns had formed a curtain of steel, killing Buck and at least thirty others. The light infantrymen had to contend with the forty wounded first, though.

With Buck dead, a young major fresh out of the Army Command and General Staff College was commanding the battalion. He spoke to the attack helicopter battalion commander, asking him to expand the security zone to the south so that the circling C-17s could land and discharge the combat troops waiting at the back ramps, rifles in hand, faces painted, adrenaline pumping, ready to go at it and kill the bastards that had once again forced them to fight and try to steady the tumbling play blocks of world power.

The C-17s came screaming in from above, landing almost atop one another. They received some small-arms fire from isolated pockets of Japanese soldiers not yet quelled. The Apaches fired Hydra rockets and let loose with 30mm chain guns on the enemy, driving them from Subic Bay Naval Base.

Two U.S. F-117 stealth bombers flew low across the water, like bats hunting insects, and dropped precision-guided munitions into each of the cargo ships that had off-loaded the Japanese weapons. Black smoke billowed high into the night, black on black, dimming the Manila City lights from Zachary's vantage point.

His troops watched the display of combined arms warfare in awe. Naval gunfire began to pound the remaining Japanese vehicles positioned along the pier where the ammunition had been stacked—and from where Ayala had attacked.

"I guess this is what they meant when they said

we were the main effort, huh, sir?" asked Slick, who had listened in on the battalion operations order earlier that afternoon.

Zachary didn't answer. He watched as he saw an F-16 explode in the sky with a bright fury that momentarily lit the entire engagement area to include the ever-resilient white Quonset huts. Like a star cluster, pieces of the jet sprinkled down, seeming lighter and less dangerous than they really were, and fizzled in the water just off the pier.

Was it theirs or ours?

Who knew? Only the pilots fighting in the skies and the AWACS airplane reading squawk signals and directing traffic.

Curiously, it occurred to Zachary that it was his company that had made all of this possible. Without his guys, America's course would have been much different. Then of course, there was Chuck Ramsey and his team to think about. And his brother, Matt.

Must get them both. Matt, where can you be? Are you safe? Chuck, has the Black Hawk found you?

CHAPTER 83

Zachary watched as Major Kooseman briefed the operations order. Kooseman had done well for being thrust into command during a raging battle. The tall major spoke nonchalantly about their next mission, a sharp contrast to the befuddlement of Colonel Buck, Zachary thought, then realized Buck was dead and squelched the thought.

"Right now, guys," Kooseman said, "we've got two Ranger battalions hiding in the jungle, pinned down by an armored division. Over two hundred tanks."

The group of captains, the commanders, collectively rolled their eyes and tightened their sphincters, waiting for the word that they were going to join the fray. The previous night's battle had given most of the soldiers in the battalion their first taste of war. Many were already battle-stress casualties, having watched Japanese helicopters fire 30mm chain guns, mowing down their buddies, killing them. Only B Company's precision fire had saved them by destroying many of the deadly attack helicopters.

The battle still raged on the perimeter. Naval gunfire popped in the offing, M1 tanks fired as if they were making headway, jets screamed overhead, helicopters came and went continuously, and, of course, the supply planes landed through it all.

They sat on the crusty, dried lava from Mount Pinatubo, amidst all the noise, just to the north of the white Quonset huts. The battalion was arrayed in the center as the brigade reserve, with the other two battalions securing the main avenues of approach into the naval base. Planes were landing every five minutes with support troops and supplies, trying to develop sufficient combat power to sustain extended operations.

Water was an issue, and it came rolling off the C-17s by the truckload. The heat had soared to over 115 degrees. The intelligence officer, Chip McCranum, had briefed that the heat was here to stay, with no relief in sight. As Zachary listened, he was reminded of George Carlin's "Hippy-Dippy Weatherman": "During the night, dark, very dark. But when the sun comes up, light, very light."

Tell me something I don't know for a change.

Kooseman stood again, rising from the white dust and brushing his army combat uniform. Wisps of white dirt exploded off his pants. He squinted as the sun tried to reach inside his eyelids and fry his pupils.

"Tomorrow morning at 0400, we attack to seize the prison at Cabanatuan." He made circling motions with his hands on the map that was positioned on an easel. "Our actions will be in concert with the Rangers, who will move from the jungles in the east as a feint to make contact with the enemy, draw their fire, allowing us to attack from the west."

He continued to describe the mission. Zachary's ears perked up when he heard his company mentioned.

"B Company will attack to secure the road that joins Cabanatuan and Fort Magsaysay," he said, pointing to a small line on the map that represented the three-mile road. "Zachary, your unit will establish blocking positions preventing enemy reinforcement either way."

"Got it," Zachary said, making a note to get with Kooseman later. He hated when other commanders interrupted the order with their parochial questions, and he had vowed never to do it.

"A Company and C Company, you'll be coming with me into the prison of Cabanatuan. We will attack to seize the prison from enemy control, then our mission will revert to one of protecting the Filipinos. D Company, you'll be in reserve, but I want you right behind us as we land and move in to attack the prison. Once we land, I expect that the Japanese will divert some forces from Magsaysay, where they have two battalions, and try to counterattack into Cabanatuan. Zachary, you've got to stop those guys."

"Got it."

Three battalions of tanks against a light infantry brigade. Zachary shook his head. *Those zoomies better get out of the O-Club and fly then, dammit.*

A hot wind blew across the hardstand, circling into a miniature funnel, picking up twigs and grass and disappearing. Zachary looked skyward, thinking that the entire operation depended on aircraft. They were using helicopters to air-assault into the objective area, and they needed attack helicopters and Air Force fighters to destroy the tanks.

Zachary squinted into the noonday sun, wondering if the air support would be able to do anything more than get them there.

CHAPTER 84

"Japs, can you believe it?" Sturgeon said to Matt and Barefoot, crouched low in the dirt behind a cluster of thick mahogany trees. The consensus was no, they could not believe it. With Japanese soldiers swarming around them, they had little time to discuss the matter. *Are they friendly or enemy? Should we give ourselves up? Is this a joint operation with the United States and Japan trying to put down the rebellion?* Even though Matt had theorized on that very occurrence, he was shocked at its reality.

But his brief stay in Mindanao was beginning to make some sense. World War I was to Germany's rise as World War II was to Japan's emergence today.

They had spent the first night lying silently on the reverse slope of the wooded knoll. Barefoot had packed his satellite gear and stashed it for fear of emitting a signal that the Japanese could detect. They were out of water and food, but the continuous procession of Japanese tanks and infantry fighting vehicles made any move impossible. It seemed that the three-mile road between Cabanatuan and Fort Magsaysay was a main supply route for the Japanese.

A small Japanese patrol had wandered aimlessly into the tree line less than a hundred meters from their hide position. The squad of seven sat in the shade, drank from their canteens, and joked in their native language. Matt could see that one was carrying a Shin Chuo Kogyo submachine gun, normally a tanker's weapon. Another had a Type 62 machine gun slung across his shoulder with two belts of

7.62mm ammunition wrapped around his body. The weapon had a small telescopic sight perched atop the rear sight assembly. The others were carrying M16A2 rifles.

They sat upon the grave, unsuspecting, and departed without incident when one of the members, probably the leader, stood and began to walk back to the west, toward Cabanatuan.

Earlier, they had witnessed the spectacular airdrop of hundreds of paratroopers at two in the morning. Barefoot had been on watch, and he awoke the others as he had spied the C-130s flying about two hundred meters above the ground discharging hundreds of soldiers. Immediately orange tracers were seeking out the elite soldiers as they fluttered to the ground. Who was friendly and who was enemy?

They could still hear gunfire as the curtain closed on a second day on the knoll. Matt was unaware that Barefoot's transmission had set the entire mission in operation. But still they were unsure. Were those American soldiers jumping in the middle of the night, or Filipinos? It had been too dark to tell. The Armed Forces of the Philippines certainly had C-130s capable of dropping soldiers. Had the insurgents pirated the airplanes? Were they now fighting Japanese forces?

"We need to try to link up with those paratroopers," Matt said.

"I'm game for anything," Barefoot added, his dark skin white from the dust.

"Okay, about two in the morning, we'll run along the ridge to the west," Matt said, pointing to his left. "We also need to find some water, so as we move, let's see if we can't find a well or something. After that, maybe we can steal a truck and haul ass."

It was risky, it was loose-knit, and it was desperate. But they were desperate men.

Matt shook Jack and Barefoot until they both wakened.

"Time to go?" Sturgeon asked in his groggy voice.

"Yeah. It's a little bit before two. The shooting's stopped some. Figured it would be a good time to bolt," Matt said, adrenaline pumping through his body, creating a sense of alertness. He held his pistol in his hand, popped the magazine out, and counted bullets. Six. He had seven shots including the round in the chamber.

"Good, let's book," Jack said.

"What should I do with this shit?" Barefoot said, patting his satellite gear. It was really too much to carry but could prove useful in the future.

"Leave it here, but bring the tape of Rathburn's burial. If we have time, we'll circle back and get the equipment. But more than likely, we'll just have to scrap it," Matt said.

"Okay," Barefoot agreed. After all, it was his equipment. He pulled the tape of Rathburn's burial out of the camera and stuffed it into his pocket, then covered the expensive gear with some leaves and branches, hoping they could come back for it. As a soldier is attached to his personal gear, Barefoot had his affections for his own equipment. He knew its minor quirks and what buttons he had to push to make the stuff work. With regret, he laid the last branch on the pile, as if he had conducted a burial.

They stood and moved in single file beneath the towering mahogany trees, stepping lightly over the high roots, following a trail that led the mile to Cabanatuan. Jack and Matt carried their pistols in hand at the ready, poised for self-defense. They slipped through the woods as silent as the wind, as if they had trained for it. They were hungry, thirsty, and tired.

They were acting on instinct, like cavemen or animals. They had to satisfy bodily needs, or they would die. It was a simple calculation. Either get up and move, or die from heat exhaustion and hunger.

Lacking energy, but full of adrenaline, somehow they managed to wind their way through the hills and find a perch from which they could survey the half-lit town of Cabanatuan. In the prone, they lay next to each other and watched as green Army trucks ambled back and forth along the white cement road less than seventy-five meters away. The trucks coughed and spit diesel into the air, masking the trio's movement down to the back of a thatch hut.

One of the drivers unprofessionally turned on his lights, making the small village visible. Matt noticed and said, "Come, this way."

Sturgeon and Barefoot followed as they ran behind a series of thatch huts.

"Over there," Matt said, pointing. "It's a school. They always have wells at their schools."

They ran, crouched low, heading toward a wooden building that contrasted with the thatch huts. Oddly, they crossed over a dirt court with two baskets at the other end. *These guys play basketball?* Matt wondered. Reaching the building, they huddled against the wall as headlights traced a line above their heads, finally turning away.

"Must be on the other side," Matt said, "I don't see shit over here."

"Let's go."

They ran to the back of the school building, which was a modest, one-room affair that looked more like an old country church without the steeple.

There it was. The pump handle was cocked high in the air above the open-lipped spout. The area beneath the spout was muddy, a good indicator the pump was functional.

The three men scampered to the device, pulling their canteens off their belts. Matt grabbed the handle and pumped hard, letting the others drink

from the spout, then fill their canteens. When they
were done, Matt stooped low, kneeling in the mud,
and drank. He drank some more. Then he gulped
down more water, letting it spill across his face.
Finally, he opened his mouth again, letting the force
of the liquid push open his throat, and race down,
nearly causing him to choke.

He felt his body rehydrate. Glistening beads of
sweat formed on his dusty arms beneath his torn
sleeves. He filled his canteen, letting the water spill
on his arms, then he stuck his head beneath the
rushing water. That was why he did not hear the first
shot.

The first shot caught Jack square in the top of the
thigh, cracking his femur. Then the gunfire came
pouring forth, kicking dirt into the air. White puffs
of dust rose into the blackness of the night.

Barefoot pulled Matt from under the pump, then
flipped Sturgeon over his shoulders with acrobatic
ease. Matt yanked his pistol from the waist of his
pants and began searching for muzzle flashes, back-
pedaling as he followed Barefoot back toward the
woods.

As they rounded the school, they saw ten Japanese soldiers coming from the other corner. They
had an opening, however small. If they could only
race back behind the thatch huts and get in the
woods, they would stand a chance.

Barefoot ran with large steps, his gait like that of a
show horse. His powerful frame seemed none the
worse from the weight of Jack. Matt saw Jack's face,
grimacing in pain, as his blood drained onto
Barefoot's shirt.

From behind the row of thatch huts jumped an
aggressive Japanese soldier, holding a Kogyo
submachine gun with folding stock. He yelled
something indiscernible to the group of Americans
and raised his weapon to fire.

Matt stopped, crouched, and fired one round into the soldier's forehead, thirty meters away. The enemy soldier—and they now knew them to be enemy—stood still, as if there were something he could do about his mortal wound, then fell back-ward to the ground, dead.

As they passed the dead man, Matt saw that his face was covered in blood. He stooped and stole the man's weapon on the fly, never breaking stride.

Matt felt a hot, stinging sensation in his lower right leg, like a snakebite. He looked down and saw that his trousers were shredded along his right calf. Other bullets punched into the ground around him. *Only a graze.*

They crested the rise and entered the wooded area, then hurriedly followed the trail, winding through the trees as if they were racing down a ski slalom.

"Go back to the equipment, I'll meet you there," Matt said. Barefoot nodded and continued to run, starting to tire from the weight. Matt pulled off the path and circled back. He quickly checked his weapon. He did not know what it was, but figured if he pulled the trigger, it would shoot.

The path to Zachary is through these bastards, Matt thought as he waited.

CHAPTER 85

They darted into a clearing, then pulled away like a ride at the local carnival. Zachary peered out of the open door, the wind beating the back of his head, and saw at least thirty other UH-60 Black Hawks performing similar maneuvers into the false insertion area.

Two minutes out, Zachary thought. He looked at his watch, then cut a gaze at Slick, who gave him a thumbs-up. The trusty RTO. In many respects, there was no better friend to a commander. Confidant, friend, lackey, supporter, idea man, humorist, the RTO was always there, always ready, always prepared. Slick was typical, with his wry sense of humor and devastating ability to make the commander laugh when he least expected it. It was tough humping the thirty pounds of radio gear and living with the commander. Often it took a special breed.

Zachary carried the company net radio in his own rucksack. He saw no need to suck another soldier away from the platoons when he was stronger than most in the company. Slick would monitor Major Kooseman and the other company commanders on battalion net, and Zachary would maneuver the company through the platoon leaders on the company net. The platoon leaders would then maneuver their squads on platoon nets.

Oh shit. Orange tracers rocketed skyward at the helicopters as they came in for a hot landing between Cabanatuan and Fort Magsaysay. The helicopters banked hard and low, pushing the envelope trying to gain cover. They touched down for a brief moment behind a large wooded knoll, discharged their passengers, then pulled away, turning toward the west to make another lift.

They would make it back in time before the first heavy storm of the wet season.

Zachary took a knee and watched the beauty of the battalion air assault. In training, they had never had the opportunity to perform entire battalion lifts, and the sight of the helicopters pulling away like a swarm of wasps impressed him. He watched and listened to the battalion radio net as McAllister's company took the lead for the assault into Cabanatuan.

McAllister's voice gave him comfort again. He was among friends. No longer was his company isolated, the world surrounding them.

"Let's move to checkpoint three-one, over," he said into his company net.

Taylor, Kurtz, and Barker acknowledged. Zachary and his platoon leaders gathered their men, formed into a series of wedges, and headed toward the wooded knoll.

Matt had decided to use the pistol first, waited until the lead soldier was less than thirty meters away, then pulled the trigger. He needed to buy Sturgeon and Barefoot some time, and this was the best way.

As he watched the man drop like a shot quail, he grabbed the submachine gun and fired into the confused mass. The weapon jumped wildly in his hands, but he was hitting his targets. He saw three others fall to the ground.

As he started receiving fire, he pulled back into the forest, ran across the trail, then doubled back to gain the flank.

It worked. The Japanese soldiers, under new direction, charged headlong into the woods where Matt had originally entered. As they melted into the sparse forest, Matt held the Kogyo tightly and sighted into the backs of the Japanese.

This is for Rathburn and Sturgeon, you bastards!

He was far more effective that time, killing at least fifteen soldiers who had bunched in their confusion. They turned on him, coming at him like a Rebel charge through the Devil's Den at Gettysburg. The enemy soldiers were screaming and firing weapons, the orange tracers blowing through the leaves, cracking branches, and temporarily painting the night sky like some wicked airbrush.

He swallowed dry spit as he felt the hammer fall on an empty chamber. He saw the barrel steaming and smoking directly in front of him when he realized he had fired all of the ammunition. There was nothing left for him to do except to move back through the woods with judicious use of his pistol.

He scurried along the reverse slope of the hill, hot lead chasing him only a step behind. He heard the helicopters come and go and assumed that they were surrounded.

A twig dug deep into his cheek, just beneath his eye, and snapped. His head turned and as he looked back toward his front, he tumbled over a large root, snapping his ankle as he fell.

In no time, three enemy soldiers were upon him, frothing at the mouth like rabid pit bulls ready to complete the kill. He shot one through the lower abdomen, actually hitting the man's testicles, then fired a shot into the face of the man to his left.

The bayonet came arching downward, piercing his abdomen. The Asian man smiled, and with the bayonet in Matt's abdomen, pulled the trigger of his M16 rifle.

Matt heard the deafening blast and felt the initial

pain, then his world began to waft back and forth in his mind as if on a pendulum. First he saw the leering Japanese soldier, delighting in the kill, then he heard the faint sound of helicopters chopping behind him. Then he thought of Sturgeon and Barefoot, and seconds later he saw Rathburn. The pendulum swung toward Meredith's face, then back again to the farm and his family. Then something about the Rolling Stones, but only briefly. Then the farm, rolling hills, the Blue Ridge, Karen, father, mother, Zachary. *Yes, Zachary. My best friend.* Fishing in the stream together. Catching trout. Then Meredith, blond hair, soft skin, sitting by the pool, telling secrets, connecting.

Then Zachary's voice.

Then nothing.

"**Bravo six, this** is White six," Kurtz said into the company radio net.

"Send it," Zachary said, recognizing the voice.

"We've got enemy contact to our left flank. Say again. Gunfire you hear is enemy contact, over."

"Roger. I want you to move to the west, through the woods, and try to develop the situation. I'll maneuver the other elements after you make contact."

"Roger."

Kurtz took a deep breath, sucked in the acrid smell of gunpowder, and told his squad leaders to move in the direction of the weapons fire. There it was again. That confident, almost cocky feeling of invincibility. *Come get me, you sons of bitches!* He spit a large wad of chaw onto the ground and tucked behind his first squad leader, ready to control the action. His chinstrap grated against his stubble beard. He carried his M4 rifle by the pistol grip at the ready with one arm, holding the platoon radio handset in his other hand. *Or I'm gonna come get you!*

"Contact," came Quinones's voice over the platoon net, followed by a brief exchange of fire. The word sent a thrill up Kurtz's spine.

"Roger," Kurtz said, moving to the squad leader's position. The point man had killed a single Japanese soldier, standing atop another man, apparently dying from a gunshot wound to the abdomen. Kurtz had first squad secure the area, while the other two squads continued to maneuver.

"Bravo six, this is White six. We've made contact. Killed three enemy soldiers and have found one civilian, looks like it anyway, with severe wounds to the abdomen. Doc says this guy's not much longer for this world. Continuing mission, over."

"Roger. I'm moving to your location now. Red six is moving to your right flank. Blue six is in reserve." Taylor was Red and Barker was Blue.

Again, there was another brief interchange of fire at the point of Kurtz's platoon. Three more enemy dead.

"Okay, Mike," Zachary said to Kurtz as he came running forward. "We're gonna move two squads abreast along this ridge and pop these guys like a zit. When they spill into the open, the rest of the battalion can have them, or we play turkey shoot."

"Got it, sir."

They were kneeling next to the wounded civilian, talking. It was dark, especially in the forest with the mahoganies blocking what little moonlight was available, their robust outlines etched against the black sky. Zachary and Kurtz had taken off their night-vision goggles to talk. It was not necessary, but seemed logical to do. Doc Gore worked feverishly on the civilian less than a meter away from them.

Something landed on Zachary's knee. At first, he thought it was a bug and brushed at it, then noticed the hand. He had no time to deal with some civilian right now. His guys were fighting. He quickly scanned the dark, shredded cargo pants, khaki shirt matted and stained with blood, and disheveled hair of the civilian. Shrouded in darkness, the dying man was unrecognizable to Zachary. *Poor guy. Medics are doing all they can, though.*

Like a penny dropped into a shallow cone, the notion or thought or idea or instinct spun around and around and around, circling wide and continuing to circle, then arching more rapidly until it dropped and Zachary had the distinct feeling that something was dreadfully wrong. Not with the mission. Hell, he could not even concentrate on that at the moment. No, especially as he looked back at the wounded figure, moving his face closer to the dying man's face. The sounds of gunfire continued but faded in Zachary's mind as he downshifted from the world of battle to another cognitive level.

He did not truly recognize his brother's face, the green eyes or the signature square jaw, but he realized with sudden and complete devastation that it was Matt reaching out to him, somehow recognizing him, almost magnetically pulled to him, grabbing his kneecap, trying to say something. He looked away in disbelief, then back, and once again saw his brother Matt lying on the ground next to him, his stomach gurgling, the pool of blood growing, the medic poised over him as if he were giving him last rites not applying medical aid.

A voice whispered, "Kill those bastards, Zachary."

Then it registered.

Christ Almighty!

Zachary scrambled to Matt's side.

"Oh Jesus Christ," he cried. "Please, Jesus, please, no."

Kurtz watched the commander completely lose it. He watched him sob and cry, hugging the civilian on the ground.

"No, no, no. Please, oh God, No!" he screamed at the heavens.

Medevac, get a medevac, you idiot!

He ripped off his helmet, then snatched the first-aid dressing from his pouch and began to press onto the bleeding area, but there was blood everywhere.

"Sir, that thing ain't gonna do much good on him. Hole's bigger in the back than in the front," Doc Gore said, matter-of-factly.

"Shut up, Gore. This is my brother and—and—this is my brother. This is my only brother," he said, his voice reaching a crescendo, then tapering rapidly as his throat knotted, and the tears gushed, his mouth turned downward. "This—is—my—brother!"

"Shit." Kurtz said, under his breath. "Break, Break," he said, grabbing the battalion net handset from Slick. "Request immediate dust-off at checkpoint three-one. We have a man dying. Need dust-off now," Kurtz said, authoritatively.

"Roger, loitering behind checkpoint three-one now. Mark with strobe." The medical evacuation pilot spoke with calm precision. Fortunately, the plan anticipated casualties and called for pre-positioning of the medical teams.

Kurtz popped the strobe from his pouch, gently nudged the commander to one side and lifted Matt Garrett's still-warm body onto his wide shoulders, blood draining down his uniform.

Zachary was catatonic. He had flipped a switch. The troops stared at him for direction. Slick, Quinones, and the others. Zachary simply watched as Kurtz hauled his brother away into the clearing behind the knoll. The company was receiving heavy fire, tracers dancing out toward Kurtz and the helicopter. Kurtz turned a steely gaze in the direction of the back-fire, as if to will it away. Zachary saw the intermittent flashing of the strobe, then watched as the helicopter lifted away. Kurtz's large shadow re-emerged into the forest. He picked up the company radio and told Taylor and Barker to continue the mission, then turned to SSG Quinones and told him to monitor the platoon net.

"Sir, sir," Kurtz said, shaking the commander. Zachary was trying to regain his composure. "We've got to get moving. He's on the medevac. They'll take care of him," Kurtz said, then looked at Doc Gore and shook his head, as if to say about the commander's brother, "He's gone."

Zachary looked at Kurtz from below and grabbed the outstretched hand. He had been there for his lieutenants so many times that it never occurred to him that they might one day be able to return the favor.

About the time he pulled himself to his feet and snatched his helmet from the ground, he heard the high-pitched squeak of mechanized vehicles moving to the east. The recognition of a large enemy presence served as a catalyst to force him to gather himself. The world shifted focus for him, like a camera zooming in, then out. With professional acumen, he understood he had a battle to fight.

"Thanks, Mike," he said to Kurtz while snapping his Kevlar.

"No sweat, sir. I'll light a candle tonight, after we kill these bastards," Kurtz said.

Zachary took notice, then grabbed Slick by the shirt collar.

"Sir, just want you to know how sorry—"

"Give me the mike," he said, cutting off Slick. There was no time for sympathy. He had already wasted valuable seconds with his little display. *Unprofessional*, he thought to himself, hardening his nerves, like steel rebar. First, Teller, then Rock, then his brother. The circle of death tightened around him as he wondered if he was next. *Who cares?* There it was again, the hand of God, hammering and forging and striking the anvil, dunking the piping-hot ore of his soul into the shallow, ever-so-shallow, pool of faith. *Please God, save him.*

"Net call, enemy moving vicinity checkpoint three-zero. Blue, I want you to move to the eastern tip of the woods and set up an anti-armor ambush now, break," he said, releasing the push-to-talk button to avoid enemy direction-finding capabilities. "Red, link up on Blue's left flank, you have the first ten vehicles, Blue has the next ten. I'll move with White. We'll maneuver onto the enemy if necessary. Acknowledge."

Barker and Taylor acknowledged, but then Barker's voice came crackling back through the handset.

"Bravo six, this is Blue six, I'm fighting about twenty enemy on the west side of the knoll! I can't break contact!" Barker screamed, the sound of machine gun fire amplified by the microphone.

"Blue six, call a fire mission to help you break contact. Make it high-explosive and willie pete. Keep fighting those guys while we set up for the ambush. Let me know when you link up with Red's left flank, over."

"Roger!" Barker sounded confused and anxious.

Zachary was placing a great burden on Barker to fight an essentially even-ratio battle, guard the company's left flank, and join the anti-armor ambush. It was too much, but he had no other choice.

Zachary moved with Kurtz along the back side of the wooded ridge. He found Taylor and told him he was in charge of the overwatch element, that he and Kurtz were going to move about three hundred meters to the east and try to extend the company's position. Taylor was already sighting his antitank weapons. Each man carried an AT-4, the successor to the light antitank weapon, and his platoon had fifteen Javelin missiles for six command launch units.

Zachary pulled Kurtz and Slick with him as they jogged down the back side of the hill. At the bottom he stopped, put on his goggles, and turned on the bright green world.

"Holy shit," Zachary said, sighting at least thirty tanks moving in single file along the road nearly two miles away. The low, flat ground made for excellent observation. In the darkness, though, the hulking beasts traveled slowly, as if they feared something.

"C'mon, follow me," Zachary said. Kurtz and his men jogged behind the commander as he raced across the level hardstand into the clearing. They ran with increasing speed, sounding like a small herd of buffalo trampling across the great open plains.

Zachary had run almost six hundred meters when he suddenly fell, his head jerking backward, and landed in a shallow pool of warm, stinking water. Some of the other troops followed suit, while others tried to stop, each man stumbling over the next like Keystone Kops.

"Rice paddies," Zachary said. "Perfect."

He could still hear Barker's platoon fighting off the enemy about a kilometer away, maybe more, as he called Taylor and changed the plan.

CHAPTER 86

Takishi was through with the games. His forces had practically destroyed the paratroopers, who had so whimsically thought they could tangle with his armored division. *Fools. They are all fools. The Americans, the Filipinos, the Rolling Stones. The world.*

But then, a report from General Nugama in Manila had given him great cause for concern. Apparently the Marines were about to close on the Presidential Palace. Losses had been heavy on both sides in the street-to-street fighting of Manila. The Americans, Nugama had told him, were bringing more troops into Subic Bay by the minute, and he had no contact with any of the other ships north of the Luzon Strait to reinforce him. The only saving grace for the Japanese was that their air force was still intact and had exacted a heavy toll on the American pilots.

That and the fact that Takishi had a fresh division.

"Quit messing around with those light forces, let the bastards have the prisoners, and come to Manila," Nugama had told him. "I need you now!"

But that had been two hours ago. It had taken Takishi that long just to organize his units for movement at two in the morning. He had decided to leave the prisoners locked in the buildings to rot. Nearly six thousand Filipinos wailing, screaming, and crying. He had a headache. He had slammed the door to the big building and locked it, drowning out the collective sounds of agony and pain. It was as if the country had been screaming in unison, shouting, *"Enough."*

Takishi spoke through the small microphone attached to his combat-vehicle crewman's helmet and told his driver to lead the column to the east. They would button up their hatches and destroy the light infantry soldiers and blow down the road to Manila to defeat the Marines. *No problem.*

His tank creaked along the cement road, crushing week-old rice that had been laid out to dry in the searing sun. The sun would rise in an hour, meaning he needed to make as much ground as possible before then. Somehow he felt safer in the darkness. Like pulling the bedspread over your head when you're scared, it seemed protective to him.

He sat inside the buttoned-down hatch and watched the world pass through the high-definition thermal sight. Slewing the turret left and right with the commander's override, he made out low ground to either side of the road.

"Be careful," he said to Private Muriami, his young driver. The driver slowed, then Takishi said, "Not that careful," realizing he needed to make time and fight the worthless light infantry, the least of his worries. They had an opportunity to deal the Americans a crushing blow.

He slewed the turret to the left as he passed through the Fort Magsaysay gate, then fully behind him, and watched with pride as all two hundred tanks of his task force were lined up, crawling slowly along the dirt road that met with the main avenue. He had left behind two infantry battalions and sixty fighting vehicles to hold off the Rangers while the tanks moved toward Manila. He had given the brigade commander instructions to maintain light contact, like a feint, while they discreetly slipped away from the Rangers until they had cleared Cabanatuan. Then he could move his two battalions along the same route, eventually effecting linkup.

As he watched, he saw a group of AH-X helicopters lift slowly off the airfield and take up positions on both flanks of his column, hovering like drone bees around the queen. He told Muriami to pick up the pace, and like an arrow, he slung the entire column to the east.

CHAPTER 87

"How many do you count, Slick?" Zachary asked, as they crouched low in the water.

"From the first one, I see about fifty, then there's a bunch of hills. Sounds like there's a helluva lot more," Slick said with a nervous edge on his voice. They could hear the tanks whining, tracks squeaking on the cement.

"No shit." Then turning to Kurtz, Zach said, "Mike, spread your guys out along these dikes. Put your men with AT4s closer to the road, about two hundred meters. Keep your other Javelin guys back about six hundred meters—about where we are now. We'll let Taylor and the boys knock out about the first twenty tanks, then the whole column will be stuck right here with nowhere to go."

"Got it, sir," Kurtz said, anxious to enact the plan. The tanks were rapidly approaching and he needed some time to brief his men. He would not have that time, though. He would only be able to tell his men where to go and when to shoot. Sometimes, that's all it took.

Zachary had called Major Kooseman for backup attack-helicopter support, but received only a "wait, out" from the major, who was busy orchestrating the fight in Cabanatuan. "There may be no fight if you don't get me those birds," Zachary had told him, "I've got tanks heading in your direction."

"Bravo six, this is Red six, over."

Zachary responded to Taylor's call.

"I've got two civilians in my AO. They're

Americans. Might be two of the hostages we heard about. One's wounded pretty badly in the leg. What should I do with them?" Taylor asked.

So far, he had successfully put the issue of his brother on the back burner. He had been cognizant of it, but had forced himself to deal with the matters at hand. Taylor's call had served to rotate the turnstile, as if his mind could only handle the array of events one at a time. First, the war, then his brother, next the war, then his brother. He envisioned an usher taking tickets as the thoughts strolled through the stile. Brother, war, brother, war, and so on.

Kneeling in the stinking mud and water, he called back to Taylor.

"I'll call a medevac for them. Have *two* troops move them to checkpoint three-one for pick up."

It was the only right thing to do. He imagined that there were two brothers back in the United States somewhere who were glad he had called the medevac for the two men.

"You okay, sir?" Slick asked, sensing his commander disconnect from the increasingly pressing events.

Zachary turned and looked at the young soldier, patted him on the back, and said, "Let's kill some bad guys."

The tanks passed to his front, only six hundred meters away. It was nerve-racking, watching them from such a short distance. Would one of his soldiers screw the plan and fire too soon, or too late? It was a distinct possibility, given the haphazard pace of events.

"They look just like M1s, sir," Slick said.

"More like the German Leopard 2, Slick. Almost an exact copy," Zachary said, releasing some nervous tension. He rested his M4 on his dry knee as he lay back against a muddy dike.

He saw the first missile strike the second tank, causing a brief fireball that lit the immediate surroundings. Successive missiles scored hits as well, stopping the column so that roughly thirty tanks, two companies, were beyond the rice paddies.

That's too many, Zachary thought to himself. But he waited. Maybe they could still do it.

Takishi slewed the turret to the right, wishing they would quickly get off the dike that was the road separating two large paddy fields. *This place will be good for factories one day*, he thought, as his tank finally passed beyond the rice paddies.

He slewed the turret back to the left, enjoying the ride. *Okay, where are these guys?* He had reports from his logistical units in Cabanatuan that they were under heavy fire from what seemed like a battalion of light infantry. *Are you kidding me? A battalion?*

"Muriami, let's go find these people and get to Manila," Takishi said as Muriami raced the jet engine, slamming Takishi's ribs into the steel seat back.

The other tank commanders followed suit, glad they were able to move faster, no longer impeded by the sudden drop on either side.

When he noticed some hot black spots burning in his thermal sight, he slewed the turret even with the road to gain perspective, then back again at the rising ground.

There they are!

"Gunner, high explosive, enemy personnel in the woods," Takishi said, mimicking the precision of a skilled soldier.

The loader slammed one round into the massive breech while the gunner took control and lased to the target. His signal came back quickly, indicating he was a mere four hundred meters away.

"Acquired," the young sergeant announced with cold acumen. He could have been on a Sunday drive for all he cared.

Takishi said, "Fire when ready," only to override the gunner when he saw the missiles screaming toward his column of tanks.

The gunner's shot flew errant, cutting a white hole into the black night, landing almost a mile away without doing any damage.

Zachary watched in disbelief as the first tank continued to roam free on the hardpan. Taylor's men had fired two volleys of Javelin missiles and three sets of AT4s. He thought he counted fifteen enemy vehicles burning. They burned a brilliant orange hue that quickly mixed with the black smoke of melting rubber.

But that's only half. Zachary was growing increasingly concerned. He did not want Kurtz to shoot his wad on the thirty or so tanks lined up to his front if Taylor needed the help.

The Japanese tanks that could turn off the road raced for the wooded knoll, offering only frontal shots, the worst kind, for Taylor's gunners and randomly spitting machine-gun fire into the edge of the forest. It was almost too late for Zachary to have Kurtz's men do anything about the advance.

Zachary checked and achieved a small measure of reassurance when he saw five tanks burning bumper to bumper at the junction in the road where the rice paddies gave way to hardstand.

No way they're getting around that.

"Bravo six, this is Red six, we're taking heavy fire, over!" came Taylor's nervous voice, almost seeming to squeak in a high pitch. He thought he could hear the bullets whipping past Taylor over the microphone.

"Roger—"

"Break, break," Barker said, loudly, short-circuiting the commander. "This is Blue six. I'm on your flank now. Engaging. Out."

Zachary watched as six missiles arched through the sky, and found targets, stopping the tanks in their tracks.

That leaves nine.

Another volley, this time AT4s disabled two more tanks.

Seven.

Zachary watched as some of the tanks stacked on the road tried to turn off and support the attack. They were unsuccessful, mostly dipping over the edge of the concrete road, then rolling into the deep mud, and sticking, unable to move forward or back. One tank turned its tread until it chewed the concrete, made partial purchase in the mud, then flipped, pinning down and ultimately drowning the tank commander, who had opened his hatch to guide the effort.

Some of the other tanks, though, turned their turrets and began to support the attack with small-arms fire and main gun blasts. Finally, his tactical patience had reached its limit.

"White, this is Bravo. Do it."

"Roger," Kurtz responded.

Kurtz's men rose from the swampy bog like Francis Marion's American Revolution cavalry, water and mud and rice stems streaming and hanging off their bodies. They fired volley after volley of antitank weapons, nearly depleting the company's entire stock, including the plus up from the ammunition pile at Subic.

The return fire was unexpectedly heavy, splashing into the mud, spraying water in all directions.

There they were again. Those damned helicopters, firing 30mm chain guns at his men.

Zachary radioed Major Kooseman and asked again about the attack helicopters, "We need support now, sir," he told him.

"Helos are five minutes out," Kooseman told him.

Five minutes? This thing'll be history in five minutes.

Zachary watched as another volley from Barker's platoon cut the attacking force down to three tanks.

"Bravo, this is Red, we're out of tank-killing systems, over," Taylor said, sounding disgusted.

"This is Blue. Likewise," Barker said, piggy-backing on Taylor's bad news.

Zachary dropped his hand into his lap after saying, "Roger, continue to fight, attack helicopters on the way."

He felt the first draft of the cool wind lift a matted hair off his forehead as he heard a helicopter in the background. Could it be? No, it was not. Only the medevac for the two civilians.

A raindrop touched his nose. At first, he thought an enemy round had kicked water into his face, but distinguished the coolness of the liquid and looked skyward. Lifting his goggles from his face, he saw heavy clouds racing across the creeping grayness of the morning like a Yankee clipper cutting through stormy seas. Then he looked at the stack of enemy tanks, some burning, some firing, some cocked crazily over the lip of the road. *What a perfect target.*

Defenseless tanks were lined up single file on the road with only a few enemy helicopters swarming for protection. The beauty of it was that the Japanese self-propelled artillery was stacked on the road as well. For the moment, they were safe from any indirect fire, but still in great danger from the enemy helicopters bobbing up and down behind the tree line near Fort Magsaysay.

The rain came with an unexpected suddenness. Cool and heavy, the drops felt larger than normal.

The wind blew sideways, making the rain feel like tiny darts against Zachary's face. It felt both hot and cold at the same time. Zachary prayed for the aberration to go away, hoping it was a simple thunderstorm. The wind gusted, spitting cold water in his face out of defiance, reporting that things were only going to get worse.

The intensity of the rain increased, pelting down in sheets.

CHAPTER 88

GREENE COUNTY, VIRGINIA

Other than being totally humiliated and having her car destroyed, Meredith's worst injury was the gash on her head from Stone's fireplace. She had crawled from the wreckage, running and not looking back, fearing that either Stone was chasing her or that her car was about to catch fire and explode.

The car, while totaled, did not burn, and thankfully she had been wearing her seat belt. She had spent one night in the Georgetown hospital, then rented a car so she could go to the one safe place she believed was still available to her.

She spoke to her assistant, Mark, over the phone from the Garrett house in Stanardsville. She told him that she would be reporting back to work in a few days, that she had an accident and needed to recover.

"Yeah, the SecDef personally came down here looking for you," Mark said.

I bet he did.

"Really, did he say anything?"

"Not really. Just said he was doing 'battlefield circulation,' otherwise known as management by walking around. He asked where you were, then split. He looked kinda nervous."

"Thanks, Mark. I'll see you in a few days," Meredith said, ready to hang up.

"Karen, can I use that computer I asked you about last night?"

"Sure thing. Do all my business on it. Have my

own server too. Went back to UVA and got a
certification in computer science. I'll do the
occasional house call for the folks around here to fix
their stuff." They walked into the study, which was
lined with pine paneling and had two bookshelves at
the back. A smallish desk was covered with mail and
books and a black-and-walnut UVA college chair
with an orange and blue seat cushion was pulled
away from the desk. A bench was underneath the
window that opened onto the north part of the farm
and offered a generous view of the mountains.

"Huh," Meredith said. "You any good with
security stuff?"

"How ya mean?" she asked, raising an eyebrow.

"I've got a thumb drive, and I can see the folders,
but can't open them."

"Password-protected. You didn't try to open
them did you? Get locked out."

"No, I figured that much out after I clicked on
one and got the password dialogue box. I never tried
a password."

"Good thing," Karen said. "Matt and I have
played around with some algorithms for code
breaking." She looked up at Meredith after she sat at
the computer and said, "Given his line of work."

Meredith dug through her purse and said,
"Well?"

"Problem?" Karen asked.

"Can't find my lipstick, but here's that thumb
drive." It was the one conscious thought she had as
she crawled from the wreckage. *Get the thumb drive.*

Karen took the device and plugged it into the
USB port and quickly pulled open the dialogue box
with the files. Then she opened another program
from her windows display and played around with it
a minute. A black screen came up and scrolled
through hundreds of lines of code and stopped.
Karen minimized that screen and said, "Interesting."

"What?" Meredith asked, hopeful.

"Did he have a problem memorizing passwords or something?"

"All the time," Meredith said, more hopeful.

"Well, he used Firefox, and all you have to do is click on the Firefox icon here in his thumb drive and you get all the passwords," Karen explained. She performed the function and a series of boxes with asterisks in them popped up.

"They're still protected," Meredith said.

"Watch this." Karen clicked on JAVA SCRIPT. Suddenly the asterisks disappeared, and the passwords appeared.

KeithRichards2002.

"He a Stones' fan?"

"You might say that." Meredith grimaced.

"Okay, I'm going to leave it with you. I never did this. And if I ever get a call about it, this computer will be in the fireplace before I hang up the phone."

"No worries. I promise. You're awesome, Karen. Thanks so much."

Karen left, and Meredith sat down to begin plowing through the files. The password worked for each folder, and what she found was, to put it mildly, shocking.

In the first file, the Pred-China folder, she read document after document that recorded financial transactions of U.S. technology sales to China totaling some $100 million. Meredith figured that at $5 million each, the Chinese had received about twenty Predators. The money, it seemed, was then funneled in two directions.

First, there was a clear chain of transactions to a man named Takishi, she presumed this was the man she had seen leaving Stone's office and with whom Stone had exchanged a Rolling Stones' code.

What could Takishi be doing with $75 million?

Well, she thought, he could be building weapons

plants on the island of Mindanao. Was this any different than selling TOW missiles to Iran, then funding the insurgency in Nicaragua? Instead of Iran-Contra, do we have China-Abu Sayyaf, she wondered? That would be a twist, fund the bad guys to start a war ... for what?

Next, she opened a file labeled "AIG." American International Group was the world's largest insurance company. In this file she found stock-trading records for early September 2001, prior to September 11. They were a combination of short sales of AIG and United Airlines stock as well as option puts. In essence, whoever the account numbers belonged to had bet in early September that AIG and United stocks were going to go down big.

Bottom line: Someone knew about the coming attacks.

Was that where it ended? she wondered. Did they know about the attacks or did they help plan the attacks? Meredith had read all of the reports of the high-ranking CIA officials who were under investigation for placing short trades on airline and insurance stocks a few days prior to 9-11. For whatever reason, the story never got much play in the press.

But the evidence was staring her in the face. The Rolling Stones, or at least Keith Richards, aka Bart Rathburn, either knew of the short trades or had placed the short trades ... or both. Rathburn, after all, was a finance major and had worked at a hedge fund before finding his way to academia and the Pentagon. Had the other $25 million gone to short trades? Or had it gone to helping the hijackers?

She remembered reading somewhere that 9-11 cost Al Qaeda somewhere around a half million dollars. That was peanuts to these guys.

Or had their cooperation, if there was coop-eration, been more subtle, such as pushing aside a report on the flight training of insurgents, for example?

She shuddered. The bottom line, she assessed, was that the Rolling Stones knew about the 9-11 attacks before they occurred.

So, let's see who they are. She opened Mick Jagger's file and saw a complete dossier on Secretary of Defense Robert Stone. She scanned through the document and closed it.

Next she opened Charlie Watts' file and saw a Harvard Business School picture of Takishi, smiling and handsome. As she read the file, Takishi was an HBS classmate of Bart Rathburn.

She had assumed that Rathburn was Keith Richards since there was no file on Richards and because Stone had once mistakenly called him Keith. So when she opened the Ronnie Wood file, she was not so much surprised when she didn't see Rathburn's face.

Instead, she was shocked at the image staring back at her.

Dick Diamond?

CHAPTER 89

ISLAND OF MINDANAO, PHILIPPINES

Chuck Ramsey could hear the helicopters circling in the distance near Cateel Bay. He saw one of the U.S. Air Force Pave Lows zipping low along the beach, then banking high into the air above the thatch huts, blowing the roof off one of them. The valiant effort of Zachary's Black Hawk had ended when the UH-60 had to make a precautionary landing on the northern tip of Mindanao because of lack of fuel. These U.S. Pave Lows were sent via the Joint Special Operations Task Force.

There was little he could do to effect linkup with this soaring, hovering angel above them, though, with no radio.

The helicopters were a welcome sign, as he had lost six more men besides Eddie in the last series of ambushes. The Abu Sayyaf was still out there chasing him. For the past week, they had walked, then fought, walked, then fought, like two boxers in the twelfth round, slinging wild punches, then moving away, circling, holding a lone fist outward to keep one another at bay, circling some more, then fighting. It was ceaseless.

Ramsey licked his dry lips and steadied his dizzy gaze as he peered through the gray-morning skies, searching for the Pave Low. A rainstorm looked to be moving to his north. He was weak from lack of water and food. The bodies of his Special Forces team littered the trail, a trail of tears, which they had cut through this unspoiled rain forest on the Mindanao eastern shore. First, there had been Peterson, then Jones, then Eddie, then one here, two there, and suddenly it was just Ramsey, Lonnie White, Randy Tuttle, Ken Benson, and Abe.

Abe had survived it all and carried a rucksack and M4 rifle from one of the fallen soldiers. He had painted his face with camouflage stick. During the last small engagement, similar to the others where they had doubled back on their own trail like some Louis L'Amour scouts often do, Abe had surged forward, bayonet fixed on his rifle, rising out of the tall grass and charging the stunned and equally tired rebels. They had fled down the mountainside as Abe had impaled a fourteen-year-old boy toting a rifle on the end of his bayonet.

The Pave Low circled back, and Ramsey briefly saw it through the top layer of the thick triple-canopy jungle. There was a small window of sky above him. He angled the metal tube in his hand toward the opening and slapped it hard on the bottom, bruising his weak palm.

The star cluster rocketed skyward, making it through to the small hole, then bursting green and sparkling back into the jungle nearly two hundred meters away.

The Pave Low reacted and tightened its search arc to about a hundred-meter area.

He pulled another star cluster from his ruck, his last, and repeated the procedure. Benson, White, Tuttle, and Abe all watched with hopeful eyes.

Ramsey turned on his strobe, holding it high in the sky, hoping that somehow it might help. The Pave Low passed the opening once, then circled back, tilting and trying to draw a bead on them.

The pilot hovered the aircraft over the opening as a steel cage called a jungle penetrator began to push its way toward them from seventy-five meters above the ground. Lowered by a hydraulic cable, the penetrator turned and twisted as it floated toward them.

Ramsey looked skyward, thankful, but still not convinced they were free. The adrenaline began to rush, though, giving him the strength to reach up and grab the metal basket. He felt a mild shock from the kinetic energy created by the massive torque of the whipping blades and transmitted along the steel cable.

Tuttle was first to go. He had been wounded in the leg and needed better medical attention than White could give him with his limited supplies.

The basket came down again, and White was next to take the ride.

Chuck's hopes began to grow, like a blooming flower in the spring, betting against the inevitable final frost of a winter not complete. Two of his men were safe aboard an Air Force helicopter. Its blades beat loudly above the jungle, which was why they did not hear the first salvo of AK-47 weapons fired their way.

A bright red spot suddenly appeared in Benson's forehead, then grew rapidly as the blood gushed outward like a fountain. Benson kicked back, eyes open, and fell against the dangling basket, knocking it crazily to the side.

Abe crouched low and immediately returned fire.

"Get in cage," he told Ramsey, who looked briefly at Abe and took him up on his offer. He pulled Benson's limp body onto his lap as he climbed into the basket, charging his M4, and began to fire as he ascended into the heights of the jungle.

Beneath him he could see Abe shooting and moving. Rolling from tree to tree, firing. He watched as Abe pulled out his bayonet and snapped it onto the front end of the rifle. Two Abu Sayyaf charged Abe with bayonets fixed as well. He felt the cage break through a tree branch, hanging momentarily on the stub, then kicking free.

Abe parried the first slash by holding his rifle above his head, then kicking at the attacker with his foot, pushing him away. The second man ran into the powerful thrust of Abe's lunging bayonet, skewering himself beyond the flash suppressor. Abe pulled the trigger, exploding the man backward into a tree, freeing his weapon to fight the dead man's partner.

Is this what it has come down to, two against four? Ramsey thought as he felt the cage strike metal. A large hand opened the top, and a voice said, "You're safe now, sir." Hands grabbed Benson's body, then him, pulling them into the aircraft.

"Send it back down," Ramsey said, weakly.

The crew chief lowered the basket as Ramsey peered over the ledge, much like Ron Peterson had done when he had saved his life. *So much has happened.*

He watched the basket twist and turn its way through the jungle.

Abe cocked his right arm and straightened it, stroking the butt of his rifle into the man's face, only to have him lower his head. His arm flew wildly against the vacant air, pulling his shoulder out of socket. Like a hot knife against his skin, he felt his right arm dangling loosely at his side.

He reached for the basket with his left arm, pulling it toward him, sliding his body into the seat.

The bayonet poked at him, glancing off the metal basket, making a spark, then finding purchase in his rib cage. He felt a rib crack, the pain sharp and pointed, like a razor in the eye. Perversely, it balanced the throbbing sensation of the separated shoulder on his other side. He kicked at the raging rebel, violently flailing his bayonet at the man lifting into the sky.

The rebel stopped, smiled, and looked down at his weapon, realizing Abe had no more ammunition. Then he watched the man slowly ascend toward the helicopter.

The young rebel lifted his rifle bringing it to port arms, and like an executioner, measured his next move, leveling the sight on the swinging basket.

Ramsey lowered his weapon and sighted the rebel. Then Abe. Then the rebel. The penetrator was oscillating, preventing Ramsey from getting a good shot.

"Pull this thing up! Pull up!" Ramsey yelled to the crew chief.

"We'll lose him, sir. We've got to get him higher!" the crew chief screamed back.

Abe looked down with fear as the basket pulled him away. On the ground, an instinct had taken charge, making him a warrior, but now as he lifted through the fog of war, sensing he was moving closer to perhaps his safety, the fear crept back into his mind. Suddenly, he had something to lose. Before, he felt as if he had already lost it. He pulled the picture of his wife and family from the breast pocket of his borrowed uniform. They were smiling at him from a photographer's studio in Tokyo.

The rebel looked away, then sighted again. The wooden stock of his Chinese rifle was covered with mud and dirt, but he was sure it would work again.

He pulled the trigger as the basket reached the bottom of the helicopter, firing one shot, then another, then stopping, flipping the selector switch to automatic, then emptying his magazine into the cage like a magician sticking swords into a basket. He was sure that one of the bullets would find its target.

Abe felt the first bullet crush his kneecap. The second burned a hole in his hamstring, cracking his femur. Some bounced off the cage, leaving hot sparks in their place.

The hand reached in and pulled him away from the cage as a series of bullets bounced off its metal frame, some catching the reinforced belly of the helicopter, others digging their way into Abe's spine.

Chuck grabbed one of Abe's arms and helped pull him into the aircraft, which banked away with the basket dangling below.

The rebel saw a green beret lying on the ground, thrust his bayonet into it, then plucked it from the blade and placed it on his head.

He had won.

Chuck looked at Abe's fading eyes. The man was dying, he was sure. Abe looked at him and grabbed his hand, rolling toward him as the helicopter banked over the ocean.

Pressing the picture of his family into Chuck's palm, he said, "Please call them and tell them I love them." He spoke with unusual clarity, his accent completely absent.

He had wanted to quote Chuck a poem to tell them, but those thoughts had been washed into the drainage pit of his mind, rushing along the gutter, finding the sewer hole and joining the morass of other peaceful, comforting notions. He had recognized his transformation from peace-loving executive to warrior-come-lately and made a mental note to write a series of poems about the gradual but persistent change in his nature. It was almost genetic, instinctual. Without cause or celebration, he did what he had to do, and he did it well. His actions were not propped by allegiance to any flag or ideals, only to the people he had toiled with for the past two weeks. His captors turned benefactors had taken him into the fold, and he had accepted them as well. The dynamics were rich with potential for beautiful prose and poetry.

But his poems were a thing of the past, and so was Abe.

Chuck watched Abe's eyes flutter, as he felt the hand close in on his, pressing the picture deeper into his palm. "Thank you, my friend."

Ramsey turned his head and his eyes caught the sight of five body bags stacked in the helicopter. Each had a name written in black marker on green tape.

He stared at one bag and the name written in bold letters: Peterson. *Ron Peterson, where it all began.*

Ramsey turned away and looked through the open door of the helicopter. His sullen gaze fixed on nothing in particular as a vivid image of Camille, his beautiful daughter, reappeared in his mind; her soft brown hair lying against her shoulders; her smooth round face grinning at him, then frowning, saying, "Come home, Daddy, I miss you. Love you, Daddy, no matter where you are."

He looked at Abe and passed out.

Abe died as the helicopter blew past Cateel Bay and raced to the north, where the hospital ship was waiting.

CHAPTER 90

ISLAND OF LUZON, PHILIPPINES

Prime Minister Mizuzawa had boarded the Shin Meiwa aircraft, flown to the site where the oil tankers were originally located, saw nothing, then landed in the mouth of the Pasig River near the Presidential Palace, using the raging storm as his cover. The pilot had balked at Mizuzawa's insistence, but gladly agreed when a Japanese "New Nambu" .38-caliber revolver was pressed against his temple. The sheering winds pushed the aircraft down, then seemingly backward, releasing its force and allowing the plane to speed forward, almost tripping over itself.

If you want something done, you have to do it yourself.

Dressed in combat fatigues, the prime minister made his way through the streets of Manila, raging with block-to-block, street-to-street, and building-to-building fighting. The entire affair was confusing. He saw M1 tanks shoot at each other, mistakenly. Filipino civilians still roamed the less chaotic streets as if times were normal. Japanese soldiers were holding the Americans back from taking the Presidential Palace and the critical financial district as well.

Mizuzawa entered the grounds of the palace practically unchallenged. The guard was huddled against the fence in a soaked poncho, the rain pelting against the porous fabric. Mizuzawa yanked his revolver from his holster, pulled back the hammer, leveled it alongside the temple of the shivering guard, then lifted it and fired a round. The blast might have made the young soldier permanently deaf in one ear, but it woke him up.

We have become too weak. It occurred to him as he strode into the palace that he was talking about himself. *I should have killed him.*

Several soldiers converged on Mizuzawa, recognizing him immediately. One summoned General Nugama, who came hustling down the steps, buckling his pants. His hair was disheveled, and the buttons to his uniform top were open. Mizuzawa could not determine if the man had been sleeping or screwing a Filipino whore.

"The spoils of war are not ours, yet, Nugama," Mizuzawa said, deciding on the latter.

"Yes, sir. Merely catching up on my sleep," Nugama said, looking virile in his old age.

Mizuzawa caught a glimpse of a beautiful Eurasian woman peering around the banister from atop the stairs. *We are getting weak.*

They walked into the operations center, where several soldiers sat before radios, television screens, and computers. All the men were wearing headsets and talking. A huge map of the Philippines hung on the wall, with red and blue markings on it indicating the location of friendly and enemy forces.

"Where is Takishi?" Mizuzawa asked Nugama.

"Sir, he is in Cabanatuan. He started moving with his division, and was stopped by"—he hated to say it—"by an infantry battalion."

"What! Fools. I didn't give him command of that division just so he could piss it away. I wanted him to be victorious. To know the smell of blood and death so that one day he could take my place as prime minister and understand necessary sacrifice." It was true. Mizuzawa wanted Takishi to return to Japan as a conquering hero. It was just another step in the mentoring process; but like all of the other steps, the mentor can only get the pupil the job. He can't ensure that he succeeds, but he could try.

"Yes, sir," Nugama said, unsure of what to say. He knew of the special relationship between Takishi and Mizuzawa. It was no secret. But Mizuzawa had never made a public declaration of it.

"How bad is it?"

"He's only lost a battalion, but all the aircraft are grounded, and he's got two brigades stuck on the road, trapped by rice paddies. He's still got two infantry battalions able to move, but they're fighting the Rangers in the jungles. Those Rangers didn't know what hit them," he said, trying his best to report some good news.

"What else is happening?" Mizuzawa asked, walking over to the map.

"We've got four divisions on the ground. Two are at about 50 percent, but holding well in the city. We had enough time to establish a decent defensive perimeter. One division was holding Subic, but I moved it over here," he said, pointing at the northern outskirts of Manila, "to flank the enemy Marines. They got caught in a pretty heavy cross fire from enemy air, then their reserve got destroyed by some light infantry to the west of Subic.

"Our intelligence was not very good," he said humbly, looking at the floor.

"So we've got three divisions at 50 percent or less, and Takishi's almost full strength," Mizuzawa said, wondering. "Where's the ship?"

Nugama paused for a moment, then it registered.

"Yes, sir. The ship is halfway between Hawaii and Los Angeles. As you know, the ship was not like the others. Its top deck looks like any other Toyota merchant ship with new cars on top. But the hull is very different. Admiral Sazaku is piloting the ship. He is very trustworthy. He will perform either mission we ask of him," Nugama said.

"Good. This thing is still a potential win. Two of our divisions against two of his. He has more aircraft, but we have more tanks and soldiers on the ground," Mizuzawa said, studying the map. He walked over to a larger-scale map of the Pacific, and traced his finger to a point midway between the Big Island of Hawaii and the big city of Los Angeles. He ran his fingernail across the map, making an indentation, then scratched an X on Los Angeles. He popped the city with his finger and turned to Nugama.

"I want you in the field, General, where you can command your soldiers, not in here sleeping with women, understand?"

"Yes, sir," Nugama replied.

"Perhaps if you had been out there, our position would not be so precarious," Mizuzawa scolded.

A young private walked up to Nugama and handed him a sheet of paper, which he read aloud. "Latest spot report has Takishi back with the main body of his division. He's lost nearly sixty tanks. The road to Cabanatuan is blocked, and the rain is still coming down too hard for the Xs to fly," he said, referring to the AH-X attack helicopters.

Mizuzawa walked back to the map and pondered. Initially, his strategy had been to take the Philippines through political surprise. They had achieved that, but something had gone wrong. Talbosa had defected, or so he thought. Then he pulled the brilliant move with the ambassador's speech to the United Nations, effectively handcuffing the Americans. There was no way they could legitimately react. Then, something else had gone wrong. Somehow, a lousy journalist had captured the death march on film. But still, he figured international opinion was split evenly between believing he had the right to restore the government of the Philippines and siding with the American response. The simple fact that they had gotten that far was a great achievement, but still far short of his goals.

Still, he needed to adjust his strategy. His presence in the operations center was a bad sign in its own right. His goals remained to reassert Japanese military power in the region. Could he do that if he lost the fight? Maybe, maybe not. The conventional fight on the ground could go either way. Japanese soldiers had softened over the past fifty years. They had rarely trained and were not used to the rigors of combat.

Mizuzawa felt the palace shudder once, then a second time.

"Can they reach us down here?" he said to Nugama.

"No, sir. We are safely deep," Nugama said.

"Okay. Let's hold with what we've got in Manila," he said, pointing at the map. "We'll focus our efforts on getting Takishi's division out of Cabanatuan. If he can break free, we pull back, deeper in the city, sucking the Americans in with us. Then Takishi comes from the north, slamming into the enemy rear."

Mizuzawa had moved from the strategic plan to operational art in a matter of seconds. It was all a mind game. Technology and soldiers were important, but the only thing that could truly tip the balance was a superior mind. Why else would theorists such as Sun Tzu and Clausewitz still be relevant today?

He needed something to maneuver with, though, and he hoped his good friend Takishi would come through in the clutch.

CHAPTER 91

Admiral Jennings walked back from the railing of his command ship, which was positioned just off Sampaloc Point near Subic Bay. The spot reports from the pilots on the airstrip were saying it was still too rough to fly. Just to be sure, hoping he could override their judgment, he had walked into the beating rain, only to be slapped in the face by a sheet of water.

General Zater had two brigades on the ground that he could not maneuver anywhere. Jennings sat back in his leather chair in the operations cell and shook his head again at his perceived lack of faith in light infantry.

Tanks were stacked on the road, waiting for the kill ... or to move on the flank of the Marines. The thought made Jennings bolt upright, his wet uniform cold against his skin. That had to be the Japanese plan. Suck the Marines deep into Manila, then slam the door shut with an operational reserve from the rear. How could they have missed it? How could his J-2 and billions of dollars' worth of satellites have missed a huge armored force stuffed into the jungle less than eighty kilometers from Manila? Those tanks would not be impeded by the rain, as were his aircraft, nor the light infantrymen. He pounded his fist into the table, cursing the light fighters.

What had been a window of opportunity for his forces had become an opening for the Japanese to drive straight through to Manila with what was beginning to look like an armored division. If only the weather would clear. The rain, his J-2 intelligence officer had told him, was a Philippine phenomenon called "phantom monsoon." They appeared from nowhere and endured either for a short period of time, or for days. *Yeah right.*

"So what you're saying is that we missed it, and we have no idea how long the son of a bitch will last," Jennings had said. The J-2 looked sheepishly at the deck of the ship and nodded.

Jennings had not come to fight the Japanese to a draw. He needed a decisive victory, one that he could have if the weather would break. Given the circumstances, his thought processes had shifted to avoiding defeat. Not a good thought. It frustrated him to have an attack-helicopter battalion, two brigades of infantry, and several advanced fighter aircraft chained to the ground by the incessant rain.

At least the Marines were tightening the noose around Manila. Three combined arms brigades had made excellent progress until they reached the inner-city core, where the Japanese defenses seemed greatest. His operational plan was rapidly to squeeze the Japanese out of Manila, toward the east, then destroy them with air power. Even that had partially failed. The Marines had been unable to unhinge either the Japanese northern or southern flank. The fight had progressed outward, mirroring the "race to the sea" in World War I, in which the French and German trench lines crept to the north as each unit tried to outflank the other.

The Japanese had the remnants of nearly three divisions hardening positions in the inner city, and a loose cannon near Fort Magsaysay ready to hammer the Marines from the rear. They had grossly underestimated the number of enemy tanks in the Cabanatuan vicinity. Initially, they had told the Ranger regimental commander that a tank company held the area. Then satellite imagery picked up what looked like a small battalion. And later it seemed like a brigade, and the latest reports showed six battalions, two full brigades. Mistakes did happen.

Jennings scurried over to the map and stared anxiously, wondering what his next move should be and how long it would take the Japanese division at Fort Magsaysay to move to Manila. He felt like a participant in a chess match. The poor weather served to strap his hands to the armrests of his chair, preventing him from moving, while his opponent moved freely about the board. He envisioned a Japanese warlord sliding a queen diagonally across the board and saying "check." *With this rain, all I've got is a bunch of pawns out there.*

It was time to take some risks.

He had to keep the pressure on the city with the Marines; it would be another week before the first tanks from Fort Carson arrived. The light division and the Rangers were well suited for the terrain, but ill prepared for the threat. If he could only do away with the division in the north, then he could throw the light infantry into the city and let them work in on the flanks. But that seemed impossible. How could he best use these lightly equipped forces so that they had the advantage? He tapped his lip with his forefinger, looking at the map.

Eighty kilometers from Subic Bay to Cabanatuan. Too far to walk. He saw that, from the east shore of Luzon, the water carved a semicircle in toward Cabanatuan, and looked to be less than twenty-five kilometers from Cabanatuan—and only fifteen from Fort Magsaysay.

He had an idea. If the rain held, it would work. If not, he might have engineered his own defeat. He reached for his radio to call General Zater and tell him about the new plan.

Zater agreed that it was worth a shot and concurred with his assessment on its chances. One thing was clear to both men: The Japanese division in the east had to be stopped.

In his mind, he looked across the table at the sneering imaginary warlord, loosened a bound wrist from the armrest, and reached for what few pieces he had left on the board.

Now, if only the rain would hold.

CHAPTER 92

Zachary moved Kurtz's platoon out of the rice paddy and sent them back to the wooded knoll near checkpoint three-one. They trudged through the pelting rain, unaware of any change in their condition, having just left the soggy rice paddy. The sky was battleship gray, vomiting rain, with a peripheral darkness that seemed prescient, like a dark circle closing in around them.

Upon approaching Taylor's position, he saw five bodies lying on the ground, covered in ponchos.

"They ours?" Zachary asked Taylor.

"Yes, sir." Taylor proceeded to list the name of each soldier and what had happened. Zachary noticed that Taylor talked with a hardened authority, as if something measurable had changed in him that morning.

One of the enemy tanks had fired multiple high-explosive rounds into Zachary's position. One soldier had caught a round in the chest, blowing a hole right through him. It impacted in the ground behind him, leaving his body still pretty much intact except for the big hole. Taylor spoke about it like it was routine. There was no edge in his voice, sort of a monotone, objective description, like what one heard on Headline News.

"About four guys jumped from one tank we hit with an AT4. We killed two, I think, and one ran in your direction. I called you, but you were on battalion net. Slick took the message," Taylor said. Water dripped in a steady stream from the front lip of his helmet. He held a map, covered in acetate, in his right hand, the water smacking it with steady rhythm like a clock pendulum.

"Yeah, he told me, but we never saw him. Bastard is probably back there right now pinpointing our position for the next attack."

Zachary walked over to Barker's position and saw three more bodies. They had been cut down during the initial action on the flank. Barker said, somewhat embarrassed, that he thought two of them were friendly-fire casualties. He had maneuvered his squads in a fashion so that they converged on each other in the darkness.

"It happens," Zachary said, remembering how the U.S. pilots had killed more than a quarter of the friendly soldiers who died during combat in the Persian Gulf War.

Kurtz was the lucky one so far. He had only lost Teller, serving as a back-up radio operator to Zach, and that seemed like an eternity ago.

Zachary huddled with his platoon leaders around a stand of mahogany trees.

"We're moving." The words were painful. Everyone knew they had to, but the logistics of moving in the rain, with dead bodies and demoralized troops, were overwhelming.

"Have your men get ready. They have an hour. I'll let battalion know what we're up to."

He walked with Slick over to a secluded spot and knelt in a pool of water, into the thick mud beneath it.

"Sir, what're we gonna do?" Slick asked, nervously. Usually, he could wait to eavesdrop on the commander and gain his information that way, but events were rapidly getting out of control.

Eight dead. Not counting Rock and Teller. Everybody counts. Make that ten dead.

"We need to move, Slick. As soon as this weather clears, this entire hill's gonna be a free-fire zone.

Arty, mortars, helicopters, tanks, you name it. We stopped them for now. But they're pissed."

The bodies had already made Slick weak and nauseous. He gave the commander the handset and turned his back. Placing his hands on his knees and leaning over, he vomited into the mud. Zachary watched without emotion. *It happens.*

He called Kooseman and gave him the word he was moving to the north side of the road and closer to the fort. He would give him an exact grid coordinate of his CP later, when he found a decent location. Kooseman reported they had secured the prison and freed the six thousand captives. His voice sounded as though he had made a mistake by doing so. Instead of setting them free into the countryside, though, he had merely unlocked their cells but kept the gates to the prison locked. Most stayed inside the protective confines of the prison simply to stay out of the rain.

Zachary told Kooseman that he needed more antitank missiles. He was all out. Kooseman obliged, gathering five Javelin missiles and ten AT4s from each company and sending them forward in a Filipino jeepney, trading the ammo for eight bodies. Zachary appreciated Kooseman's good sense.

The casualties gone, and the wounded patched, Zachary had the battalion's 105mm artillery pieces fire continuous mixtures of smoke and high- explosive rounds into the perimeter of Fort Magsaysay. All of the tanks that could move had backed along the cement road until they were out of sight.

He hoped no one would see him move. With a grim look of determination, Zachary lifted his arm, palm stretched outward, then brought it forward, saying, "Follow me."

They slogged their way across the muddy field.

Takishi rubbed the towel across the back of his wet hair. He and Muriami had been the only ones to make it back through the rice paddies. Everyone else had died from the American onslaught. *An entire tank battalion destroyed. What a waste.*

He looked in the mirror of the command-post latrine as he heard the shelling begin outside. He was frustrated. Mizuzawa had told him that commanding the division would be easy, that everything would fall into place, that it was all common sense.

But how could he have been so careless as to wander aimlessly into the American ambush? Next time, he would do better.

The rain pelted his rubber coat as he walked to the building where the hostages were supposed to have been, then trudged through the mud to a new tank. Muriami had cleaned the inside and put two more radios in it. Takishi's gear was stashed on the floor of the turret ring. Takishi gave Muriami a thumbs-up. "As soon as the rain stops, we move north to Bongabon, then"—he paused to smile—"on to Manila."

CHAPTER 93

The sun never made an appearance, the rain continuing its onslaught. Zachary had wondered if he might see Noah come floating by sometime soon. A full day of monsoon-force rains. His men waded through knee-deep mud, slipping and falling in the miserable muck. During the move, some forgot their overarching concerns of living through this war and cursed the rain and mud and weight they were carrying on their backs.

Some even cursed Captain Garrett for making them move. The wooded knoll was a perfectly good position. They had defended well from there.

By nightfall, they had found a good spot from which to defend. Zachary had purposely taken them on a circuitous route so that any Japanese intelligence collectors would have a hard time figuring their intentions. He heard the men swearing but figured it might do them some good to get their minds off the previous battle, so he said nothing.

When they reached their new defensive position, indistinguishable from any other terrain in the area, he told his men to go to 75 percent security and get some rest. Most tried, but few did.

Zachary looked into the sheets of water blowing with the wind, almost horizontal. He had led them to the northeast of Fort Magsaysay along a small ridge covered with high grass. The jungle was only three hundred meters to the rear, Fort Magsaysay about one and a half kilometers to the south. He called Kooseman and told him he was in position and gave him the grid.

Kooseman went ballistic.

"What the hell are you doing way over there?!" Kooseman screamed.

"They're coming this way next," Zachary said, without hesitation or emotion. He was not going to move, no matter what, and had decided before they moved from their previous site that he was going to ask forgiveness instead of permission, knowing he never would have received the latter.

"I need you to move back and guard my flank," Kooseman said. Zachary looked at the handset. Kooseman was a good guy, but he sounded too dry. He was in a building somewhere, Zachary was sure, as was the rest of the battalion, probably.

"Negative; have McAllister move about six hundred meters north of my old position. That way we'll be able to catch them in a cross fire," Zachary countered, unflinching.

Kooseman paused. Zachary figured he was looking at a map or weighing Zach's insubordination. He didn't care. He wasn't moving.

"Roger," Kooseman responded.

Zachary gave the radio handset back to Slick. Looking through his night-vision goggles, Zachary identified what appeared to be an airstrip, less than a mile to the southwest. He saw the faint black outlines of helicopters and had an idea.

"Think this shit'll ever stop?" Slick asked his captain, shivering in the dark night.

Zachary hardly noticed the question. He summoned Kurtz and SSG Quinones, who appeared moments later, faces painted black for the movement. He gave them instructions on his idea and told them to report back once they were prepared. The two men returned within the half-hour and Zach went over the plan again.

"It's 0200, let's go," he said.

The four of them moved through second platoon's leg of the triangular patrol base. Wearing the goggles felt good, keeping their faces dry for a change. Zachary led the men down the ridge, keeping low. Zachary, Kurtz, and Quinones had emptied their rucksacks and loaded them with the company's supply of C4, detonation cord, and other demolitions equipment.

They moved silently through the loud rain. *Infantry weather.* Wading through a small stream, engorged probably to twice its size, Zachary pulled at a root on the far bank, which dislodged, causing him to fall back into the water. Kurtz and Quinones were behind him, lifting him out immediately. Finally clawing their way to the far side, they spied a weak roll of concertina guarding fifteen helicopters parked innocently on the cement runway.

Zachary designated five aircraft for each man. When they were done, they were to shine their IR flashlights three times in his direction. Slick's job was to watch for the signals.

There appeared to be no roving guard. Zachary could make out a small shack at the far end of the runway but could see no one. He low-crawled up to the wire and nudged it with his rifle, just to be sure, then took his wire cutters and snipped the strands of razor-sharp metal, cutting his hands as he did so. The pain was sharp and unnecessary; he should have been more careful.

The task complete, they slithered like snakes through the obscure opening. Zachary had chosen the five aircraft farthest away. It was the right thing to do. As he crawled on the cement, his body armor and outer tactical vest dug into his skin, and the pools of standing water stung his hands.

He gauged the aircraft. They looked like sleek, new-model Apaches.

He slid his rucksack off his shoulders and dug into its dryness, producing a standard M112 block of C4 that they had prerigged with time fuses, blasting caps, and nonelectric firing devices.

He opened the door to the first helicopter, placing the explosive next to the control panel, leaving the door cracked slightly. He repeated the process for each of the other aircraft, then flashed his IR in Slick's direction. Slick flashed back that he acknowledged. Kurtz and Quinones did the same, then Slick flashed four times to the captain, indicating they were all ready.

Zachary knelt next to the helicopter farthest away from where they had entered the airstrip, and closest to the small hut, less than one hundred meters.

That was why he saw the light come on. A huge spotlight followed, shining in their direction.

He pulled the first nonelectric firing device, listening for the hissing of burning time fuse. Running from helicopter to helicopter, he did the same. Kurtz and Quinones followed suit. He reached his last aircraft and stooped to pick his rucksack off the wet pavement when he heard a bullet whiz by his ear, like a closing zipper, and ricochet off the helicopter. Looking back over his shoulder, he tripped, severely bruising his elbow.

The rate of fire increased as they scampered back through the wire. Quinones had gone first, but was screaming and writhing on the ground as if he was hit.

"Medic! I need a medic!" His body was bouncing wildly on the ground. Zachary approached him, sliding off his goggles and keeping below the enemy fire.

After his eyes adjusted to the night, he saw a horrible sight. Quinones had apparently slipped as he ran through the wire and fallen. One of the razors from the concertina had snagged him just beneath his left eye and ripped open the socket.

Blood was everywhere, and Zachary saw the eye, strung to Quinones's face by a thread of red membrane or muscle, nearly falling out of the socket.

"Help me, sir," Quinones whispered, watching the commander out of his remaining eye.

Zachary pulled out his first-aid dressing and wrapped it around Quinones's head, securing the eye in place. He didn't know, maybe they had the technology to fix it.

Kurtz slung Quinones over his shoulder and grabbed the man's weapon, then went to one knee, saying, "Son of a bitch."

Zachary looked at Kurtz, who groaned and stood, blood pouring from his lower right leg. The Japanese soldiers were racing across the airfield, firing their weapons.

The first explosion knocked about seven of them back. The next blasts happened almost in unison, giving Zachary, Kurtz, and Quinones enough time to melt into the high grass to the east.

They fled into the jungle, clawing their way up the hills without regard for direction, turning to check for pursuers on occasion.

"Halt, who goes there," came the American voice.

"We're Americans!" Zachary screamed.

"Advance forward to be recognized."

"Eagle."

"Viper."

"Welcome to Second Bat. What the hell are you guys doing?" the Ranger said from beneath his patrol cap, the sides of his shaved head glistening in the night.

Zachary turned and watched the Japanese try to extinguish the fires on the helicopters. It was no use. Every one of them was now destroyed.

It could make the difference.

CHAPTER 94

WHITE HOUSE, WASHINGTON, DC

President Davis looked at his friend, Bob Stone, thinking, *He's not himself.*

"What's the matter, Bob, you seem nervous? You're not getting weak on me, are you?"

"No, sir, just a little tired," Stone said, his voice shaking in the confines of the diminutive situation room. They were waiting for Jim Fleagles, the Secretary of State, and Dave Palmer, the NSA. Sewell was sitting next to the president, staring at Stone, who was looking across the table at President Davis, then Frank Lantini.

In reality, Stone had received a phone call from a female police officer saying she wanted to ask him some questions. He nervously inquired, "About what?" only for her to tell him, "We will discuss that later." They made an appointment for the following afternoon.

"Looks like the rain'll stop soon," Lantini said, trying to change the subject.

How's that for some intelligence insight, Stone mused.

"Is that good or bad?" the president asked.

"Both, depending on how you look at it," Lantini said.

That's nailing it down, Frankie old boy, Stone said to himself.

Fleagles and the NSA walked in and sat down.

"Chairman," the president said.

"We were just discussing this rain that's slowed the action some. Looks like it'll lift soon," Sewell said.

"That's good, right?" Fleagles asked in a naive sort of way.

Sewell smirked. "Could be. But Jennings has put the rest of the light division on a ship and is taking them around the other side of Luzon," he said, standing and pointing at a map. "He's got almost two brigades ready to assault from hovercraft, walk the short distance over this ridge, and come in on the enemy's flank. He reasons, and I agree, that if we can take away this guy," he said, thumping a red square symbol with two Xs at the top, then we win today. If not, then the fight goes on. And, if we don't win in the next two days, I'm afraid the international scene could get out of control. It'll be another week before we can get enough tanks over there to make a difference."

"Thanks, Chairman. Impacts on Iraq?" Davis asked.

"Significant, but we think we can be on schedule for next winter or spring," Stone said.

"If that's the math, then okay. But we've got to watch the terrorist flow into Iraq. If they've got weapons of mass destruction, then we need to accelerate."

"This Pacific Rim thing has soaked up time and talent, sir. Only way to put it," Sewell said, reinforcing Stone's position.

The president had begun to speak when a young Army captain, Stockton Ackers, stuck his head inside the room from the operations office and said, "Sir, we need you in here."

"Can it wait?" Davis asked.

"No, sir," Ackers responded, his serious eyes locked firmly with the president's.

The entourage entered the small operations cell,

where computers thrummed with messages, phones constantly rang, maps hung on the wall crazily, and young military officers dressed in civilian clothes performed yeoman's work, often clocking in eighteen- to twenty-hour days.

"Sir, we've got reports of Chinese nuclear weapons moving from the western border with Russia," Ackers said, pointing at a large map about where the Great Wall would be, "to the eastern area near Shanghai. They've never moved those missiles before. We think it's a response to the Philippine crisis."

"Is there any way we can track those things," the president asked.

"Sure, sir, but if they launch, they launch. Nothing we can do about it," Ackers responded to the simple question.

"Okay. I'll talk to President Jiang today. Anything else?"

"Yes, sir. About an hour ago a Korean destroyer sank a Japanese Kuang Hua VI attack boat. They were both in international waters, but the attack boat looked like it was trying to get inside Korean waters. We think it was the newest Japanese ship—"

"I guess I'll talk to President Park after Jiang," the president said, shaking his head, wondering what could happen next.

"Sir," Ackers said, hesitating. "Taiwan's pushed its navy out from Taipei and is poised just southwest of Okinawa, and we've still got the Chinese navy building forces in the East China Sea. This thing could blow any minute."

"Spare me the editorial, Captain," Davis snapped, causing Ackers to clench his jaw. He had been in the operations center for twenty straight hours. He had worked through the first night of Operation Enduring Freedom-Philippines and was operating on a meager four hours of sleep in the last seventy-two. He probably knew better than any of the politicians exactly what was happening.

The president thought about the implications of Ackers's information. How should he respond to China, Korea, Russia, and Taiwan? Each felt threatened, he was sure. The era of the Japanese warlord had left an indelible imprint on the minds of many of the leaders of that region, like Hitler in Germany and Napoleon in France.

But they saw Japanese culture and society as more capable of producing the racist, demagogic warrior of the past. Perhaps Germany was beyond Hitler, and France, Napoleon, but its Asian counterparts might interpret Japan to be reemerging as a nationalistic threat off the east coast of the Asian continent, driven by warlords indistinguishable from the executive auto manufacturers.

Their economic expansion during the past sixty years was the twentieth century's Trojan horse. The Japanese had funneled their historical penchant for war and aggression into highly productive endeavors such as industry, manufacturing, and other high-technology development, but sooner or later, they had reached a point of diminishing returns. Like the once-successful merchant who fell on hard times, they could either fight back or file for bankruptcy. Japan wasn't about to go for Chapter Eleven.

The men retired to the situation office conference room again burdened with the new information.

"We have to finish this thing in the next twenty-four hours," the president said, hanging up the phone. He had called the Chinese prime minister, who was his usual intransigent self.

"If Japan is not defeated by midnight tomorrow," the Chinese leader had said, "we will take matters into our own hands."

The men stared at each other, realizing how right Meredith had been. She had picked up the horseshoe and tossed a perfect ringer, the metal clanking loud through each man's ears today.

Their collective mind, though, was frozen by the news. At the strategic level, if they could not keep China and others out of the war, the United States would lose everything. The most dynamic free-market economy in Asia would wither, taking with it a large portion of the European and American markets, potentially launching the world into another depression.

China had the ability to annihilate Japan with nuclear weapons. The ultimate irony would be China's introduction into the war, and the United States siding with Japan to stop an even-more-dangerous aggressor. Even worse would be the Chinese destruction of Japan, only to witness massive American involvement to rebuild the vital trading partner.

The international community's economic interdependence made the world economy a house of cards. To pull one away might very well bring the entire house down. Worse, at the foundation were the United States, Japan, and Europe, all mingled together like a tri-colored fabric.

The men stared at each other, none knowing what to say.

Then Sewell winked at Stone, his civilian equivalent, and decided to break the ice.

"Let's just see how this thing pans out."

CHAPTER 95

PENTAGON, WASHINGTON, DC

"The move with Takishi was risky," Fox said to Diamond.

"Risky indeed," Diamond agreed.

The two men were sitting in Fox's office again; Fox in his throne and Diamond in the facing chair. Fox put his hand on the desk next to Diamond, his fingers spread casually toward his partner. Rezia's aria, "Ocean! thou mighty monster," from Carl Maria von Weber's *Oberon*, played quietly in the background.

Diamond reached out and took Fox's hand, lightly stroking the well-manicured fingers, caressing the palm as he might a wounded dove.

"But it was necessary to get China sufficiently concerned to put forth their ultimatum," Diamond said. He lifted Fox's hand and kissed it.

Fox ran a finger around Diamond's lips, smiling.

"Yes, that was a brilliant move. Now the twenty-four-hour ultimatum is in effect. We will have to complete the destruction of the Japanese, or else China and North Korea will 'take matters into their own hands.'" He pulled his hand away from Diamond, who was in the process of kissing each individual finger, in order to make quotation marks around his sentence.

Fox leaned forward and ran his delicate hand through Diamond's sparse hair.

"So we started out with Nine-eleven in order to

open the door for action in Iraq," Diamond said, nuzzling his head into Fox's hand. "Then we retaliate against Al Qaeda and the Taliban sufficiently to get them out of Afghanistan, but not sufficiently to destroy them. Brilliant suggestion by the way, Saul. The lingering threat will open so many opportunities—the possibilities are limitless."

"It *was* a good idea," Fox purred. "We haven't put more than a brigade in Afghanistan. And when that Matt Garrett crossed over and was about to get you-know-who, well, your quick action to blackmail Stone was genius. Using Stone's personal information to create an E*Trade account so that 'he' could short AIG and United Airlines was pure brilliance."

"Thank you." Diamond sighed. "It certainly got Stone to move Garrett far off the Al Qaeda trail quickly." The two men were becoming aroused, stimulated by their manipulations and grand strategy. "Matt Garrett's dead now anyway. That's what I hear."

"Good. Good. That was a loose end we didn't need," Fox said. "Not that he knew anything. But he was too aggressive, too good."

"That's right. Then, as we gathered the momentum on Iraq, we have to hand it to Stone, who worked faster than we thought he could, to get the Philippine situation to a sufficient level actually to be a diversion," Diamond said.

"But they had been working on that for two years." Fox chuckled. "The Japanese used him and outsmarted him."

"Well, we've been working on our project longer than that," Diamond moaned. He was in full arousal. The two were holding hands with both hands, fingers interlaced, appearing to be locked in some tantric yoga pose.

"Yes, we have," Fox said. "Which is why we had

to intervene with Takishi to get him to ratchet up the force levels so that there was a credible threat to the region."

"So that China and North Korea would issue an ultimatum," Diamond whispered, blowing into Fox's ear.

"Which brings us full circle." Fox sighed. "We will wrap this up soon and begin large-scale deployments to Kuwait. I've already signed the deployment orders."

"I'm just thankful that you broke the Rolling Stones' code," Diamond said, running his cheek against Fox's.

"Rather easy, Dick. We will ruin Mick Jagger, Charlie Watts will be dead soon, and Keith Richards is already dead. That only leaves the question about what we do with Ronnie Wood," Fox said.

"Problematic," Diamond agreed, kissing Fox's neck.

"We have to make sure that the Philippine action is done quickly and leave Wood intact. He may not be much, but he's what we got," Fox said.

"He's our man," Diamond agreed.

CHAPTER 96

ISLAND OF LUZON, PHILIPPINES

Zachary watched the convoy move out and called Kooseman, the acting battalion commander.

"I've got about 120 tanks, plus a shitload of infantry fighting vehicles moving north toward Bongabon," Zachary said, peering above a rotted log. He lay in the prone position, holding a set of binoculars to his face, counting. He had slipped a knee pad over his swelling elbow so that he could hold the binos steady.

The Ranger medic had done all he could for SSG Quinones, the morphine shot being the most helpful. With the rain, a medevac was impossible.

"What I'd give for a few A-10s and some F-16s," Zachary said.

"Like you always say, sir, this is infantry weather. Them zoomies can't handle this shit," Slick said, smiling, feeling safe watching the procession move away from them to the northwest. It was a comforting feeling, as if he might never see them again.

"Yeah, but they'd make short work of this. I don't see a single air-defense weapon," Zachary said.

He was right. In Zach's assessment the Japanese had gone into the conflict severely unprepared, despite their strategic and tactical surprise. They had some stinger gunners riding in the tanks and infantry fighting vehicles, but all they could do was react. There was no integrated system set up for early warning such as the Americans used.

Zachary and Slick lay against a rotted log, soft from the rain, waiting for the word from Kooseman. Zachary had played cowboy enough for one war and was growing apprehensive over his isolation from the rest of the unit. Once again, he was all alone, save for the Rangers to his left flank. It was, however, his fault. He had moved the company on his own initiative.

Something instinctual had governed him, almost forcing him to the new position, as if he was supposed to be there.

They heard wet, muffled sounds of artillery rounds leaving their tubes and cutting a path through the driving rain and high clouds. The rounds popped in the distance. Through his binos Zachary saw timber crash and mud splash on the wooded knoll they had earlier defended. The Japanese self-propelled artillery pumped round after round into the infamous knoll, then shifted its fire onto the town of Cabanatuan, indiscriminately spraying the area.

Zach could see thatch huts, the ones that had withstood the onslaught of the rain, disintegrate under the now-incessant bombardment. They had learned one lesson, Zachary figured, and that was to go nowhere without artillery support.

"Bravo six, this is Knight five, over," came Kooseman's voice over Slick's radio handset.

"This is Bravo six, over," Zachary said.

"Can you do anything about that artillery; it's getting pretty bad over here?" Kooseman asked, anger in his voice.

Zachary's mind raged white-hot *He's got a lot of balls.* Kooseman had chastised him for moving so far away but had the nerve to ask Zachary to attack the enemy formation and compromise his new position. Yesterday, he would have done it without fail, but today, he had gained a better perspective. Some of

the edge had dulled from his hate, the driving force
to kill every Japanese soldier. He recognized that he
had a larger responsibility to protect his company
and complete the mission.

"What do you want me to do? I've got about
fifteen missiles," Zachary said, hoping that would
discourage Kooseman.

The artillery volleys increased, and for the first
time Zachary heard the impotent battalion 105mm
rounds impacting near the Japanese 155mm self-
propelled guns. They landed harmlessly around the
armored hulks of the Japanese guns.

"Can you see their arty? How many guns do they
have?"

Zachary didn't like the way the conversation was
going; but then he thought of guys like McAllister
and Glenn Bush, who were probably over there
getting shelled.

"Roger. I count sixteen guns. Looks like two
batteries. All are firing," Zachary said, knowing immediately what his new mission was going to be.

"You've got enough to take them out," Kooseman
said, trying to make it sound like an order.

Water dripped steadily off the black handset that
Zachary held to his ear and mouth. His elbow had
busted a hole in the log, and he saw some maggots
crawling on his sleeve. As he brushed his elbow
against the soggy wood, he wondered about
Kooseman's mathematical capabilities. Sure, he could
get most of the artillery, but then would have to bear
the brunt of nearly two hundred armored vehicles
turned against him.

It was suicide.

"I'm not so sure it's a smart move," Zachary said
into the handset, realizing he was being insub-
ordinate.

"I'm not asking your opinion, Garrett. Shoot the
artillery. Do it now," Kooseman retorted. He heard

loud explosions amplified by the transmission. Looking through his binoculars as the gray shade of morning lightened ever so slightly, he watched as a shell tore a huge hole in the prison roof.

"What happens when these two brigades turn on my ass?" Zachary asked.

"We've got you covered. Have you shot the artillery, yet?"

"Roger. Happening now," Zachary said, tossing the handset to Slick. Zachary ordered his platoon leaders to his position, and they rapidly arrived, Kurtz limping with a large bandage around his lower leg.

"We've got orders to destroy that artillery," he said, pointing at the dark figures jumping backward each time they fired. They were nearly five hundred meters away, perfect distance for the missile gunners. Zachary hated to use the passive voice regarding an order. Normally he took responsibility for everything, but he had a hard time justifying to his men that their company was supposed to attack a two-hundred-strong armored vehicle convoy.

"Then what?" Taylor asked.

"Then we fight like good soldiers, Andy. We do our best. We've been given a mission, and we're gonna do it."

Kurtz and Barker were silent as Zachary sketched out a new plan. It was simple: Assign each gunner an artillery piece, everyone would fire simultaneously, then the company would move a kilometer to the rear, into the jungle.

He watched as his platoon leaders trod back to their platoons, and could not help wondering about that night attack they had botched in training over two weeks ago.

Just don't screw the pooch here.

"Packers," he said into the radio after receiving word from the three platoon leaders that they were ready.

He looked over his shoulder and thought he saw something, something blue, but then watched as his antitank gunners once again scored strikes on the enemy armor.

Despite the pelting rain, thirteen of the sixteen artillery pieces were burning a bright orange hue, the color of a sun.

The sun, yes. Blue skies mean the sun will come out.

Zachary looked back over his shoulder and saw a blue patch of sky moving slowly above a mountain peak, like an old man on a Sunday drive.

Hurry up!

"Knight this is Bravo. Destroyed thirteen of sixteen. Out of missiles," Zachary reported to Kooseman, ready to pack his bags and move into the jungle.

"I sent you some AT4 yesterday. Get the other three. We're still taking arty," Kooseman demanded.

Zachary wanted to tell him to pack sand, but instead obeyed, as he knew he always would.

"Roger, out," Zachary replied.

"You don't say out to me, Captain! You say, over, over."

Zachary threw the handset into the mud and stood. He could still hear Kooseman squawking, but quit listening when he noticed … something was different.

It had stopped raining.

CHAPTER 97

Takishi told Muriami to move out. They weren't going to wait for the rain to stop. Muriami gunned the jet engine, tossing Takishi's ribs into the padded rubber of the commander's hatch.

Takishi surveyed the wet, gray morning. The rain had continued through the night, and Takishi had decided to move his tanks after the enemy had destroyed his helicopters.

He radioed his commanders and told them to follow him north. He positioned an infantry battalion on each side of his column of tanks. His soldiers, all soaked to the core, revved the diesel engines and began the muddy trek north toward Bongabon, only to cut south from there toward Manila.

The light infantry had been pesky, though, and using the new route, he could avoid them. *"Just drive around the bastards!"* Mizuzawa had told him. The Marines had made a penetration in the defenses and were bearing down Roxas Boulevard with at least three companies.

He needed an operational victory to counter the weight of the tactical defeat. If Takishi could spring free, then the Americans would have to react to the threat that he posed.

Mizuzawa was desperate, so he had told Takishi if he was not successful, the ship was going into harbor. Takishi had protested mildly, but he knew there was nothing he could do. With Mizuzawa, you either signed up for the entire plan or took a hike. He had been opposed to the idea of the ship, but Mizuzawa had overruled him, saying it was necessary.

"This time, we must make it," Takishi said to Muriami, as they splashed along the muddy road. The tank tread bogged down briefly, then got a grip, gaining purchase on firmer turf. Takishi looked ahead and saw that the road was strewn with chunks of asphalt. Without a decent surface, the road would be impassable.

After an hour of tough slogging, Takishi slewed his turret 180 degrees and ordered Muriami to stop the tank. The going had been slow anyway, and a brief halt would not make a big difference one way or the other.

Frustrated, he watched the American missiles chew into his artillery, then he saw about thirty men come charging downhill toward the pieces that were still firing. They set up shoulder-launched weapons and fired, setting the remainder of the artillery ablaze.

All he had left was direct-fire capability. He pressed the toggle switch on his CVC helmet and ordered the right-flank infantry battalion commander to dismount and destroy, once and for all, the pesky light infantry.

Whether it was for glory or because of pure frustration, Takishi lifted his M4, a prize among all of his troops, and stepped out of the relative protection of the tank turret. He jogged into the fray behind hundreds of his infantry and saw a man running down the hill with a radio handset in his ear and a black coil stretching to another soldier, who was trying to keep up.

Charlie Watts was going solo!

Standing, Zachary predicted that the right-flank battalion would turn on his position. It did.

Soon, a 25mm chain gun was chewing the soggy

ground to his front. Barker's platoon, having just destroyed the remainder of the artillery, was suddenly stranded by the advancing vehicles.

Like army ants, Japanese infantry came pouring from the backs of the fighting vehicles, firing their American weapons at American soldiers.

With horror, Zachary watched as ten vehicles started driving at Barker's platoon of thirty men, caught in the open like a herd of mustangs surrounded by cowboys. Some of the troops had time to move, but many did not. The twenty-ton armored weapons crushed them, some pivoting atop the bodies.

Zachary saw Barker crouched low, firing his M4 at an oncoming tank, his bullets ricocheting wildly off its rolled steel. The tank impaled him on its front deck, as the tank commander leaned over the turret and emptied a full magazine of submachine-gun ammunition into Barker's body, leaving it glued to the tank by streaming blood. Zachary saw Barker's head bouncing crazily as the tank stopped, then backed, forcing Barker's body to slide onto the ground. It pivot-steered to gain the proper angle, finally chewing the wet turf, then Barker, mixing the mud with the blood and bones of the young lieutenant.

"I need artillery, air, and helicopters here now!" Zachary screamed into the battalion net.

"Hold on, Zach," came McAllister's voice, "I'm almost there."

McAllister's voice comforted him briefly, then the wave of charging infantrymen flushed the thought from his mind. *Must be three hundred.*

His remaining two platoons, positioned along the open ridge, began firing. The squad's automatic weapons sang through the morning air, thrumming lightly in contrast to the Japanese 7.62mm machine guns, which made loud, cracking sounds.

"Fix bayonets," Zachary said calmly into the company radio.

Some did, most already had.

The two lines of soldiers merged, one indistinguishable from the other. Zachary saw Slick's eyes grow wide with fear as he fumbled with his bayonet.

Too late. A small Japanese soldier drove the butt of his weapon into Slick's helmet, knocking him back. Zachary took his pistol and fired it almost point-blank at the man's face, leaving a mangled mass in its path, like a plate of spaghetti.

Zachary stuffed the pistol in his belt and lifted his M4, firing it at the many targets. The scene reminded him of a Civil War painting he'd seen at Gettysburg, the Union and Confederate lines locked together in combat, brother against brother.

These were no brothers, though. He knew about brothers. The thought sent a hot, violent rage surging through his body.

He stood, let out a low, guttural moan, then screamed wildly and waded into the fray, flailing his weapon back and forth, stabbing some with the bayonet, shooting others who were far enough away. Small Japanese men, clad in dark olive uniforms, mouths contorted, were screaming words foreign to Zachary. As he parried bayonet thrusts, he had a sense that he was one of seven—a man named Stanard who had fought so valiantly in a little battle near the Blue Ridge called New Market nearly 140 years ago. Stanard and his six VMI classmates had died as cadets, battling the Union invasion of their beloved Virginia countryside, and the Blue Ridge folks had named a small town after him.

He felt close to Stanard as a knife pierced his left shoulder from behind. He turned and saw the blackened face of a Japanese officer as the knife made a cracking sound cutting through his clavicle.

Zachary pulled the pistol from his holster with his right hand, dropping the empty M4, and bored a hole through his attacker's neck, bright red blood spraying in all directions.

He pulled the knife from his shoulder in time to thrust it into another enemy soldier coming at him with a bayonet. The forward momentum of the small man knocked Zachary onto his back as he slid fifteen feet through the mud, coming to rest at the feet of two men fighting.

He saw Kurtz wildly swinging his rifle, crushing a man's temple. Zachary stood and wheeled around as he pointed his pistol in Slick's face, pulling the trigger, but moving the barrel to the side just in time.

Slick grabbed the commander and pulled him from the mêlée.

The sound of gunfire and screaming men filled the air. It was a horrible noise, the decibels of death, rising into the fresh, cool morning.

"Sir, Captain McAllister's coming up the hill now. He just called on the radio!" Slick said, not sure why he thought it was important for the commander to know. More than anything, he wanted to protect the man he had grown to know and respect. They had developed a bond, a bond that vanished as soon as Zachary watched the bullet strike Slick in the gut, just beneath the outer tactical vest, causing blood to pump like a stuck water fountain.

"Medic!" Zachary screamed, realizing he would get no help. He pulled Slick's first-aid dressing, ripped open his uniform, and placed it on the wound, but blood was everywhere.

"Kill those bastards, sir," Slick said as he died, his hand holding the black handset that had practically become an appendage.

Bastards!

The circle of death, once again, tightened its noose around Zachary.

A bullet struck him in the back of his right shoulder, balancing the throbbing pain from the knife wound and knocking him onto the ground. He stared skyward, his mind fuzzy, and would have sworn he saw buzzards circling the sky.

Big black birds, hovering, and turning, arching high and low, their beaks closed tight, waiting for the kill. Some moving fast, others just circling, while even more just hovered above the trees and began to fire at the Japanese tanks.

Suddenly, AH-64 Apache helicopters and Air Force A-10s began swooping along the strung-out column and pumping 30mm depleted uranium sabot bullets into the backs of the enemy infantry climbing the ridge in order to complete the destruction of B Company.

Then he saw McAllister's men rise from the stream that bordered Fort Magsaysay and converge on the left-flank infantry battalion that had by then dismounted. Only three hundred meters away, he saw McAllister leading the charge with an M4, bayonet fixed, his head turned, screaming something over his shoulder, and pulling his arm forward with his palm open. He saw his lips form the words, "Follow me," as his troops came screaming from the riverbed and tangled with the Japanese infantry.

The Apaches and A-10s raked the Japanese column with relative impunity, concerned only with ensuring that they didn't shoot any of the American soldiers.

Zachary watched an A-10 swing low, spit its 30mm, and take a direct hit from a missile, knocking it sideways and forcing the airplane to tumble end over end through the enemy infantry.

At least he took a bunch with him.

Flaming tanks and infantry fighting vehicles burned a brilliant orange, emitting a black smoke that rose to the heavens—perhaps dusty souls escaping the dying.

Zachary stood and joined his company, still

locked in hand-to-hand combat. He had lost his weapons and used his helmet to hold at bay a charging Japanese soldier, crushing the Kevlar into the man's face. His attacker flipped backward in the mud, the man's weapon firing errantly into the sky. Curiously, Zachary noticed that the downed man was no soldier; his attacker looked more like a civilian. Perhaps he was Japanese intelligence?

Zachary pulled his K-Bar from its sheath and drove it into the man's neck until he felt it penetrate into the mud below. It hung on the civilian's trachea as he pulled it out, forcing him to grab the neck and yank hard to retrieve his knife. The jagged edge of the knife caught Zachary's hand on the way out, cutting deep into the bone of his thumb.

He felt the crushing impact of wood on his mouth as he caught a glimpse of an enemy pant leg move toward him. Teeth bounced loose into his throat, almost choking him.

He grabbed the man's thrusting weapon, slicing open his hands on the bayonet, but somehow gripping the muddy stock tightly before the pointed object could enter his body. It didn't matter, the infantryman pulled back on the weapon, leering at him from above, but Zachary held on firmly and rose as the man pulled the trigger.

Frozen in time, he saw the weapon emit a bright muzzle flash, and felt something hot burn its way through his abdomen. Another muzzle flash and he fell backward, reaching out with his knife, trying to stab at the foot of his attacker.

He could barely sense the feel of the wet, cold steel against the back of his head.

There was no time to remember the flashing images of Amanda or Matt or Riley or Karen or Slick or Rock or Teller or Father or Mother.

He heard a shot ... and saw the quail drop and looked at his brother, Matt, and smiled. They both watched their dog Ranger bounce through the high weeds and cattails along the stream in search of the fallen game. They followed, bare-chested and laughing in the cool mountain air, each looking at the other, Matt's crooked smile prominent. Thorny vines scraped at their tattered dungarees as they reached a high rock outcropping, which rose sixty feet above a deep pool in the South River. Turning their heads slowly, they looked back at the towering Blue Ridge, waved at each other, and leapt over the brink.

CHAPTER 98

The hot sun boiled onto Mike Kurtz's face as he lifted his head and saw shimmering waves of heat rising above the soggy ground like charmed cobras.

Through the ripples in the air, he noticed hundreds of bodies lying motionless, some wearing Army combat uniforms, many others clad in dark olive uniforms. Armored vehicles still burned brightly, the heat intensified by the searing sun.

He stood, or at least tried, and fell back to one knee, his weight causing immense pain to course through his body. The jungle was just to his east about three hundred meters up the hill, and it struck him that the terrain always looked different when he finally got to see it in broad daylight.

They had defended from a ridge that overlooked the road to Bongabon. It was the only place on the ground where they could have effectively engaged the Japanese. Once again, Captain Garrett had made the right choice. He lifted his eyes and tried to spot the captain walking about, motivating the troops as he did so well. He had remembered seeing him briefly during the battle, then had lost track.

Nothing. Nothing but the soft swish of helicopter blades ferrying bodies away from Fort Magsaysay to a hospital ship.

The silence was eerie, almost causing him to believe he had died, but then he saw a body roll over and try to elevate. Kurtz stood and limped badly to the man, stepping over bodies.

Andy Taylor turned and looked at Kurtz, his old

friend. A large scar ran across Taylor's chin, still damp with blood.

"What the hell happened?" Taylor said more out of exasperation than to ask a question.

"I think we won," Kurtz said, then fell forward, almost passing out.

"Geez, man, you okay?" his friend asked, concerned. Kurtz had lost a lot of blood and needed a doctor badly. But he almost fainted because he recognized a name tag on a uniform that covered a dead body. There were no facial features to recognize, as the head was basically ... gone. He prayed against all hope that the man was alive, but saw nothing to indicate so. The body was motionless, flies buzzing around his blood-soaked upper torso. Body parts were strewn about in macabre fashion. All they could recognize was the name tag and rank and identification tags that were oddly in plain view. His unspoken thought was that it looked like the man had received a direct hit of a mortar or artillery shell.

"Shit," Kurtz said, looking at Taylor. He looked at the dog tags, and the name on the identification tags matched those on the uniform. Taylor hobbled to his rucksack, pulled out a poncho, and rolled the "remains" into the rubber material. He snapped the sides and asked Kurtz to help him.

They carried the heavy poncho down the hill toward the airfield they had silently attacked last night, where an American UH-60 sat hovering. Just beyond the aircraft were General Zater and Colonel Lindsay, surveying the destruction. In their estimation, the mission had to have been a success. One or two light infantry companies had defeated an entire division, or so the awards would read.

Taylor and Kurtz hauled their precious cargo toward the aircraft, their route made circuitous by the battlefield littered with bodies and burning vehicles. Zater and Lindsay approached, looking grimly at the two men. They had been discussing the fact that the singular actions of Zachary Garrett's men had prevented the armored division from moving to Manila to destroy the Marines.

"They saved the day," Zater said.

Taylor and Kurtz acknowledged the presence of the two senior officers and continued with their business, neither wearing a helmet, nor did they have any weapons. Their uniforms were tattered and mostly a dark red from dried blood. Kurtz's dog tags lay against his hairy chest, and his matted hair was glued with blood to his forehead.

Taylor's scar seemed deeper and longer than when Kurtz had first seen it. A Japanese bayonet had carved a permanent war memory into Taylor's rugged good looks.

"Who's in the body bag, son?" Zater asked solemnly.

Kurtz looked at the man, then at Taylor.

"Just one of the soldiers, sir. Just another soldier," he said absently.

They walked past the two high-ranking officers and laid the body inside the general's helicopter.

Kurtz turned to the pilot and told him to take good care of the man they had placed in his aircraft. The pilot looked at the lumpy poncho, then out at the horrible sight of the battlefield, wishing that his aviator brethren could have made it sooner. Just five or ten minutes would have made a difference.

The pilot gave Kurtz and Taylor a sad nod and watched as the two warriors merged into the field of bodies.

General Zater walked over to the helicopter, pulled at the poncho just enough to see that Kurtz had written a name in black marker against light green tape.

A tear formed in his eye, and he thought, *You're right, just another soldier.*

CHAPTER 99

A large gold cross was perched atop the simple white building adjoined to the Malacanang Presidential Palace by a short catwalk. Beneath the cross was a stained-glass window depicting the Mother Mary holding Baby Jesus. The welcome sun shone upon the multicolored glass, diffusing its light like a prism and licking at the standing puddles of water.

Five hundred years ago, when the Spanish first colonized the archipelago, naming it after King Philip, they Christianized the natives by introducing them to the Catholic religion. Every leader of the country since that time has been a Catholic, in name at least, and after achieving independence in 1947, the chapel was erected as a monument to the religion and its important role in Philippine society. The Pope himself had visited the enclave and declared the fenced chapel the property of Vatican City.

That day, a week after the final battle at Fort Magsaysay, Mizuzawa used it for other purposes.

"Get me Sazaku," Mizuzawa said to General Nugama from the confines of the small chapel. Mizuzawa did not expect the Americans to wait much longer, but hoped they would respect the sanctity of the Catholic Church long enough for him to make one last move.

The Marines had unhinged the northern edge of the Manila defensive line, rolled the flank with one brigade, and surrounded the Presidential Palace with another brigade, while the third brigade fixed the southern flank, preventing the Japanese from reinforcing against the breakthrough.

Takishi had made a frantic call only moments before Mizuzawa and Nugama had run into the chapel with as much radio gear as they could garner.

"I'm being destroyed!" Takishi had reported. The road from Fort Magsaysay to Bongabon was littered with burning Japanese tanks and infantry fighting vehicles, some ignited internally from stored ammunition.

"You're on your own," Mizuzawa responded to his friend, hearing the sound of exploding tanks in the background of Takishi's transmission.

Mizuzawa learned from the Americans that Takishi had been found among the dead littered on the battlefield outside of Fort Magsaysay, a knife wound to the neck. Indeed, Mizuzawa was watching his plans for a new, more dominant Japanese Empire fade like the setting sun, melting into the western horizon.

But he had one more card to play. It was, after all, a game of high-stakes poker, where each country tried to read the other's bluff, raising the ante when appropriate. Mizuzawa reached into his shirtsleeve and yanked out the ace he had tucked away before he had set the deadly train of events in motion.

"Sazaku, my friend. It is time," Mizuzawa said into the satellite radio.

The transmission soared as a neat bundle of words through the atmosphere, bouncing off one satellite, then another, and finally entering the receiver screwed to a metal frame inside the cabin of Admiral Sazaku's merchant marine car carrier: the *Shimpu*.

"Yes. I figured as much," Sazaku responded, his transmission reversing the path of Mizuzawa's.

"How long until you will detonate?" Mizuzawa asked, an edge to his voice. He was anxious to deal the Americans a fatal blow, even if it was a solitary strike that might invite massive retaliation. But he doubted that would happen. Americans were always believers in just wars, just victories, and just punishments.

A nuclear explosion in Los Angeles would be devastating for sure, but Mizuzawa would have shot his complete wad, having nothing else to fight with except his meager self-defense forces.

"I'm six hours out from the harbor. As soon as I touch the pier, I will vanish in a blaze of glory for my country," Sazaku answered, reminiscent of the kamikaze pilots of World War II. Sazaku carried on the Japanese kamikaze tradition of writing a final poem before the splendid final moments of life.

I am the final victor/my country proud/the ship I steer/finishing loud/I am not alone/friends by my side/others gathered/in the ebbing tide/in the end/my floating corpse/finding safe harbor/Banzai Japan, no remorse.

"Yes, good. Continue your mission," Mizuzawa ordered, then placed the handset back in its receiver. He looked at Nugama, an old friend whom he trusted.

"Do you have misgivings, my friend?" Mizuzawa asked, hoping for an honest answer.

"We can still win, Prime Minister. We can have Sazaku enter the port, then we can sue for peace on our terms," Nugama responded, his gray hair shining bright beneath the stained-glass window. They could hear the intermittent pop of small-arms fire and the horrifying noise of American jets slicing low above the Manila skyline.

CHAPTER 100

GREENE COUNTY, VIRGINIA

While she was recovering at the Garrett farm in Stanardsville, Meredith continued to pore over the thumb drive, finding little else of use. She stood and stretched, catlike, her angora sweater providing full effect.

She went back to Matt's room, where she had been sleeping, and studied the computer notes he had typed, which gave her an idea.

"Karen," she shouted down the stairs. "Think Matt would mind if I looked at some files on his computer?"

"No, just stay away from all the sports illustrated swimsuit editions. He copies the pictures in Adobe PDF and saves them." Karen smiled.

"I always thought of him as a man who could judge quality swimwear," Meredith said, smiling. Like a Greek tragedy, the two women were able to manage pockets of humor, but overall the situation was a disaster.

Karen opened Matt's computer using all of the protocols and she was inside Matt Garrett's storage files. She was missing something—something she couldn't remember, and Meredith believed it was substantial.

She scanned his personal e-mail. Lots of Viagra offers, announcements that his Bank of America account was going to be closed if he didn't provide all of his financial data, and some that looked like stray friends, perhaps lovers.

She reprimanded herself for perusing the note from Kari Jackson from New York. Apparently they had once been an item in college. With a career like Matt's, Meredith wished Kari good luck. Well, actually, she didn't. Not the way she had grown to feel.

As she stared at the screen, a new e-mail appeared at the top in the form of a text message, meaning it was most likely sent from a cell phone. She didn't recognize the phone number but did understand the message.

Check out *Shimpu*. Contact KIA. New location. Standing by.

That was it, Meredith derided herself. The eleventh ship was out there floating in the Pacific as a wild card. Matt had mentioned this to her when they first met in Palau.

She ran downstairs and kissed Karen on the cheek, then jumped in her Prelude to make the two-hour drive to DC along Route 29 and I-66. She called Mark, her assistant, to get her the proper parking clearances and to let them know she had urgent information. She fishtailed her small car into a parking space on the Ellipse less than five hundred yards from the Washington Monument.

She could see the tall white structure pointing into the sky, and even at that urgent moment was amazed that there was nothing actually holding the granite blocks together but their sheer weight.

She ran to the southwest gate of the White House, flashing her credentials and passing through the metal detector. The guard recognized her from her few visits with Stone and allowed her to pass after phoning Dave Palmer, who told him to send her through.

Worry etched lines of concern across her soft face. Dressed in blue jeans and flannel shirt, she had driven as fast as possible from Stanardsville.

She jogged beneath the awning that led to the business portion of the White House in the West Wing, then bounced up the stairs into Palmer's corner office where Stone and Lantini were looking at a map on Palmer's desk. She steeled herself against Stone's presence and projected a determined demeanor.

"You've got to find this ship," she demanded, slapping down a piece of paper on the desk with the word *Shimpu* scribbled in large, erratic script.

The three men looked at her, then the paper, and Palmer asked, "What's the big deal, we've won this thing? We've got the Presidential Palace, and we've defeated their operational reserve. They've got nothing left. All we've got to do is root Mizuzawa out of the Catholic chapel there, and we can pack our bags." His matter-of-fact demeanor only served to ignite a simmering fire in Meredith.

"You don't understand! The ship has nukes on it and is roaming in the Pacific somewhere," she said, shaking. She tried to maintain her professionalism, fearing that Palmer might just mistake her for another woman with PMS. The barriers were still there. If she had been a man, she could have done or said whatever she wanted, but as a woman, if she got too irate, she was just another crazy bitch.

"What makes you so sure, Meredith?" Stone asked, giving her the benefit of the doubt. After all, she had predicted with certainty the reaction of Japan's neighbors. In fact, the president's policy was based in large part on Meredith's acute analysis. Thankfully, the defeat of the Japanese ground forces had kept the Chinese and Koreans in check. The Russians and Taiwanese were merely extending their security zones and never had any intention of provoking Japan beyond convincing her to put her toys back in her bag and go home.

"This is the eleventh ship. I don't know how I missed it, but remember there were ten that pulled away from Davao City. They were military sealift ships disguised as oil tankers. But look here," she said, flipping some pages to a shipping log, "the *Shimpu* docked at Zhoushan a month ago, spent one night, never off-loaded anything, then arrived in Davao City and departed port the day Matt Garrett's contact was killed on the pier. And Matt reported this."

Palmer took a minute to scan the log, a product of United States HUMINT, human intelligence and passed it to Lantini, whose organization had originally provided the document. Routinely, operators around the world tracked foreign ships, particularly among high-risk nations. Stone looked over Lantini's shoulder, and thought, *What have we done?*

"We know this ship docked in Zhoushan, loaded something, then left, then arrived in Davao, and left. Now we don't know where it is. Is that right?" Palmer said. He added before she could answer, "Christ, what happened to your head." He saw the six stitches that the Georgetown doctor had put in her forehead near the right temple.

"Jogging accident," she said quickly, staring directly at Stone. "Why don't we just try to find the *Shimpu?* And then we can hazard a guess as to what it's doing."

"You think there are nukes on the thing, really?" Lantini asked.

"Well, why don't we worst-case it, then?" Sewell said, walking into the office. He wore his green Army uniform, bedecked with medals from conflicts in Vietnam, Grenada, Panama, and Iraq. Meredith smiled. Sewell returned the nonverbal greeting, shaking her hand.

"The president called me over to discuss his

speech tonight, but I couldn't help overhearing your conversation as I walked by," Sewell said.

"We can shift our focus to this thing if you want, Chairman, but what about China and Korea? We might lose focus there just to start scanning for this one ship in the Pacific," Palmer said.

"Why don't we start looking at places like Guam, where we have most of our logistical support, Hawaii, God forbid, and even the West Coast. We can do it in that order. If it's Guam or Hawaii, we need to find it fast. Heck, depending on how long this cannon's been loose, it may already be docked somewhere," Sewell said, the thought sending chills up Meredith's spine.

She was glad that Sewell had come to the rescue. She was nervous enough with Stone in the room, but had also been beating her head against the glass ceiling of discrimination with Palmer, even though he was more understanding than most. But when there was a crisis, she couldn't understand why Palmer, or any other man for that matter, just didn't stuff it back in his underwear, zip it up, and forget that she was a woman. She appreciated Sewell's gender-neutral approach and his protective aura with the predator Stone lurking so close.

"Why can't we just tell Mizuzawa to call off the dog, or we'll level Japan?" Palmer said.

"Get real, Dave. He knows we would never destroy the Japanese economy. It would never work for us in the long run. Besides, he's probably already made up his mind," Sewell said, making good sense to Meredith.

"That's right," Meredith said, "he's probably been holding that ship in reserve somewhere, keeping his options open."

"What does *Shimpu* mean, anyway?" Palmer asked.

"*Divine Wind*," Meredith responded, and added.

"Back in the late thirteenth century, monsoons saved the Japanese from defeat at the hands of the Mongols twice. The Japanese saw it as divine intervention." Meredith shuddered once, then went on, "In World War II, the Japanese pilots who flew their airplanes into our ships were known as the *Shimpu* force, not kamikazes. Kamikaze was an American invention. Those men were supposedly divinely chosen and would ultimately provide victory for Japan. In a way, I guess they did, when you consider their economic resurgence. Now I bet Mizuzawa thinks it is providence that he can hold us hostage with a nuclear device on a ship."

They remained silent for a moment, letting the gravity of the situation settle over them, like a gray haze. There was nothing worse than good news followed by bad news. The Armed Forces had finally crumbled the Japanese juggernaut on the Philippines, a quick operation really, and the president was ready to inform the world of this success.

But now a wild card floated recklessly about, somewhere, ready to deal a horrifying blow to America. Could they find it? Could they defend against it? What were the options?

"Well, the monsoon has lifted and we need to get a message to our man in the Philippines," Sewell said, then departed.

CHAPTER 101

MANILA, PHILIPPINES

Prime Minister Mizuzawa held a glass of chilled sake high in the air, clinking it against General Nugama's crystal glass, containing the same.

"*Banzai* Japan," Mizuzawa said, his voice muffled with an air of disappointment. He had not wanted to send the *Shimpu* on her final voyage, but gladly did so once the situation had turned for the worse. Her traditional enemies surrounded Japan, and he could sue for peace using the *Shimpu*, or he could let her steam right through the harbor and send a serious message to the world.

"Who could that be?" Mizuzawa asked Nugama, who shrugged his shoulders at the sound of the knock on the door.

"Your Excellency, it is Father Sierra. I wish to speak with you," the priest said, his voice softened by the thick mahogany door. "The United Nations has asked me to come and speak with you as a neutral party."

"Yes, come in, Father," Mizuzawa said, as a guard opened the door. "But what about Father Xavier?"

"He's here," Sierra said.

Father Xavier nodded as he pushed Sierra's wheelchair through the entry. Dressed in his black suit with its standard white collar, Father Sierra was an image of holiness. His compassionate brown eyes were set deep on his face. His skin was light brown and tan, his hands callused and rough. Father Sierra hid his hurt arm by draping his black coat over the sling. On the upside, the sling hid his pistol and IV bag nicely.

"I am Father Sierra, and, of course, you know Father Xavier," Sierra said. He remained in charge of the conversation from his end, speaking Japanese and not wanting words to flow through an interpreter. His voice was firm, but wavered when he had to dig deep, which the Japanese language often required.

The priest spoke in Japanese, but could switch to Tagalog or English, whichever the men preferred.

Mizuzawa nodded at Father Xavier, with whom they had been conversing during their sanctuary in the Catholic building. Then Mizuzawa's wide, scaly paws met Sierra's as they shook hands—a Western tradition, but the wheelchair-bound man could not bow.

"The Americans have requested an audience with you, Prime Minister," Sierra said.

"You have rough hands for a priest, Sierra," Mizuzawa said suspiciously. "Anyway, what could the Americans want with me, other than to kill me?" Mizuzawa said, almost laughing. "Soon, they will surely want to do that."

Sierra looked at the two men as Xavier closed the door to the small office they occupied. The room was filled mostly with clerical equipment: old computer, desk, bookcase, the two cots the men used for sleeping, and the radio equipment. He felt Xavier's necessary presence return behind him.

Sierra scanned the room and the men, noticing that both Mizuzawa and Nugama each had a new Nambu model 60 .38 caliber revolver holstered on his right hip. Nugama's uniform was wrinkled and dirty from days of wear, and Mizuzawa looked comfortable in his olive regalia.

The two men looked at Father Sierra and took light sips from their sake.

"Gentlemen, the Americans are concerned about

a nuclear weapon that they believe you may have stored on a commercial ship," Sierra said. Mizuzawa dropped his glass on the floor, the fine crystal shattering cleanly into thousands of tiny pieces and clear sake, leaving a dark stain on the tile.

"While the Catholic Church recognizes your right to political asylum, we cannot harbor a terrorist. So please, if you have designs with this weapon of terror, reverse its course, or I must release you," Sierra said, eloquently.

"Sierra, mind your own business. You do what the Pope tells you, understand?" Mizuzawa said. "Where did you come from anyway? We've been dealing with Xavier and have had no problems until now."

Sierra ignored the question, and continued in Japanese, "The Pope wishes that you would stop the ship and turn it over to a United Nations force for boarding. The *Shimpu,* is it not?" Sierra said in a stern voice. Actually, he had never contacted the Vatican but was sure that the Pope would want the ship stopped.

"Well, then, tell the Pope to mind his own business," Mizuzawa said.

"Are you refusing to reverse the course of the ship, Prime Minister?" Sierra asked, as if he were negotiating.

"There is no ship, Sierra. Now leave," Mizuzawa shot back. His eyes darted between Fathers Sierra and Xavier, registering something, perhaps a telepathic bond between the two men.

"Wait a second, sir—" Nugama said, only to be cut off by Mizuzawa.

"Enough!" Mizuzawa screamed, grabbing the capped bottle of sake and cracking it over the computer's keyboard, the alcohol's clear liquid spreading over the gray frame.

There it was. Sierra was looking for an opening.

He could sense that Nugama might be willing to deal. Sierra's experience told him that when a man faces certain death, he will frequently seek the option that preserves his life. Nugama didn't need to know just yet that he wasn't going to live. He slightly nudged Father Xavier in the right thigh with his right elbow as the guard took a step toward them.

"Operations, this is *Shimpu*," said a static-filled voice over the radio receiver positioned next to the computer monitor. "Thirty minutes out from target, I can see the harbor."

Sierra looked at the radio, then back at Mizuzawa, who was nearly foaming at the mouth.

"Well, Prime Minister, what are you going to do?"

Mizuzawa turned the jagged edge of the sake bottle up to his lips, drinking the remainder of the liquid from the capped bottle. The sharp glass cut his lips, causing bright red streams of blood to slide down his face. Nugama watched, his eyes darting nervously toward the two priests.

Biting a chunk of the glass from the bottle, then chewing, Mizuzawa tossed the jagged glass at Sierra. Mizuzawa then drew his revolver from his holster, waving it madly in Sierra's face.

"The Americans must die! They dropped bombs on Nagasaki and Hiroshima! We drop bomb on Los Angeles! In thirty minutes, the Japanese people will have revenge for the most heinous war crimes of all time. Then we will be even!" Mizuzawa shouted, spitting wads of blood and glass into Sierra's face.

"I ask you one last time," Sierra said, calmly, his stoic countenance showing no sign of fear. "Are you going to stop the ship?"

"You idiot! Can't you see this is our destiny?! Soon my generation will go the way of the *Shimpu*. We will all be gone, taking with us the memories of the horror of Nagasaki and Hiroshima. If we do not act now, revenge will never be achieved. The West will have triumphed over the East, an unforgivable sin. I would have you tell the Americans 'no,' but now I must kill you both. I have told you too much already," Mizuzawa said, red spit bubbles forming at the corner of his mouth. He angled the revolver toward Sierra's face.

"Wait, Prime Minister, you underestimate me. I will tell the Americans nothing," Sierra said, his voice like granite.

"I wish I could trust you, but the Christian faith is useless, and, therefore, so are you."

Sierra looked at Nugama, who had turned away, awaiting the blast. He thought he saw a tear streaming down Nugama's cheek, which was a good sign.

Nugama flinched as a shot rang loudly in the close quarters of the office. He heard a man fall to the ground, dropping to one knee, then the other. Another shot echoed loudly in the small room.

"Either you turn that ship around, or you're next," Sierra said. Father Xavier's Glock was dangerously close to Nugama's temple. Sierra's Glock was wafting smoke from the bore and still aimed at the dead guard.

Nugama picked up the radio handset and said, "*Shimpu,* this is operations center. Reverse course, the worthless Americans have met our demands. Your mission is complete."

"Roger, *Shimpu* turning now. Congratulations," Sazaku said.

Father Xavier held his pistol level with Nugama's face, then backed away from the Japanese general, nodding at the man's revolver.

Sierra saw Nugama reach for his own revolver and Father Xavier let him finish the move. Nugama's hand slid slowly up his side, and he turned the weapon against his temple, pulling the trigger. The bullet bored through his brain, squeezed out the other side, and tumbled harmlessly onto Mizuzawa's body.

Nugama slumped to the floor, draped across Mizuzawa's legs, their bodies forming an X on the floor.

"Fathers Sierra and Xavier" pulled the starched collars from their black shirts, tossed them on the desk, and Xavier wheeled Sierra into the hot Philippine sun. Sierra removed the brown contact lenses and chucked them aside also. Strapping, combat-ready Marines opened the tall iron gate surrounding the chapel grounds and carried Sierra onto the hospital litter, which they placed in the UH-60 helicopter for immediate evacuation back to the *Mercy*.

"Sir, you okay?" the security detail leader asked.

"Fine. Get me back to the hospital ship."

The Marines snapped to attention and saluted the wounded warrior and his partner, as the Black Hawk departed.

CHAPTER 102

GREENE COUNTY, VIRGINIA

Karen had gone numb when she heard the news. This time, the green sedan did not carry Meredith; rather, it bore the grim reaper.

"Your brother is dead, ma'am. Killed in action. Performed magnificently. Made a difference. Made history." The man had spoken in broken sentences, or so it seemed, as Karen had collapsed on the wooden porch.

Meredith had lifted her, though, holding her up with her strong arms. "Be strong, Karen," Meredith had said. And so she was.

Reverend Early spoke that day, standing next to the fresh-tilled dirt next to Mother Garrett's grave in the shadows of the Blue Ridge. The new hole would receive her brother, and Karen had almost asked them to dig one for her. There had been no other news, except a report that a civilian had died from a gunshot wound to the stomach. She would pray and be strong though. She would try to believe that she had one brother still alive. Like walking against a gale-force wind, she would force herself to go against her instincts.

Meredith sat next to her in the cold metal chair on the cool spring morning. The fog had only recently lifted, replaced by the smell of fresh-cut hay. The old brick house was perched above them on the hill across from the barn where the horses and cows wandered, oblivious to all of the pain endured in the Garrett household during the past month.

There was more pain to follow. There always was.

The elder Garrett sat on the other side of Karen, and they all peered into the deep hole that would receive their loved one.

They couldn't help it, Meredith and Karen. They cried openly, unembarrassed, with the hundred or so well-wishers standing behind them and paying their last respects to Stanardsville's fallen hero.

"He died in the fury of combat, protecting the world from a heinous enemy. Through his personal efforts and his sacrifice, the world is truly a safer place," Reverend Early said. He spoke eloquently, as all preachers seem to do. He was emphatic at just the right moment, and soft-spoken when necessary. His words soothed and at least tried to heal the pain.

Meredith watched and couldn't help but think of when she had first met Matt in Palau. She looked away, seeing the angular wings of a dove dart back and forth along the tree line near the stream. A rabbit hopped into a hole near the barn, and the wind churned lightly atop the trees. She felt the Blue Ridge to her back, strong and powerful, full of grace. Yes, amazing grace.

She stood as the gathering began singing "Amazing Grace."

"Amazing grace, how sweet the sound, that saved a wretch like me. I once was lost but now am found ..."

The DC-9 Nightingale had landed at Andrews Air Force Base in Maryland less than fifteen miles from Washington over three hours ago.

The government car sped down Route 29 until it reached the small town of Ruckersville, then turned right onto a county-maintained road. Passing an outlet store, then Shifflett Exxon, the car sped past a Greene County police officer, who did not bother to pursue. The trees and split-rail fences that cordoned the road whipped by with monotony. The Blue Ridge stared down upon him from the west, almost seeming to smile. The rolling hills and gradual peaks adorned with trees and shrub and grass opened their arms wide, welcoming the man. It gave him a good feeling, a sense of connection. He remembered the area well, and was glad that he could visit once again.

The car turned off the paved road and dipped once to the right as it crossed the cattle guard, then found purchase in the gravel and hardstand that was the road.

The passenger could see the brick house and he felt secure. Just being on the property, the land, was enough to make him want to stop the driver and let him walk and feel the red clay beneath his feet. If only he *could* walk.

The car stopped in a circular area just outside the wooden porch, and the driver opened the door so that he could give assistance.

"**Once was blind**, but now can see!"

Meredith looked down, then over her shoulder at the Blue Ridge, rising above her like a powerfully strong man, but emanating the seductiveness and lure of a beautiful woman. The mountains gave her strength. She knew that she could be strong. She had endured.

She looked at Karen, who was also peering over her shoulder, having stopped singing as well. Beyond the throng of well-wishers, their mouths all moving in synch, they could see the source of their strength. Something so beautiful had to develop the character of its people.

A special breed.

They both turned and looked at each other, Meredith's blond hair lying softly on her black dress, Karen's reddish brown hair equally beautiful in its unfamiliar position fanned across her shoulders. Each woman, beautiful and strong. *Like the Blue Ridge.*

Their eyes connected, passing a knowing sign that they would forever endure the tragedies of the past. And that those tragedies had created an indelible link between them. Life would go on. It always did.

Meredith looked back at the coffin sitting ominously next to the rectangular hole as she felt the wind brush her face and thought she could feel Matt's presence. How fitting, she thought, as she heard a commotion at the back of the crowd.

The man used crutches to assist his movement to the graveyard, the rubber tips collecting, then kicking out, red clay. Near the back of the group, he heard one woman gasp, as if she saw a ghost, perhaps a ghost of the man who was supposed to be in the coffin.

The singing slowed, then stopped, as the man made his way to the front of the group and placed his hands on the shoulders of the blond-haired woman.

Meredith felt the wind kick at her face again, bringing a smile to her lips. Suddenly, the chorus of "Amazing Grace" grew louder, echoing distinctly through the valley below, then resonating loudly back to the Blue Ridge. It was a proud sound, a comforting one.

Then there were the comforting hands of a well-wisher upon her back. She reached and touched both hands lightly, patting them to say "thank you." Odd, though, that both hands were bandaged.

Why would Preacher Early be smiling so much, singing so loud?

Meredith thought she heard a familiar voice say, "How's my Virginian?"

There he was. Matt Garrett, flesh and blood. Scars and healing wounds ran across his face, white gauze covered his hands, and he looked *tired*.

The singing stopped at the very moment Meredith placed both her hands to her mouth, holding back the tears and the joy and the frustration and the sadness and the happiness. Her emotions tumbled through her body, coursed through her mind, causing her to shake and stretch her hands outward, seemingly unsure of what to do.

Matt managed a weak smile and laid his chin on her shoulder as he grabbed Karen and his father, who were by then standing and holding on to him.

Karen grabbed the back of his hair and held him tightly, saying, "My God, you're back. Thank you." They all held on to Matt's bandaged torso tightly, squeezing so hard it hurt him, but it didn't matter. Then Riley Dwyer, Zachary's girlfriend, was joining the group, her long, curly strawberry blond hair falling across Karen's back. And there was Blake Sessoms, his childhood friend, smiling, his ponytail shaking as he cried and joined the growing throng.

He hugged them all as best he could, looked over the shoulders and heads burrowed into his strong chest, and stared into his brother's grave, weeping. Out of the corner of his misty eyes he noticed a young girl, maybe fourteen, standing away from the group, near the fence, with her arms crossed, staring at the mountains. Amanda: Zach's daughter.

Mr. Garrett turned his head, looked at Zachary's grave, and said to his God, "My boys are home. Thank you."

CHAPTER 103

GEORGETOWN, WASHINGTON, DC

Saul Fox and Dick Diamond lay in bed in Fox's Georgetown townhouse. Fox was propped on one elbow, lightly stroking Diamond's arm. A week had passed since the Japanese general and prime minister had died in Manila's Malcanang Palace Catholic sanctuary and the *Shimpu* had been stopped. Fox had opened the window earlier in the day, allowing the cool evening air to flutter through the heavy drapes. The piano strokes of Bach's "Well-Tempered Clavier" pinged softly through the surround-sound speakers.

"This was all so very exciting," Fox said. "So close to Armageddon in Los Angeles."

"I'm not sure I can wait until next spring for Iraq," Diamond said softly. "The thrill was beyond belief."

"A long, continuous frisson of pleasure."

"Yes, a frisson."

"Afghanistan was no fun, like a bad lay," Fox said. "Just lay there, if you'll pardon my pun."

"But this was satyr-like, almost kinky." Diamond smiled. "We had no idea what was going to happen next, what nerve ending might tingle."

"The continuous ratcheting upward, like building toward a climax, was unbelievable," Fox agreed.

"This is a fun game, Saul. I'm glad I know you."

Fox looked at Diamond and smiled again, lightly stroking his bare shoulder.

"I just got confirmation that Takishi is dead," Fox said.

"Charlie Watts," Diamond acknowledged, as if going through one of his checklists.

"Stone is not going to bother us, guaranteed. He keeps his job, we keep ours. I have a police friend who has the tape of Stone trying to rape that blond woman. If anything ever happens to me, he'll run with it."

"Mick Jagger," Diamond whispered hoarsely.

"And we know what happened to Rathburn," Fox said.

"Keith Richards," Diamond whispered again, almost mournful, like a military funeral where the first sergeant calls the roll of the dead.

"The news articles about short sales and so forth have tapered off, and I want to thank you for using your media contacts to help in that regard. Though they didn't mention us, it was a bit close for comfort."

"You're welcome." Diamond smiled again.

Fox had just purchased magenta sheets that matched the chintz covering the bay window, which offered a commanding view of the Potomac River and the wooded area around the GW Parkway. Fox looked over Diamond's shoulder at the heavy mauve design on the curtains. He thought he saw one of them ruffle with the wind, however slight, that was wafting off the Potomac and into his lair.

"Which leaves only one loose end," Fox said.

"Ronnie Wood." Diamond sighed.

Fox looked away, not sure if he was ready to act, but he grasped the knife handle with his free hand beneath the pillow and made a tense fist as he pondered his next move.

"Well, actually ..." Fox began.

"Before you do something stupid," Diamond said, quickly. His arm had been hanging over the side of the bed, and he simply reached between the mattress and box springs and clutched the pistol handle in his right hand. "Who else could there be? I have enough dirt on you that, in the event of my death, you will be hanged in the media, tried in court, and most likely put to death by lethal injection when the world learns that you are at a minimum a Nine-eleven coconspirator. Or perhaps they will just put you in Guantanamo with the other terrorists, as Stone suggested."

Fox's grip on the knife relaxed a bit as he smiled at Diamond and stroked his cheek.

"Why would you say something like that to me, Dick? You know how I feel about you. We're a team. I was just going to say that, actually, Ronnie Wood is going to be okay. He's on board."

"A team," Diamond reiterated, as he relaxed his grip on the pistol.

"We have much work to do in testing our theories. We're talking changing history in a forever kind of way," Fox said, his words dueling with his instinct to kill Diamond. He had suspected for several weeks now that Diamond was Ronnie Wood, but still lacked hard evidence.

"The Brothers of Babylon. The future. Eternal fame, like Churchill," Diamond said.

"Our theory about attacks on the homeland demonstrated outcomes that would have been otherwise impossible to imagine. Who would have guessed that the American people would have contributed a billion and a half dollars to charities? That patriotism would have surged so much? That country music would be the clear winner?"

They shared a good chuckle about the country music. Fox lifted the stereo remote and increased the volume on the Bach.

"Yes, country music," Diamond said.

Fox continued, "And who would have thought that our movement would become so powerful. We

can just point the way, and they follow, like sheep."
Fox eyed Diamond as he prepared his response.

"Yes, like sheep," Diamond said dreamily as he licked his lips.

"We have navigated the most challenging possible tests. For so many years, from our university and think-tank offices, we could only dream about eternal fame. Jeffrey Sachs got all the credit for bringing capitalism to Russia and Poland after the Cold War. Now, we will be famous for what we will do in the Middle East."

"Famous," Diamond said.

CHAPTER 104

PENTAGON, WASHINGTON, DC

It had been all Matt could do to heal and survive. Being pulled off the hospital ship *Mercy* that was by now situated somewhere in the Persian Gulf, in order to play the wheelchair-bound role as Father Sierra, was challenging.

He had heard about the big battle at Fort Magsaysay, and General Zater had flown to the *Mercy* to give him the news about Zachary's death on the battlefield. Somehow, he had been able to push adrenaline through his body sufficiently to subdue the pain for one last mission. X-Ray, his protégé, had told him that there were no others who could speak Japanese as well as he or play the role required. It wasn't so much an order as it was a request, his friend had said.

There was never any doubt that he would perform the *mission*, Matt knew. But the only way to do it was in tandem with Macrini as Father Xavier and Matt playing the feeble priest. Besides, the fact that there were two of them presented the Japanese commanders a new variable, and they had been able to parlay the confusion to good effect for the country. And while the doctors had all said no, all Matt had to do was think of Zach, and he said, "Yes—make it work."

A full week after Zachary's funeral and a complete debriefing from Meredith on the Rolling Stones,

Matt thought he had pieced it together.

Stone and his cronies were fanning the flames of insurgency in an awkward move to derail the building momentum to fight in Iraq. *Create a war to stop a war?* He thought about Iran-Contra and wondered what this would be called: China-Abu Sayyaf?

But when young men and women were putting their lives on the line, Matt believed, the proffer of academic theorems by amateur political appointees about simplifying warfare were best rejected and left in the rough drafts of the professors' dissertations and class notes. *Where and why you went to war mattered,* Matt thought. *Intelligence is central to the whole discussion. And we damn sure didn't need to manufacture a war in the Philippines.* That thought had dropped another tumbler into place on figuring out the true identity of Ronnie Wood.

Every time I'm close, I'm moved.

Matt walked through the E-ring of the Pentagon and passed a man who looked the other way as they approached one another. Matt immediately recognized him as a journalist for the *Washington Post.* The book on him was that he was shady at best; dishonest, even up for grabs, at worst. Matt strode confidently past the man and now the final tumbler of the lock fell into place in his mind. He had solved the mystery.

Energized, he stopped in front of Latisha's desk directly outside of Secretary Stone's office.

"You're up next, Mr. Garrett." Latisha smiled.

"Thank you."

Matt was dressed in his usual garb: olive cargo pants, basic tan button-down cotton shirt, and dark windbreaker. His arm was out of the sling, and he could walk with minimal pain.

"Matt, come in," Stone said.

Matt followed Stone into his office and sat on a

blue leather sofa. In front of him was a small coffee table with an assortment of magazines and newspapers that were current but unread.

"How can I help you?"

Matt tossed the manila folder on the table. "Read it. Then we'll talk."

He watched Stone pick up the file and skim through the pages. Matt had to hand it to Stone; the man's expression never changed. But he guessed that anyone who could pull off the kind of charade that Stone had must have the deadened sense of morality that allowed him to appear unfazed by shocking information. Stone closed the folder and placed it back on the table.

"Okay," Stone said.

"All of this was some game?" Matt asked.

"Everything had its purposes, yes," Stone said.

"Do the people who die matter?"

"Everyone dies eventually, Matt," Stone said.

Matt stiffened at Stone's insensitive comment and said, "Your compassion is overwhelming."

"You're not here to discuss my compassion. I agreed to see you based upon what you've been through. What we put you through. You know about everything now, and I would ask that you keep confidential your knowledge of Ronnie Wood."

"But why?" Matt asked. He leaned back into the sofa, curious.

"I'll appeal to your sense of patriotism. This is a great country, and we need to avoid further embarrassment."

"I could argue that exposing Mr. Wood would help us greatly in that regard."

"Perhaps, but the short-term pain might be debilitating. We're in a very vulnerable place right now."

"He's just another bureaucrat, but I'll think about it," Matt offered.

"Speaking of vulnerabilities, have you heard about the tragic deaths of my deputy Saul Fox and Dick Diamond?"

"Not even sure I know who they are," Matt said, staring directly into Stone's liquid eyes.

Stone seemed to consider his comment and nodded.

"Yes. You're CIA, and a field agent at that. There would be no reason for you to know them."

"No reason," Matt replied. "But there is this."

He pulled a small tape recorder out of his windbreaker pocket and placed it on the table as he punched the PLAY button:

"This was all so very exciting. So close to Armageddon in Los Angeles …"

Matt let the recording play where the two lovers disclosed all the bits of the conspiracy to include Stone's participation, albeit coerced.

Stone's hand reached out for the tape, and Matt used his good arm to strike like a cobra against Stone's wrist, grabbing it and squeezing it in a viselike grip. He leveled his eyes on Stone and began to speak.

"Scumbags like you think you can live in your little soundproof world so that nothing circles back on you. I look at it differently. I'm thinking that maybe Ronnie Wood and Mick Jagger will have a similar fight over these matters? Perhaps go the way of Fox and Diamond?"

Matt squeezed Stone's arm so tight he thought he might snap the bone. Stone's eyes fluttered either at the hint that Matt had something to do with the deaths of Fox and Diamond or the palpable desire for revenge transmitted from Matt through Stone's wrist, like an electrical current.

"You send anyone after me, and I will know about it, Stone," he said, his voice like granite. "And I will personally come to your little cottage in

Orange County. I might be hiding behind the fireplace or perhaps in that nice refinished kitchen, who knows? Or maybe I'll be at your McLean mansion, where you tried to rape Meredith. But I'll be somewhere. So be smart. And being smart includes calling that slimy reporter you just told to out me and hang the bullshit failures on my back. I know how your type operates. Call him right now," Matt demanded.

"Now?"

"I've got your E*Trade account that shows you made a fortune shorting stock before Nine-eleven. Rathburn was a meticulous record keeper. Now what are you going to do? Think about it. You've got a lot riding on this one, and you are walking on the razor."

Stone stared at him for a moment, then looked away toward the window.

"I understand," Stone said. He picked up the phone and dialed a number. Shortly someone answered, and Stone said, "Call it off." There must have been a protest because Stone shouted into the phone, "I said call it off, or you're dead, are we clear?"

"Do we have satisfaction?" Matt asked, sarcastically.

In the end, Matt knew there was nothing he could do to Stone that wouldn't violate his principles or the law, but he would leave the tape behind as a tangible reminder to Stone of his influence.

And on that thought his mind spun to last night.

Matt had watched Diamond and Fox from behind the thick curtains in the bedroom. He had lined up the iron sights of his pistol on each of their foreheads with his good arm. He had a steady aim on Fox, then he would move to Diamond, and back to Fox.

When the moment came to pull the trigger, Zachary's face flashed in front of him, saying, "Don't do it. It's not worth it."

As he looked back up, though, he saw the glint of steel in Fox's hand and a pistol in Diamond's.

"What's this letter, Dick?" Saul asked angrily, shaking the white paper at his lover as he walked from the study into the bedroom. His voice raged above Diamond's favorite opera: Puccini's "Nessun Dorma" ... *None will know my name!*

"It's not mine, Saul. It's a plant," Diamond countered, holding up his hands as if to surrender.

The two men were naked except for boxer briefs in Diamond's case and tighty whiteys in Fox's. Both men had paunches that overlapped beyond the waistbands of the briefs. *Disgusting and comical at the same time,* Matt thought.

Of course, Matt had planted the letter and the dossier in Fox's study once he learned of the Rolling Stones and thought of Dick Diamond's role as Ronnie. Though he knew Ronnie was merely a cutout for a far-more-powerful person, as he had found a different picture beneath Diamond's in the file Meredith had opened. It had been password-protected, and nothing could have prepared him for the image staring back at him.

Still, he couldn't let Diamond or Fox get away with their crimes. Matt knew that, assuredly, the protective cocoon of the political-appointee bureaucracy would shield them from any accountability. Still, Matt had shaken his head at the internecine politics where there were double agents within cliques and power groups inside the Beltway and figured his ploy might work.

But what did that make him, he wondered? As he recalled the scene, he felt his own satisfaction:

"And what's this?" Fox screamed. "You're Ronnie? You're a member of the Rolling Stones? You've been double-crossing me? I knew it, you bastard!"

Matt saw him hold the knife the way an orchestra

conductor might hold an Uzi. *This should be interesting,* Matt thought.

"I'm not Ronnie!" Diamond proclaimed.

Matt was surprised to see how quickly Fox leapt toward Diamond, brandishing the knife as he shouted, "Double-crossing bastard."

This was as much a lovers' quarrel as it was a dispute about who was supporting which conspiracy. It hadn't hurt that Matt's sister Karen had transposed a photo of Diamond and Stone appearing intimate in conversation.

As Matt had watched Diamond respond, he thought, *Never bring a knife to a gunfight.* He didn't even wince as Diamond's pistol kicked back the moment Fox's knife entered his heart. The bullet from Diamond's gun caught Fox in the middle of the forehead, killing him instantly. The knife in Diamond's heart let him live long enough to say, "But I know who Ronnie really is …"

Matt had closed his eyes and lowered his head. Covering his tracks from Fox's apartment, he stole silently through the night in his old Porsche 944 and did not stop until he reached his home in Loudoun County.

"Yes," Stone said. "Yes, we have an agreement."

Stone's words brought him back to the present. He released the man's wrist, which Stone snatched back.

When Matt departed Stone's office, he put the Pentagon in his rearview mirror and the memories of last night in the recesses of his mind as he drove along the George Washington Parkway to Langley. His thoughts turned to Zachary and the daughter who would never get to know her father now … and the brother he would never see again.

When he arrived at Langley, he walked onto the giant seal of the Central Intelligence Agency in the headquarters building and he blew past the security desk, only to be stopped by two large men in gray suits. One of them was the deputy director, Roger Houghton. They had seen him coming, or perhaps someone had been following him. Either way, Houghton was prepared for him.

"Don't do it, Matt," Houghton said.

"Lantini. Where's Lantini?"

"Gone. Nobody can find him. Now go home and rest."

"I won't rest until he's dead," Matt said. Good operators always relied upon two sources, as opposed to one, to confirm intelligence. In this case Matt had three.

Matt had always wondered why he received the text to keep his 'feet and knees together' before Peterson's airplane was even shot down. Once he discovered Lantini's role as Ronnie Wood by Lantini's photo in the file, hidden by the ruse of Diamond's picture, Matt had developed a plausible theory. The fact that Lantini had fled served as confirmation to Matt that the CIA director had conspired with Stone and the others.

Every time I'm close, I'm moved.

Matt's 944 Porsche boiled smoke from the burning tires as he sped out of CIA headquarters and back onto the George Washington Parkway.

He stopped at an isolated scenic overlook, gazed across the Potomac, and leaned over the rock wall. Lifting his head, tears running down his cheeks, he shouted, "Zachary!"

EPILOGUE

A week later Matt stood by himself on a large rock that protruded above the South River at the north end of the 150 acres he called home in Stanardsville, Virginia. He had pushed his rehab a bit too hard, and an admonishing doctor had promised him she would order him to bed rest if he didn't wear the sling. So, with one arm back in a sling, with his good arm he flung flat pebbles across the bubbling water giving no evidence of the shortstop he had once been.

Just a few short weeks ago he had been in the Philippines chasing Predators and finding Japanese troops and ships. The text he had sent from his Blackberry on that incident had cued Meredith to convince the National Security Advisor to have the ship interdicted. It turned out that all of his reports had either been received by Rathburn or Lantini, and discarded. Thankfully, the United States Navy had corralled the rogue vessel with a carrier battle group, F-18s circled the sky like buzzards spying road kill. The SEALs had boarded the *Shimpu* and found the skipper on the floor of the captain's ward with a fresh bullet wound in his head.

He skipped another stone upstream, the current causing the stone to flip wildly. Not a good toss. Each time he tried to throw, the stitches in his abdomen screamed at him, pulling at healing skin.

Would the wounds that mattered ever heal?

Zachary was dead, and he wondered if he would ever be able to accept that fact. Life was never what it seemed, he understood, but the unfairness of his brother's death in that remote corner of the world might weigh on him forever. At least he hoped so. Zachary was too great a man simply to be gone. His contributions were too substantial just to be forgotten. No, Matt *would* earn Zachary's sacrifice. Once healed, he would be back in the field taking the fight to the enemy. In the meantime, he would serve in his new capacity as a special advisor to the director of the CIA ... until his physical wounds healed.

He would go back to Afghanistan or Iraq and fight there. That was his mission.

On that thought, he wondered exactly what was happening in the world. How could Diamond and Fox be so manipulative and callous? How could Stone not see what they were doing? How could Lantini betray him?

What was in store for the world? Nine-eleven, Islamic fundamentalism, and rogue nationalism were supposedly exploiting the seams of a fractured universe. But what was real and what was manufactured?

The ivory-tower conspiracies of the elite clouded the true heroism of the young men and women fighting so hard, who, in the eyes of the likes of Fox and Diamond, were truly nothing but cannon fodder.

He turned, carefully stepping along the rock, placing the stream to his back.

"Hi, handsome," Meredith said. She was standing on the bank, her arms crossed, perhaps warding off the spring chill. She was wearing a dark blue Northface jacket over lighter dungarees. Her hiking boots were crossed one over the other as she leaned against a small poplar tree. New growth.

Matt nodded at her and stepped off the rock. He approached Meredith and took her in his good arm without saying a word.

"It's okay," she whispered, hugging him back.

Matt rested his head on her hair, the sling causing his arm to press awkwardly between them as he looked west into the churning river and the mountains whence it had come.

"Don't leave me," he caught himself saying. Why, he wasn't sure. Maybe with Zachary's loss he needed to fill the empty space quickly. Perhaps it would be less painful that way.

"I'm not going anywhere you're not going," she said softly.

He pulled away and kissed her on the lips, then said, "I'm just going to refuse to believe that he's dead."

Matt's words of disbelief floated like an autumn leaf into the wind, fluttered up the hill toward the house, circled the fresh-tilled grave, and bolted skyward toward the heavens.

Want to see where Matt goes next?
Please enjoy the first two chapters of

And pick up book two of the THREAT
series on October 20, 2009!

CHAPTER 1

APRIL 2003, FRIDAY EVENING, 1700 HOURS, LOUDOUN COUNTY, VIRGINIA

Matt Garrett stood and stretched, physical scars sending waves of pain through his body. He looked at the fading blue sky from the deck of his Loudoun County home, perhaps seeking a nod, guidance—anything really—from his dead brother Zachary.

A paramilitary operative with the CIA, Matt had been wounded in the same fight in the Philippines last year, where his brother was killed. Coincidence, mostly, but the fact remained that Zachary was dead, and Matt had almost died.

He lowered his head and stared at his backyard, the terrain gently sloping away from his one-story brick rambler. Thoughts of Zachary had dominated him over the past year and had stymied his recovery. He knew he needed to move on, but he refused to let go.

Matt thought fondly of Zachary's graduation from West Point, his brother's service in Desert Storm, his agonizing decision to leave the service and work the family farm in the mid-nineties, and then, after the 9-11 attacks, his firm resolve to get into the fight. Which he had done.

Which had gotten him killed.

"If only he had stayed on the farm," Matt muttered.

It was nearly six p.m., and despite Matt's near-paralytic state regarding Zachary, he did sense an uncertain stir of change in the wind. Perhaps that was what kept him hanging on. The towering pine trees in his back yard bowed with the breeze, and Matt closed his eyes, trying to understand everything that had transpired. Operation Iraqi Freedom had kicked off and was an apparent success so far, but he had his doubts. With all the fanfare over Iraq, he couldn't help but pick at the open scab of his failure to kill Al Qaeda senior leadership when he had had the shot. Now the opportunity was lost forever. True, high ranking officials had denied his kill chain, and a JDAM bomb had struck closer to his team than to the Al Qaeda leadership, but he still blamed himself. That failure, coupled with his brother's death and Matt's own physical wounds, were enough to make him doubt himself. And in his business, there was no margin for doubt—no second guessing.

Since when did you start following orders, Garrett? Should have stayed, taken the shot.

He shook his head and looked to his left, where a small hill rose above the stream. There was nothing but forest for about three miles. The April evening was filled with the hum of spring in the Virginia countryside. Through the pine thickets Matt saw budding dogwoods and darting squirrels. The temperature hovered in that optimistically comfortable range where he would begin to wear T-shirts and shorts when relaxing at his home. He stared at the pieces of a fading blue sky that shone through the pine tips to the rear of his property. Then he looked down at his batting cage.

Matt walked down the deck steps, grabbed a Pete Rose 34-inch bat, and stepped into the rectangular mesh netting. He liked the thin handle and the wide barrel of the bat. Even if Charlie Hustle had been banned from baseball, it was still the best bat in the sport. Matt flipped a switch on a small post, and the machine hummed to life. Some people meditated, Matt figured; he hit baseballs.

Absently, he wondered if he entered the cage to duel with himself. Whether it was post traumatic stress or prolonged grieving, Matt was in persistent internal conflict. Sometimes he had gnawing at him the urge to get in his old Porsche, fill the gas tank, and drive dark, dangerous roads at high speeds. Other times he stepped into the batting cage.

His angst was no different, he figured, than the way some of his soldier buddies who were suffering post traumatic stress might wake up screaming, grab for their elusory weapon in the middle of the night, and move through the house, methodically clearing each room, calling "One up" to invisible partners, buddies who had been killed right next to them in combat.

Matt needed to fill that emptiness left by Zach's absence and burn his adrenaline. The grief welled inside him, he repressed it, and then it reappeared somewhere else like a magician's trick. One moment it was an obvious thought; the next it was a repressed memory. Post traumatic stress was tricky that way. The repressed memory went latent, seemingly forgotten, only to surge forward at the least expected time, manifesting itself as a spontaneous action, sometimes benign, often not. Only on intense reflection or therapy could the sufferer follow the byzantine trail back to the original mournful feeling.

So today, instead of a suicidal drag race in the Porsche, Matt stared down 95-mph fastballs moving with enough velocity to kill him. No helmet. That was part of the risk, the game. This way, at least, his edginess was more predictable, like Russian roulette. Which bullet, which fastball, might hit him? He never knew when one tire might catch the stitches and spit at him a left-handed curve ball hard and fast directly at his temple. Just as bad as a bullet. Maybe worse. He would see it coming. Would he duck?

Or smile and stand there, ready to join his brother?

The first ball blew past him before he could even think about swinging. With each successive pitch, his cut migrated toward what it once was. He had been an above-.300 collegiate batsman. Soon he was hitting a few frozen ropes back at the machine, which was protected by a wire mesh fence. The calm evening rang resolutely with the distinct crack of the wooden 34 against the quiet hum of the pitching machine's spinning tires.

Matt focused, and he tried to forget about Zachary's death. The War on Terror had claimed many casualties. The fact that Zachary had survived, even thrived, during Operation Desert Storm, only to succumb to a small-scale action in the Philippines, would forever confound Matt.

As he rifled balls into the far netting, his mind drifted to a few men that he politely referred to as *those bastards*, the upper-echelon Rolling Stones groupies who conspired to start a war in the Philippines simply to avert another war in Iraq.

A fastball came whipping at him, and there was Bart Rathburn, killed by Abu Sayyaf rebels. Swing. Crack. Rathburn, who had been an assistant secretary of defense using the pseudonym Keith Richards, was gone into the back of the net. The tires then spit him a slider, low and away: Taiku Takishi, a Japanese businessman turned rogue, also known as Charlie Watts. Smooth swing. Solid wood. Takishi, who led the Japanese invasion of the Philippines, was gone into right field. Another pitch knuckled straight at him. He swung defensively and swatted away the face of Secretary of Defense Robert Stone. Stone, using the nom de guerre, Mick Jagger, orchestrated the entire conspiracy. Following Stone's knuckleball was a 98-mph fastball that blew past him.

Ronnie Wood.

Though not located in the year since his disappearance, CIA director Frank Lantini, Matt was convinced, played the ever elusive Ronnie Wood.

Every time I was close, he moved me. But there were other possibilities, Matt knew. His mind briefly churned, visualizing these Beltway heroes who pulled the marionette strings of so many great Americans, using them as the fodder that they were. A bolt of anger shot through Matt when he realized that it was only those with whom you served that you could trust to be on your flank, to help you in a time of crisis. That notion brought his mind reeling back to Zachary.

Why couldn't I save him?

Like the baseballs punching into the far end of the net, Matt's angst over Zachary's death was tightly confined in his thoughts by a web of guilt and remorse.

The injuries to his body—the gunshots to the abdomen and shoulder and the bayonet slice across the forearm that screamed with every swing—had mostly healed. And with each pitch and swing Matt focused his mind on the task at hand, hitting the baseball, the action removing just a bit of the pain, working out physical and emotional scars. *Just keep swinging*, he told himself. *Stay in the game.*

"Keep your elbow up."

Matt turned toward the voice just enough to move his body into the path of one of those ninety-five-mile-an-hour fastballs—bb's, aspirin tablets, rockets, as he used to call them—whipping in high and inside. It struck him squarely on the left shoulder.

"Son of a ..." Matt took a quick knee and pressed the stop button.

A woman came running toward him. "I am so sorry."

"Aw, man." Another pitch rifled above his head punching with a demonic thud into the back of tarp. "Go get some ice out of the freezer. Back door's open." The machine spit a final ball that landed about halfway toward Matt, the rawhide rolling next to his knee.

Gotta go easy in there, Matt thought to himself. Adrenaline dumped, he shook his head. Truthfully, he had been pushing the envelope in his rehab in an attempt to get back into the fight.

Matt pulled up his shirt-sleeve and noticed a welt was already forming.

It took a minute to register that he had no idea who he had just sent into his house. An attractive woman returned with a towel filled with ice. She was wearing a blue pants suit with a white blouse. A string of Lapis beads circling her neck made Matt think back to Afghanistan, where Lapis was mined extensively.

"Who are you?" he asked through gritted teeth as she put the ice on his shoulder.

"Name's Peyton O'Hara." She showed him a badge. "The vice president of the United States requires your services, Mr. Garrett."

"So he sent you?"

"It seems your phone is—"

"I shut the phone off." Matt looked down at the welt on his shoulder.

"As I was saying, I work with the vice president. He needs your help."

Matt grabbed the towel and took a step back, registering the concern on the young woman's face.

She was a natural redhead with hazel eyes and a nice figure. Setting the towel on the deck rail, he pulled off his shirt, catching her eyes glancing at his muscular frame. At six-foot-two, he was considerably taller than she. Though he had been recovering from wounds, he had also been lifting and running almost every day. Her quick glance confirmed in his mind that he was, perhaps, in the best physical condition of his life. He reapplied the ice to the bruise.

"What happened?" She pointed at his forearm.

"Hunting accident."

"I see." Peyton looked at him suspiciously. She took in his green eyes and light brown hair, strangely glad the vice president had asked her to come find this enigma. "And there?" She pointed at his stomach where a large scar that looked like a grotesque blossoming flower had healed, revealing minor lumps of skin that never reformed in exactly the right place.

"Appendicitis," Matt said, stone-faced.

"Must have been one hell of a huge appendix," she smiled.

"What are you? A hooker or something? Blake Sessoms send you here?" Matt asked. "Like those strippers dressed as cops?"

Blake was Matt's closest childhood friend, save Zachary.

"Funny," Peyton said.

Matt looked down at the welt on his shoulder.

"Another lump for the collection?" she quipped, following his eyes to the rising lump on Matt's upper arm. "Adds some symmetry don't you think?"

Ignoring her comment, he sat in a two-dollar lawn chair he had picked up from K-Mart a few weeks earlier. It was either that or five hundred dollars for deck furniture that was not as comfortable.

"So what's Hellerman want?" Matt's voice was flat.

"He wants you to come over to his Middleburg mansion. That's where his alternate command post is now and where he's set up a special task force on terrorism. He wants you to be a part of that. He's talked to Houghton at CIA, who said you're available. With the Iraq war going well, he is making sure we're watching our six on other extremists."

Matt stared at her a moment. He had been out of action since being wounded and was now being considered by the president to serve as a special assistant to the CIA director. He figured Houghton would never say no to the president or vice president after his recent confirmation as Lantini's replacement at CIA. Matt was on a leave of absence from his position with his unit and figured Houghton thought this might be the best way to ease him back into the fight. But Matt was part mercenary and part intelligence analyst and had never participated in a special task force—other than raiding some dirtbag's hideout to kill him.

"And he wants me to ask you about your work on the Predator project," she mentioned, almost as an afterthought.

Matt calmly looked to his left and then his right, and then turned his head toward her and leveled his eyes on hers.

"Predators? What are those?" Matt asked.

She stepped toward him.

"Everyone knows about the former administration's technology transfers to China, Mr. Garrett. What I'm telling you is that we may have some new information, and we don't have much time to sort it out. We're five miles from civilization, and if it will make you feel better, we can whisper, but we really need to know what you saw in China."

Matt had spent two months touring China as a photojournalist, trying to find eighteen absent unmanned aerial vehicles (UAVs) that were not so much missed for their aerodynamics as they were for their payload capabilities. The leads had taken him to the Philippines, where he got caught up in the insurgency that had wounded him and killed his brother.

"Sounds like you should speak to somebody who knows what you're talking about. Maybe the Rolling Stones? You a groupie?" *Those bastards.* "This is a dead end." *Literally, it was for Zachary*, he thought with a wince.

She stared at him with piercing eyes. She was a cross between Julianne Moore and a Fox News anchorwoman whose name he had forgotten. She crossed her arms and looked away, thinking. Matt saw her eyes fixate on the batting cage then return to his abdominal scar. Then she looked at him with a satisfied countenance, appearing to have figured something out.

"Well, the vice president thinks you know something you're not telling us," she said.

"You're right." Matt considered her comment. "The Predators are a hockey team in Nashville, right?" He placed the towel on the deck, stood and walked over to the railing of the deck and leaned back, towering over her by at least eight inches.

She pursed her lips and said, "Funny." She showed him her National Security Agency badge again, which he agreed looked authentic enough. Then she pulled out her Top Secret White House Basement Operations Center pass.

"Impressive."

"Need my shoe size?" she asked.

Matt smirked. "Screw the vice president." Then, "Sorry, if that's in your job description, you know."

Peyton stared at him and smiled. "They told me you could be an ass. I just didn't expect it to surface so quickly."

Matt considered her a moment. He figured her

mental calculations had been to determine which course to choose: sympathetic to his loss and injuries or hard-nosed negotiator completing an assigned task? Her selection of the firm approach caused him to gain a measure of respect for her. He didn't want her sympathy.

"Who cares? I put everything in the report, and nobody believed it. We couldn't get jack past the political appointees. If you're truly working with Hellerman, then you know the Stones conspiracy set us back light years."

"I know that was a difficult time for you—"

"Difficult?" Matt asked, incredulous. "You have no idea what you're talking about, lady."

Matt picked up his baseball bat and tossed it from hand to hand, working off his anger and frustration. Who was this person interrupting his sanctuary, his ritual?

Peyton eyed the bat. He figured that she had read his dossier and knew about his mandatory shrink visits. The psychiatrist said he had a hair-trigger temper. *Good, make her think*, Matt thought.

"This is important, Matt. You know my credentials," Peyton said, keeping an eye on the bat.

"So we discuss top secret, compartmented information on my back deck? Here's a clue. Check out a warehouse in Mindanao in the Philippines. I went there, got shot, and then came home. You know the rest."

"Well, actually, I knew what you just said, but something doesn't add up."

"What's that?" He was mildly interested but tiring quickly. He had baseballs to hit. With another month of convalescent leave on his docket before his return to Langley, he needed to sort out a few more things. Unscrew his head. On that note, he flipped the bat against the deck railing, walked into the house and grabbed two Budweisers from the refrigerator, and handed one to Peyton by the top. She knew the trick and turned the bottle while he held his vice grip on the cap. With a slight sound of gas escaping they opened the bottle, and she took a sip. He popped his open with the same hand and drank half the beer in one tilt.

"Let's just say we're concerned about the location of those Predators, based upon some intercepts we've received." She looked away as she spoke, holding her amber bottle chest high.

"Oh, I get it. I share top secret information with you, and you share bullshit with me. Seems fair," he fumed, his temper edging to the surface. He took another long pull on the Bud.

"Listen, we've got traffic that says the Chinese might try to use those Predators against Taiwan, but it's not clear yet."

"Okay. But, I've told you everything I know. I tracked them to China and Mindanao by studying shipping logs, going to the ports, bribing dirt poor dockworkers, and even shooting a couple of people. I suggest you do the same," he said.

"Did you ever see any of the Predators?" she asked, ignoring his rebuff.

"It's all in the report, Peyton."

"If it was all in the report, Matt, I wouldn't be here."

They held their beer bottles in front of themselves as if they were ready to fence, Matt's tilting toward her, hers toward him.

They exchanged long, hard stares. The obnoxious ringing of Peyton's cell phone interrupted the painful silence. She answered and handed it to Matt.

"Matt, this is the vice president. I need you to meet me at Dulles Airport in an hour. VIP gate. Bring a suitcase. Tell Peyton to come along too. I'll be waiting."

"What's this all about?" he asked, handing the phone back to her.

"Beats me, but we should probably get moving."

The cool spring breeze snapped past them both. Truthfully, today he could not care less what the man wanted.

"Whatever. I'll see you there," he said as Peyton bounced down the steps. He casually followed her, a guard ushering an unwanted visitor to the exit. He stopped at the corner of his brick rambler and watched as she mounted a Ducati Street Fighter.

"Don't be late, Matt Garrett."

She shook her hair, donned the helmet, and turned the ignition. The bike roared to life. She punched the gear box and rolled away.

"Bizarre," Matt muttered and then strolled inside his house.

CHAPTER 2

DULLES AIRPORT, NORTHERN VIRGINIA

Matt yanked his "go-bag" from beneath his bed, which he always kept ready and within arm's reach as he slept. He checked the Baby Glock and ensured he had four magazines of 9mm ammunition, two with round point and two with hollow point. He opened his Duane Dieter Spec Ops knife with a quick flip of his wrist, then pressed the detent button to collapse the blade. Handling his weapons made him wonder just where the hell Lantini might be …

He then quickly stuffed a variety of clothing and toiletries in the small duffel. A few minutes later, he jumped in the fifteen-year-old Porsche 944 he had purchased from the same junk yard in which he had found the pitching machine. He ran the "black bullet" wide open, quickly covering the short distance to the airport.

Pressing speed dial on his cell phone, he listened as Blake Sessoms, his childhood best friend, answered.

"This is Blake."

"Blake, Matt here.

"Hey. How you doing?"

"Got a few things to talk about, but don't have much time right now. How about we link up in the next few." He paused, then continued, "It has been tough without Zach around."

"I miss him, too," Blake said. "It's been a year … a tough year, brother."

The two friends let a moment pass over the crackling cell phone airwaves.

"Roger that," Matt whispered.

"Going anywhere you can tell me?" Blake asked.

"I'm not sure what's happening, but wanted to let you know I am heading out of town. We'll catch up later."

"Sure thing, bro'."

"Are you going to be around in the next few days?"

"Yeah."

"I'll call you."

The two friends hung up, and Matt reflected briefly that it had been months since he had spoken to Blake, with whom he used to chat a few times a week. They had grown up together in the Blue Ridge, playing baseball and fishing. They had both started college at the University of Virginia. Matt opted for a career in the military, while Blake chose a path that eventually led him to Virginia Beach and a small fortune.

Downshifting into the arrivals/departures fork in the road leading to the airport, Matt saw the sign for the VIP gate and followed the arrows until he was stopped at a closed chain-link gate in a remote area about a half mile from the main terminal. The gate opened as he slowed..

Pulling through the opening, he saw the shiny, black scalp of Alvin Jessup, the vice president's lead Secret Service agent.

"Hey, Alvin," he said, rolling down his window.

Jessup, a hulking man dressed in a black overcoat, looked every bit the former collegiate fullback. He walked up to Matt's window with a dour face.

"Finally coming out of your hole, Garrett?" Jessup asked.

"Just following orders, Alvin. What are you complaining about? Last time I saw you, I ended up with all your money," Matt said.

"Ain't playing poker with you anymore. That's for damn sure. Whoever heard of giving all the money to a homeless shelter, anyway?"

"Well, didn't feel right keeping your life's savings," Matt said. "What's going on?"

"Not sure, but the man's been on the phone with Fort Bragg a lot."

"Okay, Alvin, let me get in here and see what's happening."

"All right, my friend. There's another land mine over there, so watch out." Jessup motioned with a turn of his head to the airplane.

Matt drove through the open gate and steered toward a U.S. Air Force Gulfstream airplane parked about a hundred meters away. He stopped next to a car that was parked against the chain-link fence. He could see the vice president's armored Suburban next to the airplane.

Matt stepped from his Porsche and walked to the folded down steps of the Gulfstream, wondering what Jessup could have meant. *A land mine?* He saw the vice president walking down the small step ladder from the jet.

Then he saw the land mine: Meredith Morris, her blond hair bouncing off her shoulders as she followed the vice president down the jet stairway.

My Virginian, Matt wanted to say, but he didn't dare utter those words. Still, he waited for Meredith to lift her eyes and notice him. Though he knew he should look away, it was impossible. He could not deny the flutter in his chest. As recently as four months ago, she had been his fiancée.

"Matt," Vice President Hellerman said. "Join me for a few seconds if you can, son."

Hellerman was motioning Matt into the back seat of his Suburban for a private chat.

"Yes, sir," Matt said without moving his eyes from Meredith's face. She looked up at him as she reached the tarmac, lifted her face slowly and smiled. His heart leapt, but his mind locked tighter than a vault door.

"Hi, Matt," she said. "Good to see you."

"Meredith," he said.

The vice president's hand pulled at his shoulder, breaking the spell. He slid into the Suburban, watching as Meredith climbed into the back seat on the opposite side. Interesting that she would be with the vice president, Matt thought, because she worked for the national security adviser, Dave Palmer.

Matt had taken the time to grab a sport coat and pulled it over his black Underarmor shirt that looked painted onto his muscular frame. He wore khaki cargo pants and lightweight brown Belleview boots. Not a typically snappy dresser, Matt figured the blazer concealed his weapon relatively well.

"Matt, glad you could make it," Hellerman said, closing the door of his vehicle. "We've got some leads on a terrorist named Ballantine, former Iraqi general."

Matt paused, thinking.

"I know the name." There was no escaping Zach's death, Matt thought. He remembered talking to Zach after his brother had returned from Desert Storm back in 1991. The detail with which Zach had described the fight that led to the capture of Ballantine was incredible. Zach, most likely the best story teller Matt knew, had painted such a clear picture that Matt had long savored the pride he felt for his older brother in securing perhaps the most prized capture of Operation Desert Storm.

"Yes, Ballantine," Hellerman continued. "I thought you might recognize the name. We think he's established a fishing guide service up in Quebec and that he uses a lightweight float plane to ferry supplies, deadly attack materials, into the United States. He may even be part of a supply chain that has funneled the WMD out of Iraq."

Matt considered what the vice president was saying. He remembered that Hellerman had served in the army reserves as a military intelligence officer, which caused Matt to place some credence in Hellerman's analysis.

"My team in Middleburg is running our own operation with limited support," Hellerman said. "We had a CIA agent have a small world moment with this guy when he was actually on leave doing some muskie fishing in Canada. Seems Ballantine opened this small enterprise a few years back and called it Moncrief Fishing Company. Flies a Sherpa into a small airport outside Burlington, Vermont, where he picks up his customers, and, we suspect, a few other things."

"We got anybody working this?" Matt asked. His mind continued to drift back to the day Zach had returned from Desert Storm. Their small hometown just north of Charlottesville, Virginia, had thrown Zachary a huge welcome home party. After the festivities, Matt and Zachary, both in their early twenties then, had sat by the river that framed their property. They drank a six pack of Budweiser while Zachary discussed the details of capturing Ballantine and then delivering him to military intelligence for interrogation. As the laundry bag full of beer, anchored to a rock next to Matt, shifted with the subtle currents of the river, Zach conveyed that he believed that Ballantine had been released in a prisoner exchange and then had mysteriously gone missing. Now, when Ballantine wasn't found in Iraq after the Americans had seized Baghdad in Gulf War II, the intelligence community dismissed his absence in favor of their vaunted deck of playing cards.

Matt, though, was intrigued by Hellerman's assessment. Ballantine was more dangerous than either Hussein or Bin Laden because he not only had means, motive, and the courage of his convictions, but he was on nobody's screen. The intelligence world dismissed him in favor of rounding up the deck of cards.

Hellerman stared at Matt a minute and said, "Yes, we're about to get an agent in there. Canada doesn't want us making a mess up there, but they also don't want to get involved."

"Screw a bunch of Canadians. Anybody I know?"

"There aren't many you don't know, but you know I can't answer that, Matt."

"Right, so what am I doing here?"

"I want you to head down to Joint Special Forces Command at Fort Bragg and talk to some of the special ops command down there. You'll be a presidential envoy. You know all those guys anyway," Hellerman said.

"Presidential envoy?" Matt chuckled. "I'll get laughed out of there. Now, maybe if I'm part of a take-down team, they'll believe *that*."

Matt's thoughts trailed off as his mind reeled with the possibilities. As an operator in the most elite counterterrorist outfit in the CIA, he was already visualizing the enemy situation. Then, as it always did, his mind spun back to that day in December 2001 when he had his sniper rifle, his team, and a good radio with communications to about a thousand airplanes all wanting to drop a bomb on bin Laden and claim victory. As he had radioed in, he received, "Kill chain denied. Say again, kill chain denied. Return to base."

Matt looked at Hellerman, letting his thoughts play out on his face.

"I had nothing to do with that, Matt. I'm one of the good guys here and I'm bringing you into this thing to get you back into the action. That's what you want right? While you can't go on the eventual raid you can work with me on this thing in my command post. Advise me." Hellerman continued, "With your injuries, you'd be no good anyway. Plus, the president would have my ass if I sent you on a tactical mission while he wants you to be preparing for this job advising the director."

"I'd much prefer to go after Ballantine." Matt's voice was stone cold.

"I've talked to the president and your director, Houghton, already." Hellerman ignored Matt's comment. "They both want you on this mission."

Matt waited a moment with his eyes fixed on the vice president, then spoke. "I'm an operator, sir. That's what I do."

"I know you're an operator. Hell, the entire world knows you're an operator, and that's part of the problem. Everyone knows you. Anyway, you'll be representing the president. Our Department of Homeland Security isn't even an agency yet. It's just some people looking for office space. You know how to wade into the middle of chaos and sort it out."

"That I do," Matt said. "What do you want me to talk to them about?"

Matt had never turned down an interesting assignment in his life, and now was not the time to start. If terrorists were coming after the country again, he wanted in on the hunt. He had made his case, so now he would just see where the situation led him.

Hellerman smiled. "Look at their plan. It's called Maple Thunder. Then see what they've got on the missing Predators while you're at it."

Matt stared at Hellerman, wondering, *Why is there so much interest in these Predators all of a sudden?*

Ignoring his thought, Matt said, "Right, so my mission is to get down to Bragg and be a spy for you, is that it?"

"Exactly. Here's a satellite phone. Keep in touch. I'll be at Middleburg, which of course is top secret. And tell Peyton everything you know about those Predators, too. That's at least as important as Ballantine." Hellerman handed Matt a small black object, which Matt promptly put in his shirt pocket.

"One thing," Matt said, returning to his personal albatross.

"What's that?"

"No Rolling Stones? No Fox and Diamond type antics? No bullshit, right?"

"We've cleaned that mess up, Matt," Hellerman said. "President Davis understands your sacrifice and appreciates your service."

"Then why does Stone still have a job as Secretary of Defense?" Matt's voice was like granite. "And where the hell is Lantini? You telling me you guys can't find a former CIA director?"

"I've got nothing to do with Lantini. Matt, get over yourself. We've got a war going on in Iraq. We need as little turbulence as possible after last year's nightmare in the Philippines, so the president decided to keep Stone in place; keep the momentum going."

Matt looked at Hellerman and then Meredith.

"I made a promise to Stone," Matt said, "that if he ever came after me because of what I know *I* would know about it. And then I would execute what I believe you people term 'preemptive actions.' I know you and Stone are close. I need you to look me in the eye with Meredith as our witness that this is a legitimate mission directed by the President of the United States."

Matt kept his cold gaze locked onto Hellerman's gray eyes, which never fluttered.

"I know you're not making a threat against the Secretary of Defense, which would be illegal. So, I'll ignore the comment and interpret 'preemptive actions' as meaning actions that are nonthreatening, in particular, nonlethal."

Matt shrugged and ran his hand along his blazer beneath which his Glock was holstered.

"This is legit, Matt. We're trying to get you back in the game. This is the first step," Hellerman said. "Trust me."

"You had me until you said, 'Trust me.' I don't trust many these days," Matt said, his eyes shifting to Meredith, who looked away, a tear possibly sneaking out of her right eye. "Produce Lantini, Ronnie Wood, for me, and then maybe we can build on our relationship."

Hellerman stared at Matt a moment and said, "I don't think we'll be seeing anymore of Ronnie Wood or the Rolling Stones. Only a select few people know about that, so let's just leave it be."

Matt shook his head, then looked at Meredith. There was something about her countenance that rang hollow, sort of a vacuous gaze.

"Then don't trust me. Trust your instincts. I'm giving you a jet to fly to Fort Bragg to get back into the game here. You can't be in Iraq right now where all of the action is and I know it's killing you."

That much was true, Matt thought, returning to Hellerman.

"Okay, if you're getting me back into the game, then *I'm* game." Matt said.

"Good," Hellerman said, then leaned back, shaking his head, as if to move on to other pressing issues. "Maybe one day this country will wake up," Hellerman added as Matt was opening the door.

Matt stopped and looked over his shoulder at Hellerman, catching the sour look on the vice president's face. *What was he talking about?*

"Excuse me, sir?"

Hellerman looked at Matt. "Just talking to myself. Damn people in this country are so complacent, take everything for granted. Not even two years removed from 9-11 and we're back to our old ways. Political infighting, stupid debates about the Iraq war, and everyone's so consumed with themselves. No sacrifice, except the military." Hellerman stopped a moment and then looked at Matt.

"You know the other day I was at Fort Bragg talking to a soldier who told me, 'Sir, the military's at war, the country's at the mall.' Pretty insightful."

Matt shrugged. Privates usually had a pretty good perspective on life, he thought. Rang true. Still, he kept his mouth shut as he watched the smoke clear off the vice president for a moment and then turned toward the Gulfstream.

"You ever read Rostow?" Hellerman's question caught Matt off guard.

"Maybe once," Matt said, lifting his duffel bag, and looking over his shoulder.

'Think about the term, 'secular spiritual stagnation.' Then we'll talk later."

Matt nodded, barely interested, then leaned back into the Suburban and said to Meredith, "Nice to see you. You look good." It was all he could allow himself.

He saw a brief flash of the woman he had once known. It was a moment of recognition in her face. He didn't know if her eyes were wistful ... or pleading. He knew full well, though, that heady politics had vaulted her into a new circle that perhaps she had been gunning for all along. Or perhaps she was operating in a realm for which she was unprepared. Either way, she had broken off the engagement four months ago and had become aloof. Not fully understanding what had happened between them hurt the most. The moment was an awkward one, with the vice president between them. Matt felt the pluck of a banjo string in his heart and then did the only thing he could do.

He turned and walked up the steps, ducking as he entered the small airplane and nodded to the two Air Force officers who would fly him to Fort Bragg. One was blond with blue eyes and looked like he had just graduated from the academy the day before. He wore lieutenant's bars. The other was a bit older, more ethnic-looking and, with eyes staring at his cockpit instruments, focused on his preflight routine. He was a captain, and, Matt presumed, in charge of the flight. He noticed a cell phone sitting in the pilot's lap and a Bluetooth headset in his ear like some Star Trek device.

As Matt turned into the small, eight-seat cabin, he was greeted with another surprise.

"So we meet again," Matt said, standing next to Peyton's seat, holding his duffel.

"How's the arm, slugger?"

"I'll live," Matt said with a shrug.

"The vice president asked me to accompany you. I couldn't get out of it."

Matt surmised that she didn't seem too disappointed.

"Well, name's Matt Garrett," he said, sticking a large hand out and giving hers a quick shake. He noticed she had firm hands. "Don't think I ever formally introduced myself."

She looked at him briefly and squeezed his hand. "Peyton O'Hara."

"Nice grip," he said, offering her a polite smile.

He walked to the back of the small airplane, sat down, put his duffel in the seat next to him, patted the weapon beneath his jacket, leaned back and shut his eyes.

"A.J. TATA IS THE NEW TOM CLANCY."
— BRAD THOR, #1 NEW YORK TIMES BESTSELLING AUTHOR OF THE LAST PATRIOT

ROGUE THREAT

A. J. TATA

BOOK TWO OF THE THREAT SERIES!

"Topical, frightening, possible, and riveting, A.J. Tata should be read by all fans of military fiction. Mixing Dale Brown's exacting detail with Stephen Coonts edge-of-the-seat pacing, here is a story that demands to be read."
-- James Rollins, New York Times bestselling author of THE DOOMSDAY KEY

AVAILABLE OCTOBER 20, 2009

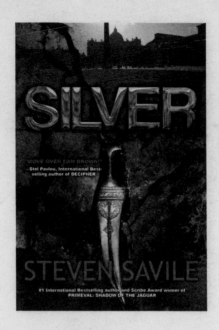

"SILVER is a wild combination of Indiana Jones, The Da Vinci Code, and The Omen. Read this book...before the world ends."
-- Kevin J Anderson, international bestselling author of THE SAGA OF SEVEN SUNS and co-author of PAUL OF DUNE

"Silver grabs you by the throat and doesn't let go. Silver is pure gold."
-- Debbie Viguie, co-author of the NY Times bestselling WICKED series

AVAILABLE JANUARY 19, 2010